Malina

Ingeborg Bachmann

Malina

Introduction by Rachel Kushner

Translated from the German by Philip Boehm

A NEW DIRECTIONS BOOK

Originally published in Germany as *Malina* by Suhrkamp Verlag in 1971.

The musical passages on pages 6 and 267 are taken from *Pierrot Lunaire,* op. 21, by Arnold Schoenberg. Lyrics by Cecil Gray.

Manufactured in the United States of America
First published as New Directions Paperbook 1440 in 2019

Design by Erik Rieselbach

Library of Congress Cataloging-in-Publication Date to come
Names: Bachmann, Ingeborg, 1926–1973, author. | Kushner, Rachel, writer of introduction. | Boehm, Philip, translator.
Title: Malina / Ingeborg Bachmann ; introduction by Rachel Kushner ; translated by Philip Boehm.
Other titles: Malina. English
Description: New York : New Directions Book, [2019]
Identifiers: LCCN 2019004327 | ISBN 9780811228725 (alk. paper)
Subjects: LCSH: Women—Austria—Fiction. | Man-woman relationships—Austria—Fiction. | Triangles (Interpersonal relations)—Austria—Fiction.
Classification: LCC PT2603.A147 M313 2019 | DDC 833/.914—dc23
LC record available at https://lccn.loc.gov/2019004327

10 9 8 7 6 5 4 3

New Directions Books are published for James Laughlin
by New Directions Publishing Corporation
80 Eighth Avenue, New York 10011

Contents

Introduction

I remember the first time I heard the title of this work, the word "Malina." Where I was standing, what room I was in, the man who said the word. It sounded so important and complete: Ma-li-na, stress on the first syllable. Stress on every syllable. So symmetrical and smoothly oblique.

"It's a novel?" I asked the man.

"Yes, a very important work by a major Austrian writer."

In "important" and "Austrian" and "work" I computed that its author, a woman, was in fact an honorary man. He didn't have to say it. He said it in the way his shoes were shined. The way he held his expensive raincoat over one arm. This was an office setting, and he was in a position above me. The way he announced the existence of Ingeborg Bachmann suggested that he believed, consciously or not, that she belonged to the world of men; perhaps she even derived from it. Anything is possible. Whether consciously or not, I put a claim on her, as someone to study, on account of her status as an honorary man.

I immediately read the novel. What I encountered in that book, which is this one, and yet not, because I will never again be the age at which I first read it, was a portrait, in language, of female consciousness, truer than anything written since Sappho's "Fragment 31." The narrative voice, first person and female, is concerned with what she calls "today," a word "only suicides ought to be allowed to use, it has no meaning for other people." "Today" is time as emergency, a present overtaken by what, elsewhere, she calls "a virus," by which I suspect she means what someone else might call love (or being in love), if by saying love, they meant a condition that suddenly renders a person incomplete.

Greener than grass I am and dead—or almost I seem to me, says Sappho (in Anne Carson's translation), lines that are open to interpretation, but from Longinus forward are generally taken to mean some profound loss of self in the desire for another. But no one knows where Sappho was going, since the final lines of the poem are lost. Bachmann's elisions, in a book about female desire and consciousness and loss of self, are intended: the elisions are brutal and internal; *Malina* is complete.

"I loved Bachmann a great deal," fellow Austrian writer Thomas Bernhard once told an interviewer. "She was a very intelligent woman. A strange combination, no? Most women are stupid but bearable, possibly even agreeable; intelligent too, but rarely."

Can a man understand this book? Completely. No less than a woman can understand Thomas Bernhard. A man can appreciate *Malina.* He doesn't have to suffer it, while a woman who reads this book might feel the same burns and itching from the wool dress the narrator puts on, late in the narrative—not by choice, by cosmic attrition, as her possessions start to go missing. But *Malina* is not a novel that is easy for anyone to understand, in a more normal sense of comprehension—the who, what, and why. I won't pretend. It's a difficult book in which to find your footing. There are all sorts of references in it, to Schoenberg, to Vienna, to historical events, not all of which the reader will catch. But once you're in, you're in. You're not decoding. Toward the end, you're racing along, deep in the rhythms of the narrator's thoughts, which are bone-true and demonically intelligent—and I mean it would be a real burden to be that mentally acute, it can't go well for a person to know that much, it can only lead to ill health, drinking, and despair—and then the novel careens over a cliff. Although "careens" and "cliff" are subjective. The narrator disappears in an inevitable and disturbing manner.

Who is she? An unknown woman, as she herself puts it, un-named, and a writer. What is the situation? It's not clear, except she lives in an apartment in Vienna with one man (Malina), and is in love with another (Ivan), who lives down the street. In the first chapter, Happy with Ivan, the joke is that she's not happy, but happiness has no share. She spends a lot of time waiting for Ivan and smoking cigarettes, and writes letters at night that she shreds instead of mails. She narrates a fantastic tale about a princess who exists in a kind of premodern utopia. In the second chapter, she dreams of hellish scenes of war-time suffering and death, of fascism and empire and very bad fathers. In the third and final section she speaks to Malina about a mailman who hoarded what he was meant to deliver, on account of an existential crisis she calls "Pri-vacy of Mail," meaning that no letter should ever, finally, be sent. She tells Malina about her former job working the night shift at a news service, which exposed her to "the swindle from up close," i.e., the meaninglessness of the churn of days, of topical news, and even of time as ordered by shared events. She talks about a hobo in Paris who was given a shower that spiritually undid him. No one should be made clean, she says, for a new life "that does not exist." The hobo and the mailman get high marks but mostly she delivers withering judgments of men. She calls intellectuals "men without true secrets." And she says that the contortions women go through to respond to male desire require a woman to invent false feelings and to shelter her real feelings "in the ones she's invented." But, she says, "for the longest time I had no feelings at all, since during those years I was entering the age of reason."

Some of her talk is embellished with musical notation, rubato, con fuoco, forte, forte, fortissimo, and so on. Why is this narrator so agitated? By the virus, which isn't exactly love, now that I think about it, but an undoing that seems almost criminal, because its grammar is so insufficient. She operates in a field of signs, an entire sensory reality, that is male. The male characters in the book, some have speculated, are mere alter egos, not "real" men, but part of her own psyche. Her troubles are deeper than plain old patriarchy, though, and derive also from Nazism, and the ways in which fascism transforms from public to private menace, a postwar specter of cruelty and destruction. She is steeped in a broad lexicon of existential issues that burn her like lit cigarettes. She's also very funny, especially in the third section of the book, when her mind goes into overdrive. Asked by Malina if she's going to a friend's funeral, she says she doesn't want to be constantly informed of that friend's—or anyone's—death. "They don't constantly tell me that someone is alive," she says. And anyhow, "it's rare that anyone is living, except in the theater of my thoughts." The idea that there are men who are good lovers, she says, is "a legend that has to be destroyed." A man might expose his bare back to her, on which some other woman has dug her nails and left traces. "What are you supposed to do with this back?" Which echoes a question in the first chapter, in a letter addressed to a "Mr. President," in which she declares that she was born with half a good-luck bonnet. "What would you do, Mr. President, with half a presidency, half an honor, half a recognition, half a hat, what would you even do with this half letter?"

Ingeborg Bachmann was born in Klagenfurt, Austria, in 1926. She was a brilliant student who completed a PhD dissertation on Martin Heidegger (whom she wanted to prove wrong), but she seems to have almost immediately transferred her intellectual attachments to Wittgenstein. She wrote radio plays and poetry and won the prestigious Gruppe 47 prize in 1953, one of only two women to be made famous by that group, which included Heinrich Böll, Günter Grass, and Uwe Johnson. Even after she quit poetry for prose, she continued to be known primarily as a lyric poet. Repeatedly she was asked in interviews to defend her decision to give up poetry. "Quitting is a strength, not a weakness," she retorted. She had a love affair with Paul Celan. Another with Max Frisch. She was something of a mentor to Thomas Bernhard, who immortalized her, as the poet Maria, in his final novel, *Extinction*.

She apparently advised Bernhard to save himself by fleeing Austria. In 1953, she herself had moved to Rome, where she remained until the end of her life, which came somewhat suddenly, in 1973, from an accident, while smoking in bed.

She was friends with Fleur Jaeggy, who described her, in a portrait of a summer journey they took in 1971 as "soignée" and smelling of roses and easy with silence. Bachmann, says Jaeggy, knew with precision "all the nuances that might hurt or wound." And It was Bachmann who "manned" the road maps on their journey. But of course she manned the maps. She's still something of an honorary man, it seems. The edition of "Understanding Modern European and Latin American Literature" devoted to her oeuvre was the only edition in the series on a woman—at least at the time my copy was printed, in 1995. Perhaps now they've added a few. No matter, Bachmann has launched a thousand dissertations, it seems, on feminist thought, and even books that interrogate the feminist thought inspired by her work.

Malina, which was published in 1971, was only to be one novel in a cycle that Bachmann called "deathstyles" or "ways of death." After she died, it was made into a film by Werner Schroeter, starring Isabelle Huppert, with a script written by Elfriede Jelinek. Critics leapt on the film as lacking in nuance. I still haven't seen it, but it's probably better than they thought.

What drove Bachmann's writing, she told an interviewer just before she died, was an unshakable belief in a utopia she knew would never come about. "It won't come and yet I believe in it," she said. The descriptions of the princess in *Malina*, who rides a black horse and follows the Danube as if the river flowed free of countries, of empires, are perhaps the most literal proof of Bachmann's version of hope. The princess, though, reaches "the edge of the world." And her story must remain nested inside another that is sardonic and bleak. The narrator has promised Ivan she would write a beautiful book, but she ends up writing, as she tells him, a book about hell. But that book—about hell—is not this one, or not entirely.

I have my own ideas on the final moment at the end, and what it means, but I don't want to give it away here, before you yourself read this letter that Bachmann—or her narrator, and it really does not matter which—did not shred, or hoard, but wrote, and sent, with the urgency of "today."

RACHEL KUSHNER

Translator's note

"I'm staring at the wall which is showing a crack, it must be an old crack that now is gently spreading because I keep staring at it."

I have been staring at Ingeborg Bachmann's *Malina* for a very long time through a crack in the wall of translation—a crack widened by thirty years of scholarship since I first attempted to render this exquisitely complex book into English. The recent German critical edition has been very helpful in revealing references that were previously obscure: I learned, for example, that the description of the Danube used in the "Princess of Kagran" fairytale contained substantial quotations from a German translation of Algernon Blackwood's *The Willows*, so it made sense to turn to the original text to recover the appropriate passages.

In the meantime, another wall has cracked open completely— and I am no longer living in Poland, behind the Iron Curtain, as I was when I first started translating this novel, with limited access to resources: today I can also roam unencumbered across the World Wide Web. Since readers, too, can turn to the Internet to indulge their curiosity (as we hope they will), we have jettisoned the notes and glosses present in the earlier version.

I further hope that three decades of translating literary texts has sharpened my discernment; I certainly have benefited from the tutelage of such great editors as Sara Bershtel and Drenka Willen.

In regard to *Malina*, I am particularly grateful to New Directions' Barbara Epler, Erik Rieselbach, and Tynan Kogane for the care they lavish on the books they publish and on all involved in their creation. I would also like to mention my indebtedness to Mark Anderson, who initially led (or lured!) me down this path, as well as remember Max Holmes, who first published this book in English. Heinz Bachmann, too, has been very kind.

My encounter with a translator who was once me has been a bit unsettling, and this is a great opportunity to do penance for past transgressions. I only hope you, gentle reader, will absolve me of any sins committed in the present.

PHILIP BOEHM

Malina

The Cast:

Ivan: born in Pécs, Hungary (formerly Fünfkirchen) in 1935.
            Has been living for some years now in Vienna, where he
            pursues his neatly ordered affairs in a building on the
            Kärntnerring. To avoid any unnecessary complications
            for Ivan and his future, this shall be designated an Insti-
            tute for Extremely Important Matters, since it deals with
            money. It is not the Credit Union.

Béla &
András: the children, aged 7 and 5

Malina: forty years old today, although it is impossible to guess
            by his appearance. Author of an "Apocrypha" no longer
            available in bookstores, but which sold a few copies in
            the late fifties. He has assumed as a disguise the status of
            a Class A Civil Servant employed in the Austrian Army
            Museum, where advanced degrees in history (his major)
            and art history (his minor) enabled him to find a good
            position. He is moving steadily up the ladder without
            motion, ambition or intrigue, and without calling atten-
            tion to himself by making demands or petty criticisms
            of the procedures and written transactions between the
            Defense Ministry on Franz-Josefs-Kai and the museum
            in the Arsenal. Although quite inconspicuous, the latter
            remains one of our city's most curious institutions.

Myself: Austrian passport, issued by the Ministry of the Interior.
            Official Austrian I.D. Eyes—br., Hair—blnd.; born in

3

Klagenfurt; some dates follow and a profession (crossed out twice and written over); addresses (crossed out three times); above which in clear block letters: Ungargasse 6, Vienna III.

Time: Today
Place: Vienna

But I had to think long and hard about the Time, since "today" is an impossible word for me, even though I hear and say it daily, you can't escape it. When people start telling me what they have planned for today—not to mention tomorrow—I get confused. My relationship with "today" is so bad that many people often mistake extreme attentiveness for an absentminded gaze. This "today" sends me flying into the utmost anxiety and the greatest haste, so that I can only write about it, or at best report whatever's going on. Actually, anything written about "today" should be destroyed immediately, just like all real letters are crumpled or torn up, unfinished and unmailed, all because they were written, but cannot arrive, "today."

Whoever has composed an intensely fervent letter only to tear it to shreds and throw it away knows exactly what is meant by "today." And who hasn't run into barely legible scribbles such as: "Please come if you can, if you want to, I might kindly request! 5:00 PM—Café Landtmann!" Or telegrams like: "Please phone right away stop today." Or: "Impossible today."

In fact, "today" is a word that only suicides ought to be allowed to use, it has no meaning for other people. It merely signifies a day like all the rest, when they have to work another eight hours or take time off, run errands, buy groceries, read the morning and evening papers, drink coffee, forget things, keep an appointment, give someone a call—in short, a day on which something is supposed to occur or, better yet, not too much is happening.

But when I say "today," my breathing grows irregular and my

heart beats a syncopation that can now be captured on an electro-cardiogram, although the graphs do not show that the cause is pre-cisely my "today," always urgent and new, however, I can prove my diagnosis is correct. In the confusing code of the medical profes-sion, the disorder precedes acute anxiety—it renders me suscep-tible, it stigmatizes me—although as of today I'm still functional, according to the experts. I'm just afraid "today" is too much for me, too gripping, too boundless, and that this pathological agitation will be a part of my "today" until its final hour.

Whereas there was nothing haphazard about establishing the Time—which I did under great duress—a charitable circumstance led me to the even more unlikely Place, which is not of my own discovery. I did discover myself there, though, and know the Place well—very well—since generally speaking it is Vienna. Really it's only a side street, more precisely a small section of the Ungargasse, as it happens that all three of us live there: Ivan, Malina and myself. But whoever sees the world from such a narrow point of view as the Third District is naturally inclined to extol the Ungargasse, to study it, to glorify it and endow it with a certain significance. It might be called a special side street since it begins at a fairly quiet, friendly spot on the Heumarkt and since not only the Stadtpark but also the forbidding market hall and the Central Customs Of-fice can be seen from where I live. At this point the houses are still dignified and uninviting, only after Ivan's—starting at Number 9 with the two bronze lions in front—does the street become more random, less calm and ordered. Despite its proximity to the diplo-matic quarter, the Ungargasse shows little affinity with the "Noble Quarter" (as the Viennese call it), which it simply leaves behind on the right. Small cafés and many old inns and taverns make the street useful: we frequent the "Alter Heller," which we reach after passing a convenient garage, the Automag, a very convenient drug store, and a cigar stand at the Neulinggasse. The great bakery on the corner of the Beatrixgasse should not be overlooked, and also, to our good fortune, there is the Münzgasse, where we can always find a parking place. Here and there one cannot deny the Ungargasse a certain atmosphere, particularly around the Consolato Italiano with the Istituto Italiano di Cultura, still the street can't claim too much of that, especially when the "O" streetcar rattles by or when the ominous postal garage looms into view. There, two inconspicuous plaques curtly pronounce: "Kaiser Franz Joseph I. 1850" and "Office and Chancellery." But these aspirations to nobility remain ignored, while the traffic calls to mind the street's distant youth, the old Hungargasse where merchants and traders returning from Hungary with horses, oxen and hay kept their lodgings. And so the Ungargasse runs its course, "along a wide bow, inbound," as it is officially described. Coming from the Rennweg, I often traverse this bow, but I can't get very far in my description, because new details are constantly arresting my attention: insulting innovations, office buildings and stores known as Modern Living—all of which mean more to me than our city's most triumphant streets and squares. Not that the Ungargasse isn't well-known, on the contrary, except a stranger would never lay eyes on it, as it is strictly residential and devoid of tourist attractions. Sightseers would turn back at Schwarzenbergplatz, or certainly upon reaching the Rennweg near the Belvedere, with which we share the honor of belonging to the Third District, but nothing more. A stranger might approach the Ungargasse from the other side, from the skating club, if he were staying in that new stone block, the Vienna Intercontinental Hotel, and happened to stray too far into the Stadtpark. Once above this same park, a chalkwhite Pierrot serenaded me in a cracking voice:

O   an-cient   scent from far -   -   off days

but we don't get to the Stadtpark more than ten times a year, though it's a mere five minutes away by foot, and Ivan, who doesn't walk on principle (despite all pleas and cajoleries on my part) only knows it from the car. It's simply too close—for fresh air we take the children to the Vienna Woods, to the Kahlenberg, to the castles at Laxenburg and Mayerling, to Petronell and Carnuntum, all the way to Burgenland. And so, because we've never had to drive there, we abstain from the Stadtpark, in fact, we treat it quite coldly, and I can't remember anything more from far-off days. Sometimes I still get a little anxious when I notice the first magnolia blossoms, but you can't always make a fuss about that. When I'm uninspired and ask Malina, like I did today: By the way, did you see the magnolias in the park? he just nods his head and responds because he's polite, but he's heard all about the magnolia before.

There's no doubt that Vienna has much prettier streets, however, they occur in other districts, and evoke the same response that overly beautiful women do: they are duly admired, but who would even consider approaching them? No one has yet claimed that the Ungargasse is beautiful, or breathtaking, or enchanting, as it intersects the Invalidenstrasse. So I don't want to be the first to make untenable assertions about my, or rather our, street. Instead, I should look to myself if I want to understand this fixation with the Ungargasse as it follows its wide bow, inbound only into me, up to Number 9 and Number 6. I should ask myself why I can't escape its magnetic field whether I'm crossing the Freyung, shopping along the Graben, taking a stroll to the National Library or standing at Lobkowitzplatz and thinking, this is where I should be living! Or at the Hof! Even when I'm loitering downtown, when I stop to leaf through an hour's worth of newspapers in some café, I'm really only pretending, secretly I'd just as soon be on my way or already home. When I do arrive in the Third District, beginning at the Beatrixgasse (where I used to live) or the Heumarkt, my blood pressure begins to rise and at the same time the tension begins to fall, the cramps which attack me in unknown places abate, and although I keep walking faster and faster, I finally attain a happy, almost urgent tranquility. I don't get sick the way I do with Time, although Time and Place suddenly converge. This little piece of side street is my greatest security, during the day I run up the stairs, at night I fall upon the outside door armed with the key, and once again that blissful moment returns, when the key twists, the locks unlock, the doors open and that feeling of having come home overwhelms me in the spray of traffic and people. This sensation radiates across one or two hundred yards where everything signals my house. Of course it isn't really mine, considering it belongs to a cooperative or some gang of investors who rebuilt it or really just patched it up. But I know next to nothing about that, since I lived ten minutes away during the repair years. In fact, for a long time I used to pass old Number 26—which remained my lucky number for many years—feeling oppressed and guilty, like a dog with a new master when he runs into his old one and doesn't know who deserves the most affection. Today, however, I can walk by Beatrixgasse 26 as if nothing had ever been there, or almost nothing—well, there was something there once, a scent from long ago, I can't sense it anymore.

For years my relationship with Malina consisted of awkward meetings, absolute follies and the biggest possible misunderstandings— I mean of course much greater misunderstandings than with other people. Certainly I was *subordinate* to him from the beginning, and I must have known early on that he was destined to be my doom, that Malina's place was already occupied by Malina even before he entered my life. I was only spared—or perhaps I spared myself— meeting him too soon, for there were numerous occasions at the E2 and H2 streetcar stop by the Stadtpark when something could have happened, and almost did. There he stood holding a newspaper, I acted as if I didn't see him, although I kept staring over my paper in his direction, without flinching. I couldn't tell whether he was really so engrossed in the news or whether he had noticed my pinning him, hypnotizing him, wanting to force him to look up. Me forcing him! I thought: if the E2 comes first, everything will be fine, but heaven forbid the unfriendly H2 or the even rarer G2 should arrive first. Finally the E2 did indeed pull up, but by the time I had jumped onto the second car Malina had vanished: he wasn't to be found in the first car or in my own and he hadn't remained behind. He must have dashed into the Stadtbahn station just as I had to turn around—after all, he couldn't have dissolved into thin air. My whole day was ruined since I couldn't find an explanation, I kept looking for him and was as much perplexed by his behavior as by my own. But that was ages ago, and today there's not enough time to talk about it. Years later the same thing happened in a lecture hall in Munich. He was suddenly standing next to me, took a few steps forward against a shove of students, searched for a seat and then retreated, while I listened—kept very alert by my fear of passing out—for one and a half hours to a lecture on "Art in the Age of Technology," while looking and looking for Malina amid this mass of people forced to sit still and be moved by the speaker. On that evening I realized beyond a doubt that I could not count on art, technology or this age to help me in any way, and that I would never have anything to do with the thoughts, themes or problems under discussion. I was also convinced I wanted Malina, and that whatever I desired to know must come from him. In the end I applauded abundantly like everyone else, then two people from Munich helped me to the back of the hall and showed me the way out. One held my arm while the other kept saying intelligent things to me, others joined in, and I kept looking over to Malina, likewise moving toward the back door, but slowly enough to allow me to gain some speed. It was then I performed the impossible: I rammed into him as if someone had pushed me, or as if I had tripped, and down I fell, right on top of Malina. This way he couldn't help but notice me, though I'm not sure he really saw me. I did hear his voice for the first time though, calm and proper, on one note: Excuse me.

I didn't know how to answer him, since no one had ever said

that to me and I wasn't sure whether he was begging my pardon or granting me his. The tears came so quickly to my eyes I lost sight of him, and because of the others I stared at the ground, took a handkerchief from my purse and pretended that someone had kicked me. When I looked up he had lost himself in the crowd.

In Vienna I stopped looking for him, assuming he was out of the country, and hopelessly retraced my way to the Stadtpark, as I did not yet own a car. One morning I found him in the paper, but the article wasn't about Malina at all, it mainly dealt with Maria Malina's funeral, the most magnificent and impressive ceremony the Viennese ever celebrated voluntarily—only for an actress, of course. Among the mourners gathered at the Zentralfriedhof could be counted the brother of the deceased, the young, highly talented and well-known writer, who wasn't well-known at all but whom the journalists quickly helped make famous for one day. For in those hours, as all Vienna marched in a long procession, from the Minister of Culture to the janitor, from critics who sit in the best boxes to high-school students who have to stand, Maria Malina had no use for a brother who had written a book that nobody knew and who was himself a "nobody." The words "young, highly talented and well-known" were necessary attire on this national day of mourning.

As if it had had nothing to do with him and even less with me, we never discussed this third, unappetizing newspaper contact, which really existed only for me. For in the lost time when we couldn't even ask each other's name, much less about each other's life, I secretly called him "Eugenius," since the first song I ever learned, and with it the first man's name, was "Prince Eugene, the Noble Knight." The name immediately held great appeal for me, also the city "Bel-ge-rad," whose significance and exotic ring didn't evaporate until it turned out that Malina was not from Belgrade but only from the Yugoslav border like myself, sometimes we still speak to each other in Slovenian or Windish, a few words, as in the first days: Jaz in ti. In ti in jaz. Other than that we don't need to talk about our good old days, because our days are getting better and better, and I have to laugh about the times when I was furious with Malina for having allowed me to squander so much time with other people and things. That's why I banished him from Belgrade, took away his name, attributed mysterious stories to him—soon he was a swindler, soon a philistine, soon a spy—and when my mood improved, I had him disappear from reality and lodged him in fairy tales and sagas, christened him Florizel, Thrushbeard, but I liked him best as St. George who slew the dragon so that my first city could be born, so that Klagenfurt could arise from the barren swamp, and after much idle play I would return discouraged to the only correct supposition, namely that Malina was indeed in Vienna, and that in this city where I had so many possibilities of running into him I had nonetheless always managed to miss him. I began to talk about Malina wherever his name came up in conversation, although this was not often. It's an ugly memory (which no longer causes me pain) but I felt compelled to act as if I knew him too, as if I knew something about him, and I was as witty as anyone else when it came to the notorious, droll story concerning Malina and Frau Jordan. Today I know that Malina never "had" anything with this Frau Jordan, as they say here, that Martin Ranner never even met secretly with her on the Cobenzl, because she was his sister—first and foremost Malina cannot possibly be considered in a context with other women. It's not out of the question that Malina knew other women before me, he knows a lot of people, so of course he knows women as well, but this doesn't mean anything at all since we've been living together, I don't think about it anymore because as far as Malina is concerned, all my suspicions and confusions have come to nothing under his astonished gaze. Moreover, the young Frau Jordan was not the woman long rumored to have uttered the famous saying, "I'm pursuing a policy for the world to come," when her husband's assistant surprised her one day on her knees scrubbing the floor and she demonstrated her full contempt for her spouse. It happened otherwise, it's a different story and one day everything will be set right. The real figures will emerge great and freed from all gossip, like Malina for me today, no longer the product of rumors, but redeemed, sitting next to me or walking with me around the city. The time has not yet come to correct the other things, that's for later. Not today.

Since everything between us has happened as it has, the only thing I still have to ask myself is what we can be for each other, Malina and I, since we are so distinct, so unalike, and this isn't a question of sex or kind, the stability of his existence and the instability of my own. Of course Malina has never lived as convulsively as I have, he's never wasted his time on trivialities, by phoning around, letting events take over, he's never gotten into trouble, much less spent half an hour staring at himself in the mirror only to rush off somewhere, always late, stammering excuses, perplexed by a question or embarrassed by an answer. I guess even today we don't have much to do with one another, we put up with each other, are mutually amazed, but my amazement is curious (is Malina really ever amazed? less and less, I think), and there's tension precisely because my presence never upsets him, since he acknowledges it as he pleases and doesn't bother when there's nothing to say, as if we weren't constantly passing each other in the apartment, impossible to overlook, performing everyday actions impossible to ignore. Then it seems to me that his calm comes from my ego being too familiar, too unimportant for him, as if he had rejected me as waste, a superfluous something-made-human, as if I were merely the dispensable product of his rib, but at the same time an unavoidable dark tale accompanying and hoping to supplement his own bright story, a tale that he, however, detaches and delimits. Thus I am the only one who has anything to settle, and above all I must and can explain myself, but only to him. He has nothing to settle, no, not him. I'm cleaning up in the front hall—I want to be near the door because he'll be here any minute—the key moves inside the door, I step back so he won't knock me down, he locks the door behind him and simultaneously, kindly, we greet one another: hello. And walking along the corridor I add:

I must talk. I will talk. There's nothing more to disturb my reminiscing.

Yes, says Malina, unamazed. I enter the living room, he heads on toward the back, since his is the last room.

I must and I will, I repeat loudly to myself, for if Malina won't ask and doesn't want to know more, then it's all right. I can be reassured.

However, if my memory only entails the usual recollections, remote, decrepit, abandoned, then I'm still far away, very far away from the silent reminiscence where nothing more can upset me.

What should upset me about a city, for example, in which I was born, without understanding why it had to be exactly there and nowhere else, but do I have to keep reminding myself about that? The Office of Tourism distributes Most Important Information on that subject, some things do fall outside its domain, but I must have learned in school where "manly courage and womanly fidelity" unite and where, according to our anthem, "the Glockner's glacier glistens." Thomas Koschat, our city's greatest native son, as attested to by the Thomas Koschatgasse, is the composer of the song: "Verlassn, verlassn, verlassn bin i," in Bismarck Elementary School I had to relearn multiplication tables I already knew, in the Benedictine school I went to religion (later not to be confirmed) with a girl from another grade, always in the afternoon—everybody else, the Catholics, had their religion before noon, and so I always had time off, the young vicar was said to have been shot in the head, the old deacon was strict, wore a mustache, and considered questions immature. The doors to the Ursuline high school (which I rattled once again) are now barred shut. Maybe I didn't get my cake at the Café Musil after the entrance exam but I wish

I had and picture myself dissecting it with a small fork. Maybe I didn't get the cake until a few years later. At the foot of the promenade overlooking the Wörthersee, near the steamboat landing, I was kissed for the first time, but I no longer see a face approaching my own, also the stranger's name must be buried in the silt of the lake, I can only remember something about ration tickets I gave to the stranger who did not return to the landing the next day, since he had been invited to visit the most beautiful woman in the city, who used to walk along the Wienergasse wearing a large hat and who really was named Wanda, once I followed her as far as Waagplatz—without a hat, without perfume and without the self-assured step of a woman of thirty-five. The stranger was probably on the run or else he wanted to exchange the tickets for cigarettes and smoke them with the beautiful tall woman, except I was already nineteen then and not just six, with a satchel on my back, when it actually happened. In a close-up you can't see the western bank of the lake, just the little bridge over the Glan, this bridge in full sun at noon with the two little boys who were also carrying satchels on their backs, the older one, at least two years older than myself, called out: You, hey you, come here, I've got something for you! Neither the words nor the boy's face have been forgotten, my first vocal challenge, so important, nor have I forgotten that first wild joy, the stopping, hesitating and the first step toward another person, all on this bridge, and all at once the hard clap of a hand on my face: There you go, now you've got it! It was the first time I had been hit in the face and my first awareness of someone else's deep satisfaction in hitting. The first experience of pain. Holding the ties of her satchel, without tears, someone who was once me trotted home with measured steps, for once not counting the pickets along the edge of the path, having fallen among humans for the very first time, and so sometimes you really do know exactly when it began, how and where, and which tears were meant for crying.

It was on the bridge over the Glan. Not the promenade by the lake.

Whereas some people are born on days like the first of July, when four extremely famous people came into the world, or on the fifth of May, crowded with great reformers and geniuses who uttered their first cries on that day, I have never been able to ascertain who was so imprudent as to begin his life on the same day I did. I do not know the satisfaction of sharing a stardate with Alexander the Great, Leibnitz, Galileo Galilei or Karl Marx, and even sailing from New York to Europe on the *Rotterdam*, where they kept a list of all passengers celebrating birthdays during passage, when my turn came the only greeting that came through my cabin door was a fancily folded birthday card from the captain, and until noon I kept hoping that among the many hundred passengers there would be some, as there had been every morning, who would be surprised with a free cake and the singing of "happy birthday to you." But as it turned out I was the only one, in vain I scanned the whole dining saloon, no, no one but me, I quickly cut my cake, distributed it hastily at three Dutch tables and talked and drank and talked, I couldn't stand the sea swells, hadn't slept the entire night, and I ran back to my cabin and locked myself in.

It was not on the bridge, nor the promenade, it wasn't on the Atlantic at night either. I was merely passing through this night, drunk, bound for the deepest night of all.

Only later did I realize that at least somebody had died on this day, which then still held my interest. At the risk of encroaching on the domain of popular astrology, since I may imagine constellations and configurations high above us merely by following my fancy, and since there isn't any science to keep an eye on me and rap my fingers, I connect my beginning with an end—why shouldn't someone start living when a human spirit expires?—but I won't mention this man's name as it is less important than the cinema behind the Kärntnerring, which has also just occurred to me, the cinema where I first saw Venice, for two hours in extravagant colors and a lot of darkness, the oars beating the water, a melody accompanied by lights passed through the water as well, and its da-dim da-dam carried me along, all the way inside the figures, the coupled figures and their dancing. In this way I arrived in a Venice I would never see, on a clanking, windy winter day in Vienna. Since then I have often heard that music again, improvised, varied, but never played the same way or so correctly, once from an adjacent room, where it was hacked to pieces during a discussion between several voices about the collapse of the monarchy, the future of socialism, and where someone began shouting because someone else had said something against existentialism or structuralism, and by listening carefully I managed to make out another beat, but by then the music had already perished in the shouting, and I was beside myself because I didn't want to hear anything else. Often I don't want to listen and often I can't look. Like when I couldn't bear the sight of the dying horse which had fallen off the cliff at Hermagor, for whose sake I walked for miles to fetch help, but I left it behind with the shepherd boy who couldn't do anything either, or the time I couldn't stand the sound of Mozart's C-Minor Mass or the gunshots in a village during Fasching.

I don't want to talk, it all upsets me, in my remembering. Malina enters the room, looks for a half-empty whiskey bottle, hands me a glass, pours one for himself and says: It still upsets you. Still. But you're upset about a different recollection.

One   *Happy with Ivan*

Having smoked and drunk again, counted the glasses and my cigarettes, saving two for today, as there are three days left till Monday, without Ivan. Sixty cigarettes later, however, Ivan is back in
Vienna, first he'll call the time service to check his watch, then dial
00 for the wakeup service, which phones right back, immediately
thereafter he'll fall asleep as quickly as he alone can do, then he'll
wake up (with the service) in a grumpy mood he always expresses
in different ways using sighs, curses, tantrums, complaints. Next
he's forgotten all about being grumpy and has jumped into the
bathroom to brush his teeth, shower and shave. He'll turn on the
radio and listen to the morning news. This is Radio Austria. The
news. In Washington ...

But Washington and Moscow and Berlin are merely impertinent
places trying to make themselves important. In my country, in Ungargassenland, no one takes them seriously or people simply smile
at such obtrusions as they would at the proclamations of ambitious
upstarts, no longer can they have any impact on my life, which once
ran into someone else's on the Landstrasser Hauptstrasse in front
of a florist whose name I have yet to discover, and I only stopped
running because there was a bouquet of Turk's-cap lilies in the window, red and seven times redder than red, never seen before, and in
front of the window stood Ivan, I don't know what else was there,

since I left with him immediately, first to the post office on the Rasumofskygasse, where we had to wait at two different counters, he at "Transfers" and I at "Stamps," and this first separation was already so painful that upon reclaiming Ivan at the exit I was speechless. He didn't have to ask me a thing because I had no doubt I would accompany him, go home with him right then and there, which to my amazement was only a few doors down from my own house. The borders were soon defined, after all only a tiny country had to be established, without territorial claims or even a proper constitution, an intoxicated land with only two houses you can find in the dark, even during total eclipses (solar and lunar), and I know by heart how many steps it takes, going diagonally, to reach Ivan's, I could even walk there blindfolded. Now the rest of the world, where I lived up to now—always in a panic, my mouth full of cotton, the throttle marks on my neck—is reduced to its petty insignificance since it is opposed by something truly powerful even if this only consists of waiting and smoking, like it does today, so no part of this force is lost. Because it's twisted I have to unwind the telephone cord ten times, carefully, with the receiver dangling off the hook, so that it may again be handled easily in case of emergency, this way I'll also be able to dial 72 68 93 before the emergency occurs. I'm aware that nobody will answer, but that's not important, as long as Ivan's phone is ringing in the darkened apartment, I know its exact location, the ringing is intended as an announcement to everything in his possession: I'm calling, it's me. And the heavy deep armchair will hear it, where he likes to sit, suddenly dozing off for five minutes, and the closets and the lamp over the bed where we lie together and his shirts and suits and the underwear he'll have tossed on the floor so that Frau Agnes knows what she has to take to the laundry. Ever since I've been able to dial this number, my life has finally stopped taking turns for the worse, I'm no longer coming apart at the seams, no longer getting into troubles I can't get out of, I'm not progressing anymore nor am I swerving from the path—because I hold my breath, stopping time, and call and smoke and wait.

If for some reason or another I hadn't moved to the Ungargasse two years ago, if I were still living in the Beatrixgasse, as during my student years, or abroad, as so often happened later, then my life would have arbitrarily taken some other course, and I never would have discovered the most important thing in the world: that everything within my reach, the telephone, receiver and cord, the bread and the butter and the kippers I save for Monday evening because they're Ivan's favorite, or the special sausage I like best, everything bears Ivan's brand, from the House of Ivan. This benevolent and powerful company must have also acquired and softened the typewriter and the vacuum cleaner which used to make such an unbearable racket—the car doors underneath my windows no longer slam shut with such a bang, and even nature must have fallen under Ivan's protection unintentionally, since the birds sing more quietly in the morning, allowing a second brief sleep.

But much more is going on since this assumption of ownership, and it seems strange to me that medicine, which considers itself a science and a very rapidly progressing one, knows nothing about the following phenomenon: the incidence of pain in my neighborhood is decreasing, between Ungargasse 6 and 9 fewer misfortunes occur, cancer and tumors, asthma and heart attacks, fevers, infections and breakdowns, even headaches and discomforts due to weather are on the decline, and I ask myself if it isn't my duty to inform scientists of this simple remedy, so that Research—which claims to be able to combat all disease using more and more sophisticated medications and treatments—could make a great leap forward. The tremulous anxiety, the high tension hovering over this city and presumably everywhere has almost completely abated here, and schizothymia, the world's schizoid soul, its crazy, gaping split, is healing itself imperceptibly.

The only remaining excitement is a hasty search for hairpins and stockings, a slight quiver while applying mascara and manipulating eyeshadow, using narrow brushes on the lids, or while dipping flimsy cotton puffs in light and dark powder. Or an insuppressible moistening of the eyes while I run back and forth between the bathroom and the hall looking for my purse or a handkerchief, a swelling of the lips—there are just these tiny physiological changes, a lighter gait which makes you taller by half an inch, and losing a little weight because it's going to be afternoon later and the offices will start to close and then these daydream-guerrillas will have infiltrated the Ungargasse and begun to incite, soon they have occupied it with their glorious proclamations and the only password they recognize, and how could that word, which even today stands for the future, be anything but Ivan.

It's Ivan. Ivan, again and again.

Against the decay and order, against life and against death, against accident, constant threats from the radio, the newspaper headlines all spreading the plague, against perfidy seeping down from upstairs or up from downstairs, against a slow devouring inside and being swallowed up by the outside, against Frau Breitner's insulted airs each morning, I hold my position, keep my early evening watch and wait and smoke, increasingly confident and safe, with unprecedented endurance and security, because in this sign I shall conquer.

Even if Ivan was created just for me, as he certainly was, I can never claim him solely for myself. For he has come to make consonants constant once again and comprehensible, to unlock vowels to their full resounding, to let words come over my lips once more, to solve problems and recreate connections long since disrupted, and I will not stray from him one iota, I will align and superimpose our identical, high-pitched first initials we use to sign our little notes, and after our names unite we could begin with the first words, cautiously, once again paying heed to this world, compelling it to respect itself once more, and since we want resurrection and not destruction, we take care not to touch each other in public, nor do we look into each other's eyes except furtively, because Ivan must first wash my eyes with his own, removing the images that landed on my retina before his arrival. Nonetheless after many cleansings a gloomy, fearsome picture reemerges, practically inextinguishable, whereupon Ivan rushes to cover it with some bright image to stop my evil eye and make me lose this horrible look—which I know how I acquired but do not remember, I do not remember ...

(You still can't, not yet, there's so much upsetting you ...)

But since Ivan is beginning to cure me, things cannot be all that bad on earth.

Even though at one time everyone knew, but since nobody remembers today, I'll disclose one reason why it has to happen secretly, why I close the door, lower the curtain, why I am alone when I present myself to Ivan. I'm not trying to keep us hidden, I want to recreate a taboo, and Malina understood this without my having to explain it, because even when I'm alone and my bedroom door is open, or when he's the only one in the apartment, he walks to his room as if there never were an open door, as if there never were a closed one, as if there weren't any room at all, so as not to profane anything and so the first bold moves and last tender submissions might have another chance. Lina doesn't clean up here either, for no one is supposed to set foot in this room, there's nothing going on that might be surrendered to dissection and analysis, because Ivan and I do not mutilate or torture ourselves, break each other on the wheel or murder one another, and in this way we shelter ourselves, protect what is our own and not to be touched. Ivan is never mistrustful, never asks questions, never suspects me, so my own suspicion disappears. Since he doesn't criticize my two obstinate chin hairs, nor notice the first two wrinkles under my eyes, since the coughing after my first cigarette doesn't bother him, since he even covers my mouth with his hand whenever I'm on the verge of saying something rash, I tell him everything I've never said before, in a different language, no holding back, because he'll never want to know what I'm up to during the day, what I did earlier, why I didn't come home until three in the morning, why I didn't have any time yesterday, why the telephone was busy for a whole hour and who I'm talking to right now, for as soon as I start with an ordinary sentence and say: I have to tell you something, Ivan interrupts me: Why, what do you have to explain to me, absolutely nothing, not a thing, who do you owe an explanation, certainly not me, nobody, it's nobody's business—

But I have to.

You're incapable of lying to me, I know that, I'm sure of that.

But only because I don't have to!

Why are you laughing? It wouldn't be a disgrace, you could still go ahead and do it. Go on and try, but you can't.

And you?

Me? Do you have to ask?

No, I don't have to.

I can try, too, but maybe I just won't tell you something from time to time. What do you say to that?

Fine with me. I have to agree. You don't have to do anything, Ivan, but you can.

While we're working things out so effortlessly, the carnage continues in the city—insufferable remarks, commentaries and scraps of gossip circulate in restaurants, at parties, in apartments, at the Jordans', the Altenwyls', the Wantschuras' or else they're distributed for the more needy in magazines, newspapers, in movies and books where things are discussed in such a way that they depart, retreat into themselves, and withdraw into us, and each wants to stand there naked, eager to undress the others to the bone, every secret disappears, forced open like a locked drawer, but where no secret existed nothing shall ever be found, and the helplessness increases following the break-ins, the strippings, the searches and the interrogations: there is no burning bush, nor is even the smallest light illumined, not in ecstatic delirium, not in fanatic sobriety, and the law of the world lies upon everyone, more misunderstood than ever before.

Because Ivan and I only tell each other good things and sometimes things intended to make each other laugh (but without ever laughing at anyone), because we're even able to smile when preoccupied and so find the right way to get back on track, to get back together, I hope we might effect a general contamination. Slowly we will infect our neighbors, one after the other, with the virus whose most likely name I know already, and if an epidemic should ensue, it would benefit all humanity. But I also realize how difficult it is to catch, how long one has to wait to be ripe for contamination, and how difficult, how completely hopeless things were for me before it happened!

Since Ivan is looking at me questioningly I must have said something, and I hurry to change the subject. I know what the virus is called, but I'll be careful not to mention its name in front of Ivan.
    What are you muttering about? What's difficult to catch? What disease are you talking about?
    It's not a disease, I'm not talking about a disease, I'm only thinking some things are hard to catch hold of.
    Either I really do speak too softly or Ivan doesn't understand what Malina would have understood, guessed, grasped long ago, and he can't even hear me—thinking or talking—and besides I've never told him anything about the virus.

A lot of things have intervened, I've accumulated more antibodies than you need to be immune—mistrust, indifference, the fearlessness which comes from too much fear, and I don't know how Ivan coped with such resistance, such impregnable misery, the nights so perfectly rehearsed for insomnia, the unbroken anxiety, the obstinate renunciation of everything. But all this came to nothing in the very first hour, when Ivan didn't exactly drop from heaven but did stand before me on the Landstrasser Hauptstrasse, his eyes smiling, very tall and slightly bowed, and for that alone I should bestow on him the highest distinctions—the absolute highest—for bumping into me and rediscovering me as I once was, my earliest layers, for retrieving me from underneath all the rubble and I shall beatify him for all his gifts—but for which gifts?—since no end is in sight and none is allowed to arrive, and so I'll begin simply, with the simplest gift of all, namely, his ability to make me laugh again.

At last I'm able to move about in my flesh as well, with the body I'd alienated with a certain disdain, I feel how everything inside is changing, how the plain and diagonally striated muscles relax, freeing themselves from their constant cramps, how both nervous systems convert simultaneously, because nothing takes place more distinctly than this conversion, an amending, a purification, the living factual proof, which could also be measured and labeled using the most modern instruments of metaphysics. It's good that I immediately grasped what had so struck me in that first hour, and, consequently, that I joined Ivan without any fuss, without any preconceived ideas. I didn't waste a moment: an event like this, which you've never known, which you can't know about in advance, which you can't have heard or ever read about, requires the utmost haste in order to occur. The slightest trifle could nip it in the bud, strangle it, stop it during takeoff, so sensitive is the genesis, the germination of this most powerful force in the world, simply because the world is sick and doesn't want a healthy force to prevail. A carhorn could have interrupted the first sentence, or a policeman ticketing a badly parked scooter, a passerby could have staggered between us, bawling, a deliveryman could have blocked our view, my God, it's impossible to think of everything that might have gotten in the way! I could have been distracted by an ambulance siren and looked down the street instead of at the bouquet of Turk's-cap lilies in the window, or Ivan could have asked someone for a light and never would have seen me. Because we were in such peril standing by the storefront, because even three sentences would have been too many, we quickly departed the danger zone, letting a lot of things just be. That's why it took us so long to get past the first small, meaningless sentences. I don't even know whether you could say today we're able to talk and converse with one another like most people. But there's no rush. We still have our whole life, says Ivan.

Nonetheless we have managed to conquer our first few sets of sentences, foolish starts, incomplete phrases, endings, surrounded by the halo of mutual consideration. Up to now most of these may be found on the telephone. We practice them over and over, as Ivan calls from his office on the Kärntnerring or again late in the afternoon or else in the evening from his home.

Hello. Hello?
It's me, who'd you think?
Oh right, of course, sorry
How I am? And you?
I don't know. This evening?
I can barely understand you
Barely? What? So you can
I can't hear you very well, can you
What ... is something?

No, nothing, later on you can
O.K., sure, I better call you later
I, I really should see these
Of course if you can't, then
I didn't say that, only if you don't
In any case let's call each other later
All right, but closer to six, since
But that'll be too late for me
Yes really for me as well, but
Maybe it doesn't make much sense today
Did someone come in?
No, just Fräulein Jellinek is here
Oh, so you're not alone anymore
But please, later on, for sure!

Ivan and I each have friends, and other people besides, and it's very
rare that he knows or I know what's going on with these other people or even know their names. We have to take turns eating out with
these friends and people, at least meet them in a café, or we have
to show foreigners around without knowing what to suggest and
most of the time we end up waiting for one more phone call. If only
fate would just once, but only once, have us meet in the city, Ivan
with people, myself with people, then he'd at least realize I, too, can
look different, that I know how to dress up (which he doubts) and
be chatty (which he doubts even more). For in his presence I grow
silent, because the smallest words—yes, now, well, and, but, then,
oh!—are so loaded, coming from me to him they have a hundred
times their meaning, they're a thousand times more effective than
the amusing tales and anecdotes, the challenging word duels that
friends and people expect of me, the gestures, the whims, the charm
put on for the sake of appearances, I don't do anything for appearances' sake for Ivan, I do nothing to appear, and I'm thankful if I can
fix him his drink and dinner, now and then secretly polish his shoes,

clean the spots on his jacket, and: Well, that's that! means more than wrinkling my forehead at a menu or dazzling people with humor and wit, leading a debate, collecting kisses on my hand and wishes for meeting again, it means more than those animated trips home with friends, another drink in the Loos Bar, kisses left and right and: see you soon! Because whenever Ivan has lunch at the Hotel Sacher, on an expense account of course and because he has to, then naturally I'll have to meet someone in the Sacher's Blue Bar later in the afternoon, and so we miss each other, whether I want to help this happen or prevent it from occurring, because tonight I'm supposed to have dinner at the Stadtkrug, but Ivan will be out in Grinzing with foreigners, and tomorrow I'm supposed to show some people Heiligenstadt and Nussdorf, the very idea makes me despair, and he'll be having dinner with some man at the Three Hussars. A lot of foreigners come to see him, a lot come to see me too, and that's what's keeping us from seeing each other today, for example, so we'll just have to phone. And within the set of telephone sentences a completely different subset may be found, while exchanging fleeting glances before going out with different friends, and these sentences have to do with "examples."

Ivan claims I'm always saying "for example." And in order to exorcise these examples, he uses some right now, for example, in the one hour we have left before dinner.

What now, for example, Miss Know-it-all? What was it like, for example, when I first entered your apartment, the next day, for example, we looked very suspicious.

I, for example, never spoke to any woman I didn't know on the street before and it would never have occurred to me that an unknown woman like that would invite a perfect stranger right away to go with—I beg your pardon?

Don't exaggerate!

For example, I'm still unclear as to what you really do. What, for example, can you do all day without lifting a finger? Let me, for example, think about that a second. No, don't say a thing.

Oh but please, I can easily explain!

I, for example, am not curious, don't tell me, I'm only trying to figure out a few things, but since I'm discreet beyond example I don't expect an answer.

Ivan, that's not the right way!

What is then?

If I, for example, came home this evening tired, but still stayed up to wait for a phone call, what, for example, Ivan, would you say to that?

I think you should go right to sleep, Miss Know-it-all.

And with that Ivan is gone.

In contrast to other men, Ivan can't bear it when I expressly wait for a call, take time for him, adjust my schedule to his, and so I do this secretly, I make accommodations and think about his various tenets and theorems, for he was the first to teach me many things. Today, however, it's late, I should have met Ivan on the way to the post office fifteen years ago. It's not too late to learn, but there's so little time for me to put this new knowledge to use. Before going to sleep at his behest, though, I consider the fact that, back then, I could not have understood the lesson in its entirety.

Since it's ringing, cooing, humming I grab the telephone because it might be Ivan, I start to say "Hello," but then hang up quietly, as today I'm not allowed a final phone call. It rings once again, then ceases at once, a cautious ringing, maybe it was Ivan, it had to be Ivan and I don't want to be dead, not yet, and if it really was Ivan, he should be pleased with me, thinking I've been asleep for a long time.

But today I'm smoking and waiting, I'm smoking by the phone till midnight, and I pick up the receiver and Ivan asks questions, and I answer.

I just have to get the ashtray
Just a minute, me too
Have you lit one as well
There. Now. No, it's not working
Don't you have any matches?
I just used the last, no I don't, on the candle
You hear that? Hey get off our line, would you
This phone has its little tics
What? Somebody's still jabbering away. You're sick?
I said "tics," it's not important, "tics" with a "t"
I don't understand: you're feeling sick?
I'm sorry, it was the wrong word
Why wrong, what do you mean?
Nothing, just that when you repeat a word so often

But even if four people are talking all at once, I can still make out Ivan's voice, and as long as I hear him and know that he hears me, I'm alive. Even if we have to interrupt the conversation, so long as the phone rings back, shrieks, buzzes, raves, sometimes a tone too loud or several tones too soft, if you add the refrigerator, the record player or turn on the water in the tub. But once it does ring—and who knows what a telephone does and what its outbursts should be called?—as long as it allows me to hear his voice then it's all the same to me whether we understand each other well, barely, or not at all due to a breakdown in the Viennese phone network, which lasts for minutes, it's also unimportant what he has to say, so expectantly, with renewed vigor or complete fatigue: I start the conversation up again with a simple "Hello?" But Ivan doesn't realize that, he either phones or he doesn't phone, yes, he phones.

It's nice you called
Nice, why nice?
Just because. It's nice of you

But I'm on the floor kneeling in front of the telephone hoping that Malina, too, never catches me in this position, nor should he ever see how I prostrate myself before the phone, with my forehead pressed to the wooden floor like a Moslem on his rug.

Couldn't you speak a little more clearly
I have to move the … better now?
So, what are you up to now?
Me? Nothing much

My Mecca and my Jerusalem! Thus have I been chosen out of all possible telephone customers, I am elected, my 72 31 44, for Ivan knows how to find me on every dial and he can find my number with greater certainty than my hair and my mouth and my hand.

Me tonight?
Well no, if you can't
But you're the one who
Right. But I don't want to go
Excuse me, but I think that's
I'm telling you I have no

You better go, I had completely forgotten
You did, so you're
All right then see you tomorrow. Sleep well!

So Ivan doesn't have any time, and the receiver feels like ice, not plastic, but metal, and it slides up to my temple, since I hear he's hanging up, and I wish this sound were a shot—short, fast, so it would all be over—I don't want Ivan to be that way today and, since he's always that way, I wish it were the end. I hang up, still kneeling on the floor, then drag myself over to the rocking chair and take a book off the table: SPACE TRAVEL—WHERE TO? I read feverishly, this is nonsense, he's the one who called, he wanted something else to happen as well, and I have to get used to the fact that he's not going to say anything more if I stop talking, the chapter's finished, the moon has been conquered, and in order not to anger Malina I gather all my letters on the living room table, in the studio I read them once again, I pile them on top of yesterday's letters, I rearrange files, VERY URGENT, URGENT, INVITATIONS, REJECTIONS, RECEIPTS, PAID BILLS, UNPAID BILLS, APARTMENT, but I can't find the unmarked file, the one I need the most, now the telephone goes off, at least a full tone too loud, it'll be long distance, and with feverish friendliness I practically scream, without knowing what I'm saying and with whom I'm forced to talk: Excuse me, operator, operator please, we've been cut off, hello! But was it Munich or Frankfurt? At any rate I've been cut off, I replace the receiver, the telephone cord is already tangled again, and I become tangled in it while I'm talking and forgetting myself, it all comes from those phone calls with Ivan. I can't untwist the cord ten times just because of Munich or whatever it was. Let it stay tangled. I keep the black telephone in view while I read, before going to sleep, when I place it next to the bed. Of course I could exchange it for a blue, red or white one, but it won't ever come to that, since I won't allow anything else in my room to change, so that nothing distracts me except Ivan, the only new thing there is, and so nothing diverts my attention from waiting, as the telephone stays still.

Vienna is silent.

I'm thinking about Ivan.
I'm thinking about love.
About injections of reality.
About their lasting only a few hours.
About the next, more potent injection.
I'm thinking in silence.
I'm thinking it's late.
It's incurable. And it's too late.
But I survive and think.
And I'm thinking it will not be Ivan.
Whatever's ahead, it will be something different.
I live in Ivan.
I will not outlive Ivan.

But all in all there can't be any doubt that Ivan and I sometimes find an hour, now and then a whole evening, that we have some time for each other which passes differently. We live two separate lives, but that's not all, as we never lose our feel for Unity of Place, and Ivan can't escape it either, even if he's never thought about it, as he certainly has not. Today he's at my place, tomorrow I'll be at his, and if he doesn't want to construct sentences with me then he'll set up his chess set or mine, in one of our apartments, and force me to play. Ivan gets annoyed, to punctuate his moves he yells words in Hungarian which must be either abusive or entertaining, up to now I can only understand jaj and jé, and on occasion I shout éljen! An exclamation which is certainly out of place but the only one I've known for years.

What in the world are you doing with your bishop, think that move over, would you please. You still haven't figured out how I play? If, in addition, Ivan says: Istenfáját! Or: az Isten kinját! I surmise that these expressions belong to a group of untranslatable Ivan-curses, and naturally he succeeds in disconcerting me with these apparent maledictions. Ivan says, you don't have any strategy, you're not bringing your pieces into play, your queen is locked in again.

I have to laugh, then I brood over the problem of my immobility once more, and Ivan winks at me. Get it? No, you don't get anything. What's in your head this time—cabbage, cauliflower, lettuce, nothing but vegetables. And now this reckless featherbrained lady wants to distract me, but I'm on to that, your dress just happened to slip off your shoulder, think about your bishop, you've been exposing your legs above the knee for over half an hour now as well, but that's not going to help, and you call that playing chess, well, fräulein, you can't play like that with me, ok, let's make our little funny face, I've been expecting that too, now we've lost our bishop, my dear girl, let me give you one more piece of advice, get the hell out of there, go from e5 to d3, but that's the last time I'm going to be so nice.

Still laughing, I lose my bishop, he's a lot better than I am, the main thing is that sometimes I manage to end with a stalemate.

Ivan asks, out of the blue: Who is Malina?

I don't have an answer for that, we play on in silence, with wrinkled foreheads, I make another mistake, Ivan doesn't believe in the "touch" rule, so he puts my piece back, I don't make any more mistakes, and the game ends in a stalemate.

For a stalemate Ivan receives his well-earned whiskey, he gazes contentedly at the chessboard, since thanks to him I didn't lose, in turn he'd like to find out something about me, but there's no rush. He still doesn't say what it is he would like to find out, not yet, he just lets me know he doesn't want to jump to any conclusion, he loves to conjecture, too much, in fact, he even presumes I have a certain talent although he doesn't know what kind, at any rate it must have something to do with "doing well."

You should always be doing well.

You don't mean me, why me!

Ivan lowers his eyelids three-quarters of the way so he can only watch me through that slit, yet his eyes are so dark, warm and large that he still sees enough of me, then he adds, unless I have another talent as well, a gift for inviting somebody to ruin things.

Ruin what? My well-being? What well-being?

Ivan moves his hand menacingly, since I've said something dumb, since there's something I don't want to be cured of although it could be cured right now. But I can't discuss this with Ivan, or explain why I wince at every brisk movement, it's still so difficult to talk to him, I'm not afraid of him, even though he's pinning my arms to my back, making me immobile. Despite this I breathe more rapidly, and even more rapidly he asks: Who's done this to you, who's put such nonsense into your head, what's inside there apart from this stupid fear of yours, I'm not anyone to be afraid of, you shouldn't be afraid of anything, what are you concocting in your head full of lettuce and beans and peas, you silly princess on your pea, I'd like to—no I don't want to know who's causing you to wince, jerk your head back, shake your head, turn your head away.

We have a lot of head-sentences, hoards of them, just like the telephone sentences, the chess sentences or the sentences about life in general, but we're still missing a lot of sentence sets, we don't have a single sentence about feelings, since Ivan never pronounces any and since I don't dare create the first one, but I wonder about this far-off, absent set of sentences, despite all the good sentences we already know how to make. For when we cross over from speech to gestures—which are consistently successful—a ritual begins for me that replaces feelings, not an empty process, nor an insignificant repetition, but rather an essence of solemn formulas newly distilled, accompanied by the only devotion of which I am truly capable.

And Ivan, what can Ivan know about that? Nevertheless he says today: So that's your religion, so that's it. His voice has changed its tone, it's less cheerful, no longer unastonished. In the end he'll find out what's going on with me, since we still have our whole life. Maybe not ahead of us, maybe just today, but we do have our lives, there's no doubt about that.

Before Ivan leaves we both sit on the bed and smoke, he has to go to Paris again for three days, I don't mind, I say casually: well ... because a vacuum exists between what I'd really like to say and each of our sparse utterances, I'd like to tell him everything, but instead I just sit here, grind the cigarette butt painfully and precisely into the ashtray and hand it to him, as if it were of the utmost importance that no ashes fall upon the floor.

It's impossible to talk to Ivan about myself. But should I just go on without dragging myself into this game?—why do I say game? why? it's not my word, it's one of Ivan's—that's impossible too. Malina knows where my concern lies, and today for the first time in ages we've been poring over atlases, city maps, leafing through dictionaries tackling words, we look up all the places and words and allow their aura to unfold, the aura which I, too, need in order to live, for then the pathos in life is lessened.

How sad I am, and why doesn't Ivan do anything about it, why does he sit there grinding out his cigarette instead of hurling the ashtray against the wall, spilling ashes all over the floor, why does he have to talk to me about Paris instead of taking me with him or staying here, not because I want to go to Paris, but so that Ungargassenland doesn't go to pieces and so I can always keep a grip on it, my own land, my country above all others. I have often been silent, speaking little, but still I talk too much. Much too much. My glorious country, not kaiserlich-königlich, devoid of King Stephen's crown and the crown of the Holy Roman Empire, my country in its new Union, my country which needs no justification or acknowledgment, but I'm tired and simply move my bishop, only to have to move it right back following Ivan's next move, I better resign right away, tell him that I've lost the game, but that I'd gladly go to Venice with him or to the Wolfgangsee this summer, or if his time really is so scarce, on a day-trip to Dürnstein on the Danube, as I know an old hotel there, and I take care to mention the wine, since Ivan really likes Dürnsteiner wine, but we'll never travel to these places, since he always has too much going on, since he has to go to Paris, since he has to get up tomorrow at seven o'clock.

Would you still want to see a movie? I ask, because by mentioning that I can keep Ivan from going home right away, I've opened the paper to the movie ads. THE THREE FANTASTIC SUPERMEN, TEXAS JIM, HOT NIGHTS IN RIO. But Ivan doesn't want to drive downtown anymore today, he leaves the chess pieces as they are, empties his glass in one move, walks very quickly to the door, as always, without good-bye, perhaps because we still have a whole life ahead of us.

I sew a button on my dressing gown and glance every now and then at the pile of papers before me. Fräulein Jellinek is waiting, sitting with her head bowed over the typewriter, she's inserted two sheets with carbon paper between them, and since I'm not saying anything, just biting off the thread, she's glad to hear the phone ring, she reaches for the receiver and I say: Please just say whatever you want, I'm not in, you have to check (but where is Fräulein Jellinek supposed to check, surely not in the closet or the storage cabinet as I can't be said to frequent either one)—say I'm sick, out of town, dead. Fräulein Jellinek looks tense and polite, covers the speaker with her hand and whispers: But it's long distance, Hamburg.

Please, Fräulein Jellinek, just say whatever amuses you. Fräulein Jellinek opts to say I'm not home, no, she's sorry, she doesn't know, she hangs up satisfied. Anyway it was a diversion. And what about Recklinghausen and London and Prague, what are we going to say there? We wanted to write them today, Fräulein Jellinek admonishes, so I quickly begin:

Dear Sirs:

thank you very much for your letter of, date, etc.

And suddenly it occurs to me that the lining is loose in the coat I call my spring coat in the spring, but which becomes my fall coat in the fall, and I run off to the closet since I have to sew in this lining, I rummage around for some dark blue thread, then inquire gaily: Where did we leave off, what was I saying? Oh, right. Just write whatever occurs to you, that I've left town or that I'm indisposed or coming down with something. Fräulein Jellinek laughs a little, she will doubtlessly write down "indisposed," because she believes in well-tempered refusals, which sound as friendly as they do neutral. One shouldn't allow people the slightest pretext, maintains Fräulein Jellinek, who always asks permission to go to the bathroom. She returns perfumed, pretty, tall, slim and consequently engaged to an intern from the Polyclinic and she uses her beautiful long fingers on the typewriter to hack out sincerely yours or every now and then best or cordial greetings.

Fräulein Jellinek waits and waits. The lining is sewn and we each take a sip from our teacups.

Just so you don't forget, the Urania, that's also very urgent. Fräulein Jellinek knows that now she's allowed to laugh as much as she wants since we're in Vienna, which doesn't fill her with awe like London and Santa Barbara and Moscow, she pens the letter all by herself, although I would say it bears a suspicious resemblance, almost word for word, to the one sent to all clubs and colleges.

Then the problem with England comes up, and I chew on the rest of the blue thread. You know what, let's quit for today and finish writing this stuff next week. Nothing occurs to me right now. Fräulein Jellinek lets me know she's been hearing this far too often and that it doesn't help in the least, she insists on starting, she wants to give it a try herself, in English.

"Dear Miss Freeman:
thank you very much for your letter of August 14th."

But now I have to explain this very complicated story to Fräulein Jellinek. I say to her, imploringly: The smartest thing would be for you to dash off two lines and then send all four letters to Dr. Richter, and I say nervously, since Ivan is going to call any minute: But no, for the tenth time, his name is Wulf and not Wolf, not like the wolf in the fairy tale, you can look it up, no, number 45, I'm almost positive, so go ahead and check, then file this junk away and we'll wait till he writes back, this Miss Freeman has caused nothing but a terrible mess.

Fräulein Jellinek shares this opinion, and she cleans the desk as I carry the telephone into the hall. The very next minute it actually does ring, and I let it ring three times, it's Ivan.

Is Jellinek gone?
Fräulein Jellinek, please!
All right Fräulein as far as I'm concerned
In fifteen minutes?
That'd be ok
No, we're just finishing up
Just whiskey, tea, no nothing else

While Fräulein Jellinek is combing her hair and putting her coat on, opening and closing her purse several times and looking for the mesh bag she uses to go shopping, she reminds me that there are three important letters I had wanted to write, and that we're out of stamps, she also wants to buy some Scotch tape, and I remind her that next time she should be sure to collect these people's names from all the little scraps of paper and write them down in the calendar, you know, all those people, there's always someone we have to keep in mind, someone who really should be in the calendar or the address book, since it's too hard to keep track of so many names.

Fräulein Jellinek and I wish each other a nice Sunday and I hope she doesn't decide to redrape her foulard around her neck once again, because Ivan really might show up any minute, I'm relieved to hear the door close and the delicate, firm heels of Fräulein Jellinek's new shoes clattering down the stairs.

Since Ivan is on his way I finish up very quickly, only the copies of the letters are still lying around, and Ivan asks just once what I'm up to there, and I say: Oh, nothing, but I look so embarrassed that he's forced to laugh. He's not interested in the letters, only in a plain piece of paper with the words "Three Murderers" which he puts back down. In general he avoids questions, but today Ivan asks, what do these notes mean, since I've left a few pages lying on the armchair. Merrily he takes one and reads: DEATHSTYLES. And from another piece of paper: THE EGYPTIAN DARKNESS. Isn't that your writing, did you write that? Since I don't answer, Ivan says: I don't like it, I suspected something like this was going on, and nobody wants all these books lying around in your crypt, why isn't there anything else, there must be other books, like EXSULTATE JUBILATE, which make you mad with joy, you're always mad with joy yourself, so why don't you write like that. It's disgusting to put this misery on the market, just adding to what's already there, these books are all absolutely loathsome. What kind of obsession is this anyway, all this gloom, everything's always sad and these books make it even worse in folio editions. Oh, right here, excuse me, but really: NOTES FROM THE DEAD HOUSE.

I say, intimidated: yes, but—

But nothing, says Ivan, and they're always suffering for all of humanity with all its troubles as well and they talk about all the wars and predict new ones, but when you're drinking coffee with me or when we're drinking wine and playing chess, then where are all the wars and where is humanity starving to death, and are you really sorry about all that or just sorry about the fact that you're losing, or because I'm about to be so hungry I could eat a horse and why are you laughing right now, does humanity have a lot to laugh about right this minute?

But I'm not laughing, I say, still I have to laugh and I allow affliction to occur elsewhere, since there isn't any here, where Ivan is sitting down with me to dinner. I can only think about the salt that isn't on the table yet, and about the butter I left in the kitchen, and I don't say it out loud but I take it upon myself to find Ivan a beautiful book, because Ivan hopes I won't write about the three murderers, he hopes I won't add to the world's misery in any book, and I'm no longer listening to what he's saying.

A storm of words starts in my head, then an incandescence, a few syllables begin to glow, and brightly colored commas fly out of all the dependent clauses and the periods which were once black have swollen into balloons and float up to my cranium, for everything will be like EXSULTATE JUBILATE in that glorious book I am thus just beginning to find. Should this book appear, as someday it must, people will writhe with laughter after only one page, they will leap for joy, they will be comforted, they will read on, biting their fists to suppress their cries of joy, it can't be helped, and when they sit down by the window and read still further they'll start flinging confetti to the pedestrians on the street below, so that they, too, will stop, astonished, as if they had walked into a carnival, and people will start throwing apples and nuts, dates and figs just like on St. Nicholas' Day, they will lean out of their windows without getting dizzy and shout out: Hear, hear! look and see! I've just read something wonderful, may I read it to you, everybody come closer, it's too wonderful!

And they begin to stop and notice, more and more people assemble, and Herr Breitner says hello for a change, he doesn't have to prove with his crutches that he's the only cripple, he croaks hello and how are you, and the fat soprano, who only leaves the house by night, coming and going in taxis, thins out somewhat, all at once she loses a hundred pounds, she appears in the stairwell, her theatrical stride carries her to the mezzanine without any shortage of breath, there she begins her coloratura, her voice twenty years younger: cari amici, teneri compagni! and no one remarks condescendingly we've heard Schwarzkopf and Callas sing that better, the words "fat cow" no longer resound in the stairwell, and the people from the fourth floor are rehabilitated, all intrigue dissolves into thin air. Everything stems from the joy following the book's appearance, a glorious book has at last arrived on earth and in Ivan's name I set out in search of its first pages, for it should come as a surprise to him. But Ivan continues to misinterpret my secrecy and today he says: You're blushing all over your face, what's happening, why are you laughing like an idiot? I only asked if I could have a little more ice for my whiskey.

When Ivan and I are quiet, because there's nothing to say, in other words when we don't talk, no silence descends, on the contrary, I notice that we are surrounded by so much, that everything around us is alive, everything becomes noticeable without being obtrusive, the whole city circulates and breathes, so Ivan and I aren't worried, because we aren't detached and locked up without contact, monadically, and we aren't stuck in some painful situation. We, too, form an acceptable part of the world, two people moving down the sidewalk idly or in haste, stepping on the zebra stripes of a street crossing, and even if we don't say a thing, even if we don't communicate with one another directly, Ivan will grab my arm in time and hold onto me so I'm not run over by a streetcar or an automobile. I always have to hurry a little to keep up with him, since he's so much taller and only has to take one step where I need two, but because of the link to the world I try to keep up with him, without falling too far behind, and in this way we arrive at the Bellaria or the Mariahilfer Strasse or the Schottenring, if there's any business to take care of. If one of us were about to lose the other we'd notice just in time, because, unlike others, we could never lose our tempers, provoke each other, be insolent, offend or reject one another. The only thing we're aware of is that we have to be at the travel agent's by six, that the parking meter might have expired, that we have to rush back to the car right this minute, and then we'll drive home to the Ungargasse, where we are safe from every conceivable danger that might threaten two human beings. I can even drop Ivan off at number 9, he doesn't have to come up to number 6 if he's so tired, and I promise to wake him with a phone call in an hour even if he's certain to swear at me, cursing and bemoaning the fact he'll be late for dinner. Because it happens that Lajos has called, the Lajos who once called my place asking for Ivan, when I answered with a secretary's voice, friendly, coolly, I'm sorry I don't know, will you please try his number, and then I have to battle a question. Where is Ivan when he's not home, not with me, and if a certain Lajos is looking for him? I just don't know, unfortunately I don't know anything, of course I see him from time to time, by chance I was even walking around town with him today, by chance we drove back together in his car to the Third District, so there's a man from Ivan's earlier life named Lajos who's being quite familiar and is even in possession of my phone number, and up to now I've only known the names Béla and András and a mother he calls his mother and whenever he talks about these three he hastily mentions he has to run up to the Hohe Warte without giving the exact street name—this happens often, just that I never hear anything about another woman, nothing about the children's mother, only their grandmother, who is of course Ivan's own mother, but

I imagine the mother of Béla and András left behind in Budapest, II. Bimbó Út 65, or in Gödöllö in an old summer cottage. Sometimes I think she's dead, shot, blown up by a mine or simply the victim of a disease in some Budapest hospital, or else she just stayed there, happy in her work, with some man whose name is not Ivan.

Long before I first heard Ivan shout the word "gyerekek!" or "kuss, gyerekek!" he told me: I'm sure you've already understood. I don't love anyone. Except my children, of course, but no one else. I nod, although I hadn't known, and it's obvious to Ivan that it should be obvious even to me. JUBILATE. Poised over an abyss, it nonetheless occurs to me how it should begin: EXSULTATE.

However, since today is the first warm day of the year we're driving to the GÄNSEHÄUFEL. Ivan has the afternoon off, only Ivan has afternoons off, or an hour off, sometimes he has a free evening. We never discuss my time, whether my hours are free or not, whether I even know what free and unfree really mean. In the little free time Ivan does have we lie in the weak sun on the lawn in front of the pool at the GÄNSEHÄUFEL, I've brought along my pocket chess set, and after an hour of wrinkling foreheads, trading pieces, castling, threats to the queen, many warnings of "check," we again arrive at a stalemate. Ivan wants to invite me for an ice cream at the Italian ice cream parlor, but there's no more time, the free afternoon is already over and we have to race back into town. I'll get my ice cream next time. While we're driving fast into town, over the Reichsbrücke and past the Praterstern, Ivan turns up the car radio very loud, though this doesn't drown out his commentary on how other drivers maneuver their cars, but the familiar places and streets we are traversing all change as the music from the radio, the speeding, the sudden stops and starts evoke in me a feeling of great adventure. I hold tightly onto the handle and, so fastened, I'd like to sing in the car, if I had a voice, or say to him faster, faster, fearlessly I let go of the handle and stretch my arms behind my head, beaming out at the Franz-Josefs-Kai and the Danube Canal and the Schottenring, for out of sheer bravado Ivan is taking a tour through downtown, I hope it will take a lot of time to cross the Ring that we're turning into now, we get into a traffic jam but force ourselves through, on our right is my old university, but it looks different somehow, less oppressive, and the Burgtheater, the Rathaus and the Parliament are all flooded by the music from the radio, this should never stop, it should last a long time, a whole film, which has never played before, but where I witness one marvel after another, because it is entitled DRIVING THROUGH VIENNA WITH IVAN, because it's entitled HAPPY, HAPPY WITH IVAN and HAPPY IN VIENNA, VIENNA HAPPY, and these rapid, dizzying sequences don't stop when he brakes hard, or when warm swaths of exhaust come stinking through the open windows, happy, happy, it's called happy, it has to be called happy, because the whole Ringstrasse is awash with music, I have to laugh at our jackrabbit starts, since today I'm not at all afraid and have no desire to jump out at the next light, I'd like to keep driving for hours, quietly humming along, just loud enough for me to hear but not Ivan, because the music is louder.

Auprès de ma blonde
I'm
You're what?
I'm
What?
I'm happy
Qu'il fait bon
Did you say something?
I didn't say anything
Fait bon, fait bon
I'll tell you later

What do you want later?
I'll never tell you
Qu'il fait bon
So tell me
It's too loud, I can't talk any louder
What do you want to say?
I can't say it any louder
Qu'il fait bon dormir
Go on, tell me, you have to tell me today
Qu'il fait bon, fait bon
That I have risen
Since I've survived the winter
Since I'm so happy
Since I already see the Stadtpark
Fait bon, fait bon
Since Ivan has arisen
Since Ivan and I
Qu'il fait bon dormir!

At night Ivan asks: why is there only a Wailing Wall, why hasn't anyone ever built a Wall of Joy?

Happy. I'm happy.

If Ivan wants it I'll build a Wall of Joy all around Vienna, where the old bastions were and where the Ringstrasse is and as far as I'm concerned, a Happy Wall as well around the ugly Vienna Belt. Then we could visit these new walls every day and be so happy we would leap for joy, for this is happiness, we are happy. Ivan asks: Should I turn off the lights?

No, leave one on, please leave one light on!

Some day I'll turn all the lights out, but now, go to sleep, be happy.

I am happy.

If you're not happy—

Then what?

You won't ever be able to accomplish anything good.

And I tell myself that if I'm happy I'll be able to.

Ivan walks out of the room quietly, turning off each light as he goes, I listen to him leave, silently I lie there, happy.

I jump up and flick on the nightlight, in terror I stand in the room with my hair mussed up, biting my lips, then I rush out and turn on one light after the other, since Malina may already be home, I have to speak to Malina at once. Why aren't there any Happy Walls or any Walls of Joy? What's the name of the wall I walk into every night? Malina has come out of his room, he looks at me astonished and shakes his head. Is it still worth it, with me? I ask Malina, and Malina doesn't answer, he leads me into the bathroom, takes a washcloth and runs warm water over it, then he uses it to wipe my face and says kindly: Just look at yourself, what's the matter this time? Malina is smearing mascara all over my face, I push him away and hunt for a makeup remover pad, go to the mirror, the smears disappear, the black marks, the reddish-brown traces of cream. Malina looks at me, thoughtfully, he says: You're asking too much too soon. It's not worth it yet, but it might be worth it later.

Downtown I saw an old desk at an antique dealer's near St. Peter's Church, he's not coming down with the price, but I'd like to buy it anyway, because then I could write something on some old, durable parchment, such as can no longer be found, with a genuine quill pen, such as can no longer be found, with some ink, such as is no longer manufactured. I would like to write an incunabulum standing up, for today twenty years have passed since I've loved Ivan, and it's been one year and three months and thirty-one days on this 31st of the month since I've known him, but then I also want to write down a year with a monstrous Roman numeral which no one will ever understand, ANNO DOMINI MDXXLI. Using red ink I would illuminate the majuscules with Turk's-cap lilies and would be able to hide myself in the legend of a woman who never existed.

The Mysteries of the Princess of Kagran

Once upon a time there lived a princess of Chagre or Chageran from a lineage known in later times as Kagran. And it happened that the same St. George who slew the dragon in the swamp so that Klagenfurt could arise after the monster's death, was active here as well in the ancient Marchfelddorf beyond the Danube, and a church in the vicinity of the flood plain commemorates his presence.

The princess was very young and very beautiful and rode a black horse whose speed exceeded that of all others. Her retainers conferred among themselves and begged her to stay back, for the land along the Danube they had entered was ever in danger, and no borders yet existed, where later there would be Rhaetia, Marcomannia, Noricum, Moesia, Dacia, Illyria and Pannonia. Neither was there yet Cisleithania nor Transleithania, because the great migrations were still under way. One day Hungarian Hussars rode up out of the Puszta, from faraway Hungaria whose expanses were yet unexplored. They overrode the land with their wild Asiatic horses which were as fast as the princess's black horse, and all were greatly afraid.

The princess lost her dominions and fell into captivity several times, for she did not fight; however, neither did she wish to be given in marriage to the old king of the Huns or the old king of the Avars. They held her as booty and guarded her with many red and blue horsemen. Because the princess was a true princess, she preferred death to allowing herself be

47

made the bride of an old king, and before the night was over she had to pluck up her courage, for her captors intended to bear her to the castle of the king of the Huns or even the Avars. She thought of fleeing and hoped her guards would fall asleep before dawn, but her hopes gradually faded. They had taken her black horse as well, and she did not know how to find her way out of the camp and back to the blue hills of her homeland. Sleeplessly she lay in her tent.

Deep into the night she thought she heard a voice, which did not speak but sang, it whispered and lulled, but then it stopped singing to strangers and sang only for her in a language which enthralled her, though she could not understand a word. Despite this she knew the voice was meant for her alone and that it was calling to her. The princess did not need to understand the words. Enchanted, she arose and opened her tent onto the unending dark night of Asia, and the first star she spied fell to the earth. The voice which had so pierced the night promised her one wish, and she wished with all her heart. Suddenly she saw a stranger before her covered in a long black cloak, he did not belong to the red and blue horsemen, he kept his face hidden in the night, but although she could not see him, she knew that it was he who had lamented her plight and had sung for her in a voice such as she had never heard before, so full of hope, and now he had come to set her free. He held her black horse by the reins and she moved her lips quietly and asked: Who are you? what is your name, my savior? how shall I thank you? He put two fingers to his mouth, she guessed this to mean she should be silent, he gave her a sign to follow and threw his black mantle around her so no one could see them. They were blacker than black in the night, and he led her and her horse, who kept his hooves quiet and did not neigh, through the camp and some way out onto the steppe. His wonderful song still rang in her ears, and the princess, who had fallen under the spell of this voice, yearned to hear it once more. She intended to ask him to head upstream with her, but he did not answer and handed her the reins. She was still in the utmost danger and he signaled her to ride on.

She had fallen in love, although she had not even seen his face, since he kept it hidden, but she obeyed him, because she had to obey him. She swung onto her black horse, stared down at him dumbly, longing to say words of parting in his language and her own. She spoke with her eyes. Then he turned and disappeared into the night.

The horse began to trot in the direction of the river, where the moist air beckoned. For the first time in her life the princess cried, and later migrants found many river pearls there, which they presented to their first king, and which were later placed together with other most ancient gems in the holy crown of King Stephen, where they can still be seen today.

When she reached the open country, she rode upstream for many days and nights until she arrived at a place where the waters spread away on all sides regardless of a main channel, and the country became a swamp for miles upon miles, covered by a vast sea of low willow-bushes. The water was still at normal level, so the bushes could bend and rustle in the perpetual wind of the plain, which kept them crippled, forever unable to raise themselves. They swayed as gently as grass, and the princess lost her orientation. It was as if everything had swirled into motion, waves of willow wands, waves of grass: the plain was alive and she was the only human living there. Happy to slip beyond the control of the stern banks, the Danube wandered about at will among the intricate network of channels intersecting the islands everywhere with broad avenues down which the waters poured with a shouting sound. Listening carefully from amid the foaming rapids, eddies and whirlpools, the princess realized that the water was tearing at the sandy banks, carrying away masses of shore and willow-clumps. Islands sank and piled up again, which shifted daily in size and shape, and so the flatland continued to live, ever in flux, until willows and islands would disappear without a trace under the rising flood. A patch of smoke could be discerned in the heavens, but nothing of the bluish hills of the princess's native land. She knew not where she was, she did not recognize the Devín heights, the still unnamed spurs of the Carpathians, nor did she see the river March as it stole into the Danube; even less did she know that one day a border would be drawn through the water, between two countries with names. For at that time no countries existed, and there were no borders.

When her horse could go no farther, she dismounted on a gravel bank, she watched the waters grow more and more turbid and she was afraid, as this foretold a flood. She no longer saw any way out of this singular world of willows, winds and waters, and she led her horse along slowly, fascinated by this forlorn, bewitched kingdom of solitude she had entered. She began casting about for a suitable camping-ground for the night, as the sun was setting, and the river, that huge fluid being, amplified its sounds and voices, its clapping, its laughter that swelled up from the rocks along the bank, its faint sweet whisperings along a quiet bend, its hissing roil and, below all mere surface sounds, the steady thundering in its bed. In the evening, swarms of gray crows approached and the cormorants began to line the banks, storks stood fishing in the water and marsh birds of all sorts filled the air with singing, petulant cries.

As a child the princess had heard of this extreme, severe land along the Danube, about the magic islands where people died of hunger, hallucinating and enjoying supreme ecstasy in the fury of their ruin. She felt the island itself was moving along with her, yet it was not the roaring waters that she feared; rather it was the willows that left her awed and anguished, imparting an uneasiness such as she had never known. Some essence emanated from them that besieged the princess's heart. She had come to the edge of the world. The princess crouched before her black horse who had stretched out exhausted and now uttered a plaintive sound, for he, too, felt there was no longer any way out, and with a dying glance begged forgiveness of the princess for no longer being able to carry her through and over the water. The princess lay down in a slight depression beside the horse, overcome with a dread she had never known, the willows whispered more and more, they hissed, they laughed, they screamed shrilly and sighed and moaned. No soldiers were pursuing her any longer, but she was surrounded by an army of strange beings, myriads of leaves fluttered over the bushy willow-heads, she was in the region where the river led into the realm of the dead, and her eyes were wide-open as an immense column of shadowy creatures advanced upon her, she buried her head in her arms to deaden the sound of the terrifying wind, then all at once she jumped up, alerted by the sounds of something brushing, tapping. She could move neither forward nor backward, she could merely choose between the water and the overpowering willows, but in this bleakest gloom a light appeared before her, and since she knew it could only be the light of a spirit, and not of any human, she strode forward, deathly afraid but wholly enchanted and enthralled.

It was no light; it was a flower which had not come from the earth but had blossomed in the raging night, redder than red. She stretched out her fingers toward the flower and at once felt the touch of another hand. The wind and the laughter of the willows grew quiet, and by the light of the moon, which rose white and strange above the stilling waters of the Danube, she recognized the stranger in the black mantle standing before her, holding her hand and covering his mouth with two fingers of his other hand so that she would not ask his name again; at the same time he smiled at her with dark, warm eyes. He was blacker than the black that had engulfed her, and she sank into his arms and onto the sand, and he lay the flower on her breast as if she were dead and covered them both with his cloak.

The sun was high in the heavens when the stranger woke the princess out of her deathlike sleep. He had quieted the elements, the true immortals. The princess and the stranger began to talk as in days of yore and when one spoke the other smiled. They exchanged bright words and dark. The flood had ebbed, and before the sun descended the princess heard her black horse rise, snort and trot through the bush. She was terrified at heart and said: I must continue up the river, come with me, never leave me again.

But the stranger shook his head, and the princess asked: Do you have to return to your people?

The stranger smiled: My people is older than all peoples of the world and is scattered in the four winds.

So come with me! the princess cried out of pain and impatience, but the stranger said: Patience, have patience, for you know, you know. The princess had acquired second sight during the night, and she therefore said through her tears: I know we will see each other again.

Where? asked the stranger, smiling, and when? for only the everlasting ride is true.

The princess looked at the faded, wilting flower left lying on the ground and said, closing her eyes, on the threshold of dreams: let me see!

Slowly she began to relate: It will be farther up the river, once again there will be a great migration, it will be in another century, let me guess? it will be more than twenty centuries from now, you will speak as people do: beloved …

What is a century? asked the stranger.

The princess took a handful of sand and let it run quickly through her fingers, she said: twenty centuries are about like that, then it will be time for you to come and kiss me.

So it will be soon, said the stranger, go on!

It will be in a city and in this city there will be a street, continued the princess, we will play cards, I will lose my eyes, in the mirror it will be Sunday.

What are city and street? asked the stranger, dismayed.

The princess began to sigh and said: Soon we shall see, I know only the words, but we shall see when you pierce my heart with these thorns, we shall stand before a window, let me speak! there will be a window

full of flowers, one flower for every century, more than twenty flow-
ers, then we shall know we are in the proper place, and all the flowers
shall resemble this one!

The princess swung onto her black horse, no longer able to endure the
clouds, for the stranger was quietly designing his and her first death.
He sang nothing to her in parting, and she rode toward the blue hills
of her country that began to appear in the distance; she rode in great
silence, for he had already driven the first thorn into her heart, and in
the castle yard, in the midst of her faithful followers, she fell from her
black horse, bleeding. But she merely smiled and stammered in a fever:
I know, I know!

I didn't buy the desk because it would have cost five thousand
schillings and came from a cloister, a fact that also bothers me,
and I wouldn't have been able to write on it anyway, since parchment and ink are not to be found, furthermore Fräulein Jellinek
would not have been very enthusiastic as she is quite accustomed
to my typewriter. I quickly stash the pages about the Princess of
Kagran in a file so Fräulein Jellinek won't see what I've written,
besides, it's more important that we finally "get something done,"
and I sit down behind her on the three steps leading to the library,
straighten some papers and dictate to her:

Dear Sirs.

Of course Fräulein Jellinek has undoubtedly put down the
heading and today's date, she's waiting, nothing occurs to me and
I say: Dear Fräulein Jellinek, please write whatever you want, although the confused woman can't possibly know what I mean here
by want. Exhausted, I say: Write, for example, that for reasons of
health, oh I see, we've already had that? write something about
other commitments, we've used that one too many times as well?
then just thank you and best wishes. Sometimes Fräulein Jellinek
is surprised but she doesn't show it, she doesn't know any dear
Sirs, just Herr Dr. Krawanja, who is specializing in neurology and

intends to marry her in July, which she confessed to me today, I'm invited to the wedding, she'll go to Venice, but while her secret thoughts are in the Polyclinic or furnishing her new apartment, she is filling out forms for me, handling my accounts which are in an incredible mess, she is now unearthing letters by the kilogram from 1962, 1963, 1964, 1965, 1966, she sees that all her attempts to establish any order with me are in vain, she invokes this order with incantations of "filing," "putting away," "organizing by subject," she wants to proceed alphabetically, chronologically, she wants to separate business from private matters, Fräulein Jellinek would be capable of all of this but I can't exactly explain to her that ever since I've known Ivan I consider any time spent on such activities wasted, that I first must put myself in order and that the idea of establishing order in this paper chaos interests me less and less. I pull myself together once again and dictate:

Dear Sirs:

Thank you for your letter of January 26.

Dear Herr Schöntal:

The person you address, claim to know and whom you are even inviting does not exist. I want to try, although it's six o'clock in the morning, which seems to me the proper time for an explanation that I owe to you and so many others, although it's six o'clock in the morning and I should have been asleep long ago, but there's so much that never permits me to sleep. You did not invite me to a children's party or just to play while the cat's away and I'm sure the parties, the banquets, the receptions all stem from a social necessity. You see, I am trying very hard to look at things from your point of view. I know we had an appointment, I should have at least given you a call, but I lack words to describe my situation, moreover, propriety demands I do not call, as it forbids me to speak of certain things. The friendly facade you see and on which I myself rely from time to time has, unfortunately, less and less to do with me. You will not think I have bad manners and thus have kept you waiting out of rudeness, manners are about the only thing I still have, and if they had ever taught "manners" in school, it certainly would have been the subject that would have appealed to me the most and in which I would have had the best grades. Dear Herr Schöntal, for years now I have been unable—this often lasts for weeks—to answer the door or pick up the telephone or call someone, it's impossible for me, and I don't know how I might be helped, I am probably beyond help already.

I'm also completely incapable of thinking about things people tell me to think about, about deadlines, work, appointments, nothing is clearer to me at six in the morning than the immensity of my misfortune, since I am completely and justly stricken with unending pain that hits each and every nerve at each and every minute of the day. I'm very tired, may I tell you how tired I am …

I pick up the phone and hear the droning voice: Telegrams, please hold, please hold, please hold, please hold, please hold. Meanwhile I scribble on a piece of paper: Dr. Walter Schöntal, Wielandstrasse 10, Nuremberg. Unfortunately cannot come stop letter follows.

Telegrams, please hold, please hold, please hold. It clicks, the lively, well-rested voice of a young woman asks: May I have your number please?

Thank you, I'll call back.

We have a whole bundle of fatigue sentences, Ivan and I, since he's often terribly exhausted, even though he's so much younger than I am, and I'm also very tired, Ivan stayed up too late, he was with some people at the Heuriger in Nussdorf till five in the morning, then he drove with them back into town where they had some goulash soup, that must have been at the same time I was writing to Lily for the two hundredth time and some other things as well, at least I sent a telegram, and Ivan calls during the day, after work, his voice barely recognizable.

Exhausted to death, completely exhausted
I'm simply dead
No I don't think so, I've just
I'm lying down, I'm simply
At least I'll be able to get some sleep this time, just this once
Tonight I'm going to bed very early, and you
I'm falling asleep already, but tonight
So go to bed earlier for once
Like a dead fly, I can't tell you
Of course if you're so tired
I was so tired just now I could have died
So it doesn't look like tonight's
Of course if you weren't so tired now
I don't think I'm hearing right
Then listen carefully for once
But you're falling asleep
Obviously not right now, I'm just tired
You have to rest
I left the downstairs door open
Maybe I am tired, but you must be even more exhausted
......
Right this minute of course, when do you think
......
I want you here at once!

I throw down the receiver, throw my weariness away, run down the stairs and across the street, diagonally. The gate to number 9 is ajar, the door to the room is ajar, and now Ivan is repeating all the sentences about exhaustion one more time, until we're too tired and too exhausted to be able to bemoan the extent of our exhaustions, we stop talking and keep each other awake despite the utmost fatigue, and in the half darkness I don't stop looking at Ivan until the wakeup service oo calls, when he can sleep for another quarter-hour, I don't stop hoping, begging and believing to have heard one sentence which did not arise from weariness, one that provides me with some insurance in this world, but something about my eyes draws tight, the secretion from the glands is so slight it won't suffice for even a single tear in the corner of each eye. Is one sentence enough to insure the person for whose sake it was uttered? There must be some insurance that is not of this world.

If Ivan doesn't have any time for a whole week, which I just realized today, I lose my composure. It comes without reason, it's senseless, I've handed Ivan his glass with three ice cubes, but immediately I get up and cross over to the window with my own glass, I want to find a way out of the room, perhaps I could leave on the pretext of going to the bathroom, just in passing, as if I were looking for a book in the library, although book and bathroom cannot be said to be connected. Before I escape from the room, before I tell myself that after all Beethoven, being deaf, did compose the Ninth Symphony in the house across the street: but I'm not deaf—actually he composed a lot of other things there as well, I could tell Ivan what else besides the Ninth—but now I can't leave the room anymore, for Ivan has already noticed, since my shoulders are tense, since the small handkerchief is no longer enough to soak up the tears, Ivan must be to blame for this natural disaster, even if he didn't do anything, after all it's impossible to cry that much. Ivan takes me by the shoulder and leads me to the table, I'm supposed to sit down and drink, and while crying I want to apologize for crying. Ivan is very surprised, he says: Why shouldn't you cry, go right ahead, cry if you want, as much as you can, a little more, you just have to cry yourself dry.

I cry myself dry and Ivan drinks a second whiskey, he doesn't ask me anything, he doesn't intervene with consolation, he is neither nervous nor irritated, he just waits the way you do for a storm to pass, he hears the sobbing diminish, five more minutes and he can dip a cloth in some ice water for me, he places it over my eyes.

I hope, my fräulein, that we're not jealous.

No, nothing like that.

I start crying again, but now only because it feels so good. Of course not. There isn't any reason.

But of course there's a reason. For me it was a week without any injections of reality. I wouldn't want Ivan to ask me the reason, but he'll never do that, he'll just allow me to cry from time to time.

Cry yourself dry! he'll command.

I inhabit this animated world of a half-wild woman, freed for the first time from the judgments and prejudices of my environment, no longer prepared to pronounce any sentence on the world, ready only for an immediate answer, for lamentation and pity, joy and happiness, hunger and thirst, because for too long I have been alive without really living. My imagination, richer than any Yagé-fantasy, is finally brought into motion by Ivan, inside me he has set off something immense, which is now radiating from me, without interruption I emit rays to the world which needs them, I beam out from this one point, which is not only the center of my life, but of my will "to live well," to be useful once again, for I would like Ivan to need me like I need him, and for the rest of our lives. Sometimes he, too, needs me because he rings the doorbell, I open the door, he's holding a newspaper, he looks around and says: I have to go right away, do you need your car tonight? Ivan has left with my car keys, and even this short appearance of his shakes reality once again, each of his sentences affects me and the oceans of the earth and the constellations, I chew on a sausage sandwich in the kitchen and put the plate in the sink, while Ivan is still say-ing "I have to go right away," I clean the dusty gramophone and gently stroke the records lying around with a velvet brush, "I want you here at once!" says Ivan as he's driving up to the Hohe Warte, because he has to see the children right away, Béla has sprained his hand, but Ivan said, "I want you here at once!" and I must accommodate this dangerous sentence between eating sausage sandwiches and opening letters and dusting, because a fiery explosion might occur at any moment among all the everyday things that are no longer everyday. I stare out into space and listen and write a list:

Electrician
Electric bill
Sapphire needle
Toothpaste
Letters to Z.K. and lawyer
Cleaners

I could put on a record but I hear "I want you here at once!" I could wait for Malina, only I better go to bed, I'm extremely tired, utterly fatigued, exhausted to death "I want you—" Ivan has to go right away, he's just bringing back the keys, it turns out Béla did not sprain his hand, Ivan's mother was exaggerating, I hold onto Ivan in the hall, and Ivan asks: What's the matter with you, why are you grinning like an idiot?

Oh nothing, it's just that I feel so idiotically good, I'm turning into an idiot.

But Ivan says: you don't mean idiotically good, just good, that's all. What used to happen when you felt good before? Did you always turn into such an idiot?

I shake my head, Ivan raises his hand in jest, as if he were about to hit me, the fear returns, I say to him, choking: Please don't, not my head.

After an hour the shivers are gone and I think I should tell Ivan, but Ivan wouldn't understand something so irrational, and because I can't talk to him about murder, I have to rely on my own resources, for evermore, I only try to cut out this abscess, to burn it off for Ivan's sake, I can't keep wallowing in this puddle of murder thoughts, with Ivan I'm sure I'll manage to get rid of them, he shall cleanse me of this disease, he shall save me. But since Ivan neither loves me nor needs me now, why should he ever love or need me? He only sees my face getting smoother and smoother and is glad when he can make me laugh, and again he'll explain to me that we're insured against everything, just like our cars, against earthquakes and hurricanes, against theft and accidents, against arson and hail, but one sentence alone keeps me insured and nothing else. No policy in the world can cover me.

In the afternoon I pull myself together and attend this lecture in the Institut Français, of course I arrive late and have to sit in the back near the door, from a distance I am greeted by François, who works in the embassy and somehow sees to it that our cultures are exchanged, reconciled or mutually fructified, he himself doesn't know exactly how, neither of us knows since neither of us needs this, but it helps our countries, he waves me closer, wants to get up, points to his seat, but I don't want to walk up to François now and cause a disturbance, because elderly ladies with hats and many old gentlemen, also some young people standing by the wall next to me, are listening as though they were in church, slowly I take in this sentence or that, and now I, too, lower my head, I keep hearing something about "la prostitution universelle," wonderful, I think, how absolutely correct, the man from Paris with a pale ascetic face is speaking with the voice of a choir boy about the 120 days of Sodom and now for the tenth time I'm hearing something about universal prostitution, the room with its pious listeners, with its universal sterility, starts spinning around me but at least I'd finally like to know whether universal prostitution will go on or not, and in this church of de Sade I cast a challenging glance at a young man who also glances back blasphemously and for an hour we keep looking at each other surreptitiously and conspiratorially, as if during mass in a church at the time of the Inquisition. Before I start laughing, with a handkerchief between my teeth, and before my stifled laughter becomes a coughing fit, I walk out, leaving a hall of indignant listeners. I have to call Ivan at once.

What did I think? Very interesting
Oh right, so-so, and you
Nothing much, it was interesting
You be sure and go to bed early
You're the one who's yawning, you should go to sleep
I'm not going to, I don't know yet
No, but tomorrow I have to
Do you really have to tomorrow?

I'm sitting alone at home and thread a sheet of paper into the typewriter, without thinking I type: Death will come.

Fräulein Jellinek has left a letter out to be signed.

Dear Herr Schöntal:
Thank you for your letter of last year, I am dismayed to note it is dated the 19th of September. Unfortunately due to many impediments it was impossible to answer earlier, and this year it will be equally impossible for me to take on any additional commitments. Many thanks and best regards.

I put in another piece of paper and toss the first in the wastebasket.

Dear Herr Schöntal:
Today I write to you in the utmost anxiety, in the greatest haste.

Since I do not know you it is easier for me to write to you than to my friends, and since you are a human being, and I deduce this from your very friendly efforts—

Vienna,…

An unknown woman.

Everyone would maintain that Ivan and I are not happy. Or that we haven't had any reason to call ourselves happy for a long time. But everyone isn't right. Everyone is no one. I forgot to ask Ivan about the tax forms on the phone, Ivan has generously promised to do my taxes for next year, I don't care about taxes and what these taxes this year want from me in some other year, my only concern is Ivan, when he talks about next year, and Ivan tells me today he forgot to mention over the phone that he's had enough sandwiches and that he'd really like to find out what I know how to cook, and now I'm expecting more out of a single evening than from all of next year. For if Ivan wants me to cook, then it has to mean something, he won't be able to scoot off so quickly anymore the way he can after a drink, and tonight while looking around my library, among all the books I can't find a single cookbook, I have to buy some at once, how absurd, what have I been reading all this time, what good is it to me now, if I can't put it to use for Ivan. THE CRITIQUE OF PURE REASON, read under 60 watts in the Beatrix-gasse, Locke, Leibnitz and Hume, in the dismal light of the National Library under the little reading lamps, beguiling my mind with concepts from all ages from the pre-Socratic philosophers to BEING AND NOTHINGNESS, Kafka, Rimbaud and Blake read under 25 watts in a hotel in Paris, Freud, Adler and Jung read at 360 watts in a lonely Berlin street, to the quiet rotations of the Chopin Études, an inflammatory speech about the expropriation of intellectual property studied on a beach near Genoa, its pages full of salt flecks and warped by the sun, LA COMÉDIE HUMAINE read with a fairly high fever, weakened by antibiotics, in Klagenfurt,

Proust read in Munich until daybreak and until the roofers burst into the attic room, the French Moralists and the Vienna Circle of Logical Empiricists with my stockings hanging loose, everything from DE RERUM NATURA to LE CULTE DE LA RAISON at thirty French cigarettes a day, history and philosophy, medicine and psychology practiced, in the Steinhof asylum work on the anamneses of schizophrenics and manic-depressives, scripts composed in the Auditorium Maximum at only 43 degrees and notes jotted at 100 degrees in the shade on de mundo, de mente, de motu, Marx and Engels read after washing my hair and V. I. Lenin when completely drunk, newspapers and newspapers and newspapers read while distraught and escaping, newspapers read while still a child in front of the stove, while lighting the fire, and newspapers and periodicals and paperbacks everywhere, at all train stations, in all trains, in streetcars, buses, airplanes and everything about everything, in four languages, fortiter, fortiter, and everything understood that can be read, and freed from all I have read for one hour, I lie down next to Ivan and say: If you really want I will write a book for you which doesn't yet exist. But you have to really want it, want it from me, and I'll never demand that you read it.

Ivan says: Let's hope it'll be a book with a happy ending.

Let's hope so.

I've cut the meat into even pieces, diced the onion very finely, measured out the paprika, because today I'm making pörkölt and even eggs in mustard sauce before that, I'm only debating whether apricot dumplings might be too much after everything else, perhaps just some fruit, but if Ivan should be in Vienna on New Year's Eve I want to try krambambuli, where you're supposed to burn the sugar, and not even my mother did that anymore. I can guess from the cookbooks which dishes are beyond my range of possibilities and which ones are still within, what might appeal to Ivan, but there's too much talk of setting aside, whipping, stirring and kneading for my taste, of top heat and bottom heat which I don't even know how to obtain in my electric oven or whether the number 200 on the oven dial is applicable for my recipes from OLD AUSTRIA INVITES YOU TO DINE or from the LITTLE HUNGARIAN KITCHEN and so I just try to surprise Ivan, who is in despair over the hundredth roast or tenderloin or tafelspitz with horseradish sauce and the eternal palatschinken for dessert offered in the restaurants. The things I'm cooking for him aren't on the menu, and I try to riddle out how to mix the good old days of lard and sweet and sour cream with the sensible new age of yogurt and lettuce lightly sprinkled with oil and lemon juice, dominated by vegetables rich in vitamins which are not supposed to be cooked, where carbohydrates, calories and moderation all count, without spices. Ivan has no idea I'm already up and running around in the morning indignantly asking why there isn't any chervil anymore, where can I find tarragon and when can I find basil, since the recipes call for it. As always the grocer has only parsley and leeks, the fish market hasn't had any brook trout for years, and so what little I do find I sprinkle at random on the meat and vegetables. I hope the onion smell won't stay on my hands, I keep running to the bathroom in order to wash my hands and wipe out with perfume all traces of any odor and to brush my hair. Ivan is only allowed to see the result: the table set and the candle burning, and Malina would be amazed that I've even managed to chill the wine in time, warm the plates, and between whisking and toasting the rolls I apply eye shadow and mascara in front of Malina's shaving mirror, pluck my eyebrows to their proper shape, and this synchronized labor which no one appreciates is more strenuous than anything I've ever done before. But for it I will receive the highest reward, since Ivan will come as early as seven and stay until midnight. Five hours of Ivan would be enough to give me a few days' confidence, a shot in the arm, get my blood going, aftercare, preventive treatment, a cure. Nothing would be too much trouble, nothing too far-fetched for me, too strenuous, in order to snatch a piece of Ivan's life: if

Ivan mentions during dinner that he used to go sailing in Hungary then right away I'll want to learn to sail, first thing tomorrow morning if possible, in the Old Danube as far as I'm concerned, in the Kaiserwasser, so that I'll be all set to accompany him if he goes sailing again some day. For it is not in my power to keep Ivan chained or shackled. Because the dinner is ready too soon, I stand in the kitchen keeping guard over the oven, pondering the reasons for this disability which has taken the place of so many erstwhile abilities. Chains imply restrictions, tactics, strategic withdrawals, what Ivan calls the Game. He challenges me to stay in the Game, because he doesn't realize that it no longer exists for me, that the Game is up. I think about my Ivan-lesson whenever I make excuses for myself, whenever I wait, for Ivan thinks that I should begin by calmly letting him wait, that I shouldn't make excuses. He also says: I should be the one to run after you, you better not ever run after me, you're in bad need of some private tutoring, who was it that failed to teach you the basics? But because Ivan isn't even slightly curious he doesn't really want to know who didn't teach me, I quickly have to sidestep and distract him, surely someday I'll succeed in producing a perfectly inscrutable smile, a mood, an annoyed air, but none of this ever works with Ivan. You're too transparent says Ivan, I can see what's going on with you every minute, you have to play the Game, so play something for me! But what should I play for him? The first attempt to reproach Ivan for not calling back yesterday, for forgetting my cigarettes, for still not knowing what brand I smoke, ends in a grimace, because before I've even reached the door, when he rings the bell, my reproaches have all evaporated, and Ivan immediately reads the weather report from my face: clearing, sunny, a warm front, cloudless skies, five continuous hours of beautiful weather.

Why don't you go ahead and say it
What?

That you want to come over again
But!
I won't permit you to say it
You see
So that you have to stay in the Game
I don't want any game
But without a game it won't work

Thus, because of Ivan, who wants the Game, I have learned a set of swearing sentences, I'm still very shocked at the first swearing sentence, but now I've almost become addicted and expect them, because it's a good sign when Ivan starts to swear.

You're a little bitch, yes you, what else?
You always get me to change my mind, that's right, you
Because it's true, please be so kind as to laugh
Don't give me those icy eyes
Les hommes sont des cochons
You're bound to know at least that much French
Les femmes aiment les cochons
I'm going to talk to you any way I want
You're a little beast
You do whatever you want with me as it is
No I'm not trying to wean you off, it's about learning more
You're too dumb, you don't understand anything
You have to become a really big beast
It'd be great if you became the biggest beast ever
Right, that's just what I want, what else?
You have to change completely
Of course with your talent, you know, you must admit
You're a witch so why not take advantage of it for once

They've really spoiled you completely
That's what you are all right, don't get so upset over every word
Don't you understand the rules?

The swearing sentences are the sole property of Ivan, since I don't respond with any answers, only outcries, or very often with a "But Ivan!" which is now no longer meant to be taken as seriously as it was in the beginning.

What does Ivan know about the rules which apply to me? but I'm still amazed that rules can be found in Ivan's vocabulary.

Despite all our differences, when it comes to our names Malina and I share the same reservations—Ivan is the only one whose name fits him completely, and since it is completely natural to him, since he identifies with his name, it is also a pleasure for me to pronounce it, to think it, to whisper it to myself. Ivan's name has become a source of pleasure, an indispensable luxury in my poverty-stricken life, and I see to it that Ivan's name is heard, whispered, and quietly thought about throughout the city. Also when I'm by myself, when I'm walking through Vienna all alone, there are many places I can say, I've walked here with Ivan, I waited for Ivan there, I had dinner with Ivan in the LINDE, I drank espresso with Ivan at the Kohlmarkt, Ivan works on the Kärntnerring, this is where Ivan buys his shirts, over there is Ivan's travel agency. He won't have to run back off to Paris or Munich again! Also the places where I haven't been with Ivan: I say to myself, some time I'll have to come here with Ivan in the evening and look down on the city from the Cobenzl or from the Herrengasse high-rise. Ivan reacts immediately and jumps up when his name is called, but Malina hesitates, and I hesitate the same way in my turn. That's why Ivan's clever not to call me by name all the time and instead use whatever pejorative comes to mind or simply say "my fräulein." My fräulein, we're letting it show again, what a disgrace, we'll be wanting to wean ourselves off that very soon now. Glissons. Glissons.

I can understand that Ivan isn't interested in Malina. I also take care they don't encroach upon each other. But I don't fully understand why Malina never talks about Ivan. He doesn't mention him, not even in passing, he very adroitly avoids overhearing my telephone conversations with Ivan or meeting Ivan in the stairwell. He acts as if he still doesn't recognize Ivan's car, although my own car is very often parked in the Münzgasse, just behind or just in front of Ivan's, and in the morning when I walk out of the house with Malina to drive him the short way to the Arsenalgasse so he won't be late for work, you'd think he'd have to notice I don't view Ivan's car as just another traffic obstacle, rather I greet it tenderly, caressing it with my hand even when it's dusty or wet and I'm relieved to discover the number has stayed the same overnight: W 99.823. Malina climbs in as I await some cathartic, mocking word, some embarrassing observation, a change of countenance, but Malina torments me with his impeccable self-control, his imperturbable trust. While I so tensely expect the great challenge, Malina pedantically explains to me what he has planned for the week, today they'll be filming in the Hall of Fame, he's having a talk with the weapons expert, the uniform expert and the medals expert, the director is away giving a lecture in London, and because of this Malina has to go by himself to an auction of weapons and pictures at the Dorotheum, but he doesn't want to make any decisions, the young man Montenuovo will receive his certification, Malina has to work this Saturday and Sunday. I'd forgotten it was his turn to work his week, and surely Malina must see that I forgot, since I said the wrong thing and showed too much surprise, but he continues to deceive himself as if there weren't anyone or anything else, as if it were just he and I. As if I were thinking about him—as always.

I've already looked for excuses several times and postponed the interview with Herr Mühlbauer, who used to be with the VIENNA DAILY NEWS and then switched without any scruples to its political competition, the VIENNA EVENING EDITION, but Herr Mühlbauer always attains his goal thanks to his tenacity, his "Küss die Hand" phone calls, at first everybody thinks, as I do, I'm just doing this to get rid of him, but what's said was said and all of a sudden the day has arrived. Whereas years ago Herr Mühlbauer still had to take written notes, he now uses a tape recorder, smokes BELVEDERES and doesn't refuse a glass of whiskey. If it's true that all interviewers ask the same questions, in his dealings with me this Mühlbauer can claim credit for having carried indiscretion to an extreme.

1st Question: ......?
Answer: What I'm doing right at the? I don't know whether I've understood you correctly. If you mean today, then I'd rather not, at any rate not today. If I may understand the question differently, at the moment in general, taking one moment to mean all moments, then I'm not qualified, no I want to say that I'm not an authority, my opinion is not authoritative, I don't have any opinion at all. Earlier you said we live in a moment of greatness, and of course I wasn't prepared for any great moment, who could even imagine such a thing in kindergarten or the first school years, later on of course, in high school as well, or even at the university, people talked about a surprising number of great moments, of great events, great people, great ideas ...

2nd Question: ......?
Answer: My development ... Oh, you mean my spiritual develop-ment. In the summer I used to take long walks on the Goria and lie in the grass. Excuse me, but this is part of development as well. No, I'd rather not say where the Goria is, otherwise it will be sold and

developed—the thought is unbearable to me. On my way home I'd have to go over the railway embankment which didn't have any crossings, sometimes it was dangerous since you couldn't see the train coming from the opposite direction because of the hazelnut bushes and a stand of ash trees, today there's no embankment to deal with, you simply walk through an underpass.

(A slight cough. Strange nervousness on the part of Herr Mühlbauer, which makes me nervous.)

On the subject of this moment of greatness, or great moments if you prefer, something does occur to me, but I won't be saying anything new to you: history teaches but has no pupils.

(Friendly nodding from Herr Mühlbauer.)

When a development does indeed begin, you will admit that... Yes, I wanted to study law, I quit my studies after three semesters, five years later I started once again and quit again after one semester, I couldn't become a judge or public prosecutor, but then I didn't want to become a lawyer either, I simply wouldn't have known whom or what I would have been able to represent or defend. Everyone and no one, everything and nothing. You see, dear Herr Mühlhofer, excuse me, Herr Mühlbauer, what would you have done in my place, since we're really all stuck in the same set of rules, the same law that no one understands, since we're incapable of conceiving how frightening this law really is...

(A nod from Herr Mühlbauer. A new disturbance. Herr Mühlbauer has to change tapes.)

... Fine, as you wish, I'll express myself more clearly and get right to the point, I'd only like to add that there are these warning signs, you know which ones I mean, since justice is so oppressingly near and what I'm saying does not exclude the possibility of its being no more than a longing for an unattainable, pure greatness, that's why it is simultaneously both oppressive and near, but in this nearness we call it injustice. Besides it pains me every time I have to walk down the Museumstrasse past the Palace of Justice or by chance I wind up near the Parliament, around the Reichsratstrasse where

I cannot avoid seeing the Palace of Justice, just consider using the word "palace" in connection with justice, it's a warning signal, not even injustice can really be administered there, let alone justice! In a development nothing is without consequence, and this daily burning of the Palace of Justice ...

(Herr Mühlbauer whispers: 1927, July 5th, 1927!)

The daily burning of such a ghastly palace with its colossal statues, with its colossal deliberations and pronouncements they call judgments! This daily burning ...

(Herr Mühlbauer stops and asks if he might erase the last bit, he says "erase" and is already erasing.)

... Which experiences have contributed to my ...? Which things have made the most impression on me? I once thought it very strange that I was born right on top of a geosyncline, you realize I don't know too much about those things, but where people are concerned a certain geotropism is inevitable. It really does affect our sense of orientation more than anything else.

(Perplexity on the part of Herr Mühlbauer. Hasty signaling to stop.)

3rd Question: ......?

Answer: My thoughts on the youth of? Nothing, really not a thing, up to now anyway I haven't given it any thought, I have to ask you to be patient with me since most of the questions you are putting to me, in fact very many of the questions people put to me in general are questions I've never asked myself. The youth of today? But then I'd have to think about the elderly of today and about people who are no longer young today but aren't yet old, it's so difficult to imagine all these categories, these specialized fields, these compartmentalized subjects—youth and old age. You know, maybe abstraction isn't my strong point, immediately I start to see all these mass accumulations, like for example children in playgrounds, granted, an agglomeration of children is particularly horrifying to me, but it's also completely incomprehensible to me how children can stand being together with so many other children. It's all right for children to be divided up among adults, but have you ever been inside a school? No child who is in his right mind or who is not utterly spoiled—although most of them probably are—no child could possibly want to live inside a hive of children, having other children's problems and having to share things other than a few diseases, for example a development, if you please. Thus the sight of any sizable agglomeration of children is enough to cause alarm...

(Herr Mühlbauer waves both hands. Apparently not in agreement.)

4th Question: ......?
Answer: My favorite what? Favorite occupation, quite right, that's what you said. I am never occupied. An occupation would be inhibiting, I would lose even the smallest overview, any view at all, by no means may I occupy myself in this ubiquitous bustle, I'm sure you see all this crazy activity in the world and hear all the infernal noises it produces. I would have occupations outlawed if I could, but I can only outlaw them as far as I am concerned, however, I wasn't so tempted, I don't claim any credit, I don't understand such temptations at all, I'm not trying to make myself seem better than I am, of course I have been tempted in ways I dare not mention, everyone is always confronted with the most difficult temptations and succumbs to them and struggles with them hopelessly, please, not in the present...

I'd rather not say that. My favorite, how did you put it now? Landscapes, animals, plants? Favorite what? Books, music, architecture, painting? I don't have any favorite animals, no favorite mosquitoes, favorite beetles, favorite worms, even with the best will in the world I cannot tell you which birds or fish or predators I prefer, it would also be difficult for me to have to choose much more generally, between organic and inorganic things.

(Herr Mühlbauer points encouragingly at Frances, who, having entered quietly, yawns, stretches and then leaps with one bound onto the table. Herr Mühlbauer has to change tapes. Small conversation with Herr Mühlbauer who didn't know I had cats in the house, it would have been so nice if you had spoken about your cats, says Herr Mühlbauer reproachfully, the cats would have added a personal note! I look at the clock and say nervously, but the cats are only here by chance, I can't think of keeping them in the city, the cats do not come into question at all, anyway not these cats, and now that Trollope is also coming in, I madly shoo them both away. The tape is running.)

4th Question: ......? (For the second time.)
Answer: Books? Yes, I read a lot, I've always read a lot. No, I'm not sure we do understand each other. I like to read best on the floor, or in bed, almost everything lying down, no, it has less to do with the books, above all it has to do with the reading, with black on white, with the letters, syllables, lines, the signs, the setting down, this inhuman fixing, this insanity, which flows from people and is frozen into expression. Believe me, expression is insanity, it arises out of our insanity. It also has to do with turning pages, with hunting from one page to the other, with flight, with complicity in an absurd, solidified effusion, with a vile overflow of verse, with insuring life in a single sentence, and, in turn, with the sentences seeking insurance in life. Reading is a vice which can replace all other vices or temporarily take their place in more intensely helping people live, it is a debauchery, a consuming addiction. No, I don't take any drugs, I take books, of course I have certain preferences, many books don't suit me at all, some I take only in the morning, others at night, there are books I don't ever let go, I drag them around with me in the apartment, carrying them from the living room into the kitchen, I read them in the hall standing up, I don't use bookmarks, I don't move my lips while reading, early

on I learned to read very well, I don't remember the method, but you ought to look into it, they must have used an excellent method in our provincial elementary schools, at least back then when I learned to read. Yes I also realized, but not until later, that there are countries where people don't know how to read, at least not quickly, but speed is important, not only concentration, can you please tell me who can keep chewing on a simple or even a complex sentence without feeling disgust, either with the eyes or the mouth, just keep on grinding away, over and over, a sentence which only consists of subject and predicate must be consumed rapidly, a sentence with many appositions must for that very reason be taken at tremendous speed, with the eyeballs performing an imperceptible slalom, since a sentence doesn't convey anything to itself, it has to "convey" something to the reader. I couldn't "work my way through" a book, that would almost be an occupation. There are people, I tell you, you come across the strangest surprises in this field of reading … I do profess a certain weakness for illiterates, I even know someone here who doesn't read and doesn't want to, a person who has succumbed to the vice of reading more easily understands such a state of innocence, really unless people are truly capable of reading they ought not to read at all.

(Herr Mühlbauer has erased the tape by mistake. Herr Mühlbauer apologizes. I'd only have to repeat a few sentences.)

Yes, I read a lot, but the shocks, the things that really stay with you are merely the vision of a page, a remembrance of five words on the lower left of page 27: Nous allons à l'Esprit. Words on a poster, names on doors, titles of books left in a store window, never sold, a magazine ad discovered in the dentist's waiting room, a gravestone epitaph that struck my eye: HERE LIES. A name while flipping through the phone book: EUSEBIUS. I'll get right to the point … For example last year I read: "He wore a Menshikov," I don't know why, but I was immediately convinced that whoever this man might have been, this sentence meant he wore a Menshikov, indeed, that he had to wear one, and that this was important for me to know, it belongs irrevocably to my life. Something will come of it. But, to get back to the point I was trying to make, even if we were to have more sessions, day and night, I couldn't list the books which have impressed me the most or explain why they made such an impression, in which places and for how long. What sticks, then, you will ask, but that's not the point! there are only a few sentences, a few expressions that wake up inside my brain again and again, begging to be heard over the years: Der Ruhm hat keine weissen Flügel. Avec ma main brûlée, j'écris sur la nature du feu. In fuoco l'amor mi mise, in fuoco d'amor mi mise. To The Onlie Begetter ...

(I signal and blush, Herr Mühlbauer has to erase that at once, no one cares about that, I wasn't thinking, I let myself get carried away, the Viennese newspaper readers wouldn't understand Italian anyway and most of them wouldn't understand French anymore, not the younger ones, besides, it's not to the point. Herr Mühlbauer wants to think it over, he couldn't keep up entirely, he, too, doesn't know Italian or French, but he's been to America twice and never once encountered the word "begetter" in his journeys.)

5th Question: ......?
Answer: Earlier I could only feel sorry for myself, I felt as disadvantaged here as someone who has been disinherited, then I learned to feel sorry for people elsewhere. You're on the wrong track, my dear Herr Mühlbauer. I get along well with this city and its diminished and disappearing surroundings which have retired from history.

(Uneasy alarm of Herr Mühlbauer. Unruffled, I proceed.)

You might also say that, as an example to the world, an empire, along with its practices and tactics embellished with ideas, was expelled from history. I am very happy to live here, because from this place on the planet, where nothing more is happening, a confrontation with the world is all the more frightening, here one is neither self-righteous nor self-satisfied, as this is not some protected island, but a haven of decay, wherever you go there is decay, decay everywhere, right before our eyes, and not just the decay of yesterday's empire, but of today's as well.

(Increasing alarm on the part of Herr Mühlbauer, I suddenly remember the VIENNA EVENING EDITION, maybe Herr Mühlbauer is already worrying about his job, I have to give a little thought to Herr Mühlbauer.)

More and more I find myself saying, as people used to say: the House of Austria, because a country would be too big for me, too roomy, too uncomfortable, I only say country when I'm talking about smaller entities. Looking out of a train window I think to myself, the country here is truly beautiful. When summer comes I'd like to drive out to the country, to the Salzkammergut or Carinthia. After all, it's easy to see what happens to people living in real countries, how heavily their consciences are burdened, even if as individuals they have little or nothing to do with the shameful deeds of their noisy countries swollen with greatness, even if they don't benefit directly from their country's increase in power and resources. Just living with other people in one house is enough to scare you. But, my dear Herr Mühlbauer, I didn't say that at all, right now I'm not saying it's the republic that is at fault—who said anything here against an inconspicuous, small, ignorant, defective yet harmless republic? certainly neither of us, there's no reason to be upset, please stay calm, the ultimatum presented to Serbia has expired long ago, a few centuries have simply passed in this rather dubious world and brought it to ruin—we accepted the new world order ages ago. That there's nothing new under the sun, no, I'd never say that, new things do exist, they do, you can bank on that, Herr Mühlbauer, it's just that seen from here, where nothing is happening anymore, and that's a good thing, too, one must tolerate the past completely, it's not yours and not mine, but who's asking whether it is, you simply have to put up with these things, in their countries other people don't have the time, they're busy, planning and dealing: sitting in their countries, they're the ones who are behind the times, because they lack a language, for always, in all ages, those without a language rule. I will tell you a terrible secret: language is punishment. Language must encompass all things and in it all things must again transpire according to guilt and the degree of guilt.

(Signs of exhaustion in Herr Mühlbauer. Signs of my own exhaustion.)

6th Question: ......?

Answer: An intermediary? A task? A spiritual mission? Have you ever tried mediating? It's a thankless role. Please, no more missions! And I don't know about missionizing in general ... We've seen what that's led to wherever it was tried, I don't understand you, but then again your vantage point must be higher, and anything above that—if it exists at all—would have to be very high indeed. It might be too painfully high for one to be taken there alone, in the thin air, for even just an hour, and how is one to pursue such heights in the company of others, while at the same time languishing in the most abject debasement, spiritual things—I don't know if you still want to follow me, since your time is so limited and so is your column in the paper, spiritual things demand constant humiliation, one must go down, not up or out on the street to attack others, it's absolutely outrageous, it should be outlawed, I don't understand how people can arrive at these high-flying expressions. Who could perform such a task anyway, and what would a mission achieve! It's unthinkable, it weighs me down completely. But maybe you were talking about administrative matters or maintaining archives? We've already made a start, with our palaces, castles and museums, our necropolis has been researched, labeled, described in great detail on enameled plaques. You never used to be sure which palace belonged to the Trautsons and which to the Strozzis and where Trinity Hospital was located and what its history was like, but now you can get by without any special knowledge, without a guide as well, and the close friends needed to obtain entrance to the Pallfy Palace or to the Leopoldine Wing of the Hofburg are no longer necessary, administrations ought to be given a boost.

(Embarrassed coughing on the part of Herr Mühlbauer.)

Naturally I'm against administration in general, surely you won't doubt that, I'm against this worldwide bureaucracy which has taken over everything from people and their depictions to potato bugs with their pictures. But here in Vienna something else is going on, the cultic administration of an Empire of the Dead, I don't know why you or I should be proud, why we should want to attract the world's attention with all these festivals: Festspiele, Musical Weeks, Commemorative Years, Festival Weeks, Days of Culture. The world could do nothing better than studiously ignore them all so as not to be frightened, because otherwise they'll see what lies in store for them—in the best case—and the more silently things proceed here, the more secretly our gravediggers go about their work, the more covertly things occur, the more quietly the requiem is played and the more inaudibly the last words are spoken, then, perhaps, true curiosity would be all the greater. Vienna's crematorium is its spiritual mission, you see, we're discovering a mission after all, you just have to keep talking until it all unfolds, but let's not speak about that, it is here, at its most fragile point, where this century sparked some minds to thought and then incinerated them, so they'd begin to have an effect, but I ask myself, and I'm sure you ask yourself too, whether every new effect doesn't effect a new misunderstanding ...

(Change of tape. Herr Mühlbauer empties his glass in one gulp.)

6th Question: ......? (For the second time. Repeat.)
Answer: "The House of Austria" has always been my favorite expression because it best explains my ties to Austria, better than

all the others at my disposal. I must have lived in this house at different times, as I can immediately call to mind the streets of Prague and the port in Trieste, I dream in Czech, in Windish, in Bosnian, I have always been at home in this House and—except while dreaming, in this dreamed House—without the slightest desire to reinhabit it, to come into its possession, to raise any claim, for the Crown Lands fell to me, I abdicated: at the Imperial Church am Hof I renounced the oldest crown. Just imagine, after each of the last wars the new border was to be drawn through the village of Galicia. Galicia, which no one knows except me, which doesn't mean a thing to anybody else, which nobody visits and which doesn't amaze a soul, always fell right in the path of the pen on Allied staff maps, and it reemerged each time, though for different reasons, with what is today called Austria, the border is only a few kilometers away, in the mountains, and for the longest time during the summer of 1945 nothing was decided, I was evacuated there, I kept wondering what would become of me, whether I would be counted as a Slovenian in Yugoslavia or a Carinthian in Austria, I was sorry I had dozed through my Slovenian classes—French came more easily to me, even Latin interested me more. Naturally Galicia would have remained Galicia under any flag, and we wouldn't have had much of an opinion, since we never worried at all about this expansion or that, at home we always said that once it's over we'll go back to Lipica, we have to visit our aunt in Brünn, what could have possibly become of our relatives in Czernowitz, the air in Friuli is better than here, when you grow up you have to go to Vienna and Prague, when you grow up …

I want to say that we always accept these realities with indifference and apathy, we were completely indifferent as to which places ended up in which countries and where they might wind up eventually. Nonetheless, traveling to Prague was different from traveling to Paris, but all the time in Vienna I wasn't truly living my life—nor can I say the time was completely lost—only that in Trieste I wasn't a stranger, but now that matters less and less. It doesn't have to be, but sometime and soon, maybe this year, I'd like to go to Venice, which I will never get to know.

7th Question: ......?
Answer: I believe there's been a misunderstanding, I could start over and answer you more precisely, if you'll be patient with me, and if another misunderstanding should arise, at least it would be a new one. We couldn't make the confusion any greater than it is, nobody's listening to us, questions are being asked and answered elsewhere now as well, people are fixing their sights on even stranger problems, new problems are ordered from each day to the next, they're invented and put into circulation, they don't really exist, you hear people talking about them and so you start talking about them yourself. I, too, have only heard about the problems, otherwise I don't have any, we could sit quietly with our hands in our laps, wouldn't that be nice, Herr Mühlbauer, sipping a drink? But at night, alone, is when the erratic monologues arise, the ones that last, for man is a somber being, only in the darkness is he master of himself and during the day he goes back to being a slave. Right now you are my slave and you have made me yours, you, a slave of your paper, which had better not call itself EVENING EDITION, your slavishly dependent newspaper for thousands of slaves...

(Herr Mühlbauer presses a button and turns off the tape recorder. I didn't hear him say: thank you for the interview. Herr Mühlbauer is in a state of utmost embarrassment, ready to redo the whole thing as early as tomorrow. If Fräulein Jellinek were here I would know what to say, I will be indisposed or sick or out of town. I would have some meeting, some appointment. Herr Mühlbauer lets me know that he's lost a whole afternoon, he packs up his tape recorder crossly and leaves saying: Küss die Hand.)

To Ivan on the telephone:

Oh, nothing much, I was just
You sound awful, were you asleep
No, just exhausted, the whole afternoon
Are you alone, have the people
Yes they're gone, also the whole afternoon
I tried the whole afternoon
I lost the whole afternoon

Ivan is livelier than I am. When he's not exhausted he's all movement, but when he's tired he is decidedly more tired than I am, and
then he gets mad about the age difference, he knows he's angry, he
wants to be angry, today he has to be especially angry at me.

Well aren't you defensive!
Why are you so defensive?
You have to attack, come on, attack me!
Show me your hands, no, not the inside
I don't read hands
You can see it on the skin of your hands
In women I can see it right away

But this time I won because my hands don't show a thing, not a
single wrinkle. Nevertheless, Ivan renews the attack.

I can often see it in your face
You looked old then
Sometimes you look really old
Today you look twenty years younger
Laugh more, read less, sleep more, think less
What you're doing is making you old

Gray and brown clothes make you old
Donate your mourning clothes to the Red Cross
Who allowed you to wear these grave-clothes?
Of course I'm mad, I want to be mad
You'll look younger right away, I'll drive old age right out of you!

Ivan, who has dozed off, wakes up, I come back from the equator, marked by a once-in-a-million-years event.

What's the matter with you?
Nothing. I'm just making something up.
That will be a fine one!

Most of the time I'm making something up, inventing. Ivan covers his mouth so I'm not supposed to notice he's yawning. He has to leave at once. It's a quarter to twelve. Almost midnight.

I've just invented a way to change the world after all!
    What? you too? society, relationships? these days that's got to be the biggest competition around.
    You're really not interested in what I'm inventing?
    Not today anyway, that's for sure, you've probably had a powerful inspiration, and one shouldn't disturb artists as they're creating.
    Fine with me, then I'll invent it all myself, but let me invent it for you.

Ivan hasn't been warned about me. He doesn't know with whom he's running around, that he's dealing with a phenomenon, an appearance which can also be deceiving, I don't want to lead Ivan astray, but he'll never realize that I am double. I am also Malina's creation. Unconcerned, Ivan sticks to the appearance, my living bodily self gives him a reference point, maybe it's the only one, but this same bodily self disturbs me, while we talk I can never allow myself to think that in an hour we'll be lying on the bed or toward evening or very late at night, because otherwise the walls could suddenly turn into glass, the roof could suddenly be lifted away. Extreme self-control lets me accept Ivan's sitting opposite me at first, silently smoking and talking. Not one word, not one gesture of mine betrays what is now possible and the fact that it will continue to be possible. One moment it's Ivan and myself. Another moment: we. Then right away: you and I. Two beings devoid of all intentions toward one another, who do not want coexistence, do not want to take off somewhere and begin a new life, do not want to break off or agree to use a dominant language. We manage just as well without an interpreter, I don't discover anything about Ivan, he doesn't discover anything about me. We do not engage in any commercial exchange of feelings, have no positions of power and do not expect delivery of any weapons to support and secure our identity. A good, easy basis, whatever falls on my ground thrives, I propagate myself with words and also propagate Ivan, I beget a new lineage, my union with Ivan brings that which is willed by God into the world.

Firebirds
Azurite
Plunging flames
Drops of jade

Dear Herr Ganz,

The first thing that bothered me about you was the way your little finger stuck out while you were showing off in front of some people and treating everyone to your witty bon mots, which were new to me and to the people there but soon no longer to me, as later I heard you repeat them many times, in the presence of other people. You had such a humorous way. What then began to bother me, and continues to bother me, is your name. Today it takes an effort to write down your name once again, and hearing it from others immediately gives me a headache. When I cannot avoid thinking about you I purposely think of you as "Herr Genz" or "Herr Gans," there have been times when I've tried "Ginz" but the best escape still remains "Herr Gonz" because it's not too far removed from your real name but can, with a little Viennese coloring, make it just a little ridiculous. I have to tell you once and for all, since the word "ganz" comes up daily, spoken by others, even I cannot avoid it, it's found in newspapers and books, in every paragraph. I should have been on my guard just because of your name with which you continue to intrude on my life and cause me undue stress. If your name had been Kopecky or Wiegele, Ullmann or Apfelböck—my life would be calmer and I could forget about you for long stretches of time. Even if your name were Meier, Maier, Mayer or Schmidt, Schmid, Schmitt it would still be possible for me not to think of you whenever the name came up, I could think about one of my friends whose name is also Meier or about any one of a number of Herr Schmidts, however their spellings might differ. In company I would feign astonishment or enthusiasm, indeed, in my haste, in the heat of these general and generally cruel conversations I could mistake you for some other Meier or some other Schmid. What idiosyncrasies! you will say. Not long ago, when I almost had to fear seeing you, shortly after the new vogue had come in—metal clothes, chain mail shirts, spiked fringes, and jewelry made from barbed wire—I felt armed for a meeting, even my ears would not have been uncovered, as my earlobes were sporting two heavy bunches of thorns in the nicest gray, which started to slip around or hurt every time I moved my head because they had forgotten to pierce holes in my earlobes when I was very young, the way they do for every other little girl in the country, mercilessly, at a most tender age. I don't understand why in the world they call this age "tender." I would have been invulnerable in this suit of armor, so armed, so ready to defend my skin, a description of which you will allow me to omit, since you once knew it so well ...

Dear Sir:
I could never pronounce your first name. You have often reproached me for this. But that is not the reason why the thought of a renewed encounter is unpleasant for me. Back then I could have spared myself this name, because the occasion so permitted. I couldn't bring myself to do this and I discovered that this inability to pronounce certain names or even to suffer excessively because of them does not stem from the names themselves but has to do with the initial, original mistrust of a person, unjustified in the beginning, but eventually, one day, always justified. Of course you were bound to misinterpret my instinctive mistrust, which could express itself only in this manner. Now that a reunion is entirely possible, sometimes I don't know for the life of me how it could be avoided, only one thought remains to cause me concern: that you can address me by my first name, calling me "Du," a "Du" that you forced upon me under circumstances you well know, and that I granted you throughout an unforgettably disgusting intermezzo, out of weakness, so as not to hurt you, so as not to show to your face the boundaries I had drawn in secret, which I was forced to draw. It may be customary to introduce a "Du" during such intermezzi, but it shouldn't remain in circulation after the episode is over. I am not reproaching you for the embarrassing and unspeakable memories you have left me. Nonetheless your thick skin, your utter inability to recognize my sensitivity to this "Du," the blackmail you used to obtain it from me and from others all make me fear that you still don't even realize it's blackmail, since it comes so completely naturally to you. Certainly you've never thought about the "Du" you use so casually, or about why it's easier for me to overlook a few corpses left in your path than the continued application

of this torture that consists in saying and thinking "Du." Since I last saw you it has not occurred to me to think of you in any but the most proper manner, to think and speak of you with "Herr" and "Sie," to be sure I do not speak of you unless it is essential, to say: I was once acquainted with Herr Ganz. My only request is that you at least trouble yourself to use the same courtesy.

Vienna,…

Very Sincerely,
An unknown woman

Dear Mr. President,
Your letter, sent in your name and in the name of all, conveys best wishes for my birthday. Please excuse my surprise. You see, this day seems to me—on account of my parents—to be part of an intimacy shared by two people whom you and the others cannot know. I myself have never had the audacity to imagine my conception and birth. Even listing my birthdate, which although without meaning for me, must have meant something to my poor parents, always seemed like the illicit mention of a taboo or exposing unknown people's joy and pain, which any thinking, feeling person considers an almost punishable offense. I should say any civilized person since our thinking and feeling is in part, in its damaged part, bound to our civilization, to the civilizing by which we have gleefully forfeited the honor of even being considered alongside the wildest savage. You, a distinguished scholar, know better than I what dignity primitive people—the last, unannihilated ones—accord to everything concerned with birth, initiation, conception and death, and in our society it is not only official arrogance that demands we surrender our last vestiges of shame, but even before surveys and data-processing a related, anticipatory spirit was already at work, confident of victory, calling for this enlightenment, which has already wreaked the greatest devastation among confused peoples not yet come of age. And when civilization has lifted

the last remaining taboos, humanity will yet be degraded to total immaturity. You congratulate me, and I cannot help but extend these congratulations, at least in thought, to a woman who died long ago, a certain Josefine H. who is listed on my birth certificate as midwife. She should have been congratulated, back then, for her dexterity and a smooth birth. Years ago I learned that this day was a Friday (it seems that by evening the time had come), information which did not exactly thrill me. If it can be avoided I don't leave the house on Fridays, I never travel on Fridays, Friday is the day of the week I find most threatening. But it is a further fact that I came into the world with half a "good-luck bonnet," half a caul, although I don't know why people still believe that this or any other peculiar feature on a newborn should augur good fortune or ill. But I already said that I apparently had only half a good-luck bonnet, and though they say half is better than none, this half cover made me deeply reflective, I was a brooding child, reflection and sitting still for hours are said to have been my most outstanding features. Nonetheless I ask myself today, too late, too late, what my pitiful mother could have made of this dusky news, half a congratulation for half a good-luck bonnet. Who would want to nurse a child, to raise it responsibly if it came into the world with only half a good-luck bonnet. What would you do, Mr. President, with half a presidency, half an honor, half a recognition, half a hat, what would you even do with this half letter? My letter to you cannot become a whole letter, because my thanks for your good wishes are themselves only half-hearted. But since one receives letters without asking for them, replies cannot be expected—

Vienna,...

An unknown woman

The torn letters are lying in the wastepaper basket, artistically messed up and mixed with crumpled invitations to an exhibition, a reception, a lecture, mixed with empty cigarette cartons, sprinkled with ashes and cigarette butts. Hastily I have put typing paper and carbons in place so that Fräulein Jellinek won't see what I've been doing in the middle of the night. She's just stopping by, she has to meet her fiancé to arrange the documents for the marriage license. She did not forget to buy two ballpoint pens, but nonetheless once again her hours have not been recorded. I ask: Why for heaven's sake didn't you write them down, you know how I am! And I rummage around in my purse and in another handbag, I'm going to have to ask Malina for some money, call him in the Arsenal, but the envelope however finally surfaces, very conspicuously stuck in the Grosser Duden dictionary, secretly marked by Malina. He never forgets, I never have to ask him to do anything. At the right time the envelopes are lying in the kitchen for Lina, on the desk for Fräulein Jellinek, in the old box in my bedroom there are a few banknotes for the hairdresser and, every few months, a few larger notes for shoes and sheets and clothes. I never know when the necessary money will appear, but if my coat has become tatty then Malina will have saved up for a new one, before the first cold day of the year. I don't know how Malina always manages, even with no money in the house, to bring us through these expensive times, he always pays the rent punctually, and for the most part also the electric bill, water bill, telephone bill and car insurance that I'm supposed to tend to. They've only cut off our telephone once or twice, but just because we were traveling and tend to be forgetful when we travel, since we don't have our mail forwarded. We got off easy again, I say with relief, it should be smooth sailing from here on, if only we don't get sick, if only nothing happens to our teeth! Malina can't give me much, but he prefers to let me save on household expenses rather than not grant me the few schillings I spend on things that mean more to me than a full refrigerator. I have my small allowance for getting around in Vienna and having a sandwich at Trześniewski's and a small coffee in the Café Sacher, for politely sending Antoinette Altenwyl flowers after a dinner, for giving Franziska Jordan MY SIN perfume for her birthday, for giving streetcar tickets, spare change or clothes to pushy or lost or stranded people I don't know, especially Bulgarians. Malina shakes his head, but he says no only if he understands from my stammering that "the cause," "the case," "the problem" is assuming immense proportions that we can't handle. Then Malina strengthens my backbone for a no that was taking shape in me as well. I still backtrack at the last moment, I say: But couldn't we really, if for example we asked Atti Altenwyl or if I asked little Semmelrock to speak with Bertold Rapatz, he has millions you know, or if you could call up Director Hubalek! At such moments Malina says decidedly: No! I'm supposed to finance the reconstruction of a girls' school in Jerusalem, I'm supposed to pay thirty thousand schillings for a refugee committee, as a small contribution, I'm supposed to come up with something for the catastrophic floods in northern Germany and in Romania, contribute to the earthquake victims' support fund, I'm supposed to finance revolutions in Mexico, Berlin and La Paz, but Martin urgently needs a thousand schillings, today, just until the first of the month, and he is reliable, Christine Wantschura urgently needs money for her husband's exhibition, but he mustn't know, she wants to get it back from her mother, but Christine has just now renewed an old fight with her mother. Three students from Frankfurt can't pay their hotel bill in Vienna, it's urgent, even more urgent is Lina's need for the next payments on her television, Malina pulls out the money and says yes, but he says no to the really big catastrophes and undertakings. Malina doesn't have any theory, for him everything divides into "to have or have not." If it were up to him we'd get by and never have any financial troubles, I'm the one who brings them into the house, along with the Bulgarians, the Germans, the South Americans, the girlfriends, the boyfriends, the acquaintances of both sexes, all these people, the geopolitical and meteorological fronts. I have never heard—and this is something Malina and Ivan have in common—of anyone going to Ivan or Malina, it simply doesn't happen, no one would think of it, I must be more attractive, maybe I simply instill a lot more trust. But Malina says: That could only happen to you, they couldn't find anyone dumber. I say: it's urgent.

The Bulgarian is waiting for me in Café Landtmann, he told Lina he came directly from Israel and needs to speak with me, I start to imagine who could be sending me greetings, who might have had an accident, what happened to Harry Goldmann whom I haven't seen in Vienna for ages, I hope it doesn't have anything to do with world affairs, hopefully no committee is being formed, hopefully no one needs a few million, hopefully I won't have to take hold of any spade, I can't bear the sight of spades or shovels since that time in Klagenfurt when they stood Wilma and me against the wall and wanted to shoot us, I can't listen to any shots at all ever since a certain Fasching, a war, a film. Hopefully it will just be greetings. Naturally it turns out to be something else entirely and luckily I still have the flu and 100° and therefore can't set out to perform new deeds and get entangled in something. I can see neither scene nor setting, but how do I say that my place is in the Ungargasse? my Ungargassenland, which I must hold, fortify, my only country, which I must keep secure, which I defend, for which I tremble, for which I fight, prepared to die, I hold it with my mortal hands, surrounded even here as I catch my breath in front of the Café Landtmann, my country that is threatened by revenge from all other countries. Herr Franz is already greeting me at the door, he looks around the overfilled coffee house with a dubious mien, but I walk past him with a brusque greeting and make the rounds, since I don't need a table, a gentleman from Israel has been waiting for me for half an hour, it's urgent. A gentleman is holding a German magazine DER SPIEGEL opened conspicuously with its title page facing anyone who enters, but the only thing I arranged with my gentleman was that I would be blond and wearing a blue spring coat, though it's not spring—but the weather does change from day to day. The gentleman with the magazine raises his hand, but doesn't rise and since no one else is watching me it might be the urgent man. It is the man, he whispers in a broken German, I ask about my friends in Tel Aviv, in Haifa, in Jerusalem, but the man doesn't know any of my friends, he is not from Israel, he was only there a few weeks ago, he's come a long way. I order a large espresso, with milk, from Herr Adolf, I don't ask: What do you want from me, who are you? How did you get my address? What brings you to Vienna? The man whispers: I come from Bulgaria. I found your name in the phone book, it was my last hope. The capital of Bulgaria must be Sofia, but the man is not from Sofia, I understand that not every Bulgarian can live in Sofia, nothing more about Bulgaria occurs to me, all the people there are supposed to live a very long time because of the yogurt, but my Bulgarian is not old and not young, his face is easily forgotten, he shakes continuously, fidgets in his chair, and keeps grabbing hold of his legs. He takes some newspaper clippings out of a briefcase, all of them from German newspapers, a large page from Der Spiegel, he nods, I'm supposed to read it, right here and now, the clippings are about a disease, Buerger's Disease, the Bulgarian drinks a small espresso and I stir my own coffee without a word, quickly read about Buerger's Disease, written for the layman of course, but even so this Disease must be very rare and unusual, I look up expectantly, I don't know why Bulgarians are interested in Buerger's Disease. The Bulgarian moves his chair slightly away from the table, he points to his legs, he is the one with the disease. The agitation rushes to my head, a terrible pain, I'm not dreaming, this time the Bulgarian succeeded, what am I supposed to do with this man and a strange disease in Café Landtmann, what would Malina do right now, what would Malina do? But the Bulgarian remains completely calm and says he just needs to have both legs amputated right away and he's run out of money in Vienna, he still has to get to Itzehoe, where they have specialists in Buerger's Disease. I smoke and keep quiet and wait, I have twenty schillings on me, it's past five o'clock, the bank is closed, the disease is there. Just before losing his temper Herr Professor Mahler shouts from the next table: Check please! Herr Franz calls cheerfully: Be right there! and runs away and I run after him. I have to phone at once. Herr Franz says: Is something wrong, gnädige Frau, I don't like the way you look at all, Peppi, bring a glass of water, but presto, for the gnädige Frau! I rummage through my handbag in the cloakroom, but the little address book isn't there, I have to look up the number of my travel agency in the phonebook, Peppi the boy waiter brings a glass of water, I rummage through my bag and find a tablet, which I can't break in my agitation, I shove the whole thing into my mouth and swallow some water, the tablet sticks in my throat and little Peppi cries out: Jesusmaryandjoseph, you're coughing, shouldn't I get Herr Franz ...! but I've found the number, I phone and wait and drink the water, I'm being connected, I'm being transferred, Herr Suchy is still in the office. Herr Suchy repeats nasally, pedantically: A foreign gentleman will come by, 1st class ticket to Itzehoe, one way, an additional thousand schillings cash, no rush, we'll take care of it, it will be a pleasure for me, no need to worry, gnädige Frau, küss die Hand!

I stand a while in the cloakroom and smoke, Herr Franz glances at me kindly as he runs by with his tails swaying, I have to smoke and wait. After a few minutes I return to the diseased table. I ask the Bulgarian to kindly go to my travel agency, the train is leaving in three hours, a certain Herr Suchy will take care of everything. I call out: Check please! Herr Professor Mahler, whose nod of recognition I repay with a confused greeting, cries out more loudly: Check please! Herr Franz rushes past us and calls back: Be right there! I leave the twenty schillings on the table and signal to the Bulgarian that that should take care of the check. I don't know what I should wish him but I say: bon voyage!

Ivan says: You've let yourself get taken in again.

But Ivan!

Malina says: Here we go again, and a thousand schillings for the road! I say: Usually you're not so petty, I have to explain it to you better, it's a terrible disease.

Malina answers thoughtfully: I don't doubt that, Herr Suchy already called me, your Bulgarian really did show up. You see! I say, and if he doesn't have any disease and both legs won't be amputated then it's a good thing, but if he does have the disease then we have to pay.

Malina says: Don't worry about it, I'll manage it somehow.

Today I couldn't have sat another hour with the leper at the Café Raimund, I wanted to jump up right away and wash my hands, not to avoid contamination but just a handshake was enough to transfer the knowledge of leprosy, at home I wanted to wash out my eyes with a solution of boric acid so my eyes would calm down after seeing such a ravaged face. Also just before my one flight of the year, Munich and back in two days because I can't stay away from the Ungargasse any longer than that, I ordered a taxi and noticed too late that the driver didn't have any nose, we were already moving because I had said frivolously: Schwechat, to the airport! and it wasn't until he turned around to ask whether he might smoke that I noticed, so I rode to Schwechat without a nose and got out there with my suitcase. But in the lobby I started to have second thoughts and canceled my flight, I went back right away with another taxi. That evening Malina wondered what I was doing home instead of in Munich. I couldn't have flown, it wasn't a good omen, and in fact the plane never made it to Munich but landed late in Nuremberg with damaged landing gear. I don't know why such people cross my path and why some of them constantly want something from me. Today two Frenchmen whose names I didn't even understand came with a recommendation, they stayed without any reason until two in the morning, I just don't understand why people come into the house and stay for hours, why they don't disclose their intentions. Maybe they don't have any intentions, but they don't leave, and I can't phone. Then I'm happy that Frances and Trollope are staying a while longer, that they are my boarders, that they give me an opportunity to get out of the room for half an hour since they have to have their Kitkat cat food and fresh chopped lung, then they parade around, satisfied, steering conversation with the strangers their way and aware that their presence is useful to me.

Of course, a month from now at the latest, the time with the cats will come to an end, they will return to the Hohe Warte or be taken to the country, Frances will grow too quickly and soon have kittens, after that she should be spayed. Ivan, with whom I discussed Frances's future, is of the same opinion, he's more for it than against, and I didn't let it show that I would prefer not to see Frances any bigger or in heat, that she should remain a little cat who never has kittens because I would like everything to stay the way it is, so that during the next few months Ivan, too, won't grow a few months older. But I can't tell that to Herr Kopecky who knows everything about cats because he once had twenty-five of them at the same time and still keeps four, who also knows everything about the behavior of Barbary macaques and rat packs and their fascinating peculiarities, but as I listen, I can scarcely take in all his very funny cat tales, about the jealousy of a Siamese named Rose of Istanbul, about the suicide of his favorite Persian named Aurora, who—he still can't grasp it—threw herself out the window. Frances isn't Siamese or Persian, just a gently caressed central European backyard cat under Viennese jurisdiction, of no race, and Trollope, her brother, came out white with a few black spots in his fur, with a phlegmatic disposition, completely at ease, never whining like Frances, an obediently purring tomcat who leaps onto my bed, sits on my back when I read, climbs on my shoulder and looks into the books along with me. For Frances and Trollope like reading with me more than anything. When I shoo them away they clamber around in the library and hide behind the books, they work hard until a few volumes come loose and fall to the floor with a crash. Then I again know where they have hidden themselves and are doing their mischief. It's high time that Béla and András get their cats back or that Ivan's mother keeps them in the country. I've only told Herr Kopecky that I'm keeping them temporarily, until friends of mine, certain friends no more clearly specified, return to Vienna from a trip. On the other hand I ask Malina to have a little more patience, he doesn't have anything against cats, but cats in our apartment who mess up his papers, clear off his desk and knock books out of the bookshelves when he least expects it, are not something he is capable of putting up with for long. Also lately the whole apartment smells of cat urine, I'm getting used to it, but Lina is in league with Malina, she delivers an ultimatum: her or the cats.

Malina says: That was another one of your great ideas, you'll never get them used to the litterbox, they don't take you seriously, get some guinea pigs or canaries or parrots, no, better not, they're too loud for me! Malina has no appreciation for stray cats that belong to two children, Malina is concerned about his peace, he doesn't think Frances and Trollope are nice or witty or droll. But whenever I forget to feed these nice cats, Malina remembers, he does it as though he'd always done it, he never forgets. That's the way Malina is, and unfortunately the way I am.

Today Lina reminds me, in all seriousness, of the fact that last year I had wanted to rearrange my apartment, naturally not the whole apartment but just three pieces of furniture and before Lina can explain to me that it's now time, I say casually: Some other time, and we'll call two men to help out! Lina snorts: Men! gnädige Frau, we don't need any men for that! She's already pushed my writing desk five centimeters and I start to lend a hand, after all it is my writing desk, it isn't budging or even tilting, it seems heavier than a thousand cubic feet of oak. I suggest to Lina that we first lighten the desk of its contents, that we take everything out of the drawers, I mumble: Couldn't you take advantage of the opportunity, of this unique opportunity and sort the drawers for once, no, I didn't say anything … I look down piously at the dust of several years.

Today Lina is not to be upset, otherwise she'd be sure to say that she "runs over it" every week anyway. Lina snorts loudly: Küss die Hand, küss die Hand, this cabinet sure is heavy!

Me: But Lina, it's best we call a couple of men now, we'll give each one a beer and ten schillings and basta. For Lina should realize how valuable she is to me, how much her strength is worth to me, that I would be prepared to buy many beers for many men, that she is essential for Malina and for me. Malina and I don't want her to have a hernia or a heart attack, she doesn't need to be moving wardrobes and cabinets around—it isn't me, it's Lina, who is stronger, together we lift the desk from one room to the other, though naturally Lina has to handle more than eighty percent of the load. Nevertheless, I'm annoyed with Lina today since she isn't giving in on anything, since she never gives in and even now she's still jealous of the men on whom I wanted to spend twenty schillings, "might as well throw it out the window" says Lina. Once again I've done everything wrong. Lina and I are dependent on each other in an inescapable way, we are closely connected although she doesn't give in to herself or to me concerning the men with the beer, although only she is allowed to criticize me out loud and not vice versa, but I do criticize her in secret. That's why I imagine the day when no one is dependent on anyone, when I live by myself in an apartment where Lina will be replaced by one or two small machines, when pressing a button will suffice to lift a desk and move it, as if it were nothing. No one will keep saying thank you to someone else, no one will help other people while secretly being annoyed by them. No one will gain or lose the advantage. But then I picture myself with the electric machines, which once a year Lina advises me not to purchase, whereas today she is again advising me to buy. She believes you can't live without an electric coffee grinder these days and an electric orange squeezer. But I drink coffee so rarely and my strength ought to suffice to squeeze Malina's orange juice. Of course I do have a vacuum cleaner and a refrigerator, but once a year Lina would like to see our apartment transformed into a machine factory, she says emphatically: But these days everybody has that, all the ladies and gentlemen have one of these!

A day will come when people will have black-golden eyes, they will see beauty, they will be freed from dirt and from every burden, they will rise into the sky, they will dive into the waters, they will forget their calluses and hardships. A day will come when they will be free, all people will be free, even from the freedom they had presumed. There shall be a greater freedom, beyond measure, a freedom to last a whole life long …

In Café Heumarkt I'm still mad at Lina since she's the dangerous accessory to certain thoughts of mine, she also sometimes hears me say sentences over the phone that she considers the purest heresy and that would give her reason to defenestrate me immediately, to send me to the guillotine, to the garotte, to burn me at the stake. But I can never fully grasp whether she only minds my going around completely exhausted in the morning, not knowing whether she should buy Ata or Imi for cleaning, or whether she just minds the fact that I can't do arithmetic correctly and don't check the sums she has painstakingly assembled, or whether it's more the sentences I utter, and whether she simply guesses these thoughts, which give her the right to kill me.

A day will come when human beings will rediscover the savannas and the steppes, they will pour forth and put an end to their slavery, when the sun is high in the heavens the animals will approach the humans who are free, and they will live in concord, the giant tortoises, the elephants, the aurochs, and the kings of the jungles and deserts will be reconciled with the liberated people, they will drink from one water, they will breathe the purified air, they will not mangle one another, it shall be the beginning, it shall be the beginning for a whole life ...

I call out: Check please! Herr Karl calls back cheerfully: Be right there! and disappears. I'm being too unfair, I crumple the paper napkin on which I've jotted a few sentence fragments, the thin paper wilts in the coffee that has slopped onto the tray. I want to go home at once, to the Ungargasse, I'll apologize to Lina, Lina will apologize to me. She'll squeeze some orange juice for me and make coffee. It doesn't have to be for my whole life. It is my whole life.

In the afternoon I'm certain I'll be able to calmly walk past Number 9, though to be sure on the opposite side of the street. I'm also certain I'll be able to stop for a minute, since Frau Agnes cleans Ivan's place early in the morning and then has to move on to the two men living on their own. I never see the couple who manage Ivan's building out on the street, no exchange of information is maintained with Herr and Frau Breitner from Number 6, I only see Frau Agnes every now and then in front of my building, deep in intimate conversation with Frau Breitner. But this time Ivan's car is not parked in front of Number 9 just by accident, as I think at first glance, since Ivan now emerges from his house and walks right up to the car, I want to keep moving quickly, but Ivan with his good eyes has already spotted me, he is waving and calling, all aglow, I run over, what's he doing here, just right now, when I'm thinking he's in his office, and then I stop glowing, because there are two small figures craning their necks, snuggled together in the front seat where by now I have sat many times. Ivan says: This is Béla, this is András, say hello! But the "gyerekek," as the children are known collectively, do not say hello, they do not answer, and when I ask, perplexed, whether they know German, they start to laugh and whisper to each other, I can't understand a word, so these are

Ivan's children—whom I always wanted to meet, whom I know a little about, for instance, that Béla is the older one and already in school—embarrassed, I talk to Ivan and no longer know what I wanted to do, where I wanted to go, oh, yes, up to the Automag in the upper Ungargasse, since my car is being lubricated and may be ready, I keep promising myself I'll visit a friend in the Nineteenth District, what's more she's sick, but I'd have to take a taxi if my car isn't ready. Ivan says: That's practically on my way, so we can take you, you'll come with us! Ivan didn't say: You'll come with me. He says something to the children in Hungarian, walks around the car, pulls the children out and opens the back door, he shoves them onto the back seat. I don't know, I'd really rather not right now, I'd like to go to the Automag or take a taxi. But how can I make Ivan understand that it's all too sudden for me? He says: So get in the car! During the drive I let Ivan talk, occasionally I glance back, I have to find a first sentence, I'm not prepared. I am not going to ask Béla which grade he's in, which school, I'm not going to ask the children how they are, what their favorite things to do are and whether they enjoy eating ice cream. There's no question about it. The children interrupt Ivan every few minutes: Did you see that? look, a fiaker! hey, a chimney sweep! did you remember my gym shoes? look, an Alfa Romeo! hey, a license plate from Salzburg! is that an American? Ivan is telling me about a difficult afternoon at work, in between he sends short, exact answers to the back seat, he talks to me about "little time," about difficulties, of all days to have to take the children to the dentist. Doctor Heer extracted one of Béla's teeth, András had to have two cavities filled. I look back, Béla opens his mouth wide, exaggeratedly so, with a grimace, András wants to do the same thing, but has to laugh, and now the opportunity is there, I don't ask whether it hurt, whether Herr Doktor Heer is a nice dentist, but open my mouth just as wide and say: But he took my wisdom teeth out, I already have wisdom teeth, you don't have those yet! Béla shrieks: Hey, she's lying.

In the evening I tell Ivan: The children don't look like you at all, maybe Béla does a little, if he didn't have that shaggy brown hair and light eyes he'd look more like you! Ivan must have guessed that I was afraid of the children, since he laughs and says: Was it that bad? You were fine, no, they don't look like me, but they also can't stand it when people start in on them, when people ask them the kind of questions people ask, then they smell a rat! Quickly I suggest: If you're going to the movies on Sunday, then I could go with you, if you don't mind, I'd like to go to the movies again, there's a film at the Apollo called THE LIVING DESERT. Ivan says: We saw that last Sunday. Thus it remained unclear whether Ivan would take me another time or whether his statement about the film was an excuse, whether I could see the children again or whether Ivan wants to keep his two worlds forever separate, in case they are no longer worlds. We begin playing chess and don't have to talk anymore, the game is tedious, involved, stagnant, we don't get anywhere, Ivan is attacking, I'm on the defensive. Ivan's attack comes to a stop, it is the longest, most speechless game we've ever played, Ivan doesn't help me a single time, and today we don't finish. Ivan has drunk more whiskey than usual, tired, he gets up, muttering Ivan-curses, he paces back and forth a few steps and keeps on drinking while standing, he doesn't want to anymore, it was a hard day, no checkmate but there hasn't been a stalemate either. Ivan wants to go home right away and go to bed, apparently I played so tediously it tired him out, his game was equally uninspired. Good Night!

Malina has come home, he finds me still in the living room, the chessboard is there, I haven't even managed to take the glasses to the kitchen. Malina can't know where I was sitting, because I'm rocking in the rocking chair in the corner next to the lamp, holding a book, RED STAR OVER CHINA, nonetheless, he bends over the board, whistles quietly and says: You would have lost by a mile! I ask what do you mean by that, and add that I might not have lost after all. But Malina thinks it over and calculates the next moves. How can he know that I was black, because black, in his opinion, would have ended up losing. Malina reaches for my glass of whiskey. How can he know it's my glass and not the glass that Ivan left, also half-full, but he never drinks out of Ivan's glass, he never touches anything Ivan has handled or used just before, a plate with olives or salted almonds. Malina extinguishes his cigarette in my ashtray and not the other one, which was Ivan's ashtray this evening. I conclude nothing.

I left China at: Enemy troops were racing up from the southeast, others approached from the North. A hurried military conference was summoned by Lin Piao.

Ivan and I: the world converging.
Malina and I, since we are one: the world diverging.

Never have I had so little use for Malina, less and less does he know where to begin with me, but had he not come home on time and found me between the Long March through China and a train of thought about children who do not look like Ivan, I would fall back into bad habits, write letters, hundreds of them, or drink and destroy, think destructively, destroy everything and then some, I would not be able to hold on to the country I have acquired, I would regress and abandon it. Even if Malina is silent, it's better than being silent alone, and it helps me with Ivan, too, when I can't grasp what's going on, when I lose my grasp on myself, because Malina is always there for me, steadfast and composed, and even in the darkest hours I am aware that Malina will never be lost to me—even if I were to get lost myself!

I say "Du" to Malina and to Ivan, but these two "Du's" differ by an immeasurable, imponderable accent in pronunciation. From the beginning I never said "Sie" to either one, as is otherwise my custom. I recognized Ivan too instantaneously and there was no time to get closer to him through speech, I had already belonged to him before a word was said. Malina, on the other hand, had been the focus of my thoughts for so many years, my longing for him had been so great that our living together one day was only the affirmation of something which should have always been, something which had only been impeded too often by other people, bad decisions and actions. My "Du" for Malina is precise and well suited to our conversations and arguments. My "Du" for Ivan is imprecise, of varying hues, darker, lighter, it can become brittle, mellow or timid, unlimited in its scale of expression, it can be said alone at longer intervals and often, like a siren, always alluringly new, but nonetheless without that tone, that expression I hear in me whenever I cannot bring myself to utter a single word in front of Ivan. Not in front of him, but inside me I will someday perfect this "Du." Perfection will have evolved.

Otherwise I say "Sie" to most people, I have an indispensable need for saying "Sie," also out of caution, but I have at my disposal at least two types of "Sie." One "Sie" is intended for most people, the other, a dangerous, richly orchestrated "Sie," which I could never say to Malina or to Ivan, is reserved for the men who might be in my life were it not for Ivan. Because of Ivan I retreat into this disquieting "Sie" and am myself withdrawn. It is a "Sie" difficult to describe, one that is sometimes—though all too rarely—grasped, yet still understood for the tension it carries, which the "Du" of camaraderies can never possess. For naturally I say "Du" to all sorts of people, because I was in school with them, because I studied with them, because I worked with them, but that doesn't mean a thing. My "Sie" might be related to that of Fanny Goldmann, who ostensibly—of course just according to rumor—persisted in saying "Sie" to all her lovers. She also said "Sie" to other men who couldn't be her lovers, and there is supposed to have been one man whom she loved to whom she said her most beautiful "Sie." Women like Fanny Goldmann, whom people are always talking about, can't do anything about it one way or the other, one day words simply begin to circulate in the city: Are you living on the moon? what, you don't know that? she's ended her biggest affairs with an absolutely inimitable "Sie"! Even Malina, who never says anything good or bad about anyone, mentions that he met Fanny Goldmann today, she was also invited to the Jordans, and he says, unsolicited: I never heard a woman say "Sie" so beautifully.

But I'm not interested in what Malina thinks about Fanny Goldmann, he's not about to make any comparisons, after all, this woman studied speech, and I never learned to breathe from the abdomen, I can't modulate words according to whim and don't know how to make artful pauses. In my anxiety over what to discuss with Malina, since it's almost bedtime, where do I begin, I've only met two children who in turn are of no interest to Malina. All that transpires elsewhere, what he calls my little stories, are never allowed to be discussed. World affairs or city events may not be rehashed, not in front of Malina, after all we're not sitting in a pub. I may talk about everything that orbits around me, that encircles me. Is there such a thing as the expropriation of intellectual property? Does the victim of such expropriation, should it indeed exist, have the right to some final difficulties in thinking? Is it still worth it?

I might ask about the most impossible things. Who invented writing? What is writing? Is it property? Who first demanded expropriation? Allons-nous à l'Esprit? Are we of an inferior race? Should we get mixed up in politics, do nothing more and simply be brutal? Are we cursed? Are we going under? Malina gets up, he's emptied my glass. I'll sleep on my questions in a deep intoxication. I'll worship animals in the night, I'll lay violent hands on the holiest icons, I'll clutch at all lies, I'll grow bestial in my dreams and will allow myself to be slaughtered like a beast.

As I'm falling asleep my head jerks, flashing inside, sparkling, casting me in darkness, I again feel threatened, it's the feeling of annihilation, and I say, very sharply, to Ivan who isn't there: Malina never, Malina is different, you don't understand Malina. I have never directed a harsh word at Ivan, will never do so out loud. Of course Ivan hasn't said anything against Malina either, he never gives him a thought, and why should Ivan be jealous of Malina's living here with me? He doesn't mention Malina for the same reasons you don't talk about someone in prison or someone who is mentally ill, out of tact, in consideration of the family, and even if my eyes do go blank for a few minutes, then it's only because a terrible tension is arising, while I'm thinking about Malina, and this benign misunderstanding, this clear confusion reigns over the three of us, it reigns and governs us. We are the only subjects to enjoy any well-being, the misapprehension we inhabit is so rich that no one ever raises his voice against the other or against the regime. That's why the other people, outside, tend to incapacitate us, because they assume rights, because they have been deprived of rights or their rights have been usurped and because they are constantly remonstrating against one another, without any right. Ivan would say: They're all poisoning one another, without any right. Ivan would say: They're all poisoning each other's lives. Malina would say: All these people with their borrowed opinions, which they've rented at such high rates, they'll wind up paying dearly.

My own borrowed opinions are already disappearing. It's becoming easier and easier for me to part from Ivan, and then to find him again, because my thoughts about him are less domineering, I can also free him for hours from my mind, so that he won't have to rub his wrists and ankles incessantly in his sleep, I no longer keep him fettered or, if I do, just very loosely. He no longer wrinkles his forehead so often, his creases are smoothing out since the dictatorship of my eyes and caresses has mellowed, when I cast a spell or a curse on him I do it briefly so we can part more easily, one of us walks out the door, one of us gets in the car and mumbles something: If it's twenty to four right now then I'll make it to the Messegelände just in time, and you? I'll be all right, no nothing special, tomorrow I'm driving to Burgenland with somebody, no, not overnight, I don't know yet what my friends ... The quietest mumbling, since neither of us knows what's going on with these friends, with the Messegelände or with Burgenland, to which life these words belong. I promised Ivan I would only wear clothes that make me both pretty and happy, I also added a quick promise to eat regularly and refrain from drinking. And even more hastily I gave Ivan my word I would get some sleep, that I would rest up, that I would sleep very deeply.

We do talk with the children, but we also quickly speak over their heads, using a desultory German full of allusions, with English sentences thrown in when it can't be avoided, though if we happen to use this English Morse Code it doesn't mean we're dealing with an SOS, everything is going well with Ivan and the children, but when the children are there I hold myself back and at the same time talk more than I would were I alone with Ivan, for then Ivan isn't so much Ivan for me as the father of Béla and András, only at first was I unable to pronounce his name in front of the children, until I noticed that they also call him Ivan (however, sometimes when he starts to whine András still cries out: Papà! it must be a word from an earlier time). At the last minute Ivan decided to take me along to Schönbrunn, naturally because András, who took to me right away, asked him: Isn't she coming? she should come with us! But both kids hang on to me in front of the monkey house, András clutches my arm, carefully I draw him closer and closer to me, I didn't know that children's bodies were warmer and nicer to the touch than the body of a grownup, jealous Béla also presses closer to me, it's only because of András, they're pushy in a way I can't get enough of, as if they had been missing someone a long time, someone they could hang on to and push and pull, Ivan has to help dole out the nuts and bananas because we're laughing and hanging on to each other and Béla is throwing the nuts, missing. Eagerly I explain about the baboon and the chimpanzees, I'm not prepared for an hour in the zoo, I should have read up in Brehm's LIFE OF ANIMALS, I'm at a complete loss when it comes to the snakes, I don't know whether the adders in there eat white mice, which Béla claims to know, or bugs and leaves, as Ivan thinks, Ivan who already has a headache, I call to him: Just go on ahead! Because Béla and András still want to see the lizards and salamanders and since Ivan isn't listening I invent unbelievable habits and stories about the lives of reptiles, unfazed by any question, I know which countries they come from, when they get up, when they go to bed, what they eat, what they think, whether they grow to be a hundred or a thousand years old. If only Ivan weren't so impatient because of his headache, his lack of sleep, since we still have to see the bears, we feed the seals, and in front of the big aviary I make up everything about vultures and eagles, there's no time left for the songbirds. I have to say that Ivan will treat us all to some ice cream at Hübner's, but only if we leave at once, otherwise nothing will come of our ice cream, I say: Ivan will be very mad at us! But only the ice cream is effective. Please, Ivan, couldn't you treat us to an ice cream, I'm sure you promised the children (over their heads, in English, "Please, do me the favor, I promised them some ice cream"), you better have a double espresso. Ivan orders grumpily, he must be exhausted, while the children and I nudge each other's feet under the table, then start kicking more and more wildly, Béla laughs hysterically: What kind of shoes does she have, boy does she have stupid shoes! For that I give Béla a gentle kick, but Ivan gets annoyed: Béla, behave yourself or we're going straight home! But we have to go straight home anyway, whether the children behave or not, Ivan tosses them onto the back seat of the car, I've stayed a second longer and bought two balloons while Ivan is looking for me in the other direction, I don't have any change, a woman helps me break a fifty schilling note, she says with a plaintive friendliness: Those must be yours, you have such nice children! And I say embarrassed: Thank you, thank you very much, how very nice of you. Quietly I get in and press a string with a balloon into the hand of each of the nice children. While driving Ivan says, in English: "You are just crazy, it was not necessary!" I turn around and say: All your quacking today! you're both unbearable! Béla and András double over laughing: We can quack, quack quack quack, we can quack! Whenever it starts to get wild like that Ivan starts singing, Béla and András stop quacking, they sing along, loudly and thinly, in and out of tune.

Debrecenbe kéne menni
pulykakakast kéne venni
vigyázz kocsis lyukas a kas
kiugrik a pulykakakas

Since I still don't know the song and can't sing anyway, I sigh to myself: éljen!

Ivan drops us off at number 9, he has to pick up some documents at the office, and I play cards with the children, András, who is always wishing me well, advises me, whereas Béla says scornfully: You're not playing right, you're an idiot, mister, excuse me, lady! We're playing Fairy Tale Quartet, but Béla is moping because the fairy tales are too stupid for him, he's past fairy tales, that's something for András and me. We play Animal Quartet and Airplane Quartet, we win and lose, I lose most often, sometimes unintentionally, sometimes on purpose, assisting the good fortune of Béla and András. When we get to City Quartet András doesn't want to play anymore, he doesn't know cities, I advise him, we whisper behind our folded cards, I say "Hong Kong," András doesn't understand, Béla throws his cards on the table, enraged, like a gentleman at a big, decisive conference who's about to burst at the seams because the others aren't up to speed, András wants to go back to fairy tales, and for a while we go back and forth until I suggest: Let's play Old Maid. They must have played Old Maid a thousand times but they're electrified once more, Béla shuffles, I cut, the cards are again dealt, drawn and played. In the end I get the Old Maid and Ivan comes in, Béla and András reel with laughter and roar with all their might: Old Maid, Old Maid! Now we have to play once again with Ivan, and in the end it's between Béla and me, unfortunately Béla draws the Old Maid from me and throws his cards down, crying out hoarsely: Ivan, she's a bitch! We exchange glances over the boys' heads. Anger begins to rumble in Ivan, and Béla pretends not to have said anything. Ivan proposes some aged cognac as a peace offering, Béla even asks if he may be allowed to fetch it, he runs twice, brings us the glasses and Ivan and I sit there in silence, our legs crossed, the children play Flower Quartet silently and cautiously at the table, and I don't think anything of it. But then I do think of something, namely that Ivan is letting his eyes drift back and forth between the children and me, musing, questioning, but for the most part friendly.

Must I forever? Must one forever? Must one wait a whole lifetime?

We're supposed to meet in the garden patio of the Italian ice cream parlor. Ivan says, so that the children don't notice anything: Hello! how are you? In front of the children I, too, act as if I hadn't seen Ivan for weeks. We also don't have much time, without asking Ivan orders four servings of mixed flavors, because Béla has to go to his infamous gym class, which is constantly causing a problem for Ivan's mother and very often for Ivan, even for Béla who doesn't like gym. Ivan criticizes our schools and their curricula, especially because of this crazy gym class, which is always held in a different place and always in the afternoon. What do you people over here think, that everybody has at least two cars and a couple of governesses! Normally I never hear Ivan say anything about living conditions in Vienna, he doesn't make comparisons, he doesn't talk about things, he seems to consider going into Here vs. There irresponsible and unproductive. He only lost his self-control because of this gym class, he said "you people over here" and said it to me, as if the gym class were the embodiment of a world to which I belong and should reject, but perhaps I'm only imagining something in my rising anxiety, I don't know what gym classes are like over there in Hungary. Ivan has paid, we take the kids out onto the street and head toward the car, András waves, but it's Béla who asks: Isn't she coming? why can't she come along? Then all three have disappeared through the Tuchlauben, rounded the corner, up to the Hoher Markt, obscured by a diplomat's limousine. I look and am still looking when there's no longer any trace of them, slowly I walk across Petersplatz to the Graben, in a different direction, I should buy some stockings, I could buy myself a sweater, especially today I would like to buy myself something nice, because they have disappeared, naturally Ivan couldn't say in front of the children whether he'd call tonight.

I hear Béla saying: She should come along!

At the Graben I bought myself a new dress, a long casual dress, for an hour in the afternoon, for a few special evenings at home, I know for whom, I like it because it's soft and long and means a lot of staying at home, even today. However I wouldn't want to have Ivan here while I'm trying it on, even less Malina, and since Malina isn't there I can only cast frequent glances in the mirror, I have to turn around in front of the long mirror in the corridor, miles away, fathoms deep, heavens high, fables removed from the men. For an hour I can live without time and space, in deep satisfaction, carried off into a legend, where the aroma of a soap, the prickle of a facial tonic, the rustle of lingerie, the dipping of puffs into pots of powder, the thoughtful stroke of a lip liner are the only reality. The result is a composition, a woman is to be created for a dress. What a woman is is being redesigned in complete secrecy, it is like a new beginning, with an aura for no one. The hair must be brushed twenty times, feet anointed and toenails painted, hair removed from legs and armpits, the shower turned on and off, a cloud of powder floats in the bathroom, the mirror is consulted, it's always Sunday, the mirror, mirror on the wall is consulted, it might be Sunday already.

One day all women will have golden eyes, they will wear golden shoes and golden dresses, and she combed her golden hair, she tore her, no! and her golden hair blew in the wind, when she rode up the Danube and entered Rhaetia...

A day will come when all women will have redgolden eyes, redgolden hair, and the poetry of their sex, their lineage, shall be recreated...

I have stepped into the mirror, I vanished in the mirror, I have seen into the future, I was one with myself and am again not one with myself. I blink, once again awake, into the mirror, shading the edge of my eyelid with a pencil. I'm able to give it up. For a moment I was immortal and myself—I wasn't there for Ivan and wasn't living in Ivan, it was without significance. The water in the tub drains away. I close the drawers, I clean up the liners, the pots, the vials, the sprays in the medicine cabinet, so Malina won't be annoyed. The dress is hung in the closet, it's not for today. I have to go outside and get some air before going to sleep. Out of consideration I turn at the Heumarkt, threatened by the proximity of the Stadtpark, by its shadows and dark figures, I make a detour over the Linke-Bahngasse, rushing because I find this section creepy, but once I reach the Beatrixgasse I again feel secure, and from the Beatrixgasse I go up the Ungargasse to the Rennweg so I won't know whether Ivan is home or not. I show the same consideration on my way back, in this way both number 9 and the informative Münzgasse remain hidden to me. Ivan should have his freedom, he should have his space, even at this hour. Racing upstairs, I take a few steps at a time, since a telephone appears to be quietly rattling, it could be our phone, it is our phone ringing in intervals, I burst through the door, leaving it open behind me, because the telephone is screeching in a state of alarm. I rip off the receiver and say breathlessly, amazed:

I was just coming, I was out for a walk
By myself of course, what else, just a few steps
So you are home, but how am I supposed to
Then I must not have noticed your car
Because I was coming from the Rennweg
I must have forgotten to look up at your window
I prefer coming down from the Rennweg
I'm afraid to go all the way to the Heumarkt
But that you're home so early
Because of the Stadtpark, you never know
Where could I have been looking
In the Münzgasse, I parked mine there today as well
In that case I'd better call you, so tomorrow I'll call

Reconciliation comes and drowsiness, my impatience softens, I wasn't secure but am once again safe, no longer walking past the Stadtpark at night, jittery as I walk along the facades of the buildings, no longer on a detour through the dark, but already a little at home, already docked safely at the Ungargasse, already safe and sound in Ungargassenland, my head's already a little above the water even. Already gurgling the first words and sentences, already commencing, beginning.

A day will come when people shall have redgolden eyes and sidereal voices, when their hands will be gifted for love, and the poetry of their lineage shall be recreated ...

Already crossing out, perusing, throwing away.

... and their hands will be gifted for goodness, with their innocent hands they will reach for the highest goodness, they shall not forever, mankind shall not forever, they will not have to wait forever.

Already insight, foresight.

I hear the key in the door, Malina looks in at me questioningly.

You're not disturbing me, sit down, would you like some tea, a glass of milk, do you want anything?

Malina himself wants to get a glass of milk from the kitchen, he makes a light, ironic bow, something amuses him enough to make him smile at me. He also can't resist saying something to annoy me: If I see correctly, nous irons mieux, la montagne est passée.

Please spare me your Prussian pronouncements, you shouldn't have bothered me now, after all everybody has the right to have things go better sometime!

I ask Ivan whether he ever thought and what he used to think and what he thinks today about love. Ivan smokes, letting the ashes fall on the floor, looks for his shoes in silence, he's found both and turns to me, he's having difficulty finding the right words.

Is that something people think about, what kind of thoughts

should I have about it, do you need words for it? are you trying to set a trap for me, my fräulein?

Yes and no. But if you don't ... And you never feel anything, no contempt, no aversion? But what if I didn't feel anything either? I ask, on the alert. I'd like to throw my arms around Ivan so he can't be far, not even a yard away from me when I ask him for the first time.

What do you mean, aversion, are you joking? Why do you want to complicate things? It's enough that I come over. My God what impossible questions you ask!

I say triumphantly: That's all I wanted to know, whether they're impossible questions. I didn't want to know anything more.

Ivan is dressed and doesn't have much time left, he says: You act pretty funny sometimes.

Not me, I answer quickly, it's the others, they're the ones who led me to such wayward thoughts earlier on, I never used to think that way, I would never have come up with contempt or aversion, and it's someone else inside me, someone who never agreed with me, someone who never allowed answers to be forced out of him to questions which had been foisted upon him.

Don't you mean foisted on her?

No, him, I don't confuse the two. Him. When I say him you have to believe me.

My fräulein, we are, after all, very female, as I was able to ascertain in the very first hour, and that's still true today, you can believe me.

You're so impatient, you don't even have the patience to let me talk for once!

Today I'm very impatient, I don't keep all my patience just for you!

You only have to have a little patience, then we'll find out.

But if you make me lose my patience!

I'm afraid it's my patience which is ultimately to blame for your impatience ...

(End of the sentences about patience and impatience. A very small sentence set.)

A day will come, when our houses will fall, all cars will have become scrap metal, we will be freed from all airplanes and rockets, renounce the invention of the wheel and the ability to split the atom, the fresh wind will come down from the blue hills and swell our chest, we will be dead and breathe, it shall be our whole life.

All water shall run dry in the deserts, once again we will be able to enter the wilderness and witness revelations, savanna and stream will invite us in their purity, diamonds will remain embedded in stone and illuminate us all, the primeval forest will take us out of the nighttime jungle of our thoughts, we will cease to think and suffer, it shall be the Redemption.

Dear Mr. President:
You wish me, on behalf of the Academy, best wishes on my birthday. Permit me to tell you how appalled I was precisely today. To be sure I have no doubt as to your tact, since I had the honor of meeting you some years ago at the opening ... since I had the honor of meeting you. However you are alluding to a day, perhaps even a specific hour and an irrevocable moment, which must have been a most private matter for my mother, my father too, as we may assume for the sake of propriety. Naturally nothing in particular was shared with me about this day, I just had to memorize a date which I have to write down on every registration form in every city, in every country, even if I'm only passing through. But I stopped passing through countries a long time ago ...

Dear Lily,

You will have heard in the meantime what happened to me and to my head. I say "in the meantime" though by now many years have already passed. Back then I asked you to come to me, to help me, it wasn't the first time, it was the second time, but you didn't come the first time either. You might know what I think about Christian love for one's neighbor. But I'm not being very articulate, I only want to say that even Christian love for one's neighbor surely does not exclude any particular possibility, though it may remain closed to someone like me, but I can also easily imagine that one acts on its account, and you might have acted on its account as well. Of course I would have preferred it had you done so on my account. Agreement is not necessary in emergencies, and this was definitely an emergency. Dear Lily, I know your magnanimity, your behavior that might be deemed extravagant in so many situations and I have always admired it. But now seven years have passed, and not even your intelligence was sufficient to avoid betraying your heart. If someone is well equipped with both heart and reason, but not quite enough, then any self-inflicted disappointment must be worse for him than the disappointment he causes his closest friends. I was completely prepared to assist Herr G. We had agreed to accept our differences of opinion on how to listen to music, at what volume, as well as what selection of course, because my sensitivity to sound had recently undergone a pathological increase, so that we would quibble day in and day out about all aspects of its use, at that point my sense of time was also beginning to suffer greatly, timing and time management struck me as pathological, but I was ready to admit that my own attitude toward time, or rather my lack of attitude, had itself acquired a diseased dimension. We had also agreed, in an emergency, to disagree on the subject of cats and dogs, I was prepared to say I was incapable of living with animals—especially cats—and him together in one apartment simultaneously, and he wanted to say that he was incapable of lying in bed with a dog or my mother and me. At any rate we had arrived at a very clear, harmonious settlement. You know my prejudices, I have carried over certain assumptions from my education, my background, but also from a certain hierarchy of premises. I was easy to deal with since I was accustomed to certain tones, to gestures, to a certain gentle manner, and the brutality with which my world—and yours as well—was injured would have itself sufficed to drive me half out of my mind. And so, because of my background, I was, in the end, beyond treatment, so to speak. I am not negotiable. I am not amenable to unfamiliar customs that cause me pain. Even the Thai ambassador, who wanted to make me take off my shoes, but you know that old story ... I do not take off my shoes. I do not advertise my prejudices. I have them. I prefer to undress myself, down to my shoes. And if my custom should one day call for it, then I will say: Cast all thou hast into the fire, even unto thy shoes.

Vienna, ...

Dear Lily,
In the meantime you undoubtedly know, against your worse judgment, for anything to be known in a bad way will have made the rounds. You yourself never believed it. Nonetheless you didn't come. Once again it's my birthday. Pardon me, it's your birthday ...

Dear Lily,
Today I've reached the point where I never want to see you again. This wish is not the result of a first or final passion felt in the heat of the moment. During the first few years I still wrote many agonizing, accusatory, reproachful letters, every one of which, however, would have revealed more of my affection, despite their tremendous reproaches, than the insignificant letters we once exchanged, equipped with the most tender greetings, mutual embraces, and many lovely wishes for one another. Nor was this wish of mine

preceded by much deliberation, I stopped deliberating long ago, but I notice that something in me is letting go of you, no longer courting you, not even looking for you anymore. Of course Herr G. or Herr W., or as far as I'm concerned Herr A., might have tried to separate us in some vile manner, but how can two people be split by one or more third parties? It would be easy to blame such a person or persons, to pin all the guilt on them—if such waggish guilt even exists, and I'm not sure it does—and anyway guilt is too unimportant. Where no wish for separation exists, it cannot occur, thus it can only have been your deep-seated desire, lying in wait for the slightest occasion. For me no occasion would have ever arisen, and therefore today there can't be any either. You have merely regressed inside of me, you have passed into the time in which we were once together, and there stands your youthful likeness, no longer vulnerable to the damage of later events and my opinions of them. It may no longer be spoiled. It is standing in the mausoleum within me, next to the images of invented characters, figures soon revived, soon dying.

Vienna,...

An unknown woman

Whenever Ivan leaves the little devils, the rascals, the bandits, the rapscallions with me, these gyerekek, because he has to run another errand, just for a moment, and because I insisted, the apartment is subjected to a turbulence beyond Lina's wildest dreams. First both demolish Lina's marble cake, scarcely eating it, and I clear away all sharp and dangerous objects, all sticks and stones. I didn't know my apartment was so full of them, furthermore, I left the door ajar for Ivan, but András has already escaped into the stairwell. I've taken on a terrible responsibility, I see new dangers arising every second, unsuspected, surprising, for if the slightest thing should happen to just one of Ivan's children, I could never look Ivan in the eye, but there are two of them, and they are faster, more inventive, quicker of mind than myself. Fortunately András hasn't run out into the street, but upstairs he rings and rings the soprano's doorbell, she can't get up and open the door because her four hundred pounds keep her in bed, later I'll slip her a note with an apology, because this must have been very upsetting to her, with her fatty degenerative heart. I drag András back into the apartment, but now the door has closed shut and I'm stranded without a key. I hammer on the door, Ivan opens, Ivan has come! with two of us the gyerekek are easier to handle, at Ivan's word Béla picks up the biggest cake crumbs without resisting, but now András has discovered the record player, already his hand is on the arm with the sapphire needle and scratching across the record. I say to Ivan happily: Let him go ahead, it doesn't matter, it's just the D-major Concerto, it's my fault! But I do put the candelabra on the tall display case out of András's reach. I dash into the kitchen and take the Coca-Cola bottles out of the refrigerator. Ivan, could you please at least open the bottles, no, the opener's lying right over there! But Béla has run off with the opener, we're supposed to guess where it is, and we play and guess: cold, lukewarm, cooler, hot, very hot! the opener is lying underneath the rocking chair. To-day the children don't want to drink any Coca-Cola, Béla empties his glass into a vase containing Herr Kopecky's roses and the rest into Ivan's tea. I say: But children, couldn't you for just one min-ute, I have to talk to Ivan about something, for heaven's sake just for a minute, please quiet down! I talk to Ivan, who tells me that he's no longer taking the children to the Tyrol after all, but to the Mondsee, and earlier than expected, because his mother no longer wants to go to the Tyrol. I don't have a chance to answer, because András has entered the kitchen on an exploratory expedition, I catch him while he's still on the balcony where he is beginning to climb the railing, I pull him down without showing any emotion, I say: Come here, please, in here, I have some chocolate for you! Ivan continues unmoved: I couldn't reach you yesterday, I would have told you sooner! So Ivan wants to go to the Mondsee, and isn't talking about the Mondsee and me, I say quickly: That works out well, I have to visit the Altenwyls' on the Wolfgangsee, I've already declined twice and have halfway accepted this time, I really should go, because otherwise they'll be insulted. Ivan says: You should go, you've got to get out of Vienna for once, I don't understand why you're always declining, you have the time. Éljen! Béla and András have now found Malina's and my shoes in the hall, they stick their little feet inside and come tottering in, András falls down bawling, I pick him up and take him on my lap. Ivan pulls Béla out of Malina's shoes, we wear ourselves out fighting with the children, keeping an eye out for the chocolate that has also disappeared, it would save us, András is clutching the remnants in his hand and smears it all over my blouse. So they're going to the Mondsee and I said I would go to the Altenwyls'. Béla cries out: Seven-league boots! with them I'll cross the whole wide world, how far have I come? all the way to Timbuktu? But, Ivan, let him stay in the shoes if he insists on walking in seven-league boots, I add in our English code, "please, do call later, I have to speak to you," the letter with the invitation to Venice, the reply, the telegram with prepaid reply, I still haven't sent any of it, it's not so important, Venice isn't important, sometime later we can ... Ivan has taken Béla to the bathroom, András is kicking and first wants to get down off my lap, then suddenly kisses me on the nose, I kiss András on the nose, we rub our noses together, I wish it would never end, that András would never get enough, just as I can't get enough of our rubbing noses. I wish neither the Mondsee nor the Wolfgangsee existed, but what's said is said, András pushes against me closer and closer, and I hold on to him, he must belong to me, the children will be all mine. Ivan comes in and sets a couple of chairs in order, he says: That's it for now, there's no more time, we have to go, once again you've behaved like two perfect little horrors! Ivan still has to buy the children a rubber boat before the stores close. I stand at the door with all three, Ivan is holding András by the hand, Béla is already romping down the stairs. Auf Wiedersehen, Fräulein! Good-bye you little brats! "I'll call you later." Auf Wiedersehen!

I take the dessert plates and glasses into the kitchen, pace up and down and don't know what else I could do, I pick a few crumbs off the carpet, Lina will run over it tomorrow with the vacuum cleaner. I wouldn't want to have Ivan anymore without the kids, I'll say something to Ivan when he calls, or else I'll tell him before he leaves, sooner or later I'll have to say something to him. But it's better I don't say it. I'll write to him from St. Wolfgang, gain some distance, think about it for ten days, then write, not one word too many. I'll find the right phrases, forget the black art of words, for Ivan I shall write in all artlessness, like the country girls back home write to their beloveds, like the queens who write to their chosen ones, without shame. I will petition for a reprieve, like the condemned who will receive no pardon.

I haven't been out of Vienna for a long time, including last summer, because Ivan had to stay in the city. I claimed that summer in Vienna was the most beautiful thing in the world, and thought there was nothing so dumb as driving into the country at the same time as everybody else, I couldn't stand vacations either, the Wolfgangsee would be ruined for me, because all Vienna goes there, and when Malina went to Carinthia I stayed behind in the apartment by myself, in order to go swimming with Ivan a few times in the Old Danube. But this summer the Old Danube has lost its charm, the most beautiful place in the world must be the Mondsee and not Vienna, dead and deserted and crisscrossed by tourists. It's as though no time had passed. In the morning Ivan will take me to the station, since they're not leaving with the car until about noon. Fräulein Jellinek drops in late this afternoon, there's still something we want to take care of.

Dear Herr Hartleben:
Thank you for your letter of May 31st!

Fräulein Jellinek waits, and I smoke, she should pull this sheet out and throw it in the wastebasket. I can't answer a letter written on a 31st of May, the number 31 may not, under any circumstances, be used and profaned. Who does this Herr from Munich think he is? How can he draw my attention to the 31st of May? What business of his is my 31st of May! I leave the room hastily, Fräulein Jellinek is not supposed to notice that I'm starting to cry, she is supposed to file and organize, she's not supposed to answer this gentleman at all. All replies can wait, they have time until after the summer, in the bathroom it again occurs to me that today I will still write one more decisive, fervent letter, but by myself, in the utmost anxiety, in the greatest haste. Fräulein Jellinek should calculate her hours, I don't have any time now, we wish each other a nice summer. The telephone is ringing, why isn't Fräulein Jellinek leaving already. Once again: have a nice summer! happy vacation! best greetings to Herr Doktor Krawanja even though I don't know him! The telephone is screeching.

I don't stutter, you're imagining things
But I told you the day before yesterday
There must be some mistake, I wanted to say
I'm really sorry, the last night
No I've already told you that today unfortunately
I don't want you to always do what I want
I'm not doing that at all, for example it's absolutely out
I'm sure I told you, just that you
But I'm the one who doesn't have any time today
Tomorrow morning I'll be sure and bring you
I'm in a terrible rush, see you in the morning, at eight!

Strange encounter. Today neither of us has any time for the other, there's always so much to do the last evening. I would have time, my bags are already packed, Malina went out to eat, for my sake. He'll come back late, also for my sake. If I only knew where Malina was. But I don't want to see him either, I can't today, I have to think about strange encounters. One day we'll have less time, one day it will have been yesterday and the day before yesterday and a year ago and two years ago. Apart from yesterday there will still be tomorrow, a tomorrow I don't want and yesterday ... Oh this yesterday, and now it occurs to me how I met Ivan and that from the very first moment and the whole time I ... and I am frightened, because I never wanted to think how it was at first, how it was a month ago, never wanted to think how times were before the children appeared, how times were with Frances and Trollope and then how it went with the children and how all four of us were in the Prater, how I laughed with András pressed against me, in the ghost train, or about the skull and crossbones. I never again wanted to know how it was in the beginning, I no longer stopped in front of the florist's in the Landstrasser Hauptstrasse, I didn't look for the name nor did I ask. But one day I will want to know it and from that day on I will stay behind and fall back into yesterday. But it's not tomorrow yet. Before yesterday and tomorrow arrive, I have to silence them inside me. It is today. I am here and today.

Ivan just called, he can't take me to the station after all, something's come up at the last minute. It doesn't matter, he'll send me a postcard, but I can't listen any longer, since I have to quickly phone for a taxi. Malina has already left and Lina still hasn't arrived. But Lina's on her way, she discovers me with my suitcases in the stairwell, we carry the suitcases downstairs, Lina does most of the lifting, she hugs me in front of the taxi: You better come back to me healthy, gnädige Frau, otherwise Herr Doktor will be disappointed!

I run around the Westbahnhof station, then behind a porter who is carting my suitcases to the end of Track 3, we have to go back since the right car is now on Track 5 and there are two trains leaving for Salzburg at the same time. On Track 5 the train is even longer than the one on Track 3, and we have to run across the ballast at the end of the platform to reach the last cars. The porter wants to be paid now, he thinks it's a scandal and typical, but then he helps me anyway because I've given him ten schillings more, it remains a scandal. I would prefer he didn't let himself be bribed by ten schillings. Then I would have had to turn back, I would have been home in an hour. The train pulls up, with my last strength I can barely slam the door which was flying open, trying to pull me out. I stay sitting on my suitcases until the conductor comes and ushers me to my compartment. On top of all this the train chooses not to derail before Linz, it makes a short stop in Linz, I've never been to Linz, I've always only passed through, Linz on the Danube, I don't want to leave the banks of the Danube.

... she no longer saw any way out of the of this singular world of willows, winds, and waters ... the willows whispered more and more, they hissed, they laughed, they screamed shrilly and sighed and moaned ... she buried her head in her arms ... She could move neither forward nor backward, she could merely choose between the water and the overpowering willows.

In Salzburg Antoinette Altenwyl is standing at the station saying good-bye to a few people returning to Munich on the train opposite. I always found this station odious with its absurd waiting times and customs clearance, but this time I don't need to be cleared, for I'm staying, I belong to DOMESTIC. But I have to wait until Antoinette has kissed and greeted her way through all the people, then she waves to the departing train, as if acknowledging entire nations with her gracious salutations, and of course she hasn't forgotten about me. Atti is really looking forward to seeing me, he's going to sail in the regatta soon, I didn't know? Antoinette always forgets other people's interests, and so Atti wants to drive me down to St. Gilgen tomorrow, because of course he's not participating in this first regatta. I listen to Antoinette with growing doubt. I don't understand why Atti is waiting for me, neither probably does Antoinette, she's invented the whole thing out of sheer friendliness. Malina sends his greetings, I say drily.

Thanks, then why aren't you here together, no, really? they're still working! and how is our lovely ladies' man?

That she considers Malina a ladies' man is such a surprise to me that I begin to laugh: But Antoinette, maybe you're confusing him with Alex Fleisser or with Fritz! Oh are you with Alex now? I say amiably: You must be crazy. But I picture to myself how Malina, alone in the apartment in Vienna, might have a hard time being a ladies' man. Antoinette is driving a Jaguar these days, English cars really are the only ones worth driving, and she maneuvers out of Salzburg with confidence and speed, along a shortcut of her own discovery. She's amazed that I arrived in one piece, one is constantly hearing such droll things about me, that I never arrive anywhere, at any rate not at the expected time and place. I launch into a long-winded description of my first time in St. Wolfgang (leaving out the main event, an afternoon in a hotel room), about how it rained the whole time and how it had been a senseless trip. Although I honestly don't remember, I let it rain so that Antoinette can make up by offering me a rainless, sunny Salzkammergut. That time I was only rarely able to see Eleonore, for an hour, because she had kitchen duty in the Grand Hotel, Antoinette interrupts me, irritated: No, what do you mean, Lore? how is that? in which kitchen? in the Grand Hotel, that doesn't exist anymore, it burned down, but it wasn't at all a bad place to stay! And I hastily draw the curtain over Eleonore and give up trying to enlighten Antoinette and hurting myself. I should never have come here again.

At the Altenwyls' five people are already gathered for tea, two more are supposed to show up for dinner, and I don't have the courage to say: But you promised me there wouldn't be anybody here, that it would be completely quiet, that we'd be all by ourselves! And so tomorrow the Wantschuras are coming, who've rented a house for the summer, and on the weekend it'll just be Atti's sister, who insists on dragging Baby along, who, are you listening to me? an incredible story, she, born swindler that she is, married this Rottwitz in Germany, apart from that she isn't very well-born, they say she had a veritable succès fou over there, Germans are always taken in by everything, they really think Baby's related to the Kinskys and to them as well, the Altenwyls, isn't it amazing. Antoinette cannot get over her amazement.

I steal away from the tea, I wander through the village and along the lake, and since I'm already here I pay my visits. The people in these parts change strangely. The Wantschuras apologize for having rented a house on the Wolfgangsee, although I wasn't reproaching them for it, I'm here myself. Christine is racing restlessly through the house, with an old apron wrapped around her so you can't see her Saint-Laurent dress underneath. It's a complete coincidence, she'd rather be in the most backward part of Styria. But here they are now, the Wantschuras—although they could do without the Salzburg Festival. Christine presses her hands to her temples, everything here upsets her. She's planting lettuce and herbs in the garden, she uses her herbs in everything she cooks, they live so simply here, incredibly simply, today Xandl is simply making some rice pudding, it's Christine's evening off. She presses her temples once again, runs her fingers through her hair. They've hardly been swimming, one is always bumping into acquaintances, and with that I get the picture. Then Christine asks: Oh? At the Altenwyls? Well you know, it's a matter of taste, Antoinette really is a charming person, but Atti, how you can stand all that, we don't have anything to do with each other, you know I really think he's jealous of Xandl. I say, astonished: But how can that be? Christine says disapprovingly: After all Atti used to draw or paint himself, what do I know, well, he just can't stand it when somebody really knows how to do something, like Xandl, that's the way they all are, these dilettantes, I don't care to deal with them at all, I scarcely know Atti, now and then I run into Antoinette in the village and at the hairdresser's in Salzburg, no, never in Vienna, basically they're so utterly conservative, which they'd prefer not to admit, and even Antoinette, although she really is charming, when it comes to modern art, not the faintest notion, and that she married Atti Altenwyl, she'll never live that down, Xandl, I'll say whatever I think, I am the way I am, you're making me furious today, you hear! And I'll give the kids something to really cry about the minute one of them shows his face again in the kitchen, please, be brave, just once, and call Atti Herr Doktor Altenwyl, I'd like to see his face then, he wouldn't think it possible, he's such a knee-jerk liberal, claiming to have a Socialist streak, and even if his calling cards do have Dr. Arthur Altenwyl printed on them a hundred times, then he's only happy because everyone knows who he is anyway. That's the way they all are!

Next door at the Mandls, who get more American with each passing year, a young man is sitting in the "living room," Cathy Mandl whispers to me that he's an "outstanding" author, if I understood correctly, and, if I understood correctly, his name must be Markt or Marek, I've never read or heard of anything by him, he must have just been discovered or is looking to Cathy to do the discovering.

After the first ten minutes he asks about the Altenwyls with un-disguised greed, and I reply only tersely or not at all. What is Graf Altenwyl up to anyway? asks the young genius, and on and on, how long have I known Graf Altenwyl and whether I'm a good friend and whether it's true that Graf Altenwyl … No I have no idea, I didn't ask what he's up to. Me? Maybe two weeks. Sailing? Maybe: Yes, I think they have two or three boats, I don't know. That might be. What is Herr Markt or Herr Marek after? An invitation to the Altenwyls? Or does he just want to keep pronouncing this name? Cathy Mandl looks plump and friendly, red as a lobster, since she doesn't tan, she speaks a Viennese-sounding American through her nose and an American Viennese. She's the big sailor in the family, the only serious "danger" for Altenwyl, if you exclude Leibl as a "professional." Herr Mandl speaks softly and seldom, he prefers to watch. He says: You have no idea what energy my wife possesses, if she doesn't get aboard her boat soon, she'll dig up our garden and turn the house upside down, some people really live and others just watch them do it, I'm one of the watchers. And you?

I don't know. I receive a vodka with orange juice. When have I had this drink before? I look into the glass, as if it contained a second one, and then I remember, I feel very hot and I'd like to drop the glass or empty it, because I once drank vodka with orange juice high up in a house, during my worst night, someone wanted to throw me out the window, and I no longer hear what Cathy Mandl is saying about the International Yacht Racing Union to which she naturally belongs, I drain my glass for the sake of the gentle Herr Mandl, he well knows what fanatics the Altenwyls are when it comes to punctuality, and I stroll back in the dusk, the vicinity of the lake is whispering and buzzing, the flies and moths flit about my face, I'm looking for the path back to the house, on the verge of collapse, and I think, I have to look good, confident, be in a good mood, no one is allowed to see me here with an ashen face, it has to stay outside, here on the path, I may only wear it in my room, alone, and I step into the illuminated house and say radiantly: Good evening, Anni! Old Josefin hobbles across the hall and I beam and laugh: Good evening, Josefin! Neither Antoinette nor all St. Wolfgang will do me in, nothing will make me tremble, nothing will disturb me in my remembering. Even in my room, however, where I'm allowed to appear exactly the way I am, I don't break down: on the washstand, next to the washbowl made of old faïence, I immediately see a letter. First I wash my hands, carefully I pour the water into the washbowl and replace the pitcher, then sit down on the bed and hold Ivan's letter, which he had mailed before my departure, he didn't forget, he didn't lose the address, I kiss the letter many times and debate whether I should carefully open the edge or whether I should slit the letter with nail scissors or a paring knife, I look at the stamps, another woman in folk costume, why are they doing that again? I'd rather not read the letter right away, I'd prefer to listen to some music first, then lie awake for a long time, holding the letter, reading my name written by Ivan's hand, lay the letter under the pillow, then pull it out and carefully open it in the night. There's a knock at the door, Anni sticks her head in: Please come to dinner, gnädige Frau, they're already all in the parlor. They call it a parlor here, and because I have to quickly comb my hair, fix my makeup and smile to myself about the Altenwyls' parlor, I don't have much time. At the sound of a gong thudding downstairs, I tear open the letter before turning out the light. I don't see any address, there are only one, two, three, four, five, six, seven, eight lines—exactly eight lines—on the page, and at the bottom of the page I read: Ivan.

I run down to the salon and now am able to say: The air is wonderful here, I was out walking and looked in on a few friends here and there, but the air in particular, the country, after the city! Antoinette calls out a few names with her sure, sharp voice and seats the guests. First there's plain leberknödel soup. It's Antoinette's policy, especially in the house at St. Wolfgang, to stick to traditional

Viennese cuisine. Nothing chic or undependable is allowed on the table, nor anything French, Spanish or Italian, one isn't surprised with overcooked spaghetti, as at the Wantschuras', or with a sad, sunken zabaglione, as at the Mandls'. Probably Antoinette owes it to the name of Altenwyl that the names and the dishes remain unadulterated, and she knows that her policy reaches the awareness of most guests and relatives. Even if everything Viennese should disappear, as long as the Altenwyls are still alive they will be serving stewed plums, duchess potatoes and husarenbraten, there will be no running water and no central heating, the linen napkins will be woven by hand, and in the house there will be no "discussions," "talking," or "get-togethers," but conversation, a dying species of weightless speaking at cross purposes, which permits proper digestion and maintains the good spirits of all. What Antoinette doesn't realize is that her artistic appreciation in these areas was developed more by the Altenwyl spirit than by her existent but somewhat confused knowledge and even less by her haphazard acquisitions of modern art. Half the table has to speak French today, because of Atti's distant relatives, a certain Uncle Beaumont and his daughter Marie. When French begins to dominate, Antoinette intervenes with a request in German: Atti, be so kind, there's a draft, but I can feel it, it's coming in from over there! Atti gets up twice and tugs on the curtains, pushes and pulls the window lock. These days everything they make is slipshod, the craftsmen around here! Mais les artisans chez nous, je vous en pris, c'est partout la même chose! Mes chers amis, vous avez vu, comment on a détruit Salzbourg, même Vienne! Mais chez nous à Paris, c'est absolument le même, je vous assure! Really Antoinette, I admire you for what you're still able to come up with these days! Absolutely, without Antoinette ... but she's able to stand her own ground! No, we had a very simple dinner service shipped from Italy, from Vietri, down in the south, you know, before you reach Salerno! And I call to mind a large, wonderful bowl from Vietri, gray-green, with a leaf design, burned and lost, my first fruit bowl, why must today bring not only vodka with orange juice but ceramics from Vietri as well? Vous êtes sûre qu'il ne s'agit pas de Fayence? Jesus, cries Antoinette, Uncle Gontran is making me completely dizzy, please help me, I never realized that faïence comes from Faenza or that it might even be the same thing, you learn something new every day. Bassano del Grappa? Il faut y aller une fois, vous prenez la route, c'était donc, tu te rappelles, Marie? Non, says this Marie froidement, and old Beaumont looks hesitatingly at his daughter and then to me for help, but Antoinette makes a quick detour because of cold Marie down into Salzburg and picks at her Viennese meat loaf, whispering to me: No, today the meat loaf's not up to par. Loudly to others: Incidentally, The Magic Flute, have you all been to see it? And what do you think? Anni, tell Josefin she has really disappointed me today, she already knows why, you don't even need to explain anything. But what do you think of Karajan? The man's always been a riddle to me!

Atti smoothes the waves between the excessively dry Viennese meat loaf, Verdi's Requiem, which Karajan conducted without Antoinette's approval, and The Magic Flute, which was staged by a well-known German director, whose name Antoinette knows exactly but mispronounces twice, confused, no different than Lina, who so often fluctuates maliciously between Zoschke and Boschke. But Antoinette is already back with Karajan, and Atti says: Of course what you all must realize is that every man is a complete riddle for Antoinette, which is exactly why men find her so beautifully unworldly and charming. Antoinette laughs with the inimitable Altenwyl laugh she acquired through marriage, for even if Fanny Goldmann is the most beautiful woman in Vienna and can claim the most beautiful "Sie," still Antoinette must be awarded the prize for the most beautiful laugh. That's Atti for you! my dear, you have no idea how right you are, but the worst thing is, she says coquettishly to her dish of blancmange from which she's removed a dainty spoonful she lets dangle between the table and her head, her hand kept at a gracious angle (Josefin is simply priceless, the blancmange is just perfect, but I'll be careful not to tell that to her)—the worst thing is, Atti, that you're still the biggest riddle of all, and please, don't contradict me! Her manner of blushing is moving, as she still colors when something occurs to her she's never said before. Je vous adore, mon chéri, she whispers tenderly and loudly enough for everyone to hear. For if a man still poses the biggest riddles after ten years, or if you prefer, twelve, we wouldn't want to importune the others with our public secrets, then we must have won the grand prize, am I not right? Il faut absolument que je vous le dise ce soir! She looks around for applause, in my direction as well and sends Anni an icy glance since Anni almost took my plate from the wrong side, but the next moment she's once again able to gaze on Atti with loving eyes. She tosses her head back, and her pinned-up hair falls down almost accidentally over her shoulder, lightly curled and golden-brown, she is sated and satisfied. Old Beaumont begins, unmercifully, to talk about the old times, those were real summer retreats back then, Atti's parents would leave Vienna with crates loaded with dishes, silver and linen, with the servants and children. Antoinette looks around sighing, her eyelids begin to flutter, for the whole story is threatening to be trotted out for the hundredth time, naturally Hofmannsthal and Strauss were with them every summer, Max Reinhardt and Kassner, and that rare Kassner commemorative album by Fertsch Mansfeld, really we should finally have a look at it today, and Castiglione's fêtes, une merveille sans comparaison, inoubliable, il était un peu louche, oui, but Reinhardt, toute autre chose, a true gentleman, il aimait les cygnes, of course he loved swans! Qui était ce type-là? asks Marie coldly. A shudder runs through Antoinette's shoulders, but friendly Atti comes to the aid of the old man, please, Uncle Gontran, tell us that incredibly droll story about your tour of the mountains, you know, when alpinism had first made its appearance, you'll just die laughing, you know, Antoinette, that Uncle Gontran was one of the first skiers to learn the Arlberg technique at the Arlberg, was that the same time as telemarks and christianas? And he was also one of the first to invent a sunflower seed diet and sunbathing, back then it was considered daringly audacious, naked, please tell us! Children, I'm dying, announces Antoinette, I'm glad I can gorge myself however I like, figure or no figure. She fixes Atti sharply, puts away her napkin, she stands up and we all move from the little parlor to the large adjacent one, wait for the mocha, and Antoinette once again stops old Beaumont from treating us to the Arlberg and the Kneipp cure, sunbathing naked or any other adventure from the turn of the century. Not long ago I was saying to Karajan, but one simply doesn't know whether the man is listening, he's in a constant trance, please, Atti, you don't have to look at me so imploringly, I'll keep my mouth shut. But what do you say to Christine's hysteria? Turning to me: Can you please tell me what has got into this woman, she's such a bore, she stares at me as if she'd swallowed a cow, I keep being friendly, but the woman seems intent on dousing me with fire and brimstone, Wantschura with his sculptures, naturally he will have driven her crazy by now, just like he did Lisel before, he's notorious in that respect, all of his muses wear out because they constantly have to stand around in his atelier, and then there's the household on top of that, I understand, but one has to have the countenance for it if one is to going to appear in public with such a man, of course he is extremely talented, Atti bought the first things he did, I'll show you, they're the best things Xandl has done!

Once another hour goes by, I'll be allowed to go to my bed and cover myself with the thick down-blanket they use in the country, as it's always cool in the evening in the Salzkammergut, outside something will be whirring around, but in the room too something will start to hum, I'll get out of bed, walk around, look for a humming, buzzing insect but not find it, and then a moth will quietly warm itself on my lamp, I could kill it, but it's not doing anything to me and therefore I can't, it would have to make noises, some agonizing sound, in order to make me thirst for murder. I fetch a couple of thrillers from my suitcase, I just have to read something. But after a few pages I realize that I already know the book. THE SIMPLE ART OF MURDER. Antoinette's scores are lying on the piano, two volumes of SANG UND KLANG, I open it to different pages and quietly try a few bars I once played as a child: Tremble, Byzantium ... Ferrara's Prince, Arise ... Death and the Maiden, the march from The Daughter of the Regiment ... the Champagne Aria ... The Last Rose of Summer. I sing quietly, but out of key and flat: Tremble, Byzantium! Then even more quietly and on key: The wine which through the eyes we drink ...

Right after breakfast, which Atti and I ate by ourselves, we take off in his motorboat. Atti has a chronometer hanging around his neck, he's handed me the boathook, I try to hand it to him at a critical moment and wind up dropping it. That wasn't very bright, you're supposed to fend us off, we're hitting the dock, push off! Normally Atti never shouts, but he feels obliged to shout whenever he's in a boat, that in itself is enough to spoil being in a boat for me. We set out in reverse, he comes about, and I think of all the years in motorboats on lakes and seas, once again I gaze at the landscape from the past, so here is the forgotten lake, it was here! Atti, to whom I try to explain how wonderful I find skimming across the water, isn't listening at all, since all he wants to do is reach the starting line before the race begins. Near St. Gilgen we kill the engine and rock for a moment. Ten minutes must pass after the first shot, then finally the second shot is fired, and now a signal ball is removed every minute. You see, they're taking down the last one! Actually I don't see anything but I do hear the starting gun. We stay behind the sailboats, which are getting underway, all I notice is that the one ahead of us is jibing, a racing jibe, explains Atti, and then we proceed very slowly so as not to disturb the regatta, Atti shakes his head at the maneuvers of these sad sailors. Ivan is supposed to be a very good sailor, we're going sailing together, next year, maybe on the Mediterranean, since Ivan doesn't think much of our little lakes. Atti is getting excited: Good God, he's not very bright, he's sailing with too much trim, that one there is drifting off course, and I point at one well underway while all the others are almost lying still. He has his own personal gust! His what? And Atti explains everything very well, but I see my forgotten lake with these playthings on it, I would like to sail here with Ivan, but far away from the other people, even if it tears the skin off my hands and I have to crawl back and forth below the boom. Atti motors up to the first buoy, which all the racers have to round, he is completely amazed. You have to sail very close and then round the buoy, the second one there has lost at least fifty meters, the sailor on that one-person boat is pinching, he's just giving wind away, and then I also learn about real and apparent wind, I like that a lot, I look at Atti admiringly and repeat the lesson: What counts in sailing is the apparent wind.

Atti's mood has mellowed thanks to my participation, the man there isn't just sitting oddly on his boat, he ought to move back more, there, finally, now he's getting it out. More, even more! It all looks like so much fun, I say, but Atti, once again annoyed, says it's not fun, the man isn't thinking about anything except the wind and his boat, and I look up at the sky, I try to remember from hanggliding what thermal wind is, what a thermal is, and I change my view, the lake is no longer the lake, light or the color of lead, but the darker patches mean something, now two boats are heeling to leeward, since once again there's not much wind, they're trying to fill their sails. We follow them a little, close to the next buoy, and it starts to get cool. Atti thinks they're going to "shoot down" the regatta, since it's not worth it, it really isn't worth it, Atti already knows why he's not taking part in this regatta. We motor home, jolting over the water, now more agitated, but suddenly Atti stops the motor, as Leibl is heading our way, he's also in St. Gilgen, and I say to Atti: What kind of big steamer is that over there? Atti shouts: That's not a steamer, that's a …

The two men start to wave. Hello Altenwyl! Hello Leibl! Our boats are next to one another, the men are talking excitedly, Leibl hasn't taken his boats out yet, Atti invites him to lunch tomorrow. Another one, I think to myself, so that's the victorious shortbodied Herr Leibl, who wins all the regattas in his catamaran, and since I can't shout like Atti I wave respectfully and occasionally look back in the mirror. This Leibl is certain to say this evening that he saw Atti without Antoinette and with some blonde. The prizewinning Herr Leibl can't know that Antoinette absolutely had to go to the hairdresser today, that she couldn't care less who's racing around the lake with Atti, for Atti's thoughts have only been about sailboats and the lake for three months now, as Antoinette will painfully, confidentially inform everyone, about this damn lake and nothing else.

Late in the evening we have to go out on the lake once again, at thirty or thirty-five knots, because Atti has an appointment with a sailmaker, the night is cool, Antoinette has gotten rid of us, she has to attend the opening of Everyman. I keep hearing some music: And dream beyond the fair horizon … I'm in Venice, I think about Vienna, I look across the water and look into the water, into the dark stories through which I'm passing. Are Ivan and I a dark story? No, he isn't, I alone am a dark story. Only the motor can be heard, it's beautiful on the lake, I stand up and hold on to the porthole frame, on the other shore I can make out a pitiful chain of lights, bleary and forlorn, and my hair is blowing in the wind.

… she was the only human living there, and she had lost her orientation … it was as if everything had swirled into motion, waves of willow wands, the Danube wandered about at will … imparting an uneasiness such as she had never known and besieged her heart …

If the fair wind weren't there I would cry bitterly, halfway to St. Gilgen, but the motor stutters, dies, Atti throws out the anchor and ground tackle, he shouts something to me and I obey, I've learned that on a boat you have to obey. Only one person is allowed to say anything. Atti can't find the canister with the extra gasoline, and I think, what will become of me, all night long on the boat, in this cold? no one can see us, we're still far away from the shore. But then we find the canister after all, the funnel too. Atti climbs forward on the boat and I hold the lantern. I'm no longer certain whether I actually want to arrive at any shore. But the motor starts, we weigh anchor and sail home in silence, as Atti also realizes that we would have had to spend the whole night on the water. We don't say anything to Antoinette, we smuggle in some greetings from the other side, invented greetings, I've forgotten the people's names. I am forgetting more and more. During dinner I can't remember what I wanted to or was supposed to have told Erna Zanetti, who was at the opening with Antoinette, I try a greeting from Herr Kopecky in Vienna. Erna is amazed: Kopecky? I excuse myself, it must be a mistake, someone in Vienna told me to say hello, maybe Martin Ranner. That can happen, says Erna considerately, that happens. Throughout the entire dinner I keep thinking about it. It really shouldn't happen, maybe it was something more important, something other than greetings, maybe I'm supposed to ask Erna for something, it wasn't a map of Salzburg, it wasn't a map of the lakes or of the Salzkammergut, it wasn't a question about a hairdresser or a drug store. My God, what was I supposed to say to or ask Erna! I don't want anything from her, but I'm supposed to ask her something. While we drink our mocha in the large parlor I keep looking guiltily at Erna, since it will never occur to me again. Nothing concerning the people surrounding me will ever occur to me, I am forgetting, already forgetting, the names, the greetings, the questions, the messages, the gossip. I don't need any Wolfgangsee, I don't need to recuperate, I suffocate whenever evening comes with all the conversation—the same situations don't really return, they're only hinted at, fear is making me suffocate, I'm afraid of losing something, I still have something to lose, I have everything to lose, it's the only important thing, I know what it's called, and I'm not capable of sitting around here at the Altenwyls, with all these people. Eating breakfast in bed is pleasant, walking along the lake is healthy, going to St. Wolfgang to buy newspapers and cigarettes is good and useless. But to realize that one day I will miss each of these days terribly, that I will cry out in horror because I have been spending them the way I have, while life is really at the Mondsee ... I will never be able to make up for that.

At midnight I return to the large parlor and raid Atti's library: THE ABC OF SAILING, FROM BOW TO STERN, WEATHER AND LEE. Somewhat fearful titles, they don't fit Atti either. I also got hold of a book, KNOTS, SPLICES, RIGGING, it seems to be the right one for me, "the book makes no assumptions ... is treated with the same systematic clarity ... easily understood instructions for tying decorative knots, from the Hohenzollern knot to chain sinnets." I read part of an easily understood book for beginners. I've already taken my sleeping pills. What will become of me, if I am only now beginning? When can I leave, how? I could still quickly learn how to sail here, but I don't want to. I want to leave, I don't think I'll need anything more, I don't think that for a whole life I need to understand what trimming, trimming in, trimming up mean. My eyes have never closed while reading before, my eyes won't close now either. I have to go home.

At five o'clock I sneak into the large parlor to the telephone. I don't know how I'm supposed to pay Antoinette for the telegram, since she shouldn't know anything about it. Telegrams please hold, please hold, please hold ... I wait and smoke and wait. There's a clicking on the line, a lively female voice asks: subscriber's name please, and number? Fearfully I whisper the Altenwyls' name and their phone number, the woman will call right back, I lift up the receiver at the first ring and whisper, so that no one in the house can hear me: Dr. Malina, Ungargasse 6, Vienna III. Text: urgently request telegram calling for urgent return to Vienna stop arrive tomorrow evening stop greetings ...

A telegram from Malina arrives the next morning, Antoinette has no time and is fleetingly surprised, I drive to Salzburg with Christine, who wants to know exactly how things were at the Altenwyls'. Antoinette is said to have become completely hysterical, and Atti is a truly kind and intelligent man, but this woman must be driving him crazy. Oh, I say, I didn't notice anything like that, it would never have occurred to me! Christine says: Naturally if you prefer such people ... of course we would have been happy to invite you, at our place you would have really had some peace and quiet, we live so terribly simply. Straining, I look out the car window and cannot find an answer. I say: You know, I've known the Altenwyls for a very long time, but no, it's not that, I like them very much, no, they're really not such a strain, what do you mean by strain?

During the drive I'm too strained, always on the verge of crying, Salzburg has to appear sometime soon, only fifteen more kilometers, only five kilometers. We're standing at the station. Christine remembers that she still has to meet somebody and has to go shopping beforehand. I say: Please don't wait, for heaven's sake, the stores are about to close! At last I'm standing there alone, I find my compartment, this person is constantly contradicting herself, I am contradicting myself as well. Why haven't I noticed before that I can hardly stand people anymore? Since when has it been like that? What has become of me? I ride bewildered past Attnang-Puchheim and Linz, with a book bouncing up and down in my hand: ECCE HOMO. I hope Malina is waiting for me at the station, but there's no one there, and I have to phone, except I don't like calling from train stations, phone booths or from post offices. Especially from booths. I must have been in prison at some time, the booths remind me of a cell, I can't call from cafés anymore either, or from friends' houses, I have to be home when I phone, and no one can be nearby, or at most Malina, because he doesn't listen. But that's something entirely different. I call from a phone booth at the Westbahnhof, sweating with claustrophobia. It can't happen to me here, I'm going crazy, it can't happen to me in a booth like a cell.

Hello you, it's me, thanks a lot
I can't make it to the station before six
Please come, I beg you, leave a little early
You know I can't, I might
Just forget it then, I'll manage
No please, what is it, you sound like
It's nothing, please, just forget it, I'm telling you
Don't complicate things so much, just take a taxi
So we'll see each other this evening, so you are
That's right, tonight I'm, we'll see each other for sure

I forgot that Malina had the night shift tonight, and I take a taxi. These days who even wants to look at that cursed automobile in which Franz Ferdinand was murdered in Sarajevo, and that bloody military cloak? I have to look it up in Malina's books, just once: Passenger car, make: Graef & Stift, license plate: A III—118, Model: Double-Phaeton body, 4 cylinders, 115 mm bore, 140 mm stroke, 28/32 horsepower, motor no. 287. Rear wall damaged by shrapnel from the first bomb, on the right wall can be seen the hole made by the bullet that caused the Duchess's death, the Archduke's standard carried on June 28, 1914 mounted to the windshield …

I carry the catalog of the Army Museum through all the rooms, the apartment looks as if it hadn't been inhabited for months, for when Malina is by himself no disorder arises. When Lina is frequently by herself in the morning, all signs of my presence vanish into the cabinets and closets, no dust falls, it's only me who causes dust and dirt to appear within hours, books to become jumbled, little notes to litter the apartment. But there's no litter yet. Before my departure I left Anni an envelope for the mail that might be sent to me in St. Wolfgang, there will be a postcard, no big surprise, still I need the card in order to place it in a drawer next to letters and cards from Paris and Munich, with a letter from Vienna on top that did go to St. Wolfgang. I'm still missing the Mondsee. I sit down by the telephone, wait and smoke, I dial Ivan's number, I let it ring, he won't be able to answer for days yet, and for days I could walk around this deserted and dead Vienna, Vienna flushed with heat, or I could just sit here, I'm absentminded, my mind is absent, what is absence of mind? Where is the mind when it's absent? Absent-mindedness inside and out, the mind here is absent everywhere, I can sit down where I want to, I can touch the furniture, I can rejoice at my escape and once again live in absence. I have returned to my own land which is also absent, my greathearted country, where I can make my bed.

It must be Malina calling, but it's Ivan.

So why did you, I tried there
I suddenly had, it was urgent, I just
Is something, we've, right, they say hello
I had wonderful weather as well, it was very
Of course you're still, but if you absolutely
Unfortunately I really have to
I have to get off, we're just about to
Did you send me a, you haven't yet, then

But I'll write you at the Ungargasse, for sure
It's not all that important, if you have time, then
Of course I have time, take care of yourself and don't
Of course I won't, I have to go now!

Malina has entered the room. He is holding me. I can hold him once again. I cling to him, cling to him more tightly. I almost went insane there, no, not just at the lake, in the phone booth as well, I almost went insane! Malina holds me until I calm down, I'm calm, and he asks: What are you reading? I say: I'm interested, it's beginning to interest me. Malina says: You don't really believe that yourself! I say: You still don't believe me, and you're right, but one day I just might become interested in you, in everything you do, think and feel!

Malina smiles peculiarly: You don't really believe that yourself.

The longest summer can begin. All the streets are empty. I can cross this wasteland in a deep delirium, the great gates at the Albrechtsrampe and at Josefsplatz will be closed, I can't recall what I once sought here, pictures, pages, books? I wander through the city aimlessly, because when I'm walking I can feel it, I can feel it most distinctly, and on the Reichsbrücke where I once threw a ring into the Danube canal, I feel it with a shock. I am wedded, it must have come to marriage. I will no longer wait for postcards from the Mondsee, I will increase my patience, if I stay bound to Ivan in this way, I can no longer shrug it off, for it has happened to my body against all reason, my body that now only moves in one continuous, soft, painful crucifixion on him. It will be this way for my whole life. In the Prater a park watchman says obligingly: You better not stay here any longer, with the riffraff that comes here at night, you better go home!

I better go home, at three o'clock in the morning I'm leaning against the entrance to Ungargasse 9, with the lions' heads on either side, and then, for some time, at the entrance to Ungargasse 6, looking up toward number 9, in my Passion, with the stations of my Passion before my eyes, stations I have again willfully traversed, from his house to my house. Our windows are dark.

Vienna is silent.

Two   *The Third Man*

Malina shall ask about everything. But I answer, unasked: This time the Place is not Vienna. It is a place called Everywhere and Nowhere. The Time is not today. In fact, the Time no longer exists at all, because it could have been yesterday, it could have been long ago, it could be again, it could be forever, some things will have never been. The units of this Time, into which other times are compressed, have no measure, and there is no measure for the non-times in which things enter that were never in Time.

Malina shall know everything. But I decide: they shall be the dreams of this night.

A large window opens, larger than all the windows I've seen, however not onto the courtyard of our building in the Ungargasse, but onto a gloomy field of clouds. A lake might lie below the clouds. I have a suspicion as to what lake it could be. But it's no longer frozen over, it's no longer Fasching and the hearty men's glee clubs which once stood on the ice in the middle of the lake have disappeared. And the lake, which cannot be seen, is lined with many cemeteries. There are no crosses, but over every grave the sky is heavily and darkly overcast—the gravestones, the plaques with their inscriptions are scarcely recognizable. My father is standing next to me and takes his hand off my shoulder, since the gravedigger has come over to us. My father looks at the old man commandingly: fearful of my father's gaze, the gravedigger turns to me. He wants to speak, but merely moves his lips for a long time in silence, and I only hear his last sentence:

This is the cemetery of the murdered daughters.

He shouldn't have said that to me, and I weep bitterly.

The chamber is large and dark, no, it's a hall, with dirty walls, it could be in the Hohenstaufen castle in Apulia. For there are no windows and no doors. My father has imprisoned me, and I want to ask him what he intends to do with me, but again I lack the courage, and I look around once more, because there must be a door, one single door leading outside, but I already understand, there's nothing there, no opening, no more openings because now each one houses a black hose, hoses are fastened all around the walls, like gigantic leeches wanting to suck something out of them. Why didn't I notice the hoses earlier, as they must have been there from the beginning! I was so blind in the semi-darkness and groped my way along the walls so as not to lose sight of my father, so that with him I might find the door, but now I find him and say: The door, show me the door. My father calmly takes the first hose off the wall, and I see a round hole, something is blowing into the room, and I duck, my father walks on, removing one hose after the other, and before I can scream I'm already inhaling the gas, more and more gas. I am in the gas chamber, that's what it is, the biggest gas chamber in the world, and in it I am alone. There's no defense against the gas. My father has disappeared, he knew where the door was and didn't show me, and while I am dying my wish to see him once more and tell him just one thing dies as well. My father, I say to him who is no longer there, I wouldn't have told anyone, I would not have betrayed you. There's no resistance going on here.

When it begins the world is already mixed up, and I know that I am crazy. The basic elements of the world are still there, but more gruesomely assembled than anyone has ever seen. Cars are rolling around, dripping paint, people pop up, smirking larvae, and when they approach me they fall down, straw puppets, bundles of iron wire, papier mâché figures, and I keep on going in this world which is not the world, my fists balled, my arms outstretched, warding off the objects, the machines which run into me and scatter, and when I'm too afraid to go on I close my eyes, but the paints—glaring, gaudy, raging colors—spatter me, my face, my naked feet, I again open my eyes to see where I am, I want to find my way out of here, next I fly high up because my fingers and toes have swollen into airy, skycolored balloons and are carrying me to the heights of nevermore, where it's even worse, then they all burst and I fall, fall and stand up, my toes have turned black, I can't go on anymore.

Sire!

My father descends from the heavy downpour of paint, he says sardonically: Go on, just go ahead! And I cover my mouth—all my teeth have fallen out, they stand in front of me as two curved mounds of marble blocks, insurmountable.

I can't say anything, since I have to escape my father and get over the marble wall, but in another language I say: Ne! Ne! And in many languages: No! No! Non! Non! Nyet! Nyet! No! Ném! Ném! Nein! For even in our language all I can say is no, I can't find any other word in any language. Some rolling structure, perhaps the giant Ferris wheel that dumps excrement from the gondolas, is headed my way me and I say: Ne! Ném! But to stop me from crying out my no, my father drives his short, firm, hard fingers into my eyes, I am blinded, but I have to go on. It's unbearable. So I smile, since my father is reaching for my tongue and wants to pull it out so no one here, too, will hear my no, although no one does hear me, but before he can tear out my tongue something horrible happens, a huge splotch of blue gushes into my mouth, so that I can no longer utter any sound. My blue, my glorious blue, in which the peacocks walk, my blue of faraway, my blue fortune on the horizon! And the blue reaches deeper down inside, into my throat, and my father now helps things along and tears my heart and entrails out of my body, but I can still walk, I first hit slushy ice before arriving at the permanent ice, and an echo within me asks: Isn't there anyone left, isn't there anybody left, in this whole world, isn't there anybody and among brothers isn't there one who is worth something, and between friends! What's left of me is frozen inside the ice, a clump, a clod, and I look up where they, the others, are living in the warm world, and Siegfried the Great calls me, at first quietly, then loudly, impatiently I listen to his voice: What are you looking for, what kind of book are you seeking? And I am voiceless. What does the great Siegfried want? He calls from above more and more clearly: What kind of book will it be, what will your book be?

Suddenly, atop a polar summit from which there's no return, I am able to shout: A book about Hell. A book about Hell!

The ice breaks, I sink beneath the pole into the center of the Earth. I am in Hell. The wispy yellow flames wreathe about, the fiery curls hang down to my feet, I spit the fires out, swallow the fires down.

Please set me free! Free me from this hour! I'm speaking with the voice of my school days, but I'm thinking with great awareness, I realize how serious it has already become, and I collapse on the smoldering ground, still thinking, I'm lying on the ground thinking that I should still be able to call for people, and with my full voice—people who could save me. I call my mother and my sister Eleonore, following the proper order exactly, so first my mother, using the first nickname from my childhood, and then my sister, then—(Upon awakening I realize I did not call my father.) Having come from the ice to die in the fire, with a melting skull I gather all my strength since I must call people in the proper order, for the sequence is the counter-spell.

It's the end of the world, a catastrophic fall into nothingness, the world—in which I am crazy—is finished, I clutch at my head the way I do so often, but am terrified to discover it is shaven and that there are metal plates and I look around in shock. Several friendly-looking doctors in white coats are sitting around me. Concurring, they state I have been saved, the plates may also be removed, my hair will grow back. They have performed electric shock therapy. I ask: Do I have to pay right now? Because my father isn't paying. The gentlemen remain friendly, there's still time. The main thing is you're saved. Once again I fall, I wake up for the second time, but I've never fallen out of bed before, and no doctors are there, my hair has grown back. Malina picks me up and lays me back on the bed.

Malina: Just keep calm. It's nothing. But will you finally tell me who your father is?

Me: (and I'm crying bitterly) Am I really here. Are you really standing there!

Malina: Good God why are you always saying "my father"?

Me: It's good you remind me. But let me think about it a long time. Cover me up. Who could my father be? Do you know for example who your father is?

Malina: Let's just drop it.

Me: Let's say I have an inkling. Don't you have any?

Malina: Are you trying to get out of it, trying to be clever?

Me: Maybe. I'd also like to dupe you for once. Tell me one thing. How did you realize that my father is not my father?

Malina: Who is your father?

Me: I don't know, I don't know, really I don't. You're the smarter of the two of us, you always know everything, your know-it-allness makes me sick. Doesn't it make you sick sometimes? Oh no, not you. Rub my feet, right, thanks, my feet are the only thing that fell asleep.

Malina: Who is he?

Me: I'll never talk. Anyway I couldn't, because I don't know.
Malina: You do know. Swear that you don't.
Me: I never swear.
Malina: Then I'll tell you, you hear, I'll tell you who he is.
Me: No. No. Never. Don't ever tell me. Bring me some ice, a
          cold damp cloth for my head.
Malina: (leaving) You'll tell me, you can count on it.

The phone whimpers quietly in the middle of the night, it wakes
me with seagull cries, then the hissing of Boeing jets. The call is
from America, and I say, relieved: Hello. It's dark, I hear crackling
all around me, I'm on a lake where the ice is beginning to melt, it
was the deep-deep frozen lake, and now I'm hanging in the water
by the phone cord, only this cable is keeping me connected. Hello!
I already know it's my father calling me. The lake may soon be
completely open, but I'm here on an island far in the water, it's cut
off, and there are no more ships. I'd like to scream into the phone:
Eleonore! I want to call my sister, but at the other end of the phone
can only be my father, I'm extremely cold and wait with the phone,
submerging, surfacing, the connection's still there, I can hear
America well, in the water you can still phone across the water.
I say quickly, gurgling, swallowing water: When are you coming,
I'm here, yes, here, you know where, it's really awful, there's no longer any connection, I'm cut off, I'm alone, no, no more ships! And
while I'm waiting for an answer, I see how gloomy the island of the
sun really is, the oleanders have keeled over, the volcano is covered
with ice crystals, even it is frozen, the old climate no longer exists.
My father laughs into the phone. I say: I'm cut off—come here,
when are you coming? He laughs and laughs, he laughs as they
do in the theater, that's where he must have learned to laugh so
hideously: HAHAHA. Nothing but: HAHAHA. Nobody laughs like
that anymore, I say, nobody laughs like that, stop it. But my father
doesn't stop his stupid laughing. Can I call you back? I ask, just to

put an end to this theater. HAHA. HAHA. The island is going under, you can see it from every continent, while the laughter continues. My father has gone to the theater. God is a show.

My father came home once more just by accident. My mother is holding three flowers, the flowers for my life, they aren't red, or blue, or white, but they must be for me, and she throws the first one in front of my father, before he can approach us. I know she's right, she has to throw him the flowers, but now I also know that she knows everything, incest, it was incest, but I'd still like to ask her for the other flowers, and I watch my father in deadly fear as he tears the other flowers from my mother's hand, to take his revenge against her as well, he tramples them, he stomps on all three flowers, as he has often stomped about when enraged, he treads on them and tramples, as if he were trying to kill three bugs, that's how much my life still means to him. I can't look at my father anymore, I cling to my mother and start to scream, yes, that's what it was, it was him, it was incest. But then I notice that not only is my mother silent and unmoved, but from the beginning my own voice has been without sound, I'm screaming but no one hears me, there's nothing to hear, my mouth is only gaping, he's taken away my voice as well, I can't pronounce the word I want to scream at him, and as I am straining with my dry, open mouth it comes once more, I know I'm going crazy, and in order to stay sane I spit into my father's face, but there's no saliva left, hardly a breath from my mouth reaches him. My father is untouchable. He is unmovable. My mother sweeps away the trampled flowers in silence, the little bit of filth, to keep the house clean. Where is my sister right now? I haven't seen my sister in the entire house.

My father takes away my keys, he throws my clothes out the window onto the street, but I pass them on to the Red Cross immediately, after I've shaken off the dust, for I have to go back in the house once more, I saw the accomplices going inside, and the first one is breaking glass and plates, but my father has a few glasses set off to the side, and as I walk in the door, trembling, and come closer to him, he takes the first one and hurls it at me, next hurls one on the ground in front of me, he throws and throws all the glasses, his aim is so exact that only a few splinters hit me, but the blood trickles from my forehead in little rills, it runs down my ear, it drops off my chin, my dress is smeared with blood because a few tiny pieces of glass have forced their way through the material, it drips more peacefully from my knees, but I want to, I have to say it to him. He says: Just stay where you are, stay put, and watch! I don't understand anything anymore, but I know there's reason to be afraid, and then it turns out the fear was not the worst thing, since my father orders my bookshelves to be torn down, in fact he says "tear them down," and I want to place myself in front of the books, but the men block me, smirking, I throw myself at their feet and say: Just leave my books in peace, just these books, do what you all want with me, do what you want, go ahead and throw me out the window, go on and give it another try, the way you did back then! But my father acts as if he didn't remember the previous attempt, and he begins taking five, six books at a time like a stack of bricks, and hurls them so they land on their heads into an old wardrobe. With cold, clammy fingers, the accomplices pull out the bookshelves, everything collapses, Kleist's deathmask flutters in front of me for a while and Hölderlin's portrait, underneath which is written: dich Erde, lieb ich, trauerst du doch mit mir! and I can only catch these pictures and hold them close to me, the small volumes of Balzac whirl around, the Aeneid gets bent and buckles, the accomplices kick Lucretius and Horatio, but someone else begins neatly stacking some things in a corner, without knowing what they are, my father pokes the man in the ribs (where have I seen this man before: he destroyed a book of mine in the Beatrixgasse) and says to him amiably: That would suit you fine, wouldn't it, with her too, huh? And now my father blinks at me, and I understand him, because the man smiles sheepishly and says he'd like to all right, and for my sake he also acts as if he'd like to treat my books well again, but full of hate I wrest the French books from his hand, since Malina had given them to me, and I say: You won't get me! And to my father I say: You always did sell off each one of us. But my father roars: What, now suddenly you don't want to? Then I will, I will!

The men leave the house, each has been given a tip, they wave their large handkerchiefs and shout: Heil Book! They tell the neighbors and all the curious onlookers: Our work is finished. Now HOLZWEGE has fallen down, also ECCE HOMO, and I squat amid the books, benumbed and bleeding, it had to come to this, for I caressed them every evening before going to sleep, and Malina had given me the most beautiful books, my father will never forgive that, and they've all become illegible, it had to come to this, there's no order anymore, and I'll never know where Kürnberger was or Lafcadio Hearn. I lie down among the books, I again caress them, one after the other, in the beginning there were only three, then there were fifteen, then over a hundred, and I ran to my first bookcase in my pajamas. Good night, gentlemen, good night, Mr. Voltaire, good night, Fürst, may you rest well, my unknown authors, sweet dreams, Mr. Pirandello, my respect, Mr. Proust. Chaire, Thukydides! For the first time the gentlemen are saying good night to me, I try to avoid touching them so as not to stain them with blood. Good night, says Josef K. to me.

My father wants to leave my mother, he's returning from America as the driver of a covered wagon snapping his whip, sitting next to him is little Melanie, who went to school with me, grown up. My mother would prefer we didn't become friends, but Melanie doesn't stop pressing close to me, with her large, excited breasts that my father likes and which make me cringe, she gesticulates, laughs, she has brown braids, then long blond hair again, she fawns on me so that I'll leave her something, and my mother keeps moving farther back inside the wagon, silently. I let Melanie kiss me, but just on one cheek, I help my mother climb out and already have my suspicions, since we are all invited, we are all wearing new clothes, even my father has shaved and changed his shirt after the long journey, and we make our entrance into the ballroom from WAR AND PEACE.

Malina: Get up, move around, walk up and down with me, breathe, take a deep breath.

Me: I can't, I'm sorry, and I can't sleep anymore if it keeps going on like this.

Malina: Why are you still thinking "War and Peace"?

Me: It's called that because one follows the other, isn't that the way it is?

Malina: You don't have to believe everything, you better think about it.

Me: Me?

Malina: It isn't war and peace.

Me: What is it then?

Malina: War.

Me: How am I ever supposed to find peace. I want peace.

Malina: It's war. All you can have is this little intermission, nothing more.

Me: Peace!

Malina: There is no peace in you, not even in you.

Me: Don't say that, not today. You're terrible.

Malina: It's war. And you are the war. You yourself.

Me: Not me.

Malina: We all are, you included.

Me: Then I don't want to be anymore, because I don't want war, then put me to sleep, make it end. I want the war to end. I don't want to hate anymore, I want … I want …

Malina: Breathe more deeply, come on. There, there, it's better, you see, I'm holding you, come over to the window,
breathe more calmly, more deeply, take a break, now
don't talk.

My father is dancing with Melanie, it's the ballroom from WAR
AND PEACE. Melanie is wearing the ring my father gave to me, but
he lets everyone think he'll leave me a more valuable ring after his
death. Next to me my mother is sitting upright and silent, next
to us are two empty chairs, two more empty chairs at our table as
well, since those two don't stop dancing. My mother is no longer
speaking to me. No one asks me to dance. Malina comes in and
the Italian singer sings: Alfin tu giungi, alfin tu giungi! And I jump
up and embrace Malina, I implore him to dance with me, I smile
at my mother with relief. Malina takes my hand, we stand leaning
against each other at the edge of the dance floor, so that my father
can see us, and although I'm certain neither of us can dance, we try,
we have to succeed, at least in deceiving everyone, we keep stopping as if we had enough to do just looking at one another, only
that doesn't have anything to do with dancing. I keep saying thank
you to Malina quietly: Thank you for coming, I'll never forget it,
oh, thank you, thank you. Now Melanie would also like to dance
with Malina, of course, and for a moment I'm afraid, but then I
hear Malina say calmly and coolly: No, unfortunately, we're about
to leave. Malina has avenged me. At the exit my long white gloves
fall on the floor, and Malina picks them up, they fall to the floor
on every step, and Malina picks them up. I say: Thank you, thank
you for everything! Let them fall, says Malina, I'll pick everything
up for you.

My father is walking along the beach in the wasteland where he
has enticed me, he has gotten married, in the sand he writes the

name of this woman who is not my mother, and I don't notice it right away, only after he has drawn the first letter. The sun shines cruelly on the letters, they lie like shadows in the sand, in the depressions, and my only hope is that the writing will be quickly blown away, before evening comes, but my God, my God, my father is returning with the great golden, gem-inlaid scepter of the University of Vienna, upon which I swore: spondeo, spondeo, and I shall to the best of my knowledge and belief, and never and under no circumstances use my knowledge to ... He actually dares use this venerable scepter, which does not belong to him, where I placed my fingers and swore my one and only oath, this staff still burning with my oath, to write the name again, this time I can also read it, MelaNIE and once again MelaNIE—with NIE like NEVER and I think in the twilight: never, never should he have been allowed to do that. My father has reached the water, satisfied, he uses the golden scepter to support himself, I have to run away, even though I know I'm weaker, but I could catch him by surprise, I jump on his back from behind to make him fall, I only want to knock him down because of the scepter from Vienna, I don't even want to hurt him, for I can't use this scepter to strike him, for I have taken an oath, I stand there with the scepter raised, my father snorts in fury, he curses me because he thinks I want to break the scepter over his head, he thinks I want to kill him with it, but I only hold it up to the sky and shout to the horizon, over the sea, to the Danube: I bring this back from the holy war. And with a handful of sand that is my knowledge, I walk across the water, and my father cannot follow me.

In my father's grand opera I am supposed to take over the lead role, supposedly it's the wish of the artistic director, who has just announced it, because then the public will come in droves, says the director, and the journalists say the same. They're waiting with notepads in hand, I'm supposed to say something about my father, also about the role, which I don't know. The director himself forces me into a costume, and since it was made for someone else, with his own hand he fastens it with pins that slit my skin, he's so clumsy. I say to the journalists: I don't know anything at all, please ask my father, I don't know anything, it's not a role for me, it's only designed to get the audience to come in droves! But the journalists write down something completely different, and I don't have any more time to scream and tear up their notes, for it's the last minute before curtain, and I run through the entire opera house, screaming in despair. There isn't a libretto to be found anywhere, and I hardly even know two entrances, it's not my role. I'm very familiar with the music, oh, do I know it, this music, but I don't know the words, I can't play this role, I'll never be able to, and, more desperately, I ask one of the director's assistants what is the first sentence from the first duet, which I have to sing with a young man. He and all the others laugh enigmatically, they know something I don't, what is it they all know? I have a suspicion, but the curtain rises, and below is this huge crowd, these droves, I start to sing at random, but in despair, I sing "What help for me, what help for me!" and I know the text can't go like that, but I also notice that the music is drowning out my desperate words. There are many people on stage, some of whom are silent, some of whom sing quietly when they make an entrance, a young man sings confidently and loudly and sometimes confers with me quickly and secretly, I realize his voice is the only one audible in this duet anyway, because my father wrote the whole part for him, and nothing for me of course, since I don't have any training and am only supposed to be shown. I'm just supposed to sing to bring in the money, and I don't break character, I don't step out of the role that isn't mine, far from it: I sing for my life, so that my father can't do anything to me. "What help for me!" Then I forget the role, I also forget I have no training, and finally, although the curtain has fallen and the accounting completed, I actually do sing, but something from a different opera, and I hear my voice, too, ringing out in the empty house, rising to the highest highs and falling to the lowest lows, "Thus would we die, thus would we die ..." The young man is faking, he doesn't know this role, but I sing on. "All dead then. All dead!" The young man leaves, I am alone on stage, they turn off the lights and leave me completely alone, in my ridiculous costume full of pins. "Can you see my friends, do you not see it!" And with a great resounding lament I plunge off this island and out of this opera into the orchestra pit, now devoid of any orchestra, still singing: "So would we die, that together ..." I have saved the performance, but am lying between the empty chairs and music stands with a broken neck.

My father is beating Melanie, then, because a large dog begins to bark in warning, he beats this dog who completely submits to his thrashing. In the same way my mother and I also allowed ourselves to be thrashed. I know that the dog is my mother, absolute submissiveness. I ask my father why he's beating Melanie as well, and he says he won't stand for such questions, she doesn't mean anything to him, it's shameless of me to even ask about her, he keeps repeating that Melanie doesn't mean anything to him, he only needs her for a few more weeks, for a little refreshment, I ought to understand that. I think the dog has no idea that it could put an end to the beating if it only gave my father's leg a little bite: the dog howls quietly and doesn't bite. Afterward my father chats with me, satisfied, relieved by the opportunity to do some beating, but I'm still despondent, I try to explain to him how sick he's made me, he'll have to find out sooner or later, with difficulty I list the hospitals I've been in and hold up the bills from all the treatments, since I think we should share the costs. My father is in the best of moods, he just doesn't understand the connection, neither with the beating nor with his actions and my wish to finally tell him everything—it remains pointless, senseless, but the atmosphere between us is not tense, rather good and jovial, because now he wants to sleep with me, drawing the curtains so that we won't be seen by Melanie, who's still lying there whimpering, but who as always has understood nothing. I lie down with a pitiful hope, but get back up immediately, I just can't, I tell him it doesn't mean a thing to me, I hear myself saying: It doesn't mean anything to me, it's never meant anything to me, it doesn't mean anything! My father is not exactly indignant, since it doesn't mean anything to him either, he's reciting one of his monologues, in which he reminds me that I once said it's always the same thing. He says: Same thing, so no excuses, don't make excuses for yourself, here with the same thing, if it's the same thing! But we will be interrupted as always, it doesn't make any sense, I can't explain to him that it's only a matter of being interrupted and never the same thing, and only with him, since I can't see that it means anything. It's Melanie who is moaning and causing the disturbance, my father steps onto the pulpit and holds his Sunday sermon, about the same thing, and all listen to him quietly and piously, as he is the greatest Sunday preacher far and wide. In the end he always pronounces a curse on something or someone, to strengthen his sermon, and he's doing it again, today he curses my mother and me, he curses his sex and mine, and I walk over to the holy water used by the Catholics and moisten my forehead, in the name of the Father, leaving before the sermon is over.

My father has come swimming with me into the kingdom of the thousand atolls. We dive into the sea, I encounter schools of the most magical fish, and I'd like to move on with them, but my father is already after me, I see him now beside me, now below me, now above me, I have to try and reach the reefs, because my mother has hidden herself in the coral reef and is staring at me in silent warning, she knows what's going to happen to me. I dive deeper and scream underwater: No! And: I don't want to anymore! I can't anymore! I know it's important to scream underwater since it drives away the sharks, so it should also drive away my father who wants to attack me, to tear me to pieces, or he wants to sleep with me again, to take me on the reef so that my mother can see it. I scream: I hate you, I hate you, I hate you more than my life, and I have sworn to kill you! I find a place with my mother, in her ramified, thousand-limbed deep-sea coral torpor which is growing constantly, I cling to her branches, fearful and afraid, I cling to her, but my father grabs at me, again he grabs at me, and it wasn't me after all, he was the one who had just screamed, it was his voice, not mine: I have sworn to kill you. But I did scream: I hate you more than my life!

Malina isn't there, I straighten out my pillow, I find the glass with the mineral water, Güssinger, ready to die of thirst I drink this glass of water. Why did I say that, why? More than my life. I have a good life, it's become better and better because of Malina. It's a gloomy morning, but already light outside. What am I muttering, why is Malina asleep now? Just right now. He should explain my words to me. I don't hate my life, so how can I hate something more than my life. I can't. I only come undone at night. I get up carefully, so that my life stays good, I put water on for tea, I have to drink tea, and in the kitchen where I'm cold despite my long nightgown, I make the tea I need, because at least making tea keeps me occupied whenever I can't do anything else. When the water comes to a boil, I am not in an atoll, I warm the pot, count the spoonfuls of Earl Grey, I pour the tea, I can still drink tea, can still conduct the boiling water to my pot. I'd prefer not to wake Malina, but I stay up till 7 in the morning, wake him up and make him breakfast. Malina isn't exactly in the best shape either, maybe he came home late, his egg is too hard, but he doesn't say anything, I mumble an excuse, the milk is sour, but why after only two days? After all it was in the ice box, Malina looks up since small white clumps are appearing in his tea, and I pour out the cup, today he has to drink his tea without milk. Everything has turned sour. I'm sorry, I say.

What's the matter? asks Malina. Get going, please, go, get ready, otherwise you'll be late, I can't talk this early in the morning.

I'm wearing the Siberian Jewish Coat like everyone else. It's the middle of winter, more and more snow is falling on us, and my bookcases are collapsing underneath the snow, the snow is burying them slowly, while we all await deportation, and the photographs on the bookshelf are getting wet, pictures of all the people I have loved, and I wipe away the snow and shake the photographs, but the snow keeps falling, my fingers are already numb, I have to let the snow bury the photos. I only despair because my father is watching my last attempts, for he doesn't belong to us, I don't want him to see my efforts and guess who is in these photographs. My father, who would also like to put on a coat, even though he's too fat for it, forgets the pictures, he confers with someone, takes his coat off again to look for another one, but fortunately there are no longer any coats around. He sees me leaving with the others, and I'd like to have one more word with him, to finally make it clear to him that he doesn't belong to us, that he has no right, I say: I don't have any more time, I don't have enough time. There's just not time for that. All around some people are criticizing me for not showing solidarity, "solidarity," what a strange word! I don't care. I'm supposed to put my signature on something, but my father is the one who signs, he is always in "solidarity," but I don't even know what it means. Very quickly I say to him: Farewell, I don't have any more time, I'm not in solidarity. I have to look for someone! I don't exactly know who it is I have to find, someone from Pécs, whom I am seeking among these people, in this terrible chaos. Moreover, the time I have left is quickly running out, I'm afraid he was already deported before me, although I can only talk to him about it, to him alone and unto the seventh generation, which I cannot vouch for, since I won't have any descendants. Among the many barracks I find him in the very last room, where he is waiting for me, exhausted, a bouquet of Turk's-cap lilies is standing next to him in the empty room, he is lying on the floor in his sidereal mantle, blacker than black, in which I saw him several thousand years ago. He sits up sleepily, he's aged a few years, and his fatigue is great. He says with his earliest voice: Ah, at last, at last you have come! And I drop down and laugh and cry and kiss him, it really is you, if only you are here, at last, at last! A child is there as well, I only see one, although it seems to me there should be two, and the child is lying in a corner. I recognized him at once. A woman is lying gently and patiently in another corner, the mother of his child, she doesn't have anything against our lying down together here before the deportation. Suddenly the order is given: Get up! We all stand up, we start off, the little one is already on the truck, we have to hurry so we can also get aboard, I just have to find our protective umbrellas, and I find them all, for him, for the gentle woman, for the child, for me as well, but my umbrella doesn't belong to me, someone once left it behind in Vienna, and I am dismayed because I always wanted to give it back, but I just don't have any time for that now. It's a dead parachute. It's too late, I have to take it so that we can get through Hungary, for I have found my first love once again, it's raining, it's pouring, pelting down on all of us, above all on the child who is so cheerful and composed. It's starting again, I'm breathing too fast, perhaps on account of the child, but my beloved says: Stay completely calm, stay as calm as we are! The moon will rise now any minute. Only I'm still deathly afraid since it's starting once again, since I'm going crazy, he says: Just stay calm, think about the Stadtpark, think about the leaf, think about the garden in Vienna, about our tree, the princess tree is blooming. At once I calm down, for the same thing has happened to both of us, I see how he points to his head, I know what they have done to his head. The truck has to cross a river, it's the Danube, then it's another river, I try to remain completely calm, for here in the Danube wetlands we met for the first time, I say I'm all right, but then my mouth opens wide without screaming, because my voice simply doesn't come. He says to me, don't forget it again, it's called: Facile! And I misunderstand, I scream, voicelessly: Facit! In the river, in the deep river. May I speak with you, madam, for a moment? asks a gentleman, I have some news for you. I ask: For whom, whom do you have to deliver this news? He says: It's only for the princess of Kagran. I snap at him: Do not pronounce this name, ever. Don't tell me a thing! But he shows me a desiccated leaf, and I know he has spoken the truth. My life is over, for during the transport he has drowned in the river, he was my life. I loved him more than my life.

Malina is holding me, he's the one saying: Just stay calm! I have to stay calm. But I walk up and down the apartment with him, he would like me to lie down, but I can no longer lie down on the bed that is too soft for me. I lie down on the floor, but am on my feet again at once because I had lain that way on another floor, underneath the warm Siberian coat, and I pace up and down with him, speaking, talking, leaving words out, letting words in. Despondently I lay my head on Malina's shoulder, where there must be a piece of platinum following an accident in which he broke his collarbone, so he once told me, and I notice that I'm getting cold, I'm beginning to shake again, the moon is coming out, you can see it from our window, do you see the moon? I see a different moon and a sidereal world, but it's not the other moon I want to speak about, I simply have to talk, talk without stopping, in order to save myself, in order not to do that to Malina, my head, my head, I'm going crazy but Malina isn't supposed to know. Nevertheless Malina does know, and I implore him as I race up and down in the apartment, clamped to him, I let myself fall down, get up again, undo my shirt, then fall down once more, because I'm losing my mind, it's coming over me, I'm losing my mind, with no consolation, but Malina repeats: Just stay calm, let yourself slump down all the way. I slump down and think about Ivan, I start breathing a little more regularly, Malina massages my hands and my feet, the area around my heart, but I'm going crazy, just one thing, I'm only asking you for one thing ... But Malina says: Why ask then, you don't have to ask. But again in my voice of today I say: Please, Ivan must never find out, never know (dazed, I realize that Malina doesn't know anything about Ivan, why talk about Ivan now?)—Ivan must never, promise me, and as long as I can still talk, I'll talk, it's important that I talk, you know I'm only talking, and please talk to me, Ivan must never, never know, please tell me something, tell me about dinner, where did you eat, with whom, talk to me about the new record, did you bring it with you, O ancient scent! Talk to me, it doesn't matter what we talk about, just something, talk, talk, talk, then we'll no longer be in Siberia, no longer in the river, no longer in the marshes, the Danubian wetlands, we'll be back here, in the Ungargasse, you my Promised Land, my Ungarland, talk to me, turn on all the lights, don't worry about the electric bill, there has to be light everywhere, turn on all the switches, give me some water, turn on the lights, turn on all the lights! Light the candelabra!

Malina turns on the lights, Malina brings the water, my disorientation abates, the dazedness increases, did I say something to Malina, did I mention Ivan's name? Did I say "candelabra"? You know, I say, less agitated, you shouldn't take everything too seriously, Ivan is alive and was alive once before, strange, isn't it? Above all, don't let it upset you, just that today it's upsetting me a lot, that's why I'm so tired, but do leave the lights on. Ivan is still alive, he'll call me. When he calls I'll tell him—Malina is once again walking up and down with me, because I can't lie still, he doesn't know what he's supposed to tell Ivan, I hear the telephone ring. Tell him, tell him, please tell him! Don't tell him anything. Best of all: I'm not at home.

My father has to wash our feet, like all our Apostolic Kaisers have to wash the feet of their poor, one day a year. Ivan and I are already taking a footbath, the water is running, foaming black and dirty, we haven't washed our feet for a long time. We better wash

them ourselves, as my father is no longer performing this honor-
able duty. I'm glad our feet are now clean, glad they smell clean, I
dry Ivan's feet and then my own, we sit on my bed and look at each
other full of joy. But now someone is coming, too late, the door
flies open, it's my father. I point to Ivan, I say: He's the one! I don't
know whether that will get me the death penalty or only send me
to a camp. My father looks at the dirty water from which I lift my
white, nice-smelling feet, and I proudly show him Ivan's clean feet.
Despite everything, even though he has neglected his duty once
again, my father is not supposed to notice how happy I am to have
washed off everything after the long journey. The journey from
him to Ivan was too long, and my feet got dirty. Next door a radio
is playing: da-dim, da-dam. My father roars: Turn off that radio!
You know good and well it's not the radio, I say with certainty,
because I've never owned one. My father roars again: Your feet are
completely filthy, and what's more I've now told everyone, too.
Just so you know. Filthy, filthy! Smiling, I say: My feet are washed,
I wish that everyone had feet as clean as mine.

What kind of music is that, enough of that music! My father
fumes as never before. And tell me at once, on what day did Co-
lumbus reach America? How many primary colors are there? How
many hues? Three primary colors. Ostwald lists 500 hues. All my
replies come quickly and correctly, but very quietly, I can't do anything about it if my father doesn't hear them. He's screaming again,
and each time he raises his voice a piece of plaster falls from the
wall or a slat of wood bursts up from the floor. How can he ask like
that if he doesn't even want to hear the answers.

It's dark in front of the window, I can't open it and so I press my
face against the pane, it's almost impossible to see. Slowly I realize
that the gloomy puddle could be a lake, and I hear the drunken
men sing a chorale on the ice. I know my father has stepped in
behind me, he has sworn to kill me, and I hurriedly place myself

between the long heavy curtain and the window, so that he doesn't surprise me while I'm looking out, but I already know what I'm not supposed to know: that on the shore of the lake lies the cemetery of the murdered daughters.

On a small ship my father is beginning to shoot his great film. He is the director, and everything runs the way he wishes. Once again I've had to give in, for my father would like to film a few sequences with me, he assures me I won't be recognized, he has the best mask-makers in the world. My father has adopted a name, no one knows which one, it's been seen occasionally in neon letters at movie marquees across half the globe. I sit around waiting, not yet dressed or made up, with curlers in my hair, only a towel over my shoulders, but suddenly I discover that my father is taking advantage of the situation and is already filming, in secret, and I jump up indignantly, can't find anything to cover myself, nonetheless I run up to him and the cameraman and say: Stop that, stop that at once! I demand the reel be destroyed immediately, this has nothing to do with any film, it's against my contract, the reel has to be removed. My father answers that that's precisely what he wanted, it will be the most interesting part of the movie, he continues filming. Horrified, I listen to the humming of the camera and again demand he stop and hand over the footage, but unmoved he continues to shoot and once again says no. I am becoming more and more agitated and cry out that he has one second to think it over, I'm no longer afraid of blackmail, I'll be able to look after myself if no one comes to my aid. Since he doesn't react and the second is over, I look out over the ship's smokestacks and all the equipment lying on the deck, I stumble over the cables and search and search, just how can I stop him from doing this, I rush back to the dressing room, the doors have been taken off their hinges to prevent me from locking myself inside, my father laughs, but at that moment I see the small manicure dish with soapy lye water in

164

front of the mirror, and quick as lightning I have an idea, I take the dish and pour the lye onto the cameras and into the ship's pipes, everything starts steaming, my father stands there paralyzed, and I tell him that I had warned him, that I no longer have to do his bidding, that I've changed, from now on I'll treat everyone the way I'm treating him, with immediate retaliation for any breach of contract. The whole ship is steaming more and more, the filming is ruined, the work has to be hastily broken off, everyone is standing in groups, anxiously discussing, but they're saying they didn't like the director anyway, they're glad this movie isn't going to be made. We abandon our ship using rope ladders, then rock away in little lifeboats and are brought aboard a big vessel. As I sit exhausted on a bench aboard the big ship, watching the rescue operations for the small ship, some human bodies float by, they're still alive but burnt, we have to make room, all of them are to be taken aboard, because another boat has exploded beyond our own sinking ship, one which also belonged to my father, with many passengers on board and where many people were wounded. Without reason I began to fear that my little soapdish also caused the explosion in the other boat, I'm already expecting to be indicted for murder as soon as we land. More and more bodies wash up against us, they have to be fished out, the dead ones as well. But then I'm relieved to hear that the other boat went down for entirely different reasons. I have nothing to do with it, it was negligence on the part of my father.

My father wants to take me away from Vienna, to another country, he's quite persuasive, I have to leave here, my friends are all bad influences, but I realize he doesn't want any witnesses, he doesn't want me to talk to anybody, he doesn't want anything coming out. But it could come out. I no longer defend myself, I only ask whether I'm allowed to write home, he says that remains to be seen, it doesn't look favorable for me. We have left for a foreign country, I do have permission to walk on the street, but I don't know anyone and I don't understand the language. We live high up where I get dizzy, no house can be that high, I've never lived that high and spend the whole day in bed as a preventive measure, I am imprisoned and not imprisoned, my father looks in on me only rarely, most of the time he sends a woman with a bandaged face, all I can see are her eyes, she knows something. She gives me food and tea, soon I can no longer get up, because everything starts spinning the first step I take. Similar cases come to mind, I have to get up, since the food must be poisoned or the tea, I make it to the bathroom and pour the food and tea down the toilet, neither the woman nor my father have noticed, they're poisoning me, it's terrible, I have to write a letter, but can only manage some beginnings, which I hide in my handbag, in the drawer, under the pillow, but I have to write and get a letter out of the house. I shudder and drop the pen, for my father is standing at the door, he's guessed long ago, he looks for all the letters, he takes one out of the wastebasket and screams: Speak up! What's this supposed to mean! Pipe up, I say! He screams for hours and doesn't stop, he won't let me speak, I start crying louder and louder, he screams better if I cry, I can't tell him I'm no longer eating, that I throw my food away, that I've already caught on, I hand him the crumpled letter from under the pillow as well and sob. Pipe up! With my eyes I tell him: I'm homesick, I want to go home! My father says mockingly: Homesick! That's a fine thing, homesick! And even if these are letters I'll make sure they'll never be dispatched, your dear letters to your dear friends.

I am emaciated to my bones and can't support myself, but then I manage, I take my suitcases down from the attic, quietly, in the middle of the night, my father is sleeping soundly, I hear him snore, he's gasping and wheezing. In spite of the altitude I have leaned out and looked down, Malina's car is parked on the other side of the street. Although he didn't receive any letters, Malina must have understood, he sent me his car. I put the most important things into the suitcase, or just whatever I can grab, it has to be done quietly and with the utmost haste, it has to be tonight, or else it will never succeed. With the suitcases I stagger onto the street, I have to put them down every few steps and wait until I catch my breath and can carry them again, then I sit in the car, I've shoved the suitcases onto the back seat, the key is in the ignition, I start the car, I zigzag down the empty nighttime street, I have a vague idea where the main road to Vienna must be, I know the direction, but I can't drive and so I come to a stop, it won't work. I should at least make it to a post office and immediately telegraph Malina to come get me, but it won't work. I have to turn around, it's already getting light, the car is no longer under my control, it glides back to the place where it was parked and stops there, stands there facing the wrong way, just once more I'd like to give it some gas and drive into the wall, into my death, since Malina isn't coming, it's day, I'm slumped over the steering wheel. Someone pulls my hair, it's my father. The woman, who shifts the cloth wrap on her face, drags me from the car and leads me back into the house. I have seen her face, she hastily covers herself again as I start to howl, I know who she is. Both of them are going to kill me.

My father has brought me inside a tall house, there's even a garden upstairs, to pass the time he lets me plant flowers in it and little trees, he makes jokes about the many Christmas trees I'm cultivating, they're from the Christmases of my childhood, but as long as he's making jokes it's all right, there are silver ball ornaments and everything is blooming violet and yellow, but they aren't the right flowers. I also plant many things in ceramic pots, I sow seeds, but the flowers which result always have the wrong, undesired colors, I'm not satisfied, and my father says: You must think you're a princess! Who do you think you are, you think you're better than everybody else, don't you! You'll get over that, you'll be cured of that, and that and that—he points at my flowers—all that's also going to end soon, what a ridiculous waste of time, all this green stuff! I hold the garden hose in my hand, I could aim it at him so his face would catch the full force of the water, so that he'd stop insulting me, because he did leave the garden to me, but I drop the hose, covering my face with my hands, he should go ahead and tell me what I'm supposed to do, the hose is running on the ground and I no longer want to water the plants, I turn off the water and go inside. My father's guests have arrived, I struggle to carry all the plates and trays with glasses back and forth, then I sit there and listen, I don't even know what they're talking about, moreover I'm supposed to converse, but whenever I search for a reply, they look at me sharply, I stutter, nothing is right anymore. My father smiles and treats everyone with charm, he claps me on the shoulder, he says: She wants you to think she's only allowed to work in my garden, look at this hardworking gardener, show your hands, child, show your beautiful little white paws! Everybody laughs, I, too, force a laugh, my father laughs the loudest, he drinks a lot and a lot more after the guests have left. I have to show him my hands once again, he turns them over, twists them and I jump up, I'm still able to break away from him since he's drunk and starts swaying when he gets on his feet, I run out and want to slam the door, hide myself in the garden, but my father comes after me, and his eyes are terrifying, his face has turned reddish-brown with rage, he chases me up to a railing, it can't be that same house once again, so high up, he tears at me, we wrestle with each other, he wants to throw me over the railing, we both start to slide, and I lunge to the other side, I have to make it to the wall or jump on the roof next door or even run back into the house, I start to lose my mind, I don't know how to escape, and my father, who may also be afraid of the railing, doesn't want to follow me any closer to the edge, he picks up a flowerpot and hurls it at me, the pot breaks on the wall behind me, my father takes another, soil splashes in my face, the pots crash and splinter, my eyes are full of dirt, my father can't be like that, he is not permitted to be like that! The doorbell rings, fortunately for me someone must have been alarmed, it rings again, or else one of the guests has returned. Someone is coming, I whisper, stop it! My father says with sarcasm: Someone's coming to see you all right, for you of course, but you are staying, do you hear! Since it goes on ringing, since it's bound to be my rescue, since I can't see anything with my face smeared with dirt and since I'm trying to find the door, my father starts throwing whatever flowerpots he can find over the railing, so that the people leave instead of coming to my rescue. Nonetheless I must have escaped, for suddenly I'm standing by the entrance on the street, with Malina before me in the darkness, I whisper, he still doesn't understand, I whisper, don't come now, not today, and Malina, whom I have never seen pale and bewildered, asks, bewildered, what's the matter, is something wrong? I whisper: please go, I have to calm him down. I hear the police sirens, the policemen are already jumping out of a squad car, utterly afraid, I say: help me now, we must get rid of them, we have to. Malina speaks to the policemen and explains that there's a party going on, that spirits have become just a little too high, high spirits and very good ones, too. He has pushed me into the darkness. The police actually drive away, Malina comes back, he says urgently, now I understand, he sent that thing flying down, it missed me by a hair, you're coming with me now, or else we'll never see each other again, this has got to stop. But I whisper, I can't come, let me try just once more, I want to calm him down, he did that because you rang the bell, I have to go back at once. Please don't ring anymore! But understand, says Malina, we'll see each other again, but not before all this is over, because he wanted to kill me. I contradict him quietly, no, no, I'm all he has, I start to cry because Malina has left, I don't know what I am supposed to do anymore, I have to remove all the traces, I gather the shards from the street, with my hands I shovel all the flowers and soil into the gutter, tonight I lost Malina and Malina almost had to die tonight, both of us, Malina and myself, but this is stronger than me and my love for Malina, I will go on in denial, a light is burning in the house, my father has fallen asleep on the floor, in the middle of the devastation, everything has been laid waste, destroyed. I lie down beside my father, amid the devastation, for my place is here next to him, who is sleeping, limp, sad and old. And although it disgusts me to look at him, I must, I have to know what danger still is written in his face, I have to know where the evil originates, and I am frightened, but in a different way than usual, because the evil is in a face I do not recognize, I am crawling over to a strange man whose hands are sticky with dirt. How did I get into this, how did I fall into his power, in whose power? In my exhaustion I have a suspicion, but the suspicion is too great, I strike it down at once, he cannot be a stranger, this cannot have been in vain and can never have been a deceit. It cannot be true.

Malina is opening a bottle of mineral water, but at the same time holds a big glass with a swallow of whiskey in front of my face and insists I drink it. I don't like drinking whiskey in the middle of the night, but since Malina looks so worried and since his fingers are pressing into my wrist, I assume I'm not doing so well. He feels for my pulse, counts and seems dissatisfied.

Malina: You still don't have anything to say to me?
Me: Something is dawning on me, I'm beginning to see some logic, but I don't understand anything in particular. Some things are half-true, such as my waiting for you, or that I once ran down the stairs to stop you, the business with the police is also almost correct, except you weren't the one who told them they should go, that there'd been a misunderstanding, rather I told them myself, I sent them away. Isn't that right? In my dream the fear was greater. Besides, would you ever call the police? I couldn't. In fact

	I didn't, the neighbors did, I covered up all the tracks, I gave false testimony, that's what you're supposed to do, isn't it?
Malina:	Why did you cover up for him?
Me:	I said it was a party, a turbulent one like any other. Alexander Fleisser and that young guy Bardos were standing downstairs, they were on their way out when Alexander was almost hit by something, I won't tell you what it was, just that it was big enough to kill a person. Bottles were also thrown down but no flowerpots, of course. I said it was by mistake. Things like that happen. Admittedly not often, not in every family, not every day, not everywhere, but it does happen, at a party, just imagine the mood everyone was in.
Malina:	I'm not talking about everybody, you know that. And I'm not asking about moods.
Me:	What's more you're not afraid when you know it might actually happen, it's not like that at all, the fear comes later, in another form, it will come tonight. But naturally you want to know something else. The next day I went to Alexander's, something might also have hit Bardos whom I hardly knew, but he was a hundred yards away by that time. I told Alexander I was extremely, somewhat, to some extent, devastated, absolutely speechless, nonetheless I talked a whole lot, Alexander already had his own ideas, you see, and I felt he might notify the authorities but you have to understand that couldn't be allowed to happen! I also said that "whoever" was throwing things had thought the street was empty, who could have imagined Bardos would be standing there as well at that late hour, and maybe "whoever" had seen him, I'm sure "whoever" did, but I was the only one who knew that, so I started going on about hard times, except you could read in Alexander's face he didn't think hard

times could excuse that type of behavior, so in addition to the hard times I invented a critical illness and kept on making things up. Alexander wasn't convinced. I hadn't intended to convince him but just wanted to prevent the worst thing from happening at that moment.

Malina: Why did you do that?

Me: I don't know. I just did. At the time it was the right thing for me to do. Later you don't remember anything anymore. Not even a single reason, since they're moot anyway.

Malina: How would you have testified?

Me: I wouldn't have. At most I'd have said the one word I was still able to pronounce—although I didn't know what it meant anymore—I could have shot down any and all questions. (Using my fingers I sign to Malina in the International Language of the Deaf.) Don't you think that would have been enough to get me through all right? Or I could have claimed I was related and not obliged to testify. It's easy for you to laugh, nothing happened to you, you weren't standing right there by the gate.

Malina: Am I laughing? You're the one who's laughing. You should get some sleep, there's no sense talking to you as long as you're holding back the truth.

Me: I gave the police some money, they don't all take bribes, but these did, that's for sure. They were happy they could go back to the station or back to bed.

Malina: What do I care about these stories? You're dreaming, you know.

Me: I'm dreaming but I can assure you I'm beginning to understand. That's when I also started distorting everything I read. Instead of "Summer Fashion Exhibition" I would read "Summer Fashion Execution." That's just one example. I could name hundreds of others. Can you believe it?

Malina: Of course I can, but then I can believe a lot of things you still don't want to.

Me: Such as ...

Malina: You forget that tomorrow I'm on stand-by. Please get up on time. I'm dead tired. And I'd appreciate it this time if my egg weren't too soft or too hard. Good night.

The winter fashion executions showing the latest designs are on display in all the important execution houses. My father is the city's number one couturier. Despite my refusals I'm supposed to model the bridal gowns. In any event white dominates all the executions this year, with very few black lines, the white ones are kept at 60 degrees below zero in the Ice Palace, there the models are wed alive in public and for the public, with frozen veils and ice-flowers. All bridal couples must be naked. The Ice Palace is located where the skating club used to be and where they hold wrestling matches in the summer, but my father has rented the entire area. I'm supposed to be joined in matrimony to young Bardos, they've booked an orchestra which is scared to death of playing at such temperatures, but my father has the widows insured. They are still the wives of the musicians.

My father returned from Russia damaged. He didn't see the Hermitage but he did study techniques of torture and did bring back the tsarina Melanie. Bardos and I are to make our entrance in a gracious, artistically designed pavilion of ice, applauded by all Vienna and the whole world because the performance is being carried by satellite and is happening the same day the Americans or the Russians or everybody together are flying to the moon. My father's only concern is that the Vienna Ice Show make the whole planet forget about the moon and the superpowers. He races up and down the First and Third Districts in his fur-lined coach, letting himself be admired with the young tsarina one more time before the grand spectacle commences.

First the loudspeakers call everyone's attention to the ingenious details of the palace, the windows with their panes of the thinnest ice, as transparent as the most beautiful glass. Hundreds of ice chandeliers illuminate the entire hall and the furnishings are astounding: sofas, tabourets, cabinets displaying incredibly delicate china, glasses and tea services, everything made of ice and in brilliant colors, painted like Augarten porcelain. Ice logs coated with naphtha seem to burn in the fireplace, and over the magnificent four-poster bed you can see through lace curtains made of ice. The tsaritza, who calls my father her "bear," teases him, exclaiming what a pleasure it must be to live in this palace, perhaps a trifle too cold for sleeping. My father leans in my direction and remarks indecently: I'm sure you won't freeze tonight, with your Herr Bardos to warm your bed, after all he's supposed to make sure the fires of love are never extinguished! I throw myself at my father's feet and beg not for my own life, but for mercy on young Bardos whom I hardly know, who hardly knows me and who is looking at me uncomprehendingly, already beginning to freeze, he has already lost his senses. I have no idea why he has to be sacrificed at this public circus as well. My father explains to the tsaritza that my accomplice must also undress and together with me be doused with water from the Danube and the Neva for as long as it takes us to become statues of ice. But that's terrible, answers Melanie in an affected voice, you big big bear, certainly you'll have the poor souls killed first. No my little bearess, replies my father, because then they wouldn't have their natural movements, which are essential components of the Law of Beauty, no, I'm going to have them doused alive, how could I possibly amuse myself with just the fear of death! You're cruel, says Melanie, but my father promises her ecstasy, he knows how closely cruelty is bound with lust. It's easy to enjoy when you're wrapped in fur, he assures her and hopes that someday Melanie will exceed all other women in her cruelty. People from off the street, joined by Viennese society, begin to shout: It's not every day you see something like this!

Standing naked before the palace at 60 degrees below zero, we are ordered to assume our positions, some members of the audience sigh, but since they've already begun pouring icy water on us everybody must be convinced that Bardos is guilty as well, even though he really isn't. I can still hear myself whimpering and uttering one final curse, the last thing I see is my father's smile of triumph and the last thing I hear is his sigh of satisfaction. No longer can I beg for Bardos's life. I become ice.

My mother and sister have sent an international intermediary, wanting to know whether I'd be willing to resume relations with my father "after" this incident. I tell the envoy: Not for anything in the world! The man, who must be an old friend of mine, is baffled by my reply and thinks it's a real pity. In his opinion I'm being too hard. Afterward I leave my mother and sister standing helpless and mute and go into the next room to discuss this face-to-face with my father. Although my thinking, judgment and entire body have become inflexible, I can't rid myself of my notion of duty: I will sleep with him again, my body unmoved, my teeth frozen shut. But he has to realize I'm only doing this out of love for the others and in order to prevent an international scandal. My father is extremely dejected, he indicates he's not feeling well, he's no longer up to all this, and I can't get him to discuss matters, he's getting worked up about a disease he doesn't have at all just so he won't have to think about Melanie and me. Suddenly it dawns on me why he's pleading every possible excuse—he's living with my sister. I can't do anything more for Eleonore, she sends me a note: Pray for me, beg for me!

Sitting on my bed, I'm too hot and too cold, I reach for a book—CONVERSATIONS WITH THE EARTH—I had left on the floor before falling asleep. I've forgotten which chapter I was on, aimlessly I look through the table of contents, the appendix, glossaries, the subterranean forces and processes, inner dynamics. Malina takes the book out of my hand and puts it away.

Malina: What's your sister doing here, who is your sister?

Me: Eleonore? I don't know, I don't have a sister named Eleonore. But we all have some sister, don't we? I'm so sorry. How could I! But you probably want to know something about my real sister. Naturally when we were little we were always together, then for a while in Vienna, Sunday mornings we used to go to concerts at the Musikverein, sometimes we went out with the same men, she also knew how to read, once she wrote three sad pages, which didn't suit her at all, in the same way many things don't suit us, and I didn't take it seriously. I missed something. What will my sister have done by now? I hope she got married soon after.

Malina: You shouldn't speak that way about your sister, it's only costing you a lot of stress to keep her concealed. And Eleonore?

Me: I should have taken it seriously, but then I was still so young.

Malina: Eleonore?

Me: She's a lot older than my sister, she must have lived in another time, even another century, I've seen her picture, but I don't remember, I don't remember ... She also read books, once I dreamed she was reading to me, in a voice from beyond the grave. Vivere ardendo e non sentire il male. Where's that from?

Malina: What happened to her?
Me: She died in a foreign land.

My father is holding my sister captive, not letting his intentions show—he demands that I give her my ring, because my sister is supposed to wear this ring, he pulls it off my finger and says: That should do, that should be enough! you're all alike, I've got something in store for you both. He has "deposed" Melanie, sometimes he says "dismissed," he saw through her, realized her ambition and her craving to glow in his own light. However, the tirades he uses to explain her craving are peculiar, they frequently mention the word "snow," she had wanted to ride through my snow with him, also through our common snow from the Alpine foothills, and I ask whether he's already received my letters, but as it happens they got stuck in the snow. Once more I ask him for the few things I'll need until the end, the two Augarten coffee cups since I want to drink coffee once again, otherwise I wouldn't be able to perform my duty, they're missing you see, that's the worst thing, I'll have to tell my sister she should at least return the cups. My father has set off a small avalanche to frighten me and silence this wish of mine, the coffee cups are buried in the snow. But he just wanted to mislead me, he unleashes a second avalanche, slowly I understand that the snow is meant to bury me and no one is supposed to find me anymore. I run toward the trees which offer support and salvation, like a coward I try to scream that I don't want anything more, he should forget it, I don't want anything at all, there's an avalanche threatening, I have to row with my arms, I have to swim in the snow to stay afloat, there's no choice but to drift on the snow. Nonetheless my father steps out onto a snow slab and unleashes a third avalanche, which tears down all our forests, the oldest and strongest trees are felled by its incredible force, I am no longer able to do my duty, I agree, the battle's finished, my father treats the search party to a free beer, they might as well go home now, there's nothing to be done until next spring. I am caught in my father's avalanche.

In the light snow on the slope behind our house I am skiing for the first time. I have to twist and turn so as not to hit the bare patches and so I'll stay within a sentence that is written in the snow as I glide down. The sentence could be from my early days, written in a child's clumsy handwriting stretched out across the snow left from my youth. I recall vaguely that it's in the brown notebook where on New Year's Eve I wrote on the first page: He who has a Why to live for will bear almost any How. But the sentence also states I'm still having difficulties with my father and can't count on being able to escape this misfortune. An older woman, a soothsayer, is teaching me and a nearby group of people how to ski. She makes sure everyone stops at the end of the slope. Where I stop, utterly exhausted, I find a letter, it concerns the 26th of January and has something to do with a child, the letter is folded together very intricately and sealed many times. It must be kept unopened for a while still—it's completely encrusted with ice—because it contains a prophecy. I start down the path through the great forest, climb out of my skis and leave my poles with them, I continue on foot, toward the city, up to the houses of my Viennese friends. All the men's names are gone from the name plates. With my last strength I try ringing Lily's doorbell, I ring although she has never come before, I'm still puzzled as to why, but I keep calm and inform her through the door that my mother and Eleonore are coming today to put me in some reputable institution, I don't need a place to stay and have to leave immediately for the airport, but suddenly I don't know whether I have to drive to Schwechat or to Aspern, I can't be at both airports simultaneously, I no longer know whether my mother and sister really are coming by plane, whether there are any planes today, whether my mother and sister can come at all and whether they have been informed. Lily was the only one who had been informed. I cannot manage the sentence, I'd like to scream: You were the only one who was informed! And what did you do, you didn't do anything, you only made everything worse!

Since all the men have vanished from Vienna I have to rent a room from a young girl, a room no larger than the one I had as a child, my first bed is standing there as well. I suddenly fall in love with the girl, I embrace her while Frau Breitner, the caretaker from the Ungargasse (or the baroness from the Beatrixgasse), is lying next door, fat and heavy, she notices us embracing, although we're covered by my big blue blanket. She's not indignant but she does say that she never would have thought that possible, after all she knows me and also knew my father well, except that she didn't know until today that my father had gone to America. Frau Breitner is complaining, for she considered me a "saint," she says repeatedly "some sort of saint" and to prevent her from giving me notice I try to explain that it's understandable and natural, after all, following the tremendous misfortune with my father, I couldn't do otherwise. I study the girl more closely, I've never met her before, she is very tender and very young and tells me about a promenade at the Wörthersee, I am overwhelmed because she's talking about the Wörthersee, but don't trust myself to say "Du" to her, because then she'd find out who I am. She isn't ever supposed to find out. Some music begins—how softly, gently—and we take turns trying to sing some words to this music, the baroness tries as well, she is the caretaker of my building, Frau Breitner, we keep making mistakes, I sing "Now all my sorrow is dispelled," the girl sings "Can you see my friends, do you not see it?" But Frau Breitner sings "Beware! Beware! Night soon melts away!"

On the way to my father's I meet a group of students who also want to see him, I can show them the way, but I wouldn't want to arrive at his door at the same time they do. Pressed against the wall, I wait while the students ring the doorbell. Melanie opens, she's wearing a long housedress, her bust is once again excessively large and there for all to see, she greets the students effusively and pretends to remember each one, she's seen them at all the lectures, and says effusively that today she is still Fräulein Melanie, but not for long, since she wants to become Frau Melanie. Never, I think to myself. Then she catches sight of me, I have ruined her performance, we greet one another superficially, shaking hands so lightly they barely touch. She leads me down the hall, it's already the new apartment, and it's obvious to me that Melanie is pregnant. Inside the apartment my Lina is standing with her head bowed, she hadn't counted on my coming anymore, in this apartment she is known as Rita so that nothing will ever remind her of me. The apartment is gigantic, consisting solely of one very narrow and one immense room, the layout goes back to my father's notions of architecture, I know his ideas, they can't be mistaken for anyone else's. Among the pieces of furniture I see my blue sofa from the Beatrixgasse, and since my father is busy arranging things I speak to him in the large room. I make some suggestions about the blue sofa and a few other things, but my father isn't listening, he's walking back and forth with a yardstick, measuring the windows, walls and doors, as he is once again planning something grand. I ask him if I should now explain to him orally or later in writing which arrangement I desire, what would he prefer. He carries on, occupied and indifferent and only says: Busy, I'm busy! Before I leave the apartment I look at a few things, high up on the wall is a strange feathered decoration, many small dead birds are standing stuffed in a niche which is lit red, and I say to myself, how distasteful, as distasteful as always. It was always taste which separated us, lack of caring and his lack of taste, both get muddled and merge into a single phrase for me, and as Lina, who lets herself be called Rita, sees me out, I say: distasteful, nothing here has any taste, it's all so uncaring, my father will never change. Lina nods, embarrassed, she gives me her hand in secret, and now I'd like to have the courage, I want to and have to slam the door loudly, like my father always slammed all doors, so that for once he will know what it is like to have someone SLAM THE DOOR. But the door clicks shut quietly, I am still unable to slam it. In front of the house I press myself against the wall, I shouldn't have come here, ever, now that Melanie is here, my father has already had the house rearranged, I can't go back and I can't get away, but I could still climb over the fence where the bushes are very thick, and deathly afraid, I run up to the fence and clamber up, it's salvation, it would be salvation, but once on top I get stuck, it's barbed wire, the barbs carry 100,000 volts, I receive the 100,000 electric jolts, my father has charged the wires, the countless volts scorch every fiber of my body. I am incinerated and die in my father's frenzy.

A window opens, revealing a sinister, cloudy landscape with a lake that is growing smaller and smaller. A cemetery surrounds the lake, the graves can be clearly discerned, the earth opens up above the graves, and for a moment the dead daughters stand with blowing hair, their faces remain indistinct, their hair falls down below their hands, each woman is raising her right hand, which can be easily seen in the white light, they spread their waxen fingers, the rings are missing, the ring fingers are missing on every hand. My father has the lake swell beyond its banks so that nothing comes out, so that nothing can be seen, so that the women drown above their graves, so that the graves drown, my father says: It's a performance—WHEN WE DEAD AWAKEN.

When I wake up I know it's been years since I've been in a theater. Performance? What performance, I don't know any performance, but it has to have been a performance.

Malina: Your imagination always did overperform.

Me: But back then my mind couldn't perform at all. Or else we're talking about perform and performance and not meaning the same thing.

Malina: I'll get to the point. Why is your ring missing? Did you ever wear a ring? Of course you didn't. You told me it was impossible for you to wear anything on your finger, or around your neck or around your wrist or as far as I'm concerned around your ankles.

Me: In the beginning he bought me a small ring, I wanted to leave it in the box but every day he'd ask how I liked the ring and was always reminding me that he had given it to me, for years he talked about this ring incessantly, as if I could live off a ring, and if I didn't volunteer to mention it each day he would ask, where do you have my ring, child? And I, the child, I said, for heaven's sake, there's no way I—no, I'm absolutely certain, I just left it lying in the bathroom, I'll go get it immediately and put it on my finger or place it next to me on the little dresser near the bed, I can't fall asleep without this ring nearby. He put on a whole horrible show about this ring, he also told everybody that he had given me a ring, and finally they all thought that, along with the ring, he had given me my life or at least a monthly allowance or a house and a garden and the air to breathe, I could hardly wear the damn ring anymore, and once the ring was said to have lost its validity I would have gladly thrown it in his face, since moreover he hadn't really given it to me at all, not of his own free will, I had pressured him for some confirmation, because no sign ever came, because I wanted a sign, and in the end I received the ring he kept on talking about. But you can't really throw a ring in someone's face, throwing one at someone's feet would have worked in a pinch, but that's easier said than done, for if someone is sitting or pacing up and down you can't very well throw something that small at their feet and achieve your goal. That's why I first went to the bathroom with the intention of throwing it down the toilet, but then that seemed too easy, too practical and too proper, I wanted my performance, furthermore I now wanted to give the ring some meaning, and I drove to Klosterneuburg, where I stood for hours on the bridge over the Danube, in the first wind of winter, then I took the little ring box out of my coat pocket and took the ring out of the box—I hadn't worn the ring for weeks—it was the 19th of September and I threw it into the Danube on that cold afternoon, while it was still light.

Malina: That doesn't explain a thing. The Danube is full of rings, every day someone takes a ring off a finger and tosses it into the Danube somewhere between Klosterneuburg and Fischamend in the cold wind of winter or the hot wind of summer.

Me: I didn't take my ring off my finger.

Malina: That's not the point, I don't want your story, you keep evading me.

Me: The strangest thing was that I knew all the time he was going around with thoughts of murder, I just didn't know how he was planning to get rid of me. Anything was possible. But he could have only come up with one possibility, and that's exactly what I couldn't guess. I didn't know such a thing still existed here and now.

Malina: Maybe you didn't know, but you were in agreement.

Me: I swear to you I was not in agreement, there's no way you can agree, you want to get away, escape. What are you trying to make me believe? I was never in agreement!

Malina: Don't swear. Don't forget, you never swear.

Me: Naturally I knew he'd want to hit me where I'm most
         vulnerable, because then he wouldn't have to do any-
         thing more except wait, wait until I myself, until I took
         my own ...
Malina: Stop crying.
Me: I'm not crying, you want to make me think I am, you're
         going to make me cry. It was completely different. Then
         I took a good look around, and I noticed that everybody
         was biding their time, both in my vicinity and also far
         away—they don't do anything else, at least nothing in
         particular, they put sleeping pills in people's hands, or
         razor blades, they make sure you lose your head while
         you're walking along the edge of a cliff, that you're com-
         pletely drunk when you open the door of a moving train,
         or simply let you come down with some disease. If they
         wait long enough a breakdown is bound to occur, your
         end will be long or short. Some people survive that, but
         only just barely.
Malina: But how much consent is required?
Me: I've suffered too much, I don't know anything anymore,
         I confess nothing, how am I supposed to know, I don't
         know enough, I hate my father, God only knows how
         much I hate him, I don't know why.
Malina: Whom have you made into your idol?
Me: No one. This can't go on, I'm not getting anywhere, I
         can't see anything, I just keep hearing a voice to fit the
         images, sometimes louder, sometimes softer, saying: In-
         cest. It's unmistakable, I know what it means.
Malina: No, you really don't. Once one has survived something
         then survival itself interferes with understanding, and
         you don't even know which lives came before and which
         is your life of today, you even mix up your own lives.
Me: I only have one life.
Malina: Leave it to me.

I've reached the Black Sea, and I know that the Danube has to flow into the Black Sea. I will flow like it does. I've floated past all the riverbanks safe and sound, but before I reach the delta then I see a fat body half-covered with water, I cannot avoid it by wading into the middle of the river, since the river is too deep here and too broad and full of whirlpools. My father has hidden himself in the water before the mouth of the river, he is a gigantic crocodile, with tired, drooping eyes that will not let me pass. There are no longer any crocodiles along the Nile, they brought the last ones to the Danube. Now and then my father opens his eyes slightly, he looks as though he were simply lying there idly, as if he weren't waiting for anything, but naturally he's waiting for me, he knew I wanted to come home, that for me coming home means salvation. Sometimes the crocodile opens his huge, craving jaws, shreds of flesh are hanging inside, flesh from the other women, and I think of the names of all the women he has devoured, old blood is floating on the water, but fresh blood as well: I don't know how hungry my father is today. Suddenly I see lying next to him a small crocodile, now he has found a crocodile after his own heart. But the small crocodile's eyes are sparkling and it is not idle, it swims up to me and wants to kiss me on both cheeks in false friendliness. Before it can kiss me, I scream: You're a crocodile! Go back to your other crocodile, after all you belong together, both of you are crocodiles! For I recognized Melanie at once, who once again lets her eyes droop hypocritically and who is no longer sparkling with her human eyes. My father screams back: Say that again! But I don't say it again, although I should since he so commands. I can only choose between being torn to pieces by him or entering the deepest part of the river. At the mouth of the Danube I disappeared into my father's jaws. But three drops of my blood, my last ones, did flow into the Black Sea.

My father enters the room, he is whistling and singing, standing there in his pajama bottoms, I hate him, I can't look at him, I pretend to be busy with my suitcase. Please get dressed, I say, put something else on! For he is wearing the pajamas I gave him for his birthday, he is wearing them intentionally, and I would like to tear them off, but suddenly I have an idea, and I remark casually: Oh, it's only you! I start to dance, I dance a waltz all by myself, and my father looks at me somewhat surprised, because his small crocodile is lying on the bed, dressed in silk and velvet, and he begins writing his will for silk and velvet, he writes on a large sheet of paper and says: You won't inherit a thing, you hear, since you insist on dancing! I actually am dancing, di-dam da-dam, I dance through all the rooms and start to twirl on the carpet which he cannot pull out from under my feet, it's the carpet from WAR AND PEACE. My father calls to my Lina: Take the carpet away from her! But Lina has the day off, and I laugh, dance, and suddenly call out: Ivan! It's our music, now it's a waltz for Ivan, for Ivan again and again, it's salvation, because my father has never heard Ivan's name, he's never seen me dance, he no longer knows what to do, they can't pull away the carpet during this whirling dance, they cannot stop me in my quick rotations, I call to Ivan, but he must not come, must not hold me, for with a voice no human has ever had before, with the voice of the stars, the sidereal voice, I beget the name Ivan and his omnipresence.

My father is beside himself, he screams indignantly: This lunatic should either stop or disappear, she should disappear at once, or else she'll wake my little crocodile. Dancing, I come closer to the crocodile, I take back the Siberian shirt which had been stolen from me, and my letters to Hungary, remove whatever is mine from its sleepy, dangerous jaws, I also want my key back, and I am laughing already as I take it off the crocodile's tooth and continue dancing, but then my father grabs the key away from me. He takes away my key on top of everything else, it's my only key! I'm speechless, I can no longer cry out: Ivan, help me! He wants to kill me! A letter of mine is still hanging on the crocodile's largest tooth, not a

Siberian letter nor a Hungarian one, with horror I realize to whom the letter is addressed, since I can read the beginning: My beloved father, you have broken my heart. Crackcrack broken dam-di-dam my broken my father crack crack rrrack da-di-dam Ivan, I want Ivan, I mean Ivan, I love Ivan, my beloved father. My father says: Take this woman away!

My child, who is now about four or five years old, comes over to me, I recognize him immediately since he looks like me. We look in a mirror and assure ourselves. My child tells me quietly that my father is getting married, to this masseuse who's very beautiful but also pushy. Because of this my child would prefer not to stay with my father any longer. We're in a large apartment belonging to some strangers, I hear my father talking to some people in another room, it's a good opportunity, and quite suddenly I decide to take the child to my place, although I'm sure he won't want to stay with me either, since my life is so disorganized, since I don't have an apartment yet, as I must first leave the homeless shelter, and pay for the rescue service and the search party, and I don't have any money, but I hold my child very close and promise him that I'll do everything. He seems to be in agreement, we assure each other that we must stick together, I know that from now on I will fight for my child, my father doesn't have any claim to our child, I don't understand myself anymore, he just doesn't have any right, now I take the child by the hand and want to see my father at once, but there are other rooms in between. My child doesn't have a name yet, I feel he is nameless like the unborn, I have to give him a name soon and my name as well, I whisper a suggestion: Animus. My child would prefer not having any name, but he understands. In every room the most disgusting scenes are taking place, I cover my child's eyes because I have discovered my father in the piano room, he's lying with a young woman underneath the piano, it could be this masseuse, my father has unbuttoned her blouse and is taking off her bra, and I am afraid my child has seen this despite my efforts. We push our way into the next room through the guests who are all drinking champagne, my father must be completely drunk, otherwise how could he forget the child like that. In the other room, where we are seeking shelter, another woman is lying on the floor, threatening everyone with a revolver, I presume it's a danger party, a revolver party, I try to play along with the woman's ludicrous ideas, she aims at the ceiling, then through the door at my father, I don't know whether in earnest or in jest, maybe she is this masseuse, since all of a sudden she asks, nastily, what am I doing here and who is this little bastard, and while she's pointing her revolver at me, I ask whether it isn't the other way around, whether she isn't the one who doesn't have any business here, but she shrieks in reply: Who is this bastard standing in my way? In mortal fear I don't know whether to pull my child close to me or whether to send him off, I want to cry out: Run, run! Run far away from here! For the woman is no longer playing with the revolver, she wants to have both of us out of the way, it's the 26th of January, and I pull my child close so that we die together, the woman ponders a moment, then takes exact aim and shoots the child. After that she no longer has to hit me. My father had only authorized one shot. The bells ring out the New Year as I fall over my child, and everyone clinks glasses and spills champagne, the champagne from New Year's Eve runs over me, and I have buried my child not in the presence of my father.

I have entered the Falling Age, the neighbors sometimes ask if something has happened. I have fallen into a small grave and hit my head and wrenched my shoulders, everything has to heal before my next fall, and I must spend this time in the crypt, I'm already scared of the next fall, but I know the prophecy: I shall fall three times before I can rise again.

My father has taken me to prison, I'm not very surprised, since I know what good connections he has. At first I hope they'll treat me well and at least allow me to write. After all, I do have plenty of time here and I am safe from my father's persecution. I could finish the book I found earlier, on the way to the prison, I saw a few sentences in the rotating blue light of the police van, I saw some hanging between the trees, floating in the waste water, pressed by many car tires into the overly hot asphalt. I took note of all the sentences, and some I still remember, but from earlier times. I am led down long corridors, they want to try different cells to see which one I fit, but then it turns out I won't receive any privileges. There's a long back and forth between different officials. My father is behind it all, he's had some of the files disappear, more and more documents in my favor vanish, and finally it turns out I'm not allowed to write. To be sure I do receive a solitary cell, as I had secretly wished, they also shove in a tin bowl with water, and although the cell is too dark and dirty my thoughts are only on the book, I ask for paper, I drum on the door for paper, because there's something I have to write. It will be easy for me in the cell, I don't regret being imprisoned here, I get used to it right away, only I keep trying to talk with the people passing outside who don't understand me, they think I'm protesting and resisting arrest, whereas I want to say the arrest doesn't matter, but I would like a few sheets of paper and something to write with. A guard rips open the door and says: It's no use, you're not allowed to write to your father! He slams the door shut against my head, although I'm already screaming: But not to my father, I promise, not to my father! My father has had it rumored about in the judiciary that I'm dangerous because I again want to write him. But it's not true, I only want to write the sentence from the ground up. I am destroyed and so I even tip over the tin bowl with the water, I'd rather die of thirst because it isn't true, and as I'm thirsting away the sentences rejoice around me, growing and growing in number. Some can only be seen, others only heard as in the Gloriastrasse, after the first injection of morphine. Crouched in a corner, without water, I know my sentences won't leave me and that I have a right to them. My father looks through a peephole, all that can be seen are his glazed eyes, he'd like to copy my sentences and take them from me, but in the greatest thirst, after my last hallucinations, I know he is watching me die without words, I have completely hidden the words inside the sentence, sufficiently grounded, which is forever safe and secret from my father, so tightly do I hold my breath. My tongue is dangling far out, but it does not reveal a single word. Because I am unconscious they search me, they want to moisten my mouth, wet my tongue, so they can find the sentences and place them in custody, but then they find three stones beside me and don't know what they mean or where they come from. They are three hard, luminous stones which have been thrown to me by the highest authority, where even my father has no influence, and I alone know what message each stone contains. Young lightning is constantly flashing inside the first reddish stone, which has fallen from heaven into my cell, it says: Live in wonder. The second blue stone, flashing with all possible hues of blue, says: Write in wonder. And I am already holding the third stone in my hand, white and radiant, whose fall can be stopped by no one, not even my father, but the cell grows so dark that the third stone's message cannot be read. The stone can no longer be seen. I shall discover this final message after I am freed.

Now my father has my mother's face as well. It's an old, gigantic, washed-out face, in which the crocodile eyes may still be seen, but the mouth resembles the mouth of an old woman, and I don't know whether he is she or she is he, but I have to speak to my father, probably for the last time. Sire! At first he doesn't answer, then he grabs the telephone, then dictates to someone, and in the meantime he says it's too early for me, I have no right to live yet, and I say, still straining, with difficulty: But it doesn't matter to me, you should know I no longer care what you think. People are there once more, Professor Kuhn and Docent Morokutti force themselves between me and my father, Herr Kuhn attests to his humble devotion, and I say aggressively: Would you please leave me alone with my father for ten minutes? All my friends have appeared as well, the Viennese are lining the street in eager expectation, but quietly, on the edge of the street, a few groups from Germany are craning their necks impatiently, they always think everything in Vienna takes too long. I say resolutely: It must be possible to speak for ten minutes with one's own mother about something important, at least just once. My father looks up in amazement, but still doesn't understand. Now and then I lose my voice: I have permitted myself to live nevertheless. Sometimes my voice returns and can be heard by all: I am living, I will live, I claim my right to live.

My father signs a document that once more undoubtedly has to do with depriving me of my rights, but the others begin to notice me. Panting heavily, he sits down to eat with relish, I know that once again I won't get anything to eat, and I watch him in all his boundless egotism, I see the bowl of frittatensuppe, next he is handed a plate of schnitzel and a dish of our apple compote, I lose control, I have come unarmed but I notice in front of me the large glass ashtrays found in all offices and the paperweights, I take the first heavy object and throw it right into the soup bowl, my mother is surprised and uses her napkin to wipe her face, I take a heavy object and aim it at the schnitzel, the plate breaks and the schnitzel goes flying into my father's face, he jumps up, pushing away the people who have come between us, and advances toward me before I can throw a third object. Now he is prepared to listen to me. I am completely calm, no longer afraid, and I say to him: I only wanted to show you that I can do anything you can. Just so you know, nothing more. Although I didn't throw a third object, the sticky compote is running over my father's face. Suddenly he has nothing more to say to me.

I've woken up. It's raining. Malina is standing by the open window.

Malina: You could suffocate in here. Besides, you were smoking too much, I've covered you up, the air will do you good. How much of all that did you understand?

Me: Almost all of it. One time I thought I didn't understand anymore, my mother had me completely confused. Why is my father also my mother?

Malina: Why do you think? If one person is everything for somebody, then that person can be many people in one.

Me: Are you suggesting that someone was ever everything for me? What a mistake! There's really nothing more bitter!

Malina: Yes. But you will act, you will have to act, you will have to destroy all the people in that one person.

Me: But I am the one who has been destroyed.

Malina: That's also true.

Me: It's getting so easy to talk about, already it's a lot easier. But it's so difficult to live with.

Malina: It's not supposed to be discussed, just lived with.

This time my father again has the face of my mother, I don't know exactly when he is my father and when he is my mother, then the suspicion intensifies, and I know he's not either one, but some third thing, and so I wait among the other people, extremely agitated, for our meeting. He is overseeing an enterprise or a government, he is staging a play, he has Daughter Rights and Daughter Societies, he is constantly giving orders, speaking on several telephones at once, and because of this I still can't make myself heard, not until the moment he lights a cigar. I say: My father, this time you are going to talk to me and answer my questions! My father waves me off, bored, he's heard it all before, my coming and asking questions, he keeps on phoning. I walk over to my mother, she is wearing my father's pants, and I say to her: You're going to speak with me before the day is over and give me some answers! But my mother, who also has my father's brow, which she raises the same way he does—in two folds over tired, indolent eyes—mumbles something about "later" and "no time." Now my father is wearing her skirts, and I say for the third time: I think I will soon know who you are, and I'll tell you myself tonight, before the night is over. But the man sits down at the table serenely and signals for me to go, however when I reach the door, which is opened for me, I turn around and slowly walk back. I walk with all my strength and stop at the large table in the courtroom, while the man on the table opposite begins to carve his schnitzel underneath the cross. I don't say anything, just show my disgust at the way he is using his fork to play with his compote, smiling at me jovially, just as he is smiling at the audience that must suddenly leave the room, he is drinking red wine, next to that is yet another cigar, still I say nothing, but he cannot mistake the meaning of my silence, since it now carries weight. I take the first heavy marble ashtray, heft it and hold it high, the man continues eating quietly, I aim and hit the plate. The man drops his fork, the schnitzel flies onto the floor, he is still holding his knife, he raises it, but at the same time I pick up the next object, because he still isn't answering, and aim exactly at the dish of compote, he wipes the juice off his face with a napkin. Now he realizes that I no longer have any feelings for him and that I could kill him. I throw a third time, I take my time aiming, and I aim exactly, and the object wipes the table clean, so that everything goes flying off—bread, wine glass, plate shards and a cigar. My father is holding his napkin in front of his face, he has nothing more to say to me.

Well?

Well?

I wipe off his face myself, not out of pity but in order to see him better, and I say: I will live!

Well?

The people have scattered, they hadn't come at their own expense. I am alone with my father under heaven, and we are standing so far apart our words echo in space:

Well!

My father first takes off my mother's clothes, he's standing so far away I don't know which costume he's wearing, he's constantly changing them, one minute he's wearing the bloodstained apron of a butcher standing before a slaughterhouse at dawn, next he's wearing a hangman's red coat and climbing up the steps, next he's wearing silver and black, with shiny black boots, in front of electric barbed wire, in front of a loading ramp, inside a watchtower, he's wearing his costumes for the riding crops, the rifles, the execution pistols, his costumes are worn in the deepest night, bloodstained and hideous.

Well?

My father, who does not have my father's voice, asks from far away:

Well?

And I speak across the distance, since we're moving farther and farther away from one another and farther away and farther:

I know who you are.

I have understood everything.

Malina is holding me, he's sitting on the edge of the bed, and for a while neither of us speaks. My pulse isn't any faster or any slower, I show no signs of paroxysm, I am not cold, I'm not breaking out in sweat, Malina is holding me and holding me, we do not separate, for his calm has passed over to me. Then I disentangle myself from him, straighten out the pillows by myself, clasp my hands around his—it's just that I cannot look at him, I stare down at our hands as they clasp one another tighter and tighter, I cannot look at him.

Me: It's not my father. It's my murderer.
Malina doesn't answer.
Me: It's my murderer.

Malina: Yes, I know that.

I don't answer.

Malina: Why were you always saying: my father?

Me: Did I really say that? How could I possibly say that? I
          didn't really mean to say it, but you can only talk about
          what you see, and I told you exactly what was shown to
          me. Also I wanted to tell him something I've now under-
          stood for a long time—namely that people don't die here,
          they are murdered. That's why I also understand how he
          could have entered my life. Somebody had to do it. He
          was the one.

Malina: So you'll never again say: War and Peace.

Me: Never again.

          It's always war.

          Here there is always violence.

          Here there is always struggle.

          It is the everlasting war.

Three   *Last Things*

At the moment my greatest fear may be the fate of our postal officials. Malina knows that for many reasons I have a particularly soft spot for mailmen, in addition to an affinity for street repairmen. This latter should make me ashamed, although I've never done anything I shouldn't have, I've always contented myself with a friendly greeting or a fleeting glance back through a car window at a group of suntanned sweating men with bare chests pouring gravel, spraying asphalt or devouring their lunches. In any case I was never so bold as to stop, nor have I ever asked Malina to help me get into conversation with a street repairman, even though Malina knows about and sympathizes with my ultimately inexplicable weakness.

My affinity for mailmen, however, remains completely untainted by impure thoughts. Years pass without my ever even recognizing their faces, for I sign the receipt they hand me at my door quickly, often with one of those old-fashioned pens they still carry. I also thank them cordially for telegrams and special deliveries and am not stingy with tips. But I can't thank them as I would like for letters they do not deliver. Nevertheless my cordiality, my exuberance at the door is also intended for undelivered, lost or mixed-up mail. In any case from early on I was quick to appreciate the wonder of mail, the delivery of letters and packages. Also the mailbox in the front hall, set within a row of mailboxes fashioned by the most modern designers for the very farsighted mailbox industry, presumably for skyscrapers the likes of which Vienna has yet to discover, and standing in sharp contrast to the marble fin de siècle Niobe and the roomy, ceremonious entrance hall—this mailbox, too, prevents me from ever thinking indifferently about the men who fill my own with death notices, invitations from galleries and institutes, brochures from travel agencies beckoning to Istanbul, the Canary Islands and Morocco. Even registered letters are deposited by a sensible Herr Sedlacek or the younger Herr Fuchs so I won't have to run to the post office in the Rasumofskygasse, and the money-orders which cause my heart to rise or sink are brought so early in the morning that I'm barefoot and in my nightgown, but always ready to sign. Evening telegrams, on the other hand, either reach me in a state of disintegration or recomposition, if they're delivered before eight o'clock. I dash to the door with a towel thrown over my head on account of my freshly washed hair, one eye still red from the eyedrops, and am afraid that Ivan might have come too soon, but then it's only some new friend or an old one with an evening telegram. What I owe these marsupial men, who carry in their pouches tidings of most precious joy or unbearable calamities, who wheel about on bicycles, who rattle up from the Heumarkt on motorcycles, who climb stairs, ringing doorbells despite their burdens, completely uncertain as to whether the trip will have been worth the effort, whether the addressee will be present, whether the addressee thinks the news is worth one schilling or four—what we all owe these men remains to be said.

A sentence was finally uttered today, not by Herr Sedlacek and not by the young Fuchs, but by a mailman I don't believe I know, who has never appeared between Christmas and New Year's with season's greetings, and who thus has little reason to be friendly to me. Today's mailman says: I'm sure all the mail you get is good, but I sure have to work hard getting it to you! I replied: Yes you do work hard, but we'll first have to check to see if all the mail you bring really is good, since unfortunately your mail sometimes makes me suffer, just as my mail makes you suffer. If not a philosopher, this mailman is most certainly a rascal, for he enjoys placing four envelopes edged in black on top of two regular letters. Maybe he's hoping a particular death notice will please me. But that one never comes, I don't even need to look, I toss the four envelopes into the wastebasket, unread. If the right one were there I'd feel it, and maybe this wheedler of a mailman has seen through me, true confidants can only be found among people you scarcely know, among irregular mailmen like this one. I never want to see him again. I'll ask Herr Sedlacek why we still need an extra postman who hardly knows our houses, who hardly knows me and who cannot keep his observations to himself. One letter contains a past due warning, in another someone writes that he's arriving at the Südbahnhof tomorrow at 8:20 AM, I don't recognize the writing and the signature is illegible. I'll have to ask Malina.

There are days when mailmen see us turn pale or red, and that may be precisely why they aren't asked to come in, sit down, drink some coffee. They are too well initiated into the terrible things that they nonetheless bear through the city fearlessly and so they are dismissed in the doorway, with or without a tip. Their fate is completely undeserved. Such treatment, which even I expose them to, is foolish, arrogant and completely unreasonable. Not even Ivan's postcards are enough for me to invite Herr Sedlacek to have some champagne. Of course Malina and I don't have a single bottle of champagne in the house, but I should keep one on hand for Herr Sedlacek, for he sees me turning pale and turning red, he suspects something, he must know something.

That one might feel called to become a mailman, that delivering mail is not an occupation haphazardly chosen, that it is a mistake to even consider it one, was proven by the famous mailman Kranewitzer of Klagenfurt, who in the end was brought to trial and sentenced to several years' imprisonment for malfeasance and misappropriation of funds, a completely misunderstood man, mistreated by the press as well as the court. I have read the reports of Kranewitzer's trial more carefully than those of the most shocking murder trials of all these past years, and the man himself, who then merely amazed me, now has my deepest sympathy. From a certain day on, without being able to explain why, Otto Kranewitzer ceased distributing the mail and for weeks and months he accumulated it in the old three-room apartment where he lived alone, piling it up to the ceiling, he sold most of his furniture to make space for the growing postal mountain. He did not open letters or packages, he did not appropriate checks or bonds, nor did he filch any banknotes sent from mothers to their sons, nothing of the sort could be proven against him. He simply, suddenly could no longer deliver the mail, a sensitive, tender, great man who realized the full momentousness of his work, and precisely because of that the low official Kranewitzer was discharged from the Austrian Postal Service in disgrace and dishonor, as it takes pride in employing only reliable, energetic mailmen of stamina. But in every profession there must be at least one man who lives in deep doubt and comes into conflict. Mail delivery in particular would seem to require a latent angst, a seismographic ability to receive emotional tremors, which is otherwise acknowledged only in the higher and highest professions, as if the mail couldn't have its own crisis, no Thinking—Wanting—Being for it, no scrupulous and noble renunciation otherwise granted all sorts of people, better paid, occupying academic chairs, people who are permitted to ponder the proofs of divine existence, to reflect on the Ontos On, the Aletheia or as far as I'm concerned the origins of the Earth or of the Universe! But the unknown and poorly paid Otto Kranewitzer was only accused of base behavior and dereliction of duty. No one realized that he had begun to ponder, that he had been gripped by the amazement which is, of course, at the root of all philosophical inquiry and anthropogenesis, and in light of the things which caused him to lose his composure he could in no way be pronounced incompetent, for no one could have been more capable than he—who had spent thirty years delivering letters to Klagenfurt—in recognizing the problem of mail, its problematic essence.

He was fully familiar with our streets, it was clear to him which letters, which packets, which printed matters were postmarked correctly. In addition, more and most subtle differences in the writing of addresses, a "Rt. Hon. Sir," or a name unaccompanied by "Herr" or "Frau," a "Prof. Dr. Dr." told him more about attitudes, generational conflict, signals of social alarm than our sociologists and psychiatrists will ever discover. By a false or insufficient return address he realized everything immediately, naturally he could distinguish a family letter from a business letter without a moment's hesitation, somewhat friendly letters from those wholly intimate, and this distinguished mailman, who took whatever risks his profession required as a cross to bear for all others, must have been seized by horror, faced with the postal mountain rising in his apartment, he must have suffered indescribable pangs of conscience, inconceivable to others, to whom a letter is just a letter and printed matter merely printed matter. On the other hand, whoever even simply attempts, as I am doing, to assemble and confront his own mail from several years (and even such a person would not be unbiased, faced with his mail alone, and thus incapable of seeing the larger connections) would probably understand that a postal crisis, even if it only did occur in a smaller city and only for a few weeks, is morally superior to the accepted onset of one of the public worldwide crises so often thoughtlessly conjured up, and that thinking, which is becoming rarer and rarer, is not solely the property of a privileged class and its dubious representatives, the authorized ruminators, but also belongs to an Otto Kranewitzer.

The case of Kranewitzer changed me greatly, internally, imperceptibly. I have to explain this to Malina, and so I do.

Me: Since that time I know what is meant by Privacy of Mail. Today I am able to picture it in its entirety. After the case of Kranewitzer I burned my letters of many years, then began writing completely different letters, mostly late at night, till eight in the morning. I didn't send all these letters, but they're the ones I'm concerned about. Over these four, five years I must have written ten thousand letters, just to myself, letters that contained everything. I also leave many letters unopened, in my attempt to practice Privacy of Mail, in my attempt to approach the height of Kranewitzer's thinking, to comprehend what could be unlawful in reading a letter. But now and then I'll have a relapse, all of a sudden I'll open one and read it, even leave it lying around so that you, for example, could read it while I'm in the kitchen—that's how poorly I guard the letters. So it isn't a crisis of mail or writing that I'm not quite equal to, it's that I backslide and revert to curiosity, every now and then I tear open a package, especially at Christmas, blushing as I take out a scarf, a beeswax candle, a silver-plated hairbrush from my sister, a new calendar from Alexander. I'm still so inconsistent, although the case of Kranewitzer could have helped me mend my ways.

Malina: Why is this Privacy of Mail so important to you?
Me: Not because of this Otto Kranewitzer. For my own sake.

For yours as well. And in the University of Vienna I swore upon a scepter. It was my only oath. I was never able to swear anything to any person, any representative of any religious or political doctrine. Even as a child I would immediately fall very ill, since I had no other defense, I would get downright sick, with high fever, and couldn't be sent anywhere to take an oath. But people who've only sworn once have it harder. Several oaths can certainly be broken, but not just one.

Since Malina knows me and is familiar with my stumbling about from one topic to another, it's easy for him to believe that I nevertheless have the willpower to carry things further than I let on, confined as I am to the limited possibilities of our everyday existence, that Privacy of Mail is also something I would like to get to the bottom of and something I will uphold.

Tonight all the mailmen in Vienna are to be tortured, people want to test if they are equal to the Privacy of Mail. However some are only to be examined for varicose veins, flat feet and other physical deformities. It's possible that as of tomorrow they'll call in the military and have it deliver letters, because the mailmen will be maltreated, injured, tormented, tortured, or broken down by injections of truth serum—and no longer capable of delivering anything. I am considering an inflammatory speech, a letter, yes, an inflammatory letter to the Minister of Postal Affairs, to protect all mailmen including my own. A letter that may already have been intercepted and burned by the soldiers, the flames will burn the words or blacken them, and it could be that the messengers in the Ministry of Postal Affairs are pursuing the Minister down the corridors to hand him what is nothing but a charred piece of paper.

Me:	You understand, my inflammatory letters, my inflammatory appeals, my inflammatory stance, this entire fire I have put on paper with my burned hand—I'm afraid it could all become a charred piece of paper. Ultimately all the paper in the world is charred by fire or melted by water, since they douse fire with water.
Malina:	The ancients used to say of someone stupid that he had no heart. They placed the seat of intelligence in the heart. You don't have to hang your heart on every single thing and have all your speeches flame and blaze and all your letters.
Me:	But how many people have just a head and nothing more, and no heart at all? I'll tell you what's really going on now: tomorrow Vienna is being relocated to the Danube, with whatever force it takes, including the military. They want to have Vienna on the Danube. They want water, not fire. One more city with a river flowing through. That would be horrible. Please, call Department Director Matreier at once, call the Minister!

But Vienna doesn't have much time left, it's slipping away, the houses are falling asleep, people are turning their lights off earlier and earlier, no one is awake anymore, entire districts are gripped by apathy, people aren't coming together or splitting apart, the city is slipping into decline although isolated thoughts and erratic monologues still occur at night. And from time to time the final dialogues between Malina and myself.

I am at home alone, Malina is keeping me waiting for a long time, I'm sitting with CHESS FOR BEGINNERS in front of the board and am in the middle of a game. No one is sitting opposite, I keep switching places, this time Malina won't be able to say that I'm about to lose, since ultimately I both win and lose at the same time. But Malina comes home and sees only one glass, he doesn't look at the chessboard, this game doesn't interest him.

Malina says, as I expected: Vienna is burning!

I've always wanted to have a younger brother, better still a younger husband, Malina should understand that, after all everybody has a sister, but only some people have brothers. Even as a child I kept a lookout for these brothers, placing not one but two pieces of candy by the window at night, since two pieces are for a brother. Besides I already had a sister. Every older man horrifies me, even if he's only older by a day, and I would never bring myself to confide in an older man, I'd rather die. The face alone tells nothing. I have to know the dates, I have to know he's five days younger, otherwise I'll be haunted by these doubts that attachments could ensue, that I could fall under the supreme curse, because it's possible that something could happen to me once again, and I have to work harder and harder to avoid the hell I must once have inhabited. But I do not remember.

Me: I have to be able to submit voluntarily, after all you're a
        little younger than I am, and I didn't meet you until later.
        Sooner or later wasn't so important, but this difference
        was. (And I don't even want to mention Ivan, so Malina
        won't find out anything, because even though Ivan wants
        to drive old age right out of me, I would still like to keep
        it so that Ivan won't age in relation to me.) You're just
        a tiny bit younger than I am, that gives you enormous
        power, take advantage of it, I will submit, I can do that
        on occasion. And this is not the result of any rational
        deliberation. It stems from either affinity or aversion, I
        can no longer change it. I am afraid.

Malina: I may be older than you.
Me: You certainly are not, I know that for a fact. You came
          after me, you can't have been there before I was, you're
          completely inconceivable before me.

I don't especially trust the last days of June, but I've often determined that I especially like people who were born in summer. Malina rejects observations of this kind with disdain, I might sooner come to him with questions about astrology which I don't understand at all. Frau Senta Novak, who is very much in demand in theatrical circles, but who is also consulted by industrialists and politicians, once drew all my configurations and possible tendencies into circles and quadrants, she showed me my horoscope which struck her as incredibly curious, I should have a look myself and see how sharply it is defined, she said that at first glance my chart shows an incredible tension, it's really not a picture of one person but of two people standing in extreme opposition to one another, which must mean that I am always on the verge of being torn in two, with configurations like these, if all the dates I had given were accurate. I asked hopefully: The torn man, the torn woman, right? If they were separated it would be livable, maintained Frau Novak, but scarcely the way it is, furthermore male and female, reason and feeling, productivity and self-destruction also stand out in an unlikely manner. I must have made a mistake with my dates, since she liked me right away, I'm such a natural woman, she likes natural people.

Malina treats everything with a uniform seriousness, he doesn't find superstitions and pseudosciences any more ridiculous than the sciences, which themselves were based on superstitions and pseudosciences, as every passing decade reveals more and more clearly, and which are compelled to renounce so many conclusions in order to progress. Dispassionate is the best way to describe how

Malina devotes himself to everything, people as well as ideas and things, and thus he belongs to that rare breed of men who, without being entirely self-sufficient, have neither friend nor foe. He also devotes himself to me, sometimes biding his time, sometimes paying close attention, he lets me do what I please, he says you only understand people if you don't press them, if you don't demand anything and don't let them provoke you, everything is revealed without all that. This balance inside him, this equanimity, will eventually drive me to despair, since I react to every situation, submit to every emotional upheaval and suffer the losses—which Malina notices, detachedly.

There are people who think that Malina and I are married. We never once considered that we might be, that such a possibility could exist, nor even that other people might think we were. For the longest time it never even crossed our minds that wherever we go, like other people, we appear as a man and a woman or even man and wife. This was a complete surprise for us, we had no idea what to make of it. We laughed a lot.

On a given morning, for example, while I'm walking around exhausted and absentmindedly fixing breakfast, Malina is capable of showing interest in the child who lives across the courtyard and for a whole year has been shouting only two words: Helloo, Helloo! holla, holla! Once I was on the verge of interfering, I wanted to go over and speak to the mother, since she apparently doesn't talk to the child at all, since what's happening here makes me worry about the future, and since this daily helloo and holla is torture to my ears, worse than Lina's vacuuming, running water or breaking plates. But Malina must hear something different and doesn't think I have to call the doctors or the child welfare representatives right away, he listens to this child's calling just as if another kind of being had arisen, one which seems no stranger to him than those beings whose vocabulary contains more than a hundred or a thousand or several thousand words. I believe Malina is completely indifferent to change or transformation, since nowhere does he see anything good, bad or least of all better. The world seems to exist for him exactly as it is, exactly as he first discovered it. And nonetheless he sometimes scares me because his view of a person is informed by the greatest, most comprehensive knowledge, impossible to acquire at any given place or time and impossible to impart to others. His listening insults me deeply, because behind everything that's said he also appears to hear things unsaid—as well as what's said too often. I myself often imagine too much, and Malina often points out my delusions, still I can't imagine how precise and how extraordinary his sight and hearing really are. I suspect he doesn't see through people or unmask them, as that would be very common and cheap, even vile in its attitude toward others. Malina beholds people, and that is something entirely different, since that does not diminish, but rather enlarges them, they become more unearthly, and my imaginative faculty, which he ridicules, is probably a very inferior variant of what he himself uses to develop, fill out, distinguish and perfect everything. So I no longer discuss the three murderers with Malina and have even less desire to talk about the fourth, about whom I don't have to tell Malina a thing, for although I have my own form of expression I have only very little skill at description. Malina doesn't want any descriptions and impressions of some dinner or other I once spent in the company of murderers. He would have gone all the way and not contented himself with a mere impression or this dull unease, he would have presented me with the real murderer and used this confrontation to force me into a realization.

Since I let my head droop, Ivan says: You just don't have anything that requires you to be there!

He'll win his case, because who wants anything from me, who needs me? But Malina should help me find a reason for my being here, since I don't have an old father to support in his old age, I don't have any children always needing something, like Ivan's: warmth, winter coats, cough syrups, gym shoes. Nor does the law of conservation of energy apply to me. I am the first perfect example of waste—extravagant, ecstatic and incapable of putting the world to any reasonable use, able to show up at the masked ball of society, or stay away like someone who has been detained, or has forgotten to make a mask, or can no longer find his costume out of carelessness, and so one day will no longer be invited. When I stand in front of a familiar door in Vienna, perhaps because I am invited, it occurs to me at the last moment it might be the wrong door, or day or hour, and I turn around and drive back to the Ungargasse, too quickly tired, too much in doubt.

Malina asks: Have you never thought how much trouble other people have often gone to because of you? I nod thankfully. They have indeed, they didn't spare themselves the trouble of providing me with character traits either, they equipped me with stories, and even with money as well, so that I can run around in clothes and eat leftovers, so that I can continue to make do and so it won't be too obvious how I am doing. Too quickly tired I can sit down in the Café Museum and leaf through newspapers and magazines. Hope springs up inside me once again, I am animated and excited because there's now a direct flight to Canada twice a week, you can fly to Australia in comfort on Qantas, safaris are getting cheaper, in Vienna we should soon see Doro-coffee with its unique aroma from the sunny high plains of Central America, Kenya is advertised, Henkell Rosée lets you flirt with a new world, no building is too high for Hitachi elevators, men's books are now available which are just as inspiring for women. To make sure your world never gets too confined, there's PRESTIGE, a breath of wide-open space and the sea. Everyone is talking about mortgages—You're in good hands with us, proclaims a mortgage bank. You'll go a long way in TARRACO shoes. We coat your Flexalum blinds twice so you'll never have to varnish them again, a RUF-Computer is never alone! And then the Antilles, le bon voyage. That's why the Bosch EXQUISIT is one of the best dishwashers in the world. The moment of truth is coming when customers ask our experts questions, when process technology, calculation, rate of return, packaging machines, delivery times are all up for debate, VIVIOPTAL to jog your memory. Take it in the morning … and the day belongs to you! So all I need is Vivioptal.

I wanted to conquer in a sign, but since I am not needed, since I have been told this, it is I who have been conquered by Ivan and these gyerekek whom I might be allowed to accompany to the movies once again, Walt Disney's MICKY MAUS is playing in the Burg cinema. Who should conquer if not they. But it may not just be Ivan, perhaps something greater has conquered me, it must be something greater, since everything is driving us to one destiny. Sometimes I still wonder what I might do for Ivan, since there's nothing I wouldn't do for him, but Ivan doesn't demand that I jump out the window, that I leap into the Danube for his sake, that I throw myself in front of a car, perhaps to save Béla and András, he has so very little time and no needs. Nor does he want me to replace Frau Agnes and clean his two rooms and wash and iron his clothes, he only wants to drop by, receive three cubes of ice in his whiskey and ask how things are, he'll also let me ask how things are with him and how things are at the Hohe Warte. On the Kärntnerring it's always the same thing: a lot of work, but nothing special. There isn't enough time to play chess, I'm no longer making any progress since we play less and less. I don't know when we started playing so much less, we really don't play at all anymore, the chess sentence sets are lying fallow, other sentence sets are also suffering

losses. It just can't be that the sentences which we discovered so
slowly are also slowly leaving us. A new group emerges.

Unfortunately I'm, my time's a little
Of course if you're so pressed for time
It's just today my time is particularly
Naturally if you don't have any time now
When I have some more time
In time we'll manage, it's just right now
Then we'll be able to, once you have time
Just right at this time, when it's on again
Over time you'll just have to be a little less
If I only make it on time
Oh my, time is really flying, you shouldn't stay too late
I've never had so little time, it's unfortunately
Maybe when you have more time then
I'll have more time later!

Every day, sometimes even cheerfully, Malina and I muse on what
horrible things might yet still happen tonight in Vienna. Because
once you've let yourself get carried away reading the newspaper,
once you've accepted the credulity of a few reported events, then
your powers of imagination shift into high gear (not my expression
and not exactly Malina's, but it did amuse Malina enough that he
brought it back from a trip to Germany, since words like "high
gear" can only be found in countries of such motion and activity). But I can never manage to abstain from reading newspapers
for long, although I am experiencing increasingly longer periods
when I read none at all or at most one I've removed from the storage room where a stack of old magazines and newspapers is lying
next to our suitcases, I look at the date with dismay: July 3, 1958.
What arrogance! Even on this day long past they drugged us with

unwanted news, with commentaries on the news, they informed us about earthquakes, airplane crashes, domestic political scandals, foreign policy blunders. When I look down today at the paper from July 3, 1958, trying to believe in the date and a day to go with it, a day which may have indeed existed, but on which I can find nothing written in my calendar, no abbreviated marks—"3 PM R! 5 PM called B, evening Gösser, Lecture K."—all entered under July 4 but not under July 3, where the page remained completely blank. Perhaps a day without riddles, certainly without headaches too, without states of fear, without unbearable memories, with only a few memories at all, derived from various times, but perhaps just a day on which Lina performed a big summer cleaning and drove me out of the house into various cafés, where I read a newspaper from July 3, which I am again reading today. And with that this day does become a riddle: an empty, robbed day when I grew older, when I didn't resist and when I allowed something to happen.

I also find a magazine from a certain July 3, and on Malina's shelves the July issues of a journal for culture and politics, and I begin to read every which way since I'd like to learn all about this day. Books are announced I never saw. WHERE TO WITH ALL THE MONEY? is one of the least understandable titles, not even Malina will be able to explain that to me. Where then is the money, and where would anyone go with what money? That's a good start all right, titles like that can make me shiver and shake. HOW TO STAGE A COUP D'ÉTAT. Written with authoritative expertise and dry, casually sarcastic humor ... Reading tips for readers who want to think politically, who want to be enlightened ... Do we need that, Malina? I take a pen and begin filling out a questionnaire. I am satisfactorily, well, very well, better than average informed. The pen first smears, then seems to be empty, then again writes in a fine line. I make x's in little empty boxes. Does your husband give you presents never, seldom, to surprise you, or only on birthdays and anniversaries? I have to be very careful, everything depends on whether I'm thinking about Malina or Ivan, and I go on writing x's for both, for example giving Ivan a never, Malina a to-surprise-me, but that's not a reliable answer. Do you dress to look good for others or to please HIM? Do you visit the hairdresser's regularly, weekly, once a month or only when you absolutely need to? What kind of absolute need is meant? Which coup d'état? My hair is hanging over the coup d'état in absolute need, since I don't know whether I should have it cut or not. Ivan thinks I should let it grow. Malina thinks it has to be cut. With a sigh I count the x's. In the end Ivan has a total of 26 points, Malina also has 26 points, although I had to make x's in completely different boxes for each. I add again. The totals of 26 points for each remain. "I am 17 years old and feel I cannot love. I get interested in a man for a few days but switch to another right away. Am I a monster? My boyfriend of the moment is 19 years old and is desperate because he wants to marry me." Blue Blitz Express crashes into Red Blitz, 107 dead and 80 wounded.

But that was years ago, and now it's being dished out once more, automobile accidents, a few crimes, announcements of summit meetings, conjectures about the weather. Today no one knows anymore why that all had to be reported. Back then they recommended Panteen Spray, which I've only been using for the past few years, I don't need their advice on a July 3 so long forgotten, and even less today.

In the evening I say to Malina: A hairspray might be all that's left, and maybe that covers everything, as I still don't know where to go with all the money and how to stage a coup d'état, and at any rate I am throwing too much money away. Now they've done it. Once this can is empty I'm not buying another. You have 26 points, you can't ask for any more, I just can't give you any more. Do with them what you want. Do you remember when the Blue Blitz crashed into the Red Blitz? Thank you very much! That's what I thought, so that's how much you care about catastrophes, you're no better than I am. But it's probably all an unbelievable swindle.

Because Malina hasn't understood a word, while I'm see-sawing in the rocking chair and he's making himself comfortable, and after he brings us something to drink I begin to explain:

It's all an unbelievable swindle, I once worked for a news service, I saw the swindle from up close, the origin of the bulletins, the indiscriminate pasting together of sentences flowing off the tele-type. One day I was supposed to switch to the night shift because someone was sick. At eleven o'clock in the evening a big black car picked me up, the chauffeur made a small detour in the Third District, and somewhere near the Reisnerstrasse a young man climbed in, a certain Pittermann, we were driven to the Seidengasse, where all the offices were dark and abandoned. Only rarely did someone appear, even at the night desks of the editorial office located in the same building. The night porter led us to the farthest rooms, over planking since the corridors were torn up, on some floor I have forgotten, I can't remember, I don't remember anything . . . Four of us were there every night, I made coffee, sometimes we had ice cream delivered around midnight, the night porter knew where to get ice cream. The men read the sheets of paper spat out by the teletypes, they cut, pasted and collated. We didn't actually whisper, but it's almost impossible to speak loudly at night when the whole city is asleep, the men must have laughed now and then, I just quietly drank coffee by myself and smoked, they would toss reports on my small table with the typewriter, random reports chosen by whim, and I would rewrite them into clean copy. Because I didn't know of anything to laugh about with the others, I wound up becoming thoroughly familiar with whatever news would wake people up the following morning. The men always closed with a short paragraph concerning some baseball game or boxing match from across the Atlantic.

Malina: What was your life like back then?
Me: At three in the morning my face would turn grayer and

grayer, I slowly deteriorated, it bowed me down, I was bowed down at the time. I lost a very important rhythm, you can never regain that. I would drink another coffee, and another, my hand often started shaking while I wrote, and later my handwriting went completely to pieces.

Malina: That's probably why I'm the only one who can still read it.

Me: The second part of the night doesn't have anything to do with the first, two different nights are housed in one night, you have to picture the first night as high-spirited, jokes are still being told, fingers are hitting the keys quickly, everybody's still in motion, the two small slim Eurasians fancy themselves smarter and more ex-travagant than the fussy Herr Pittermann, who moves so clumsily and loudly. Movement is important, because it's easy to imagine that elsewhere during the night people are still drinking and shouting, possibly embracing or wearing themselves out dancing—all out of boredom with the present day and revulsion at the next. In the first night it's still the day, with all its excesses, which is the decisive factor. You don't realize it's really night until the second night comes, everyone has grown calmer, here and there someone has gotten up to stretch, or secretly find some other movement even though all of us had ar-rived at the news service well rested. Around five o'clock in the morning it was horrible, everyone was weighed down by some burden, I would go wash my hands and rub my fingers with a dirty old handtowel. The build-ings in the Seidengasse were as eerie as a murder scene. Where I heard steps there would be none, the teletypes would be still, then again start to rattle, I would run back into our big room where you could already smell the perspiration, even through the cigarette fumes. It was the beginning of fatigue. At seven in the morning we scarcely said good-bye to one another, I climbed into the black car with young Pittermann, we looked out the windows without saying a word. Women were carrying fresh milk and fresh rolls, men were walking with purposeful, confident steps, with briefcases under their arms and coat collars upturned and puffing out small early morning clouds. In the limousine we had dirty fingernails and our mouths were brownish and bitter, once again the young man climbed out near the Reisnerstrasse while I got out at the Beatrixgasse. I dragged myself upstairs by the railing and was scared I'd run into the baroness who left the building at this time, on her way to the municipal welfare office, because she disapproved of my mysterious coming home at this hour. Afterward it took me a long time to get to sleep, I'd lie on the bed in my clothes, smelling foul, around noon I'd manage to discard my clothes and actually sleep, but it wasn't a good sleep, since it was constantly interrupted by everyday noises from outside. The bulletin was already in circulation, the news reports were already having an effect, I never read them. I went without news for two whole years.

Malina: So you weren't living. When did you try to live, what were you waiting for?

Me: Esteemed Malina, there must have also been a few hours and one free day a week for very limited undertakings. But I don't know how people live the first part of their life, it must be like the first part of the night, high-spirited, it's just hard for me to gather those hours up, because that's when I entered the age of reason, that must have claimed the rest of my time.

I dreaded the big black car, which called to mind secret drives, espionage, sinister intrigues, at that time there were always rumors floating through Vienna that there was a loading ramp—an

Umschlagplatz—that there was a slave trade, that people and papers disappeared wrapped up in rugs, that everyone was working for some side or another, without even knowing it. No side revealed anything. Everyone who worked was a prostitute without knowing it, where have I heard that before? Why did I laugh at that? It was the beginning of universal prostitution.

Malina: Once you described it to me completely differently. After the university you found work in some office, it paid all right but not really, so later you took the night shift, since you could earn more money than during the day.

Me: I'm not telling, I won't talk, I can't, it's more than a mere disturbance in my memory. Tell me instead what you did today in your Arsenal.

Malina: Nothing much. The usual things, and then some film people came, they need a battle with Turks. Kurt Swoboda is looking for something to use as a model, he has a commission. Besides we've already given permission for another film that the Germans want to shoot in the Hall of Fame.

Me: Someday I'd like to watch a movie being made. Or be an extra. Wouldn't that make me think of something else for a change?

Malina: That's just boring, it goes on for hours, days, you trip over cables, everyone's just standing around, and most of the time nothing is happening. Sunday I'm on duty. I'm only mentioning it so you can make your plans.

Me: So now we can go eat, but I'm not quite ready. Let me make one phone call, please, it'll just take a minute. Just one minute, ok?

There is a disturbance in my memory, I shatter against every memory. Back then in the ruins there was no hope at all—so people said and kept repeating—they tried to sound convincing by describing a time they called the first postwar era. You never heard anything about a second one. That too was a swindle. I almost believed it myself—that once the window and door frames are reinstalled, once the mountains of rubble disappear, then all of a sudden everything will be better, people will again live in their homes and be able to continue living. But just the fact that for years I wanted to say how strange I found this living—and continued living—is very revealing, though no one wanted to listen to me. I would never have thought that everything would first have to be plundered, stolen, pawned and then bought and sold three times over. The biggest black market was supposedly at the Resselpark, because of its many dangers you had to give it plenty of room, beginning in the late afternoon, all the way up to Karlsplatz. One day the black market ostensibly ceased to exist. But I'm not convinced. A universal black market resulted, and whenever I buy cigarettes or eggs, I know—but really only as of today—that they come from the black market. Anyway the whole market is black, it can't have been that black before because it still lacked a universal density. Later on, after all the display windows were full and while everything was piling up, the cans, the boxes, the cartons, I could no longer buy anything. Scarcely would I step into the large department stores on the Mariahilfer Strasse, for example Gerngross, than I would feel nauseous, Christine had advised me to avoid the small expensive shops, Lina was more for Herzmansky's than Gerngross, and I did try, but I just couldn't, I can't look at more than one thing at a time. Thousands of fabrics, thousands of tin cans, of sausages, shoes and buttons, the whole mass of items before my eyes blackens each single thing. In large numbers everything gets much too threatened, a quantity needs to remain something abstract, has to be the postulate of a theory, has to remain operable, it has to have the purity of mathematics, only mathematics allows billions to be beautiful, a billion apples, on the other hand, is unpalatable, a ton of coffee in itself testifies to countless crimes, a billion people is inconceivably depraved, pitiful, loathsome, entangled in a black market, daily needing billions of potatoes, rations of rice and loaves of bread. Long after there was plenty to eat I still couldn't eat well, and even now I can only eat when someone else is eating with me, or if I'm alone and there's just an apple lying there and a piece of bread or a leftover slice of sausage. It has to be something left over.

Malina: Well we probably won't eat at all today if you don't stop talking about it. We could drive up to Cobenzl, get up, get dressed, otherwise it'll be too late.

Me: Please not up there. I don't want to have the city at my feet, why do we have to have a whole city at our feet when we only want to eat dinner. Let's just go someplace nearby. To the Alter Heller.

It began as early as Paris, after my first escape from Vienna, for a while I couldn't walk very well on my left foot, it hurt, and the pain was accompanied by groaning, oh God, oh God. Dangerous impulses of great consequence are often felt first in the body, where they cause certain words to be pronounced: previously my only acquaintance with God was a conceptual one from philosophical seminars, along with being, nothingness, essence, existence, the Brahma.

In Paris I mostly had no money, but always, whenever the money was coming to an end, I had to spend it on something special, incidentally this is still true today, after all it can't be spent on just anything, I have to have a final inspiration as to how it should be spent, for if an idea does come to me I know at least for a moment that I too, populate the world, that I am a part of a constantly, heavily increasing, lightly decreasing population, and am aware that this world, overcrowded with a needy population, an insatiable population living in a constant state of emergency, is spinning through the universe, and as long as I am hanging on to it by means of gravity, with nothing in my pocket and an inspiration in my head, I know what is to be done.

Back then, in the vicinity of the Rue Monge, on the way to Place de la Contrescarpe, I bought two bottles of red wine in a little bistro that was open all night, then a bottle of white wine as well. I thought to myself, maybe somebody doesn't like red wine, after all you can't sentence a person to red wine. The men slept or acted as if they were sleeping, and I crept over to them and placed the bottles near enough to avoid misunderstanding. They had to understand the bottles were legally theirs. When I did it again another night, one of the clochards woke up and said something about God, "que Dieu vous …" and later I heard something in England like "… bless you." Naturally I've forgotten the circumstances. I assume that those who have been wounded sometimes talk that way to others equally blessed with such wounds, and then go on living somewhere, just as I, too, go on living somewhere, blessed with all kinds of wounds.

Among the men in Paris, but I don't know whether it was he who had woken up in the night, there was one called Marcel, his name is all I remember, a key word next to other key words like Rue Monge, like the name of two or three hotels and room number 26. But I do know that Marcel is no longer alive, and that the style of his death was most unusual …

Malina interrupts me, he is protecting me, but I think that his wanting to protect me is preventing me from telling. It's Malina who isn't letting me talk.

Me: Do you think nothing else will ever change in my life?
Malina: What are you really thinking about? About Marcel, or
          still about the same one thing, or about everything that's
          made you feel like you've been double-crossed.
Me: What's that again about a cross? Since when do you use
          the same figures of speech as everyone else?
Malina: Up to now you've always understood perfectly well, with
          or without figures of speech.
Me: Give me today's paper. You've spoiled the whole story for
          me, later on you'll regret you didn't hear the very amaz-
          ing end of Marcel, since I'm the only one left who can tell
          it. The others are either living somewhere or they've died
          somewhere. Marcel is certainly forgotten.

Malina has handed me the newspaper he sometimes brings back
from the museum. I skip the first pages and look at the horoscope.
"With a little more courage you will be able to master upcoming
difficulties. Be careful in traffic. Obtain abundant sleep." In Malina's horoscope there's something about affairs of the heart taking
a stormy turn, but that should hardly interest him. Apart from that
he should spare his bronchia. I never thought that Malina might
even have bronchia.

Me: What are your bronchia doing? Do you really have bron-
          chia?
Malina: Why not? Why shouldn't I? Everybody has bronchia.
          Since when are you concerned about my health?
Me: I'm only asking. How were things today, was it very
          stormy?
Malina: Where? Certainly not in the Arsenal. Not that I would
          know. I was filing documents.

Me: Not even a little stormy? Maybe if you think back really
          hard, wasn't it just a tiny bit stormy?
Malina: Why are you looking at me so suspiciously? Don't you
          believe me? This is ridiculous, and why are you staring
          that way, what is it you see? That's not a spider and it's
          not a tarantula either, you made that stain yourself a few
          days ago, when you were pouring coffee. What do you
          see?

I see that something is missing from the table. But what? Something used to lie here. There was almost always a pack of Ivan's
cigarettes, half-full, he always forgot one on purpose, so that if he
needed a cigarette he could have one right away. I realize he hasn't
forgotten a pack for quite some time.

Me: Haven't you ever considered living somewhere else?
          Where there's more green. For example in Hietzing a
          very nice apartment will be opening up soon, Christine
          knows about it from friends whose friends are moving
          away from there. You'd have more room for your books.
          Here there's no more room at all, the bookshelves are all
          overflowing because of your mania, I don't have anything
          against your mania, but it is manic. And you also claim
          you still smell cat urine in the hallway from Frances and
          Trollope. Lina says she doesn't notice anything anymore,
          it's just your sensitivity, you're so sensitive.
Malina: I haven't understood a word you're saying. Why should
          we pack up and move to Hietzing? Neither one of us ever
          wanted to live in Hietzing or the Hohe Warte or in Dö-
          bling.
Me: Please not the Hohe Warte! I said Hietzing. I never imag-
          ined you had anything against Hietzing!

Malina: One is just like the other, and they're both out of the question. So don't start crying right away.

Me: I didn't say a word about the Hohe Warte, and don't think I'm starting to cry. I just have the sniffles. I have to obtain more abundant sleep. Of course we're staying in the Ungargasse. Anything else is out of the question.

What would I like to do today? Let me think! I don't want to go out, I don't want to read or listen to music either. I'll just have to content myself with you. But I'm going to keep you entertained, since it occurred to me that we've never talked about men, that you never ask about the men. However you didn't do a very good job hiding your old book. I was reading it today, it's not good, for example you describe a man, presumably yourself, just before he falls asleep, but really I'm the only one who could have been your model. Men always fall asleep right away. Furthermore why don't you find men as profoundly interesting as I do?

Malina says: Maybe I imagine all men are like myself.

I reply: That's the most absurd thing you could imagine. A woman could sooner imagine she's like all other women, and a woman would have more reason to do so. Once again it has to do with men, you see.

For show, Malina throws up his hands indignantly: But please no stories or at most just a few fragments, if they're amusing enough. Say what you can without committing any indiscretion.

Malina really should know who I am!

I continue: Men differ from one another, you see, and every single one should actually be considered an incurable clinical case, consequently the textbooks and treatises don't come close to explaining and understanding even a single man in his rudimentariness. It's a thousand times easier to understand a man's cerebral aspect, at least for me. And although this is supposed to be their common trait, it most assuredly is not. What a mistake!

The material required to make such a generalization could not be compiled in centuries. A single woman has to come to terms with too many peculiarities as it is, and no one ever told her before-hand what symptoms she would have to accommodate and brace up for, you could say the whole attitude of men toward women is diseased, what's more it's so exceptionally diseased that men will never be completely freed from their diseases. At most it might be said of women that they are more or less marked by the contamina-tions they've contracted by sympathizing with the suffering.

You're in a very ornery mood today. It's beginning to entertain me after all.

I say happily: It must make a person sick to have so few new experiences that he has to constantly repeat himself, for example a man bites my earlobe, but not because it's my earlobe or because he's crazy about earlobes and absolutely has to bite them, he bites them because he's bitten the earlobes of all the other women, whether small or large, purple, pale, sensitive or numb, he doesn't care what the earlobes think about it. You have to admit that this is a serious compulsion if a man—who may be equipped with more or less knowledge but always only a limited possibility of putting this knowledge to use—if a man like that feels obliged to pounce on a woman, possibly for years and years, once would be all right, any woman can stand it once. That also explains this secret, vague suspicion men have, since they can't imagine that a woman naturally has to behave completely differently with some other diseased man, since he has nothing but a shallow, superfi-cial awareness of these different variations, mostly the ones passed around from mouth to mouth or those which science casts in an exacerbatedly evil light. Malina really doesn't have a clue. He says: I thought that some men must be especially talented, at any rate you occasionally hear talk about someone in particular or else more generally—about the Greeks for instance. (Malina looks at me slyly, then laughs, then I laugh as well.) I try to stay serious: In

Greece I happened to be lucky, but just that once. Sometimes a person gets lucky, but I'm sure most women are never lucky. What I'm talking about has nothing to do with the supposition that there are some men who are good lovers, there really aren't. That is a legend that has to be destroyed someday, at most there are men with whom it is completely hopeless and a few with whom it's not quite so hopeless. Although no one has bothered to inquire, that is the reason why only women always have their heads full of feelings and stories, with their man or men. Such thoughts really do consume the greatest part of every woman's time. But she has to think about it, because without her unflagging pushing and prompting of feelings, she could literally never bear being with a man, since every man truly is sick and hardly takes any notice of her. It's easy for him to think so little about women, because his diseased system is infallible, he repeats, he has repeated, he will repeat. If he likes kissing feet, he'll kiss the feet of fifty more women, why should he risk dwelling on or worrying about a creature who is right now enjoying letting him kiss her feet, at least that's what he thinks. A woman, however, must come to terms with the fact that now, because her feet happen to have their turn, she has to invent unbelievable feelings and all day long has to shelter her real feelings in the ones she's invented, on the one hand just to stand the whole business with the feet, but above all to stand the greater part that's missing, because anyone who's so hung up on feet is bound to be greatly neglecting something else. In addition to this there are the sudden readjustments, from one man to another a woman's body must unlearn everything and once again adapt to something entirely new. But a man simply continues his habits in peace, sometimes that works out, if he's lucky, mostly it doesn't.

Malina is not pleased with me: Now that is something completely new to me, I was so convinced you liked men, and you have always found men attractive, their company alone was indispensable for you, even if no longer ...

Of course men have always interested me, but that's precisely why they don't have to be liked, in fact I didn't like most of them, they always only fascinated me, just because of the thought: what's he going to do once he's finished biting my shoulder, what does he expect will happen next? Or else someone exposes his back on which, long before you, some woman once took her fingernails, her five claws, and left five stripes, forever visible, so you get completely distraught or at least discombobulated, what are you supposed to do with this back, which constantly reminds you of some ecstatic moment or attack of pain, then what pain are you still supposed to feel, what ecstasy? For the longest time I had no feelings at all, since during those years I was entering the age of reason. Nonetheless, like all other women I naturally always had men on my mind, for the abovementioned reasons, and I'm sure that in turn the men gave very little thought to me, only after work, or maybe on a day off.

Malina: No exception?
Me: There was just one.
Malina: How was there just one exception?

That's simple. You only have to make someone unhappy enough, just by chance, for example, by not helping someone make up for some stupidity. Once you're sure you've really made someone miserable then he's bound to be thinking about you. However, most men usually make women unhappy, and there's no reciprocity, as our misfortune is natural, inevitable, stemming as it does from the disease of men, for whose sake women have to bear so much in mind, continually modifying what they've just learned—for, as a rule, if you have to constantly brood about somebody, and generate feelings about him, then you're going to be unhappy. What's more, your misfortune will grow with time, it will double, triple, increase a hundredfold. All someone who wants to avoid unhappiness needs to do is call things off every time after a few days. It's impossible to be unhappy and cry over somebody unless he's already made you thoroughly unhappy to begin with. No one cries over a man after just a few hours, no matter how young or handsome, intelligent or kind. But half a year spent with a full-blown blabbermouth, a notorious idiot, a repulsive weakling given to the strangest habits—that has broken even strong and rational women, driven them to suicide, just think if you will of Erna Zanetti, who on account of this lecturer in theater studies (can you imagine, on account of a theatrical scholar!) is said to have swallowed forty sleeping pills, and I'm sure she's not the only one, he also got her to stop smoking, because he couldn't stand the smoke. I don't know whether she had to become a vegetarian or not, but I'm sure some other horrible things happened as well. Now instead of being glad that this idiot left her, instead of going out the next day and enjoying twenty cigarettes or eating whatever she wanted, she loses her head and tries to kill herself, she can't think of anything better since she's been thinking about him incessantly and suffering because of him for months, naturally also because of nicotine withdrawal and all those lettuce leaves and carrots.

Malina pretends to be horrified but has to laugh: You're not claiming that women are more unhappy than men, are you!

Of course not, I'm only saying that women face an unhappiness which is particularly inevitable and absolutely unnecessary. I was only talking about the kind of unhappiness. You can't compare, and today we weren't claiming to talk about general unhappiness, which seems to hit all people so hard. I'm just trying to keep you entertained and tell you what's funny or odd or amusing. I, for example, was very dissatisfied that I was never raped. When I arrived here the Russians had lost all desire to rape the Viennese women, and there were also fewer and fewer drunk Americans, whom nobody really considered proper rapists anyway, which is why there was so much less talk about their deeds than those of the Russians, for naturally there are reasons for a sanctioned, devoutly practiced terror. From fifteen-year-old girls to ninety-year-old grandmas, so the saying went. Sometimes you could still read something in the papers about two Negroes in uniform, but please, two Negroes roaming around Salzburg is richly inadequate for one province with so many women, and the men I met or didn't meet and who only walked by me in the woods or saw me sitting on a stone at a brook, alone and defenseless, never had the idea. You wouldn't believe it, but apart from a few drunks, a few sex murderers and others who get into the papers where they are designated as sex offenders, no normal man with normal drives has the obvious idea that a normal woman would like to be quite normally raped. Part of it is that men aren't normal, but people lose sight of the full extent of the male pathology, so accustomed have they become to men's aberrant behavior and their phenomenal lack of instinct. In Vienna, however, it could be different, it must not be that bad, since the city is made for universal prostitution. You probably can't remember the first years after the war. Vienna was, to put it mildly, a city equipped with the strangest institutions. But this time has now been expunged from the city's annals, no one talks about it anymore. It's not exactly forbidden, but even so people don't talk about it. On holidays, even church holidays such as Marian feast days or Ascension or days commemorating the republic, citizens were forced to the Stadtpark, on the side bordering the Ringstrasse, the Parkring, they had to go to this horrible park and do in public whatever they wanted or were able to do, especially when the horse chestnuts were blooming, but later as well, once the nuts ripened and opened and fell to the ground. There was hardly anyone who hadn't run into every man with every woman. Although it all took place in silence, almost with complete indifference, you could still describe what went on as a nightmare, the whole city participated in this universal prostitution, every woman must have lain on the trampled lawn with every man or else they leaned against the walls, moaning and groaning, panting, sometimes several at a time, by turns, promiscuously. Everyone slept with everyone else, everyone used each other, and so today no one should be surprised that there are hardly ever any rumors, for today the same men and women greet one another politely, as if nothing had happened, the men doff their hats and kiss the hands of the ladies, who in turn stroll past the Stadtpark with a light gait and whispered greetings, looking flattered as they carry their elegant purses and parasols. But the round dance continues, this La Ronde that stems from that time, and which today is no longer anonymous. The relations which reign today must be seen as part of this epidemic, for instance why Ödön Pataki was first seen with Franziska Ranner, but then Franziska Ranner with Leo Jordan, why Leo Jordan later married twice more after his marriage to Elvira, who in turn helped young Marek, why young Marek ultimately ruined Fanny Goldmann, and why beforehand she had gotten along all too well with Harry and then went off with Milan, but young Marek started seeing Karin Krause, that petite German woman, but later on Marek was also with Elisabeth Mihailovics, who then fell in with Bertold Rapatz, who in turn ... Now I know all that, and I know why Martin had this grotesque affair with Elfi Nemec, who later also ended up with Leo Jordan, and I know why everybody is connected with everybody else in the most peculiar way, even if only a few of them actually realize it. Of course no one knows the reasons, but I see why already, and one day everyone shall see! But I can't tell everything, since I don't have time for that. Even if I just consider the role the Altenwyls' house played in all this, although they themselves were never aware—generally speaking none of the hosts ever knew, including Barbara Gebauder—of what was germinating and to what end, what all the foolish chatter was wreaking and to what end. Society is the biggest murder scene of all. In it the seeds of the most incredible crimes are sown in the subtlest manner, crimes which remain forever unknown to the courts of this world. I didn't discover that because I never looked and never listened very exactly, and now I listen less and less, but the less I listen, the more I am shocked by the connections I am beginning to see. I was living immoderately, which is why I felt the full effects of these peace games—that's how they're passed off, as if they weren't really war games—in all their monstrousness. By comparison all the worldwide and world-famous crimes—as well as the ones known all over town—seem simple by comparison: brutal, devoid of mystery, something for psychiatrists and mass psychologists, who are also unable to curb the misdeeds, since the riddles these crimes pose to the all-too-diligent experts are so terrifically primitive. But what was and still is happening here on the other hand was never primitive. Do you remember that one evening? Fanny Goldmann went home surprisingly early and unaccompanied, she got up and left the table, nothing had happened, but today I know, I know the reason. There are words, looks that can kill, no one notices, everybody is clinging to a facade, a complete distortion. And Klara and Haderer, before he died, but I'll stop here ...

For some time, it was in Rome, I only had eyes for sailors, on Sundays they stand around some plaza, I think the Piazza del Popolo, where at night people from the countryside would try to walk to the Corso in a straight line, blindfolded, starting at the fountain with the obelisk. It's an impossible task. Sailors can also be seen standing around in the Villa Borghese, but many more soldiers. They stare into space with this serious, greedy gaze fixed on a Sunday which will be over at any minute. It's fascinating to watch these young men. And then for a while I was completely captivated by a mechanic from the Erdberg, he had to hammer out one of my car's fenders and respray the body. For me he was impenetrable, of a deeply serious demeanor, just imagine these glances and those tedious, slow thoughts! I went back a few times and watched him at all sorts of jobs. I have never seen so much anguish in someone, so much earnest ignorance. Completely impervious. Sad hopes flashed up inside me, sad, oppressive desires, nothing more: after all, these men would never understand it, but then who really wants to be understood anyway. Who in the world wants that!

I was always very timid, not bold by any means, I would have had to leave my telephone number and my address with him, but in his presence I was too engrossed in a riddle and couldn't do it. It may be easy to guess, if not every thought, then every second thought of an Einstein, a Faraday, some shining beacon, a Freud or a Liebig, as they are men without true secrets. But beauty is far superior, as is its wordlessness. This mechanic was more important to me, this mechanic, whom I'll never forget, to whom I made pilgrimages, only to ask for the bill in the end, nothing more. He was important to me. For it is precisely beauty that is more important, beauty which I lack and which I want to seduce. Sometimes I'll be walking down a street and scarcely do I see someone superior to me than I feel myself being drawn in that direction, but is this natural or normal? Am I a woman or something dimorphic? Am I not entirely female—what am I, anyway? The news is often filled with such ghastly reports. In Pötzleinsdorf, at the Prater, in the Vienna Woods, in every outskirt of the city a woman has been murdered, strangled—it almost happened to me, too, but not in the outskirts—strangled by some brutal individual, and then I always think to myself: that could be you, that will be you. An unknown woman murdered by some unknown man.

I've made up a pretext and have dropped in at Ivan's. I love to play with his transistor radio. Once again I've gone for days without news. Ivan advises me to at last buy a radio if I like hearing the news or listening to music so much. He thinks it would help me get up in the morning, the way it helps him for example, and at night I'd have something against the silence, I try turning the knob slowly, carefully searching for what might emerge against the silence.

An excited male voice is in the room: Dear listeners, we now have London on the line, our permanent correspondent Doctor Alfons Werth, Herr Werth will be right here reporting to us from London, just a moment's patience, we take you now to London, dear Herr Doktor Werth, we hear you loud and clear, I'd like to ask you in the name of our listeners in Austria about the mood in London following the devaluation of the pound, Herr Werth is now on the air ...

Turn that box off would you please! says Ivan, who right now has no interest in opinions from London or Athens.

Ivan?

What are you trying to say?

Why don't you ever let me talk?

Ivan must have some history behind him, must have been in a cyclone, and he thinks I have my own story as well, the usual one, containing at least one man and an appropriate disappointment, but I say: Me? Nothing, I'm not trying to say anything at all, I only wanted to say "Ivan" to you, nothing more. I could also ask you what you think about insecticides.

Do you have flies at home?

No. I try to imagine myself as a fly or a rabbit being abused in some laboratory experiment, or a rat, which has been injected but which, full of hate, makes one final jump.

Ivan says: Thoughts like that won't make you happy either.

I'm just not happy right now, sometimes I don't feel any happiness or joy. I know I should be happy more often.

(I just can't bring myself to say to Ivan, who is my joy and my life: you alone are my joy and my life! since then I might lose Ivan even more quickly, I'm losing him on occasion as it is and that's clear to me from the constant diminishment of joy these days. I don't know how long Ivan has been shortening my life, and I have to start talking to him about it sometime.)

Because someone has killed me, because someone has wanted to kill me all the time, and then I started killing someone in thought, that is to say, not in thought, it was something else, it never does have much to do with thoughts, so it happened differently, I overcame it, too, besides I no longer do anything in thought.

Ivan looks up and says incredulously, as he loosens a screw with a screwdriver in his efforts to repair the telephone extension cord: You? Why you, my sweet little lunatic? And who did you have in mind! Ivan laughs and bends down over the phone outlet, once again twisting the wires carefully around the screw.

Does it surprise you?

Not in the least, why should it? In thought I already have dozens on my conscience, people who've annoyed me, says Ivan. His repair job is a success, now he couldn't care less about what I wanted to say concerning myself. I dress hurriedly, I mumble that I have to be home earlier today. Where is Malina? My God, if I were only with Malina already, because once again I cannot stand it, I shouldn't have started talking, and I say to Ivan: Please forgive me, I'm just not feeling well, no, I've forgotten something, do you mind, would you mind? I have to go home right away, I think I left the coffee on the burner, I'm sure I didn't turn it off!

No, Ivan never minds.

At home I lie on the floor and wait and breathe, I hyperventilate more and more, causing more than a few extra systoles, and I'd rather not die before Malina arrives, I look at the alarm clock, hardly a minute goes by, and here my life is passing away before my eyes. I don't know how I made it to the bathroom, but I'm holding my hands under the cold running water, it runs up to my elbows, I rub my arms and feet and legs with an ice-cold cloth, moving up toward my heart, time doesn't pass, but now Malina has to come, and then Malina is there, and then I collapse at once, finally, my God, why are you so late getting home!

Once I was on a ship, we were sitting around in the bar, a group of people bound for America, I knew a few already. But then one began burning holes in the back of his hand with a glowing cigarette. He was the only one laughing about it, we didn't know whether we were allowed to laugh too. Most of the time you don't know why people do such things to themselves, they simply don't say or else they tell you something completely different so you never actually discover the real reason. In a Berlin apartment I once met a man who was drinking one glass of vodka after the other but without ever getting drunk, he kept talking to me for hours, terribly sober, and when no one was listening, he asked me whether he could see me again, because he wanted to see me again at all costs, and I said nothing so clearly it indicated agreement. Then people started talking about the world situation, and someone put on a record, ASCENSEUR POUR L'ÉCHAFAUD. While there were only a few notes quietly purring and the conversation turned to the hotline between Washington and Moscow, the man casually asked me—as casually as he had before when he inquired whether I wouldn't be better off wearing velvet, he'd like to see me dressed in velvet best of all—Have you ever murdered someone? I said equally light-heartedly: No, of course not, and you? The man said: Yes, I am a murderer. For a while I didn't say anything, he looked at me softly and spoke once again: You can believe me, it's true! I believed him, too, since it had to be true, he was the third murderer I'd sat with at a table, but he was the first and only one to admit it. The two other times were at parties in Vienna, and I only found out later, on my way home. Occasionally I've wanted to write something about these three evenings, which were spaced out over many years, and in an attempt to do so I wrote on top of a page: Three murderers. But then I didn't manage any more, since I only wanted to sketch out these three murderers in order to hint at a fourth, for my three murderers don't really constitute a story, I never saw any of them again, they're still alive somewhere, eating with other people at dinner parties and doing things to themselves. One of them is no longer interned in the asylum at Steinhof, one is living in America under an assumed name, one is drinking to become increasingly sober, and is no longer in Berlin. I can't talk about the fourth, I don't remember him, I forget, I do not remember ...

(But I did run into the electric barbed wire.) I do remember one detail. Day after day, I kept throwing away my food, and secretly pouring out my tea, I must have known why.

Marcel, however, died in the following manner:

One day all the clochards of Paris were to be removed from the city. The welfare office, which is also responsible for the city's maintaining a decent image, entered the Rue Monge accompanied by the police, all they wanted to do was reassimilate the old men into life, first by washing them and getting them cleaned up for the same life. Marcel rose and went with them, a very peaceful man, moreover a wise, docile man after a few glasses of wine. Presumably their coming that day didn't matter to him in the least, and maybe he also thought he'd be able to return to his good place on the street, where the warm air of the Metro wafted up through the ventilation shafts. But inside the washroom, with its many showers for the common good, his turn came too, they placed him underneath the shower which was certainly not too hot and not too cold, just that he was naked for the first time in many years and under water. Before anyone could understand what was happening and reach out to him, he had fallen dead on the spot. You see what I mean! Malina looks at me a little unsure, although otherwise he's never unsure. I could have spared myself the story. But I can feel the shower once again, I know what it was they should not have been allowed to wash off Marcel. When someone is living in the vapors of his happiness, when he no longer has many words at his disposal, simply "God bless you," "May God reward you," then people should not attempt to wash him, should not wash off what is good for him, should not try and clean him up for a new life that does not exist.

Me: In Marcel's position I would have dropped dead at the first drop myself.

Malina: So happiness was always …

Me: Why do you always have to anticipate my thoughts? Right now I'm really thinking about Marcel, no, I hardly ever think about him anymore, it's just an episode, I'm thinking about myself and now already about something else, Marcel just showed up to help me.

Malina: —it's the spirit's beautiful tomorrow that never dawns.

Me: You don't have to keep reminding me about that school notebook of mine. It must have contained a whole lot more, but I burned it in the washhouse. I still have to have at least a thin patina of happiness, let's just hope no shower comes to wash away a certain smell I can't be without.

Malina: Since when are you getting along so well with the world, since when are you happy?

Me: You keep everything under observation and that's why you don't notice anything.

Malina: It's the other way around. I've noticed everything but I've never kept you under observation.

Me: But occasionally I've even allowed you to live the way you wanted, without bothering you—that's more … that's more generous.

Malina: I've noticed that as well, and someday you'll know whether it was a good thing to forget me, or whether it isn't better to take notice of me again. Except you'll probably never have a choice, you already don't have one.

Me: Forget you, how could I ever forget you! I was only making an attempt, just pretending, to show you that I can get along without you.

Malina doesn't consider this hypocrisy worth an answer, and although he won't enumerate all the days and nights I have forgotten him, he's a hypocrite, too, since he knows that for me his being so considerate was and still is much worse than any reproach. But we manage to find our way back together, for I need my double existence, my Ivanlife and my Malinafield, I cannot be where Ivan isn't, just as I cannot return home when Malina isn't there.

Ivan says: Just cut it out!

I say once again: Ivan, someday I'd like to tell you something, it doesn't have to be today, but someday I have to tell you.

You're out of cigarettes?

Yes, that's what I wanted to tell you, I'm out of cigarettes again.

Ivan is prepared to drive around the city with me to look for cigarettes, and because they are nowhere to be found we stop in front of the Hotel Imperial, Ivan finally gets some from the porter. Once again I'm in good standing with the world. It's still possible to love the world, even if it is only love on demand, and there's someone in-between acting as a transformer, but Ivan doesn't have to know that, because once more he's beginning to fear that I love him, and now as he is giving me a light and I can once again smoke and wait, I have no need of saying: Don't worry a bit, as far as I'm concerned you're just here to give me a light, thanks for the light, thanks for every cigarette you've lit for me, thanks for driving around the city, thanks for driving me home!

Malina: Are you going to Haderer's funeral?

Me: No, why should I go to the cemetery and catch a cold? Tomorrow I can read in the papers what it was like, what they said and besides I don't like funerals, these days no one knows how to behave at someone's death or at a cemetery anymore. I also don't want people constantly telling me that Haderer or someone else has died. They don't constantly tell me that someone is alive. It's all the same to me anyway, whether I liked someone or not, and the fact that there are only certain people I can and do meet, since some are no longer alive, doesn't surprise me, though for other reasons. Do you want to tell me why I have to be informed that all of sudden as of yesterday Herr Haderer or some other famous person, some conductor or politician, some banker or philosopher is dead. I'm not interested. No one has died as far as I'm concerned and it's rare that anyone is living, except in the theater of my thoughts.

Malina: So for you I'm not living most of the time?

Me: You are living. You're even alive most of the time, but you also provide evidence that you're alive. What proof do the others give me? None at all.

Malina: "Heaven is black as pitch."

Me: That could be used. It sounds as if whoever wrote it were alive. At last a surprise.

Malina: "Heaven is an almost inconceivably dark black. The stars are very bright, but do not twinkle because there is no atmosphere."

Me: Oh! This one's very precise.

Malina: "The sun is a dazzling disk pressed into the black velvet of heaven. I was very moved by the infinity of cosmic space, by its inconceivable expanse ..."

Me: Who is this mystic?

Malina: Alexei Leonov, who went into space for ten minutes.

Me: Not bad. But velvet, I don't know whether I would have used the word velvet. Is he also a poet on the side?

Malina: No, he paints in his free time. For a long time he didn't know whether he wanted to be a painter or an astronaut.

Me: An understandable difficulty when choosing a profession. But then to talk about space like a romantic journeyman ...

Malina: People don't change very much. As long as something's inconceivable, inexplicable or pitch black, it moves them, they go walking in the woods or rocketing into space, bringing their own world of secrets into the secrets of the world.

Me: And that brings us to the world hereafter. We may as well stop letting progress amaze us. Later on Leonov will be given a dacha and he'll plant roses, and years afterward people will smile at him gently, listening to him tell about Voskhod II one more time. Grandfather Leonov, please tell us what it was like back then, those first ten minutes out there! Once upon a time there was a moon that everyone wanted to fly to, and the moon was far away and inhospitable, but one day Alexei in Luck arrived, and behold …

Malina: It's rather strange he didn't notice the Urals, because he was out in space doing somersaults next to the ship.

Me: It was bound to happen like that. You're usually doing somersaults whenever there's something you really want to see or grasp, be it the Urals or the word for them, a thought or the words for those. I'm in the same predicament as our Grandfather Leonov, something is always eluding me, but internally, whenever I explore this infinite space inside me. Nothing much has changed since the good old days when people first started going into space.

Malina: Infinite?

Me: Of course. How could this space be anything but infinite?

I have to lie down for just an hour, which then turns into two, for I can't bear talking to Malina for very long.

Malina: You really have to clean up your room sometime, all these yellowed pages and scraps of paper completely covered with dust, someday no one will be able to find his way around in them.

Me: What? What's that supposed to mean? Nobody needs to find his way around here. I have my reasons for making things messier and messier. But if anyone has a right to see these "scraps" it's you. But you won't be able to find your way around, my dear, since years from now you wouldn't understand what one thing or another means.

Malina: Let me try, just once.

Me: Then explain why an old piece of paper has resurfaced, I could even tell where I bought it from the paper's format—A4 Standard—it was in a shop in the country, near a lake, and there's talk of you, of a trip to Lower Austria. But I'm not letting you read it, you can only look at the words which are written above it.

Malina: Deathstyles.

Me: But on the next note, format A2, written two years later, are the words "Deathstales." What was I trying to say? I might have made a mistake in writing. How, when and where? But guess what I wrote about you and Atti Altenwyl! You won't be able to! That time a large logging truck was ahead of you, going slowly uphill along a curve, you noticed how the poorly chained logs started to slide, you saw the whole load beginning to slip out behind, toward your car, and then and then ... So go ahead and say it!

Malina: How do you come to imagine that? You must have been crazy.

Me: I don't know myself, but I'm not imagining things, because something else happened shortly after that, you had gone swimming in the Wolfgangsee with Martin and Atti, you swam out the farthest, and developed a cramp in your left foot, and then and then ... Do you know anything more about that?

Malina:	Where did you get that, it's absolutely impossible for you to know anything about that, you weren't even there.
Me:	But if I wasn't there, then you're admitting that I could have been there, even if I wasn't. And what about the plug? Why didn't you want to put it in the socket anymore, that night in your room, why were you sitting in the dark, what had happened to all the switches that you had to sit in the dark so often.
Malina:	I often sat in the dark. Back then you were in the light.
Me:	No, I just thought I was.
Malina:	But it's the truth. So how is it that you know it?
Me:	It's impossible for me to know, so how can it be true?

I can't say anything more, because Malina takes two pieces of paper, crumples them and throws them in my face. Although a paper ball doesn't hurt and immediately drops to the floor, I fear its coming. Malina takes me by the shoulders and shakes me, he could also take his fist to my face, but he won't do that, and in any case he'll be hearing from me. But then comes a slap that brings me to my senses and once again I know where I am.

Me:	(accelerando) I'm not falling asleep on you.
Malina:	Where was it, on the way to Stockerau?
Me:	(crescendo) Stop it, it was someplace on the way to Stockerau, don't hit me, please don't hit me, just before Korneuburg, but stop asking me. I was the one who was crushed, not you!

I sit there with my face burning hotter and hotter and ask Malina to bring me the compact from my handbag. I step on the crumpled papers and shove them away with my foot, but Malina picks them up and carefully smooths them out. Without looking at them he puts them back in the drawer. I have to go to the bathroom after all, we won't be able to go out with me looking like this, hopefully I won't get a black eye, there are just a few red splotches on my face, and my heart is set on going to the Three Hussars, since Malina promised and Ivan doesn't have any time. Malina thinks it'll be ok, I should put more of this brownish cream on my face, I dab a little more foundation on my cheeks, he's right, it'll be ok, and it will all disappear in the fresh air. Malina promises me asparagus with Hollandaise sauce and schneeball pastries with chocolate sauce. I no longer trust this dinner. As I'm applying mascara for the second time, Malina asks: Why do you know all that?

He shouldn't ask me any more today.

Me: (presto, prestissimo) But I want asparagus with Mousse-
         line sauce and crème caramel. I'm not clairvoyant. I only
         put up with it. I was the one who almost drowned, not
         you. I don't want crème caramel, I want crêpes surprise
         instead, something with surprise.

For life may still arise out of such desires, in these minutes, whenever my own life comes up short next to Malina's.

Malina: What do you mean by life? I think you still want to call
         somebody or maybe it's better if three of us go to the
         Three Hussars. Who would you like to bring along, Alex-
         ander or Martin, maybe then you'll remember what you
         mean by life.
Me: If I still do mean anything by life … You're right, someone

	else ought to come along. I'm going to put on my old black dress, with the new belt.
Malina:	But take your scarf as well, you know which one I mean. Do me this one favor, since you never wear the striped dress. Why don't you ever wear it?
Me:	I'll wear it again. Please don't ask now. I have to bring myself to that. But otherwise the only thing I still like is this life with you, with the scarf you first gave me, with all the objects afterward. Life is reading a page that you have read, or reading over your shoulder, reading with you and not forgetting, because you don't forget anything. Life is also walking around in this void, which has space for everything. It's a path to the river Glan and the paths along the Gail, I lie stretched out with my notebooks on the Goria, once again I'm filling them with scribblings: He who has a Why to live for will bear almost any How. As if it had always been like that, I'm living the earliest times with you, always simultaneously with today, passively, without assailing anything or conjuring anything up. I'm just letting myself live more. Everything just has to come up at the same time and make an impression on me.
Malina:	What is life?
Me:	Whatever can't be lived.
Malina:	What is it?
Me:	(più mosso, forte) Leave me alone.
Malina:	What?
Me:	(molto meno mosso) Whatever you and I could pool together, that's what life is. Is that enough for you?
Malina:	You and I? Why not just say "we"?
Me:	(tempo giusto) I don't like "we," "one," "both" and so on and so on.
Malina:	For a minute I almost thought that what you liked least of all was "I."

Me: (soavemente) Is that a contradiction?

Malina: It certainly is.

Me: (andante con grazia) It's not a contradiction as long as I
           want you. I don't want myself, just you, and what do you
           think about that?

Malina: That would be your most dangerous adventure. But it's
           already begun.

Me: (tempo) Exactly, it began long ago, that's what life has
           been for a long time. (vivace) Do you know what I just
           noticed about myself? That my skin isn't like it was be-
           fore, it's simply different, although I can't discover so
           much as a single new wrinkle. The same ones are always
           there, the ones I got when I was twenty, they're only get-
           ting deeper, more distinct. Is that a clue, and what does
           it mean? Generally speaking it's pretty clear where it's
           pointing—namely to the end. But where is this clue tak-
           ing you and me? Into what wrinkled faces will each of
           us disappear? It's not growing old that amazes me, but
           the idea of one unknown woman succeeding another
           unknown woman. What will I be like then? I ask myself,
           like people used to ask in ages past, and with an equally
           large question mark, what will there be after death—but
           the question is senseless since it's impossible to imagine
           the answer. I can't reasonably imagine it either, I only
           know that I am no longer the way I used to be, I don't
           know myself a whit better and I haven't grown closer
           to myself at all. I've just watched one unknown woman
           slide further and further into another.

Malina: Don't forget that today this unknown woman still has
           something in mind, she still has someone on her mind,
           maybe she loves, who knows, maybe she hates, maybe
           she'd like to make one more phone call.

Me: (senza pedale) That's none of your business, that's not
           part of the same problem.

Malina: It is very much part of the same problem, since it will accelerate everything.

Me: You'd probably like that. (piano) Witness one more defeat. (pianissimo) This one.

Malina: I only said it would accelerate things. You won't need yourself anymore. I won't need you anymore either.

Me: (arioso dolente) Someone already said to me that I just don't have anyone who needs me.

Malina: That someone probably meant something different. Don't forget that I think differently. You've forgotten for too long the way I exist alongside you in this time.

Me: (cantabile) Me, forget! Me, forget you!

Malina: How well you are able to lie to me with your tone of voice and be slyly telling the truth at the same time!

Me: (crescendo) Me, forget you!

Malina: Come on, let's go. Do you have everything?

Me: (forte) I never have everything. (rubato) You're supposed to think of everything. About the keys, locking up, turning off the lights.

Malina: Tonight we'll talk about the future for a start. Your room absolutely must be cleaned up. Otherwise nobody will be able to find a way through all that mess.

Malina is already at the door, but I rush back down the hall, since I have to make one more phone call before leaving, and for this reason we never make it out of the house on time. I have to dial the number, it's a compulsion, an inspiration, I have only one number in my head, it's not the number of my passport, not a room number in Paris, not my date of birth, not today's date, and despite Malina's impatience I dial 72 68 93, a number not in anyone else's head, but I can say it aloud, sing it, whistle it, weep it out of me, laugh it in, my fingers are able to find it on the dial in the dark, without any prompting.

Yes, it's me
No, only me
No. Really?
Yes, just about to leave
I'll call you later
Right, very much later
I'll call you even later!

Malina: So tell me finally how you came across ideas like that. Because I've never driven to Stockerau with Atti, and I've never gone swimming in the Wolfgangsee at night with Martin and Atti.

Me: I always see everything very clearly laid out before me, I picture it to myself, that's what they say isn't it, for example all these long tree trunks starting to slide off the truck, and I'm sitting with Atti Altenwyl in the car as they start tumbling down on top of us and we can't back away because cars are backed up behind us one after the other, and I realize that now all those cubic tons of wood are going to come rolling down right on me.

Malina: But we're both sitting here right now, and I'm telling you one more time that I've never been to Stockerau with him.

Me: How do you know that I was thinking about the road to Stockerau? Because in the first place I didn't say a thing about Stockerau, I just mentioned Lower Austria in general, and only thought about that because of Aunt Marie.

Malina: I really am afraid you're crazy.

Me: Not too crazy. And don't talk like (piano, pianissimo) Ivan.

Malina: Don't talk like who?

Me: (abbandonandosi, sotto voce) Love me, no, more than

that, love me more, love me completely, so it will soon be over.

Malina: You know everything about me? And everything about everybody else as well?

Me: (presto alla tedesca) No I don't, I don't know anything. And nothing about anybody else! (non troppo vivo) That was only talk about picturing things, I didn't want to talk about you at all, not specifically about you. Because it's you who's never afraid, who's never been afraid. We really are both sitting here right now, but I am afraid. (con sentimento ed espressione) I wouldn't have asked you for something a minute ago, if you'd ever been as afraid as I am.

I've laid my head in Malina's hand, Malina doesn't say a word, he doesn't move, but neither does he caress my head. With his free hand he lights a cigarette. My hand is no longer on his palm, and I try to sit up straight and not let anything show.

Malina: Why are you putting your hand on your neck again?

Me: You're right, I think I do that a lot.

Malina: Does it stem from that time?

Me: Yes. Yes, I'm sure of it now. I'm certain that's where it started, and then more and more kept coming. It just keeps on coming. I have to hold my head. But I try my best not to let anybody notice. I run my hand underneath my hair and prop up my head. Then the other person thinks I'm listening especially carefully and that it's a gesture like crossing your legs or resting your chin on your hands.

Malina: But it can look like a bad habit, bad manners.

Me: It's my own manner of clinging to myself when I can't
         cling to you.
Malina: What did you achieve in the years afterward?
Me: (legato) Nothing. At first nothing. Then I started clearing
         away the years. That was the most difficult thing, since I'd
         become so absentminded, I no longer had the strength to
         clear away even the accidental properties of my unhappi-
         ness. Since I was unable to reach the unhappiness itself,
         there were many incidental things I needed to remove:
         airports, streets, pubs, shops, certain dishes and wines,
         very many people, all types of chitchat and babble. But
         mostly, falsification. I was a complete fake, I was handed
         false papers, deported hither and yon, then reemployed
         just to sit by, to agree where I had never agreed before, to
         confirm, consent, concede. I was surrounded by ways of
         thought I had to imitate although they were completely
         alien to me. In the end I was one big fake, underneath
         which I remained recognizable probably only to you.
Malina: What did you learn from that?
Me: (con sordina) Nothing. I got nothing out of it.
Malina: That's not true.
Me: (agitato) But it is true. I again started to speak, to walk,
         to feel things, to remember an earlier time which existed
         before the time I don't want to remember. (tempo gi-
         usto) And one day things started going well for the two
         of us once again. Since when do we get along so well with
         each other?
Malina: Since forever, I think.
Me: (leggermente) How courteous, how nice, how lovely of
         you to tell me that. (quasi una fantasia) I've sometimes
         thought you were often—three hundred sixty days of
         the year at least—so deathly afraid on my account. You
         would recoil every time the doorbell rang, you would see
         a dangerous person hidden in every nearby shadow, the

timber on the truck in front of you was especially men-
acing. You almost died if you heard steps behind you. If
you were reading a book, the door would seem to open
suddenly, and then you'd drop the book in mortal terror—because I was not allowed to read any more books.
I thought you were so extraordinarily calm because you
had died hundreds, no thousands, of times. (ben mar-
cato) How wrong I was.

Malina knows very well that I like going out with him in the evening, but he doesn't expect me to, he's not surprised when there's
some reason for my refusal, one time because my stockings have a
run, then of course it's often Ivan who's to blame for my hesitation,
since Ivan doesn't know, not yet, what his plans are for the evening,
and then there's a further difficulty in choosing a restaurant, because there are some Malina refuses to enter, he can't abide noise,
he can't stand gypsy music or old Viennese songs, the poor lighting
and stale air found in night clubs are not to his taste, he can't eat
unwisely like Ivan, for no obvious reason he eats in moderation,
he can't drink like Ivan, he only smokes occasionally, almost out
of kindness to me.

On the evenings when he's gone to visit people without me, I know
that Malina says little. He'll sit there in silence, listening, he'll get
someone to talk and finally give everybody the feeling that at one
point they've said something more intelligent than all the other
sentences, that they've shown more substance, because Malina
raises others to his own level. Even so he always keeps his distance—he is distance personified. He will never utter a word about
his own life, never talk about me, but at the same time he won't
arouse the slightest suspicion he might be hiding something. And
Malina really isn't hiding anything, for in the best possible sense

he has nothing to hide. He is not weaving his contribution into the grand text, expanding the texture of the network, the Viennese net has a few small holes solely thanks to Malina. That is why he is the extreme negation of anything that offends, of anything that provokes, anything that spreads or breaks out or vindicates—what would Malina ever do that would require vindication! He can be charming, he pronounces courteous, glittery sentences which are never too friendly, he displays a tiny bit of cordiality, which pops out of him whenever he takes his leave, for instance, then goes back into hiding right away, because he immediately turns and leaves, he always leaves very quickly, he kisses women's hands, and whenever the situation calls for him to help women, he takes them by the arm for a minute, he touches them so lightly that not one of them can think anything of it and yet all of them must think something. Malina is on the verge of leaving, the people just look at him in surprise, they don't know why he's leaving, since he doesn't say, embarrassed, why, where or how come right now. Nor does anyone dare ask him. It's unthinkable that anyone would approach Malina with the same questions people are always asking me: What are you doing tomorrow night? For heaven's sake, you're not thinking of leaving already! You absolutely must meet so-and-so! No, that kind of thing doesn't happen to Malina, he has a cloak of invisibility, his visor is almost always closed. I envy Malina and attempt to imitate him, but I can't pull it off, I'm caught in every net, I induce all types of blackmail, from the very first hour I am Alda's slave, by no means just her patient, although she's supposed to be a doctor, I immediately find out what Alda is up to and what she's going through, and after thirty more minutes I'm having to look for a voice instructor for a certain Herr Kramer, no, for his daughter, since she doesn't want to have anything more to do with her father, this Herr Kramer—all for Alda's sake. I don't know any voice instructors, I've never needed one, but I've already half admitted to knowing someone who I'm sure does know, must know some voice instructors, after all, I do share a building with an opera singer, of course I don't really know her, but there has to be some way to help Herr Kramer's daughter, since Alda wants to help him or really his daughter. What should I do? A Doktor Wellek, one of the four Wellek brothers, the very one who hasn't amounted to anything yet, now has his big chance in television, everything is riding on this, and if I might just put in a small word, although I've never put in even the smallest word to any of the gentlemen in the Austrian Television Network, then...Should I go to Argentinierstrasse and put in a small word? Can't Herr Wellek live without me, am I his last hope?

Malina says: You're not even my last hope. And Herr Wellek will manage to make himself unpopular enough without you. If one more person helps him he'll completely forget how to help himself. All you'll do is kill him with your small word.

Today I'm waiting for Malina in the Blue Bar of the Sacher Hotel. He doesn't come for a long time and then shows up after all. We enter the large dining hall and Malina confers with the waiter, but then I hear myself suddenly saying: No, I can't, please not here, I can't sit at this table! Malina thinks the table is quite pleasant, the small one in the corner I've often preferred to the larger tables, since I sit with my back to the protruding bit of wall, and the waiter agrees, he does know me after all, and he knows that I like this protected place. I say breathlessly: No, no! Don't you see! Malina asks: What is there to see, especially? I turn around and walk out slowly, so as not to cause a scene, I greet the Jordans and Alda who is sitting at the large table with some American guests, and then a few other people whom I also know but whose names escape me. Malina walks quietly behind me, I feel he is simply following me and greeting in turn. At the coat check I let him drape my coat over my shoulders, I look at him in despair. Doesn't he understand? Malina asks quietly: What did you see?

I still don't know what I saw, and I reenter the restaurant, thinking that Malina is bound to be hungry and that it's already getting late, I explain hastily: I'm sorry, let's go back inside, I can eat something now, it was only for a minute that I couldn't stand it! I actually do sit down at that table, and now I realize it's the table where Ivan will sit with someone else, Ivan will sit in Malina's place and order, and someone else will be sitting at his right hand, just as I am sitting to the right of Malina. They will sit on the right hand, and one day the seating shall be rightful. It's the table where today I'm eating my last meal before the execution. Once again it's tafelspitz, with horseradish and a chive sauce. Then I can drink one more espresso, no, no dessert, today I want to forgo dessert. This is the table where it happens and where it will happen, and this is the way it is before they chop off your head. Beforehand you're permitted one last meal. My head rolls onto the plate in the restaurant of the Sacher Hotel, spraying the lily-white damask tablecloth with blood, my head has fallen and is exhibited to the guests.

Today I stop at the corner of the Beatrixgasse and the Ungargasse, unable to continue. I look down at my feet which I can no longer move, then over to the sidewalk and the street crossing, where everything has become discolored. I know for a fact that it will be this important place, the brown discoloration is already wet and oozing, I'm standing in a puddle of blood, it is very distinctly blood, I can't go on standing here forever, gripping my neck, I can't stand the sight of what I see. I cry out, now softly, now loudly: Hallo! Please! Hallo! Would you please stop! A woman toting a shopping bag who has already passed by turns around and stares at me, questioningly. I ask in desperation: Could you please, please be so kind, please stay with me for just a moment, I must have lost my way, I can't figure out where to go, I don't know my way around here, can you please tell me where I can find the Ungargasse? And perhaps the woman does know where the Ungargasse is, she says: You're already on the Ungargasse, what number did you want? I point around the corner, down the street toward the Beethoven house, I cross to the other side, with Beethoven I feel safe, and there from number 5 I look over at an entryway which has now become strange to me, marked with the number 6, I see Frau Breitner standing in front, I'd rather not run into Frau Breitner now, but Frau Breitner is a human being, I am surrounded by human beings, nothing can happen to me, and I look over at the other shore, I must descend from the sidewalk and attain the other shore, the O-streetcar runs ringing by, it's the O-car of today, everything is as always, I wait for it to pass, and quivering with the strain I take the key from my purse and set off, donning a smile for Frau Breitner, I've reached the other shore, I saunter past Frau Breitner for whom my beautiful book is also supposed to be written, Frau Breitner doesn't smile back, but she does greet me, and once again I have made it to my house. I didn't see a thing. I'm home.

In the apartment I lie down on the floor, thinking about my book, it's gotten lost, there is no beautiful book, I can no longer write the beautiful book, I've stopped thinking about the book long ago, there's no foundation, nothing more comes to me, not a single sentence. But I was so sure the beautiful book existed and that I would find it for Ivan. No day will come, people will never, poetry will never and they will never, people will have black, dark eyes, their hands will wreak destruction, the plague will come, this plague which everyone is carrying, this plague which has infected all, this plague will snatch them up and carry them away, soon. It will be the end.

Beauty is no longer flowing from me, it could have flowed from me, it came in waves to me from Ivan, Ivan who is beautiful, I have known one single beautiful human being, nonetheless I have seen beauty, in the end I, too, became beautiful one single time, through Ivan.

Get up! says Malina, who finds me on the floor, and he means it. What are you saying about beauty? What's beautiful? But I can't get up, I've propped my head on THE GREAT PHILOSOPHERS, who are quite hard. Malina takes away the book and lifts me up.

Me: (con affetto) I really have to tell you. No, you have to explain it to me. If someone is consummately beautiful and ordinary, why is he the only one capable of inspiring fantasy? I've never told you, I was never happy, never ever, only in a few moments, but in the end I did see beauty. You'll ask what that's good for. It doesn't need to accomplish anything, it's enough in itself. I've seen so many other things, but they were never enough. The mind doesn't move any other mind, only ones of the same mind, I'm sorry, I know you consider beauty to be the lesser of the two, but it does move the mind and the spirit. Je suis tombée mal, je suis tombée bien.

Malina: Stop falling down all the time. Get up. Go out, have fun, ignore me, do something, anything!

Me: (dolcissimo) Me? Do something? Abandon you? Leave you?

Malina: Did I say something about me?

Me: No you didn't, but I'm talking about you, I'm thinking about you. I'm getting up for your sake, I'll eat one more time, but I'm only eating to please you.

Malina will want to go out with me, want to distract me, he'll force me, he'll be forceful, up to the end. How am I to make him understand any of my stories? Since Malina is probably changing his clothes, I change as well, once again I can continue, I pull an appearance out of the mirror and smile at it dutifully. But Malina says: (Is Malina saying something?) Malina says: Kill him! Kill him!

I say something. (But am I really saying something?) I say: He is the only one I cannot kill, the only one. To Malina I say sharply: You're wrong, he is my life, my only joy, I can't kill him.

But Malina says in a tone which is both inaudible and unmistakable: kill him!

I'm trying to have fun, and am reading less. Late in the evening, with the record player on low, I tell Malina:

In the Psychological Institute in the Liebiggasse we always drank tea or coffee. I knew a man there who always used shorthand to record what everyone said, and sometimes other things besides. I don't know shorthand. Sometimes we'd give each other Rorschach tests, Szondi tests, thematic apperception tests, and would diagnose each other's character and personality, we would observe our performance and behavior and examine our expressions. Once he asked how many men I'd slept with, and I couldn't think of any except this one-legged thief who'd been in jail, and a lamp covered with flies in a room in Mariahilf that was rented by the hour, but I said at random: seven! He laughed surprised and said, then naturally he'd like to marry me, our children would certainly be intelligent, also very pretty, and what did I think of that. We went to the Prater, and I wanted to go on the Ferris wheel, because back then I was never afraid, just happy the way I felt while gliding and later on while skiing, I could laugh for hours out of sheer happiness. Of course then we never spoke about it again. Shortly afterward I had to take my oral examinations, and in the morning before the three big exams all the embers spilled out of the furnace at the Philosophical Institute, I stomped on some pieces of coal or wood, I ran to get a broom and dustpan, since the cleaning ladies hadn't come yet, it was smoldering and smoking terribly, I didn't want there to be a fire, I trampled the embers with my feet, the stench stayed in the institute for days, my shoes were singed, but nothing burned down. I also opened all the windows. Even so I managed to take my first exam at eight in the morning, I was supposed to be there with another candidate but he didn't come, he'd had a stroke during the night, as I found out just before going in to be examined about Leibnitz, Kant and Hume. The Old Privy Councillor, who was also the rector at the time, wore a dirty robe, earlier he'd been given some award from Greece, I don't know what for, and he began asking questions, very annoyed that a candidate had missed an exam due to demise, but at least I was there and not yet dead. In his anger he had forgotten what subjects had been agreed upon, and during the exam someone phoned—I believe it was his sister—one moment we were discussing the neo-Kantians, the next moment we were with the English deists, but still quite far from Kant himself, and I didn't know very much. After the phone calls things improved a little, I launched straight into what had been agreed upon, and he didn't notice. I asked him a fearful question relating to the problem of time and space, admittedly a question without meaning for me at the time, but he felt quite flattered that I had asked, and then I was dismissed. I ran back to our institute, it wasn't burning, and went on to the next two exams. I passed all of them. But I never did solve the problem relating to time and space. Later it grew and grew.

Malina: Why are you thinking about that? I had the impression that that time was completely unimportant as far as you were concerned.

Me: There's a reason they call the oral exams the Rigorosum, and they were unimportant but rigorous nonetheless, and the other candidate had died of a stroke, twenty-three years old, and afterward I had to walk from the

Institute to the Universitätsstrasse, past the university, groping my way along the entire wall, I also managed to cross the street, since Eleonore and Alexander Fleisser were waiting for me in the Café Bastei, my face must have looked very downcast, I must have been on the verge of collapse, they'd already spotted me through the window before I caught sight of them. As I approached the table no one said a word, they thought I hadn't passed the exams—and as it was I really only passed in a certain sense—then they shoved a cup of coffee in my direction, and I said, into their dismayed faces, that it had been extremely easy, child's play. For some time they kept on asking questions, then they finally believed me, I was thinking about the embers, the possible fire, but I don't remember, I don't remember exactly ... I'm sure we didn't celebrate. Shortly thereafter I had to place two fingers on a scepter and say some words in Latin. I was wearing a black dress that I'd borrowed from Lily, too short, a few young men and I stood lined up in the Auditorium Maximum, then I heard my own voice, just once, loud and clear, the other voices were scarcely audible. But I wasn't alarmed at myself, and later on I again spoke quietly.

Me: (lamentandosi) So what have I learned or discovered in all these years, considering all the sacrifices, and think about the effort I've gone to!

Malina: Nothing at all of course. You learned what was already inside you, what you already knew. Isn't that enough?

Me: Maybe you're right. I sometimes think now that I'm recovering myself, the way I used to be. I'm all too glad to think about the time when I had everything, when my cheerfulness was truly full of cheer, when I was serious in the good sense of the word. (quasi glissando) Then everything became worse for the wear, damaged, used and used up and ultimately destroyed. (moderato) I slowly improved myself, more and more I made up for what was missing, and I consider myself healed. So now I'm almost like I used to be. (sotto voce) But what purpose did the journey serve?

Malina: The journey doesn't serve any purpose, it's available to everyone but not everyone must take it. However someday people should be able to switch back and forth between their newly-recovered self and a future version that can no longer be the old one. Without strain, without sickness, without regret or pity.

Me: (tempo giusto) I no longer pity myself.

Malina: I expected at least that, you were bound to come to that conclusion. Who wants to cry over you, to cry over the likes of us.

Me: But why do people cry over others at all?

Malina: That too should stop, for other people deserve to be cried over as little as you deserve my crying over you. What good would it have done you back then if someone in Timbuktu or in Adelaide had cried about a child in Klagenfurt who'd been covered with rubble, who had lain down on the ground under the trees along the lake promenade during an attack of low-flying aircraft, and who then had to see dead and wounded bodies for the first time, all around her. So don't cry over others, they have enough to do saving their skin or getting through the few hours left before they're murdered. They don't need tears Made in Austria. Besides, the tears come later, in the middle of peace, as you once called this time, in a comfortable armchair, when no shots are being fired and nothing is burning. People go hungry at other times too, on the street, among the well-fed passersby. And fear is first felt during some stupid horror film. People don't freeze in winter, but at the beach on a summer's day. Where was it? When did you feel the most cold? It was a beautiful, unseasonably warm October day by the sea. So you can either stay calm for the others or be constantly agitated. You won't change a thing.

Me: (più mosso) But even if there's nothing to be done, even if we are powerless to intervene, the question nonetheless remains: what is to be done? It would be inhuman to do nothing.

Malina: Calm the commotion. Disturb the calm.

Me: (dolente, molto mosso) But when will the time finally come for me to accomplish this, when I can do and do nothing more, all at once? When will the time come when I can find time for that? When will it be time to stop all false differentiation and categorization, to stop false fear and suffering, senseless empathy, this constant, senseless pondering and musing! (una corda) I want to think my way out slowly. (tutte le corde) Is that the way it is?

Malina: If that's how you want it.

Me: Should I no longer ask you?

Malina: Even that is another question.

Me: (tempo giusto) Go and work until supper, then I'll call you. No, I'm not going to cook, why should I waste my time with that. I'd like to go out, that's right, walk a few steps to a small place to eat, somewhere loud, where people are eating and drinking, so that I can again imagine the world. To the Alter Heller.

Malina: I am at your command.

Me: (forte) I'll command you yet. Even you.

Malina: We'll see about that, my dear!

Me: Because in the end I will be in command of everything.

Malina: That is megalomania. So you're only passing from one mania to another.

Me:	(senza licenza) No. To act is to abstain from action, if it keeps going on the way you're demonstrating. In which case my mania is no longer growing but decreasing.
Malina:	No. On the whole you are gaining, and if you stopped weighing it over and over, if you stopped weighing yourself, you'd be able to gain even more, and more and more.
Me:	(tempo) Gain what, if there's no strength left?
Malina:	You gain in fear.
Me:	So I frighten you.
Malina:	Not me, but yourself. This fear stems from the truth. But you will be able to watch yourself. You'll hardly be participating, you'll no longer be here.
Me:	(abbandonandosi) Why not here? No, I don't understand you! But then I don't understand anything anymore … I'd have to get rid of myself!
Malina:	Because you can only be of use to yourself by hurting yourself. That is the beginning and the end of all struggle. You have hurt yourself enough. It will help you a lot. But not the you you're thinking of.
Me:	(tutto il clavicembalo) Oh! I'm somebody else, you're trying to say that I'll become someone completely different!
Malina:	No. That's nonsense. You most certainly are yourself, and you can't change that either. But a self is moved, is carried away, and a self does things, it acts. However you will act no longer.
Me:	(diminuendo) I've never liked acting anyway.
Malina:	But you have acted. And you have allowed others to act on you, against you, use you in their own actions and transactions.
Me:	(non troppo vivo) But I never wanted that. I've never even acted against my enemies.
Malina:	Don't forget that not one of your enemies has ever seen you, and you have never seen one of them.

Me: I don't believe that. (vivacissimamente) I have seen one of them, and he has seen me, but not properly.

Malina: What a strange endeavor! You really want to be seen properly? Maybe even by your friends?

Me: (presto, agitato) Stop it, who ever believed that, there are no friends, maybe temporary ones, friends of the moment! (con fuoco) But people do have enemies.

Malina: Maybe not even that ... not even that.

Me: (tempo) Oh yes, I know.

Malina: So you might be looking at your enemy this very minute.

Me: Then you would have to be my enemy. But you're not.

Malina: You should stop fighting. Against what? You should now go neither forward nor back, just learn a new style of combat. The only style of combat you're allowed.

Me: But I already know how to fight. Ultimately I'll strike back, since I'm gaining ground. I've gained a lot of ground in these years.

Malina: And that makes you happy?

Me: (con sordino) Pardon me?

Malina: What a charming way you have of avoiding questions! You have to stay where you are. This must be your place. You should neither press forward nor retreat. Because then you shall conquer, in this place, the only place where you belong.

Me: (con brio) Conquer! Who's talking about victory anymore or conquering anything, now that the sign is lost in which to conquer.

Malina: Nevertheless the word is: conquer. You will succeed without a single trick and without force. Furthermore you will not conquer with your self, but rather—

Me: (allegro) But rather—you see?

Malina: Not with your self.

Me: (forte) What makes my self worse than anybody else's?

Malina: Nothing. Everything. Because your actions are only ever
           futile. That is what's unforgivable.
Me: (piano) Even if it is unforgivable, I'm still always wanting
           to spread myself too thin, to lose my way, to lose my self.
Malina: What you want doesn't count anymore. In the proper
           place you'll have nothing more to want. There you will
           be yourself so much you'll be able to give up your self.
           It will be the first place where someone has healed the
           world.
Me: Do I have to start with that?
Malina: You've started with everything, that's why you have to
           start with this as well. And you'll stop with everything.
Me: (pensieroso) Me?
Malina: You still want to take this into your mouth, this "Me"?
           Are you still weighing it over? Go ahead and weigh it on
           a scale!
Me: (tempo giusto) But I'm just now beginning to love this
           self.
Malina: How much do you think you can love it?
Me: (appassionato e con molto sentimento) Very much. All
           too much. I shall love it as my neighbor, as you!

Today I walk through the Ungargasse and think about moving elsewhere, an apartment's supposed to be opening up in Heiligenstadt,
someone's moving out, friends of friends, but the apartment isn't
very roomy by any means, and how am I supposed to inflict this on
Malina, to whom I wanted to suggest a larger apartment before, on
account of his many books. But he'll never leave the Third District.
A single tear forms, just in the corner of one eye, but it doesn't roll
down my cheek, it crystallizes in the cold air, then grows bigger
and bigger into a second giant globe that doesn't want to orbit
with the world—it breaks off from the planet and plunges into
infinity.

Ivan is no longer Ivan, I look at him like a clinician studying an X-ray, I see his skeleton, spots on his lung due to smoking, but I no longer see Ivan himself. Who will give Ivan back to me? Why does he let me look at him like that so suddenly? I'd like to collapse on the table when he asks for the check, or under the table, tearing off the tablecloth with all the plates and glasses and silverware, and even the salt, although I'm very superstitious. Don't be that way with me, I'll say, don't do that to me, or else I'll die.

I went dancing yesterday, in the Eden Bar.

Ivan is listening to me, but is he really listening? He ought to hear me telling him that I went dancing, I wanted to destroy something, because I ultimately danced with a disgusting young man and I looked at him in a way I've never looked at Ivan, since he kept dancing more and more wildly and with increasing precision, clapping his hands and snapping his fingers. I say to Ivan: I'm dead tired, I was up too late, I can't keep it up anymore.

But is Ivan listening to me?

Ivan asks in passing, since we haven't seen each other in a long time, if I wouldn't like to go with him and the children to the Burgkino, they're showing Walt Disney's MICKY MAUS. Unfortunately I don't have any time, because now I don't want to see the children anymore, especially not the children, Ivan anytime, but not the children he's going to take away from me. I can't see Béla and András anymore. They'll have to get their wisdom teeth without me. I'll no longer be around when they're removed.

Malina whispers inside me: Kill them, kill them.

But inside me there is a louder whisper: never Ivan and the children, they belong together, I can't kill them. When it happens—as it will happen—when Ivan touches someone else, then Ivan will no longer be Ivan. At least I have never touched a soul.

I say: Ivan.

Ivan says: Check please!

There must be some mistake, after all it is Ivan, only I keep glancing past him at the tablecloth, the salt shaker, I stare at the fork, I could poke my eyes out, I look over his shoulder out the window and give perfunctory answers to his questions.

Ivan says: You look pale as death, aren't you well?

Just lack of sleep, I ought to take a vacation, friends of mine are driving to Kitzbühel, Alexander and Martin are going to St. Anton, otherwise it's getting impossible for me to recover, the winters are getting longer and longer, who can possibly survive these winters!

So Ivan must really think it's the winter, for he strongly advises me to leave soon. I'm simply not looking at him anymore, I see something else, a shadow is sitting next to him, Ivan is laughing and talking with a shadow, he's a lot funnier, more exuberant, he was never so awfully exuberant with me, and I say that I'm sure Martin or Fritz ... but that I still have so much to do, no, I don't know. We'll phone each other.

Is Ivan also thinking how different it used to be, or does it only seem so to me, that things used to be different than they are today. An insane laughter sticks in my throat, but since I'm afraid I'd never stop laughing I don't say a thing and grow more and more sullen. After coffee I am completely silent, I smoke.

Ivan says: You sure are pretty blah today.

I ask: Really? Really? Was I always like that?

In front of the entrance to my building I stay seated in the car, hesitating, and suggest we phone each other when we get a chance. Ivan doesn't contradict me, he doesn't say, you're crazy, what are you talking about, what do you mean when we get a chance. He already thinks it's normal for us to phone each other when we get a chance. He'll agree if I don't get out right away, but I'm already getting out, I slam the door shut and shout: I'm really incredibly busy these days!

I never sleep anymore except for late in the morning. Who would want to sleep inside a forest of the night teeming with questions? With my hands clasped behind my head, I lie awake in the night and think how happy I was, happy, and after all I did promise myself I'd never complain again, never accuse anyone, if I might be allowed to be happy just once. But now I want to prolong this happiness, like anyone who's experienced this good fortune. I want this happiness which has had its time and is now departing. I am no longer happy. It's the spirit's beautiful tomorrow that never dawns ... But it wasn't my tomorrow by any means, it was my spirit's beautiful today, the today of my waiting after work between six and seven, of my waiting by the phone until midnight, and this today cannot be over. It can't be true.

Malina looks in on me. Are you still awake?

I just happened to be awake, I have to think about something, it's awful.

Malina says: I see, and why is it awful?

Me: (con fuoco) It's awful, it's awful beyond words, it's too awful.
Malina: Is that all that's keeping you awake? (Kill him! kill him!)
Me: (sotto voce) Yes, that's all.
Malina: And what are you going to do?
Me: (forte, forte, fortissimo) Nothing.

Early in the morning I've collapsed into the rocking chair, I'm staring at the wall, which is showing a crack, it must be an old crack that now is gently spreading because I keep staring at it. It's late enough, I could get a chance to make a phone call, and I pick up the phone and want to say, are you already asleep? Then it occurs to me just in time that I'd really have to ask, are you already awake? But today it's too hard for me to say good morning, and I quietly replace the receiver, I can feel the scent so distinctly with my whole face, so strongly that I think I'm buried in Ivan's shoulder, in that indispensable scent I call cinnamon, the scent which always sustained me, which staved off all drowsiness, the only scent that let me breathe more easily. The wall doesn't yield, it doesn't want to give in, but I will force the wall to open along this crack. If Ivan doesn't call me at once, if he never calls me again, if he doesn't call until Monday, what will I do then? What has set the sun and all the other stars in motion is not some law of physics, I alone was capable of moving them, as long as Ivan was close by—not only for me and not only for him, but for the others as well, and I have to speak, I have to tell, soon there will be nothing more to disturb my remembering. Except the story of Ivan with me will never be told, since we don't have any story, there won't be any 99 x Love and no sensational revelations from Austro-Hungarian bedrooms.

I don't understand Malina, who is now serenely eating his breakfast before leaving the house. We will never understand each other, we're as different as night and day, he is inhuman with his whispered suggestions, his silences and his detached questions. For if Ivan should no longer belong to me, the way I belong to him, then he will one day exist in some normal life, which will make him become quite normal, he will no longer be celebrated, but maybe Ivan doesn't want anything other than his simple life, and I have only complicated a piece of his life with my silent stares, my flagrantly bad playing, my confessions constructed out of fragmented phrases.

Ivan says laughingly, but just once: I can't breathe where you place me, please not so high, don't ever bring anyone else up here where the air is so thin, take my advice, learn your lesson! I didn't say: But after you who else am I supposed to ... But you can't think that after you I'd ... I'd still prefer to learn every lesson for your sake. Not for anyone else.

Malina and I have been invited to the Gebauers, but we're no longer talking to the other people standing around the salon, drinking and getting into heated discussions, instead we suddenly find ourselves alone in the room with the Bechstein grand piano, where Barbara practices when we're not there. I recall what Malina first played for me, before we really began talking to one another, and I'd like to ask him to play it once again. But then I go to the piano myself and clumsily begin to look for a few notes, still standing.

Malina doesn't move, at least he acts as though he were looking at the pictures, a portrait by Kokoschka ostensibly portraying Barbara's grandmother, a few drawings by Swoboda, the two small sculptures by Wantschura, all of which he's known for a long time.

Malina turns around after all, crosses over to me, pushes me away and sits down on the piano stool. Once again I place myself behind him, like back then. He really does play and half speaks and half sings and is audible only to me.

Now all my sor-row I dis-pell; and dream be-yond ____ the fair ho-

ri-zon... O an-cient scent from far-off days!

We quickly say good-bye and are heading home on foot and in the dark, even crossing through the Stadtpark, where the heavy, gloomy, giant black moths circle and the chords are heard more distinctly underneath the ailing moon, once again there is wine in the park, the wine which through the eyes we drink, again the ne-nuphar serves as a boat, again there is nostalgia and parody, atroc-ity and a serenade before the journey home.

After a long hot bath in the morning I notice that my cabinets are empty, also only a few stockings and a bra are to be found in the wardrobe. A lone dress is hanging on a hanger, the last dress Malina gave me, which I never wear, it's black, with some colorful diagonal stripes on top. Another black dress is lying in the ward-robe, in a plastic bag, black on top with colorful vertical stripes below, it's an old dress I was wearing when Ivan saw me for the first time. I've never worn it since then and have preserved it as a relic. What has happened in my apartment? What has Lina done with all my dresses and my clothes? There wasn't that much to take to the laundry or the dry cleaning. I walk around deep in thought, dress in hand, and I feel cold. Before Malina leaves the house, I say: Please take a look at my room, something incredible has happened.

Malina comes in carrying a cup of tea, he's in a hurry, he sips at the tea and asks: What is it then? I pull the dress over my head in front of him and start breathing too quickly, I'm hyperventilating, I can scarcely speak. It's this dress, it has to be because of this dress, all of a sudden I realize why I've never been able to wear it. Don't you see, the dress is too hot for me, I'll melt in it, the wool must be too warm, isn't there any other dress here! Malina says: I think it looks good on you, you look good in it, if you really want my opinion, it suits you exceptionally well.

Malina has finished his tea and I hear him walking around, tak-ing the usual few steps, gathering his raincoat, the house key, a few books and some papers. I go back in the bathroom and look at the mirror, the dress crackles and makes my skin red down to my wrists, it's awful, it's too awful, some hellish thread must be woven into this dress. It must be my Nessus tunic, I don't know what it's been soaked in. I never did want to wear it, I must have known why.

And how long have I been living with a dead telephone? No new dress can provide adequate consolation for that. Whenever the phone screeches or cries out, I still sometimes get up with a foolish hope, but then say: Hello? with a disguised voice, deeper than my own, as it always turns out to be someone with whom I can't or don't want to talk. Then I lie down and wish I were dead. But today the phone is ringing, the dress is chafing my skin, apprehensively I approach the telephone, I do not disguise my voice, and it's a good thing I didn't, because the phone is alive. It's Ivan. It couldn't happen otherwise, eventually it had to be Ivan. After one sentence Ivan has lifted me up again, he has uplifted me, has soothed my skin, gratefully I assent, I say yes. Yes, I said yes.

I have to get rid of Malina for this evening, I say something to persuade him, he does have his obligations after all, he can't always decline, he promised Kurt he'd drop by one of these evenings, Kurt would be really happy if it were today, he'd like to show Malina his new drawings, and the Wantschuras are going over to Kurt's, for that reason alone Malina really has to go, because if Wantschura starts to drink then things will get complicated, and without Malina all the old arguments will reemerge. In return I promise Malina that I'll come along to the Jordans one of these evenings, after all we can't keep declining, we have to visit Leo Jordan twice a year. Malina doesn't cause any difficulty, he immediately realizes that he has to spend the evening at Swoboda's. I am always right of course. If I hadn't thought about it Malina would have simply forgotten. He's really glad he has me, he never leaves home without a grateful glance, and I say to him as tenderly as I can: Please forgive me all that nonsense with the dress, today I want to wear it very much, I feel great in it! How do you always manage to get the right size, how is it you know the measurements? Thank you so much for the dress!

I read a book until eight o'clock. Because dinner is all ready, I've put on makeup and combed my hair. "For it is futile to try to feign indifference concerning inquiries whose object cannot be indifferent to human nature."

Then I got embroiled in the struggle against innate ideas, already decided. I'm also sulking because I no longer have all my books, whether it be the moral sense of Hutcheson or else of Shaftesbury, but today I have no sense of orientation, but for that I do have a summa cum laude, even if I do always look as though I'd failed. Language palatalization. I still know the words, they've been rusting on my tongue for many years, and I know very well the words which dissolve on my tongue daily or which I can scarcely swallow or get out. And it wasn't the things that I was less and less able to buy and look at as time went on, it was the words for these things that I could not bear to hear. Half a pound of veal. How can you get that past your tongue? Not that I'm especially concerned about calves. But also: Grapes, one pound. Fresh milk. A leather belt. All made of leather. For me a coin, such as a schilling, doesn't bring up the problem of cash commerce, devaluation or the gold standard, it's just that suddenly I feel a schilling in my mouth, light, cold, round, an annoying schilling that I need to spit out.

Ivan is still lying on the bed with an expression on his face I've never seen before. He is brooding, straining over something, he doesn't seem to be in a hurry, all of a sudden he has time to lie here quietly, and I lean over him, my arms folded over my chest, but then collapse so that Ivan can say: Today I've absolutely got to talk to you.

Then he again says nothing. I cover my face with my hands so as not to disturb him, because he has to talk to me.

Ivan begins: I have to talk to you. Do you remember? I once said there are some things I just won't tell you. But if I ... what would you, if I—?

If you? I ask. It can hardly be heard.

And if you? I repeat.

Ivan says: I think I have to tell it to you now.

I don't ask: What do you have to tell me? Because otherwise he might go on talking. But even if I stay silent a little longer he might ask: What would you, if ...

Since the silence can't be allowed to go one for too long, I shake my head and lie down beside him, I keep stroking his face gently, so that he has to stop speculating, and so he won't find the words for the end.

Does that mean, that you ... what do you know?

I again shake my head, it doesn't mean a thing, I don't know anything either, and if I were to know or he were to tell me there would still be no reply, not here and not now and no more on earth. As long as I live there will be no answer to that. This lying quietly has to end sooner or later, I have to find one cigarette for him and one for me, I have to light both, and we're allowed to smoke one more time, for ultimately Ivan has to go. I can't watch the way he avoids looking at me, I look at the wall and try to find something there. It shouldn't take so long for a person to get dressed, it might be longer than I can survive, and while Ivan, still straining, doesn't know how he should go, with what word, I snap off the light and he manages to find his way out, since the hall light is still on. Behind Ivan I hear the door closing.

I am frightened by the more familiar noise of Malina's unlocking the door. He stops for a minute outside my bedroom, and since I'd like to say something friendly, and since I'd also like to know if I've lost my voice, I say: I just went to bed, I was just about to fall asleep, you must be very tired yourself, go get some sleep.

But after a while Malina comes back from his room and comes to me through the darkness. He snaps on the light, and once again I'm frightened, he picks up the small tin box with the sleeping tablets and counts them. They're my sleeping pills, he's making me furious, but I don't say anything, today I'm not saying another word.

Malina says: You've already taken three, I think that's enough.

We start to argue, I see it coming, we're going to butt heads. That is now inevitable.

I say: No, just one and a half, you can see that one's been cut in half.

Malina says: I counted them this morning, there are three missing.

I say: At most I took two and a half, and a half doesn't count as a whole.

Malina takes the tablets, sticks them in his jacket pocket and walks out of the room.

Good night.

I jump out of bed, speechless, helpless, he's slammed the door, I can't bear a door being slammed, I can't bear his counting things, I didn't ask him this morning to check, of course it's possible I asked him earlier to count them during these days, since I'm no longer able to keep track of things. But how dare Malina come to me now to tally up these tablets, he has no idea what's happened, and suddenly I cry out, ripping open the door: But you don't have any idea!

He opens his door and asks: Did you say something?

I ask Malina: Give me just one more, I really need it!

Malina says once and for all: You're not getting any more. We're going to bed.

Since when has Malina been treating me that way? What does he want? For me to drink water and pace up and down, make tea and pace up and down, drink whiskey and pace up and down, but there isn't a bottle of whiskey to be found in the whole apartment either.

One day he'll even demand that I stop phoning, that I stop seeing Ivan, but he'll never accomplish that. I sneak quietly into Malina's room, I look for his jacket in the dark, reach inside all the pockets, but I can't find the tablets, I feel my way around the room, touching every object and then finally locate them on top of a stack of books. I slide two out of the tin onto my hand, one for now and one for later in the night, as a precaution, and I even manage to close the door so quietly he cannot possibly hear me. Both tablets are lying next to me on the bedside table, the light is on, I don't take them, they're far from enough, and I have broken into Malina's room and deceived him, he will soon know. But I only did it to calm down, for no other reason. Soon we will know everything. Because it can't go on like this for very long. A day will come. A day will come, and there will be the dry cheerful voice of Malina, but no more beautiful words from me, pronounced in great excitement. Malina worries much too much. Simply for Ivan's sake, so that Ivan is not affected, so that Ivan isn't even grazed by a shadow of guilt, for Ivan isn't guilty, I would not consume forty tablets, but how do I explain to Malina that all I want is to stay calm, that I won't harm myself so as not to harm Ivan. I simply have to calm down more, because it isn't out of the question that Ivan might call when he gets a chance.

Excellency, Generalissimo, Malina Esq., again I must ask you something. Is there a legacy?

What do you want with a legacy? What do you mean by that?

I would like to keep and preserve the Privacy of Mail. But I would also like to leave something behind. Are you deliberately not understanding me?

Since Malina is sleeping, I begin to write. Fräulein Jellinek has been married for a long time, no one is around anymore to write letters for me, organize and file.

Esteemed Herr Richter:

You were kind enough to assist me, in the most friendly manner, with a few legal questions which I considered completely insignificant. Mostly I have in mind the case of B. Of course this case is not important to me. However since you are a lawyer, and since back then I could turn to you in complete trust, and since you were so extremely generous with your help, without even charging me, and since today in Vienna I have no one I might turn to, I would like to ask you how one goes about writing a will. There are some things I must put in order, I have always lived in the utmost disorder, but it seems the time has come when even I have to come into some kind of order. Do you think, for example, that it's enough to write longhand, or that I should meet with you or that I …

Dear Herr Doktor Richter:

I am writing you in the utmost anxiety, in the greatest haste, because … I am writing you in the utmost anxiety, I would still like to put some things in order, it doesn't involve much, only my papers, a few objects to which I am, however, very attached, and I wouldn't want these objects to fall into the hands of strangers. Unfortunately I am at my wits' end, I may only assure you that I've thought everything through very exactly. Since I have no dependents, I wish (is this legally valid?) for some things to belong to a certain person forever: a blue glass cube, particularly a small coffee cup with a green edge and an old Chinese good-luck charm which depicts the heavens, the earth, the moon, and nothing more. I will then specify the name. My papers, on the other hand, and this much you yourself may know about my untenable position … I haven't eaten anything for days, I am no longer able to eat or sleep, moreover it has nothing to do with money, since I don't have any left, I am fully isolated in Vienna, cut off from the rest of the world where people earn money and eat, and since my situation may already be …

Esteemed and dear Herr Doktor Richter,
No one will know better than you that I am forced to make out a
will on account of various circumstances. Testaments, cemeteries,
final dispositions have always, in every case, from the very beginning, filled me with the greatest horror, probably no one needs a
testament anyway. Nevertheless I am turning to you today, because
you, as a lawyer, may be able to understand my position, which is
completely unsettled and unexplained and perhaps inexplicable
as well, and put it in some kind of order, which I greatly long for.
All my personal, my most private things are to be passed on to a
certain person, the name is enclosed on a separate piece of paper.
Another question occurs to me concerning my papers. Every page
has been written on and they are all without any value, to be sure,
I've never owned any papers of value, no stock certificates or secu-
rities. Even so it is very important to me that my papers be handed
over only to Herr Malina, whom, if I remember, you once saw during your all too brief stay in Vienna. But I no longer remember very
exactly, I could be mistaken, in any case, in case of emergency, I
give you the name of this person ...

Dear Herr Doktor Richter:
I am writing you in the utmost anxiety, in the greatest haste, I am
completely incapable of thinking straight, but who ever did think
straight? My situation has become completely untenable, perhaps
it always was. But in the end it should be said: It was not Herr Malina, nor was it Ivan, a name which says nothing to you. Later I will
explain to you what he has to do with my life. Whatever happens to
my most personal belongings has no meaning for me today.

Esteemed and dear Herr Richter, Esq.
I am perhaps presuming too much of you, but I am writing to you
in the utmost anxiety, in the greatest haste. Can you, as a lawyer so

well versed in the law, reveal to me how one composes a valid will? Unfortunately I don't know, but I am forced for various reasons ...

Please answer me immediately, if possible immediately upon receipt of my letter!

Vienna, ...

An unknown woman

It's Malina's day off, I would have preferred to spend the day by myself, but nothing can move Malina out of the house, even though there's some hostility between us. It starts with his being annoyed and hungry, we eat earlier than usual, I light the candelabra that otherwise burns only for Ivan. The table seems to me to be properly set, but there's only cold meat, unfortunately I forgot the bread. Of course Malina doesn't say anything, but I know what he is thinking.

Me: Since when do we have a crack in the wall?
Malina: I don't remember, it must have been there a long time.
Me: Since when do we have that dark patch over the radiator?
Malina: We have to have something on the walls if we don't hang any pictures.
Me: I need white walls, harmless walls, otherwise I immediately see myself living in Goya's last room. Think about the dog poking his head out of the depths, all the dark sinister things on the wall, from his last period. You should have never been allowed to show me that room in Madrid.
Malina: I was never in Madrid with you. Don't tell stories.
Me: That doesn't matter in the least, in any case I was there, Monseigneur, with or without your permission. I'm finding spider webs up on the walls, look how they've woven everything together!
Malina: Don't you have anything to wear, why are you wearing my old robe?

276

Me:	Because I really don't have anything else to wear. Didn't you ever come across the sentence: siam contenti, sono un uomo, ho fetto questa caricatura.
Malina:	I believe it's sono dio. The gods die many, many deaths.
Me:	People do, not gods.
Malina:	Why do you always make corrections like that?
Me:	I'm allowed to make them because I have become a caricature, in spirit and in flesh. Are we satisfied now?

Malina goes to his room, and comes back with a box of matches. The candles have burned down. I forgot to buy new ones. Malina simply has to do without. I could again ask him for advice, ask what's going on and how it's going on, although I'm feeling the tension and hostility more and more distinctly.

Me:	Something must have gone wrong with the primates and later with the hominids. A man, a woman … strange words, a strange madness! Which of the two of us will pass summa cum laude? I, me, myself—that's all been a mistake for me. Is "I" perhaps an object?
Malina:	No.
Me:	But is it here and today?
Malina:	Yes.
Me:	Does it have a story?
Malina:	Not anymore.
Me:	Can you touch it?
Malina:	Never.
Me:	But you have to hold on to me!
Malina:	Do I have to? How do you want to be taken?
Me:	(con fuoco) I hate you.
Malina:	Are you speaking to me, did you say something?
Me:	(forte) Herr von Malina, Your Grace, Magnificence! (crescendo) Your Lordship, Omnipotence, I hate you,

sir! (fortissimo) Exchange me as far as I'm concerned, let's trade, your Honor! (tutto il clavicembalo) I hate you! (perdendo le forze, dolente) Please, keep me all the same. I've never hated you.

Malina: I don't believe a single word you're saying, just all your words at once.

Me: (dolente) Don't leave me! (cantabile assai) You—leaving me! (senza pedale) I wanted to tell a story, but I won't do it. (mesto) You alone are disturbing me in my remembering, (tempo giusto) You go and take over the stories—from which the big story is constructed. Take them all away from me.

I've cleared off the table, but there's still more to clear up. There will be no more letters, telegrams and postcards. Ivan won't be leaving Vienna in the near future. But even afterward and still later—nothing more will come. I am looking for a special place in the apartment, for a secret drawer, because I'm walking up and down carrying a small bundle. There has to be a drawer in my desk which will never again pop out, which no one will be able to open. Or else I could pry up part of the parquet floor with a crowbar, hide the letters there, put the flooring back in place and seal it, as long as I'm still sovereign of my dominion. Malina is reading a book, presumably: "For it is futile to try to feign indifference concerning inquiries whose object cannot be indifferent to human nature." Every now and then he glances up, annoyed, as if he didn't know I'm walking around with a bundle of letters, looking for a place to hide them.

I am kneeling on the floor, it is not Mecca and not Jerusalem I am bowing to. I no longer bow to anything, all I have to do is to pull out the lowest drawer of the desk, the one that catches and is so hard to open. I have to be very quiet, so Malina won't see which place I've chosen, but then the knot comes undone, the letters slide out in a mess, I tie them back together clumsily and force them through a crack into the drawer, but then take them right back out, fearful that the letters might have disappeared already. I forgot to write something on the wrapping paper, something in case these letters wind up being found by strangers after all, following an auction where my desk was on the block. The importance would have to be conveyed with very few words: These are the only letters ... these letters are the only letters ... the letters, which reached me ... My only letters!

I can't find the words for the uniqueness of Ivan's letters, and I have to give up before I am discovered. The drawer gets stuck. I press it shut with all my weight, but quietly, lock it, and slip the key into Malina's old robe which is flopping around me.

I sit down in the living room opposite Malina, he shuts his book and looks at me inquisitively.

Are you finished?

I nod, I am finished.

Why are you just sitting there instead of finally making us some coffee?

I look at Malina gently, thinking that now I ought to tell him something terrible, something which will separate us forever and render any further word between us impossible. But I stand up and walk slowly out of the room, I turn around in the door and do not hear myself saying anything terrible, just something else, cantabile and dolcissimo:

As you like. I'll put the coffee on at once.

I am standing in front of the stove, waiting for the water to boil, I spoon some coffee into the filter and think and am still thinking, I must have reached a point where thought is so necessary it is no longer possible, my head sinks into my shoulders, I get hot since my face is too near to the burner. Nous allons à l'Esprit! But I can still make this coffee. I'd just like to know what Malina is doing in the room, what he's thinking about me, since I'm wondering a little about him, too, although my thoughts are traveling far beyond him and me. I bustle about, warm the coffee pot and place the two little Augarten cups on the tray in front of me, where they are impossible to overlook, just as it's impossible to ignore the fact that I'm standing here, still thinking.

Once upon a time there was a princess, once the Hungarian Hussars rode up from the vast land whose expanses were yet unexplored, once upon a time the willows hissed on the Danube, once upon a time there was a bouquet of Turk's-cap lilies and a black mantle ... My kingdom, my Ungargassenland, which I have held with my mortal hands, my glorious land, now no larger than the burner on my stove, which is beginning to glow, as the rest of the water drips through the filter ... I have to watch out that I don't fall face-first onto the stove, that I don't disfigure myself, burn myself, then Malina would have to call the police and the ambulance, he would have to confess his negligence at having let a woman burn halfway to death. I stand up straight, my face glowing from the red plate on the stove, where I so often burned scraps of paper at night, not so much to burn something written, but to light one last and one very last cigarette. But I no longer smoke. I've given it up as of today. I can turn the knob back to o. Once upon a time, but I'm not burning, I keep myself upright, the coffee is ready, the lid is on the pot. I'm finished. From a window overlooking the courtyard you can hear music, qu'il fait bon, fait bon. My hands aren't shaking, I carry the tray into the room, I pour the coffee obediently, as always—two spoonfuls of sugar for Malina and none for me. I sit across from Malina and we drink our coffee in dead silence. What's the matter with Malina? He doesn't thank me, doesn't smile, doesn't break the silence and he makes no suggestions for the evening. But it's his day off, and he doesn't want anything from me.

I stare unwaveringly at Malina, but he doesn't look up. I stand up, thinking that if he doesn't say something immediately, if he doesn't stop me, it will be murder, and I step away since I can no longer say it. It's not so frightening anymore, just that our falling apart is more frightening than any falling out. I have lived in Ivan and I die in Malina.

Malina is still drinking his coffee. You can hear a "Helloo" from the other window overlooking the courtyard. I've stepped over to the wall, I walk into the wall, holding my breath. I should have written a note: It wasn't Malina. But the wall opens, I am inside the wall, all Malina can see is the crack we've been seeing all along. He'll think I've left the room.

The phone rings, Malina picks it up, he plays with my sunglasses and breaks them, then he plays with a blue glass cube that actually belongs to me. Sender never thanked, donor unknown. But he's not just playing, since he's already moving my candelabra out of the way. He says: Hello! For a while nothing, then Malina says coldly, impatiently, you've dialed the wrong number.

He's broken my glasses, he tosses them into the wastebasket, they are my eyes, he hurls the glass cube in after them, it is the second stone from a dream, he makes my coffee cup disappear, he tries to break a record, but it doesn't break, it just bends, giving the greatest resistance before it finally does crack, he clears the table, he tears up a few letters, he throws away my legacy, everything lands in the wastebasket. He drops a tin box with sleeping tablets in between the scraps of paper, looks around for something else, he moves the candelabra even further away and finally hides it, as if the children could ever reach it, and there is something inside the wall, something that can no longer cry out, but cries out nonetheless: Ivan!

Malina looks around meticulously, he sees everything but no longer hears. Only his small green-rimmed cup is still there, nothing more, proof that he is alone. The telephone rings again. Malina hesitates, but then goes back to answer it after all. He knows it's Ivan. Malina says: Hello? And again for a while says nothing.

Excuse me?
No?
Then I didn't express myself clearly.
There must be some mistake.
The number is 723144.
Yes, Ungargasse 6.
No, there isn't.
There is no woman here,
I'm telling you, there was never anyone here by that name.
No one else is here.
My number is 723144.
My name?
Malina.

Steps, Malina's incessant steps, quieter steps, the most quiet steps. A standing still. No alarm, no sirens. No one comes to help. Not the ambulance and not the police. It's a very old wall, a very strong wall, from which no one can fall, which no one can break open, from which nothing can ever be heard again.

It was murder.

New Directions Paperbooks—a partial listing

*BILINGUAL EDITION

For a complete listing, request a free catalog from New Directions, 80 8th Avenue, New York, NY 10011
or visit us online at ndbooks.com